BETSY'S FOR

When her mother is dying, Betsy Kramer makes the uncharacteristic decision to return to her home at Windy Hill to work on her tattered relationships and spend time gathering driftwood with her mother Margaret. Before she dies, Margaret admits to Betsy that she knows about the treehouse, but she doesn't reveal anything about who Betsy's father is. At her mother's funeral, Tom, the only man Betsy ever loved, returns and reminds her that daffodils were once her favorite flower, but she avoids him. Lingering at Windy Hill, Betsy finds letters from her estranged father hidden in a hatbox and realizes the enormity of the lie perpetrated by her mother. Her mother could have saved her from sexual harassment, from being fatherless, and from making the worst choice of her life, if she'd not kept secrets. As Betsy and Tom start spending time together, picking peaches and antiquing, Betsy faces her biggest demon, and even the fireflies hovering over the Magical Pond can't help her. With vivid imagery and deep feeling, *Daffodils and Fireflies* chronicles one woman's journey home again.

"*Daffodils and Fireflies* is written with style, power and grace...An emotional voyage that hurts and enlightens."—*Les Roberts, author of the Milan Jacovich Mysteries.*

"...a thoughtful and moving novel...vivid detail and emotional depth..."—*Trudy Brandenburg, author of the Emma Haines Kayak Mystery Series.*

"Claudia is a superb writer with an authentic voice..."—*Betsy Muller, Artist's Way study group leader, author of Energy Makeover.*

"Compelling characters drive this well-written novel. Clever. Vivid. Claudia pulls you right into the story." —*Christine Benedict, author of the mystery thriller Anonymous.*

"...tragedies as well as the triumphs. You'll be moved by this touching book of women's fiction."—*Deanna Adams, author of Peggy Sue Got Pregnant.*

DAFFODILS AND FIREFLIES

Claudia J. Taller

Moonshine Cove Publishing, LLC
Abbeville, South Carolina U.S.A.

FIRST MOONSHINE COVE EDITION APRIL 2015

This book is a work of fiction. Names, characters, places and incidents are products of the author's imagination or are used fictitiously. Any resemblance to actual events, locales or persons, living or dead, is entirely coincidental.

ISBN: 978-1-937327-64-4
Library of Congress Control Number: 2015936436
Copyright © 2015 by Claudia J. Taller

All rights reserved. No part of this book may be reproduced in whole or in part without written permission from the publisher except by reviewers who may quote brief excerpts as part of a review in a newspaper, magazine or electronic publication; nor may any part of this book be reproduced, stored in a retrieval system or transmitted in any form or by any means electronic, mechanical, photocopying, recording or any other means, without written permission from the publisher.

Book interior and cover design by Moonshine Cove; cover illustrations public domain; images by http://www.forestwander.com/ and Jeff the Quiet.

Acknowledgment

My pen is raised to Julia Cameron, who said, "When we open ourselves to something or someone greater than ourselves working through us, we paradoxically open ourselves to our own greatest selves."

I could not begin to name all the people who helped me write and finish this book, but I acknowledge Skyline Writers Group and Word Lovers Retreat writers, as well as various friends and family members who have read portions of the book and helped me through problems the story presented. And Joy Held pointed me in the direction of Moonshine Cove Publishing, which I would not have found on my own.

As always, this book is for Paul, who stills my heart and grounds me, who reminds me of who I am, every day, and forever.

Dedication

This book is dedicated to my three daughters, Allison, Melissa, and Claire: May you know the solace of letting go of pain, the wisdom of forgiveness, and the poignancy of opening to possibilities.

Also by Claudia J. Taller

Ohio's Lake Erie Wineries (2011)

30 Perfect Days, Finding Abundance in Ordinary Life (2014)

Ohio's Canal Country Wineries (Forthcoming 2015)

DAFFODILS AND FIREFLIES

WATER'S EBB AND FLOW
At Willow Beach

My mother died a year ago during daffodil days.

Now, as the bright yellow and white flowers brighten the hillside above Willow Beach, I think about how the daffodils drooped near the back stoop of Windy Hill, our family's farm, right after Mom died. Maybe those daffodils had been a sign that things were going to change, a reminder that life would go on, and I had some decisions to make. Windy Hill had just become mine.

The rippling waves of Lake Erie wash over the sandy shore and claim it with the sigh of letting go, here at the beach. Moments after it succumbs to the land, the water pulls back and under, rolling out again, collecting energy and vigor, like a long intake of breath. The water falls into the depths then reaches for the far horizon, a falling and rising that is incessant and urgent, not to be ignored. The ancient rhythm of water calms and rejuvenates me.

On the day my mother died, I walked those miles from Windy Hill to Willow Beach without thinking about my feet. I needed to be by the water.

My mother liked to touch her forehead against mine as I rested my face on her lilac-scented pillow. On the night before she died, she playfully brushed my cheeks with butterfly kisses. She wanted me home again, away from the clanging life that kept me from sleep. The memory of that moment floats in and out of dreams and through my daylight hours, yet its true meaning eludes me. There is much to know about Mom, her love affair with my father, and what she knew and didn't know about Jerry and me. I linger in the familiar childhood places of Willow Beach and Windy Hill not quite knowing why.

The voices of the men on the other park bench rise over the roar of the surf. "Yeah, I've lived in these parts nigh sixty years. You cain't always see the horizon," the shriveled old man sits with his legs crossed, revealing white socks tucked into black shoes. His smoky voice reminds me of my mother's husband Ben.

The fit but not young cyclist's bicycle leans against the clock tower wall. "You can almost believe Lake Erie's an ocean. I'm cycling around the state trying to figure out what to do next." He raises his hands in supplication like he's letting the world decide his fate. "Got laid off, my wife divorced me, the kids are gone."

"Well, it's a new time for you then," says the old man, nodding. "Yep. You've a life ahead, but what's it going to be, you wonder."

That was the question I started with after Mom died. Death has a way of helping you know life's short. And forcing choices.

"I'm 44 years old and I'm starting over," the younger man said.

"The way it was meant to be, God's will."

The menacing call of the gulls and the squawking of the migrating geese fill the stillness of a conversation ended. I close my eyes. I started over in mid-life too. Was it God's will or the result of mistakes made along the way? I'm not sure that they were my mistakes and I'm not sure how much God's hand has been in it.

Before I found out Mom was sick, I was in the middle of living the life of an editor living in a downtown Cleveland warehouse apartment. Every month, I escaped to exotic jungle-tangled and God-infused places as I put together *Leisure Travel* magazine. Sometimes, I went to Alaska or Paris or Australia on assignment. But mostly, I was an armchair traveler.

And then I got the phone call from Cassie. If you knew me then, you would have been surprised that I went home at all. My story begins a few months before Mom died. I'll find some answers in the retelling of it.

CHAPTER ONE – HOUSE OF GOD

December's "Home for the Holidays" issue wasn't done yet. Even though I had the feeling that this was the year I would win the International Magazine Association's editorial prize, nothing was guaranteed. I'd been tense with worry for weeks, waiting. And my staff moved like prehistoric tortoises.

I hit the intercom on my office telephone and yelled, "Jamie, where's the cover spread? I haven't seen it yet. I don't care what your excuse is, get me the mock-up as soon as you can. Like, yesterday."

"But Elizabeth, I'm still waiting for the designer to get it to me."

"I don't care. It needs to be done. And it better be impressive."

She sighed audibly. "I'll see what I can do."

I shook my head and stood up to walk over to the glass windows thirty floors above street level. Against the background of the steel-gray waters of Lake Erie, a petite woman with dark shoulder-length hair came into focus and stared back at me. I exhaled slowly, trying to gain composure. The more I worked, the stronger the tug of wanting something new pulled on me. I expected an answer for my restlessness from my reflection in the glass, but I had none.

Mo startled me. She must have walked in without knocking. "Hey, I need you to sign these reimbursement forms."

"Didn't I tell you to knock before you enter my office? What's wrong with you? Can't you follow simple instructions?" I plopped down into my chair.

"I did knock." Mo sat down on the other side of my desk.

"No, you didn't."

She shook her head with an almost imperceptible roll of her eyes.

"Attitude will get you nowhere." I shook my head. "You're impertinent."

Her eyes opened wide. "I didn't mean anything." Her chestnut hair cascaded onto the shoulders of her immaculate black suit as she laid the papers in front of me. She made me feel ancient and untidy.

"You need to stay late. I haven't gotten to any of my correspondence yet."

"How late do you think it will be?" Her voice belied her compliance.

"Could be seven, eight, not as late as nine."

"My parents want to take me to dinner at six."

"That can be changed. I'm sure your job is important to you."

She sighed. "I'll see what I can do." Her lips pursed in consternation. She held back, posed her pen over her notebook. "What about Greece? Do you want to avoid Thanksgiving and go the following week? Anthony's schedule works with that."

"I'm not sure I want to work with Anthony. I didn't like his images of Russia last month."

"Who do you want then?"

The photos had been so blurred, they were almost unusable. I wondered how we could have such a bad photographer on our staff. "Do you think I should fire his ass?"

She pulled back and sat up straight. "No."

"I guess we can let him prove himself in Greece. I'll try to look at the pictures as we go along. Let's do it the week of Thanksgiving."

"But . . ."

I'm not suggesting travel on Wednesday. I'm suggesting we leave next Saturday and return to the States on Thursday. We should be home in time for dinner."

Mo's pen was gliding across her notepad. "Where do you plan to go?"

"I have an itinerary right here." I turned to my computer. "Yes, it's all here. I'll send it to you. Sending it . . . now. Get on it."

She scurried out, shoulders back, not looking at me. Two minutes later, I received an e-mail from her that read, "It won't make any difference if we do the letters tonight or tomorrow. They'll go in the mail the same day."

She had a point. Because she did, I relented even though I was anxious to get some documents out. "Have a nice dinner," I typed back.

I looked up when small, olive-skinned Jamie, flustered by the rush, walked through the doorway. "I have what he gave me. I think you can get a feel for it, but it's not done yet. Just so you know."

The cover was beautiful. Jerusalem's Holy Trinity Cathedral turrets glowed against a star-filled sky. A bevy of parishioners waited to get inside. What could be better than Jerusalem at Christmas time, Christianity in the heart of the land of Judaism and

Islam?

Jamie was smiling. "You like it, don't you?"

My shoulders relaxed. Thank God it was done. "I do. Do you think I can win the award?"

She nodded. I could tell she didn't really want me to win. There wasn't any reason for her to care. She didn't like me.

"Tell what's-his-face to complete it. I have no changes."

"Will do." She walked out the door fast, as if she had to leave before I changed my mind.

They don't get me. They don't know it takes absolute perfection at every step to get it right.

I had two weeks to make sure all the articles, photos, and ads flowed well. I was going to Greece in the middle of it. Mom would flip out, again, that I was arriving on Thanksgiving Day.

The phone rang. I stared at the number, almost let it go into voicemail, but the number looked familiar. "Elizabeth Kramer."

"Betsy?"

I didn't recognize the voice. "Yes?"

"I'm in town. How about meeting me for dinner?"

Robert. He wasn't wealthy or connected but he was beautiful in every way. His brown hair was always a bit rumpled and a little too long, his dark eyes were warm under thick lashes, and he carried himself with light confidence. He thought about the problems of war, the state of Catholicism, and the way African women were mutilated. He was a photographer with a heart and lots of talent. He believed in perfection as much as I did. "I can. What are you doing here, in Cleveland?"

"Hoping you'll have dinner with me."

My heart sank. "That's not good."

"Why not?"

"I'm not really available."

There it was, his marvelous loose laugh. "Yes, you are. You're very available. You're all grown up and you have no ties and you've been divorced forever."

I loved his voice. It was like chocolate laced with brandy, smooth and deep. "I guess you remember me."

There was an uncomfortable silence until he said, "Of course I remember you. We had a fabulous time together last month. Did I misinterpret how it was?"

"No. It's just . . . I don't expect things to go anywhere."

"Why not?"

"I don't know."

A moment later, he said, "Your address—5690 W. 9th—is that right?"

"Yes."

"I'll pick you up at seven."

Then I felt sorry for myself, working so hard, pushing, always pushing, and all I really wanted was to have dinner with Robert. Why couldn't I just have fun?

I thought I loved my work with all my heart. Right then, I knew I didn't.

I walked the nine blocks to my condo. I liked Robert, but I couldn't imagine why we were doing this thing, this going-out-on-a-date thing. He didn't know the real me, the person who failed at baking cookies with my daughter, who didn't stay married to a man that only needed to be loved, who didn't respect her mother. I was a disaster in relationships.

I took the elevator to the third floor and walked the wooden floors to the end unit. After living my life on a dairy farm, the converted warehouse felt like a cavern. Winifred wrapped around my legs when I opened the door, and I reached down to pick her up before walking down the hallway to the floor-to-ceiling windows overlooking the Cuyahoga River. The cavern opened up to a view of a timeless world.

Down from where I stood, Moses Cleaveland found the mouth of the Cuyahoga and landed on Settler's Landing. Warehouses and small manufacturing facilities dotted the winding river, and railroad tracks crossed on iron lift bridges. The mounds of salt from the mines rose beyond the boats docked near the riverfront. Further south, new condos sat high above the riverbank. On the valley floor, the tracks and roadways striated the land. The gathering darkness was pierced with points of light from surrounding buildings. The river was glimmering, a meandering luminous pink ribbon colored by the lingering sunset.

My city was beautiful. Looking out at my view, I thought back to the feeling I had earlier, that my job wasn't enough. I almost felt like I didn't LIKE my job.

It wasn't enough. What was enough? How does anyone know that their one small life, their little world in their head, their daily routines, their projects and accomplishments are the best that one can do?

Why ask these questions now? Why had Robert's invitation to dinner taken me in this direction?

I was middle-aged. My life was half gone. The sole goal had been to win an editorial prize, and I was on the brink of that accomplishment. Then what? The feeling that I would cry rested on my chest and bubbled up as gasping dry heaves. For the first time in many years, I was crying. *Why am I crying?* I angrily brushed away the tears and went into the bathroom, dropping my tabby cat to the floor. Naked, standing in the shower, I gave into the tears, astonished that I was crying and not knowing what was wrong.

I was wrung out, emptied, and somehow restored to equilibrium when toweling off. I felt calmer than I had in a long time.

Robert kissed me lightly, his hand on the small of my back. He looked down at the slim black dress, the long strand of pearls, and the neat high heels, and said, "You look lovely." I took his hand and lead him into my space, showing it off.

"How wonderful," he said, as I knew he would when he took in my space of floor-to-ceiling windows and book shelves and travel memorabilia. He lingered by the windows until he sensed I was anxious to leave. "I'll have to come back and get pictures of the Cuyahoga from here some time. You must love this view."

"It's the best thing about this place. That, and that it's all mine."

We walked to the Blue Point Grille and once seated in the dim light, Robert ordered fresh grilled salmon with risotto and corn confetti. I sipped my wine, still wondering at my crying earlier. *Am I having a breakdown?*

"Tell me about the current issue of the magazine." He sat back with his gin and tonic.

"The cover is a cathedral in Jerusalem. I like the idea of Jerusalem being the centerpiece for going home for the holidays. It cuts right through the nativity, champagne toasts, and gifts to get to just plain old religion."

"I'm surprised you didn't choose Bethlehem."

"Bethlehem's too Christian."

He nodded.

"Is it trite?"

"No. It might be too serious though."

I pulled my wheat roll apart. "That's what I'm afraid of. I go back and forth between thinking it's too trite and thinking it's too deep."

"Jerusalem's war ravaged."

"It's holy. The cover article starts by describing holiday rituals in the Russian Orthodox Church, at the nearby mosque, and the old Jewish synagogue."

"Well done. Did you write it?"

"No. I wish I had."

"Last month's magazine turned out well," he said. "All that blue in Bermuda splashed across the cover was eye-catching. You liked my photos, then?"

"Loved them."

"I think of you every time I see it on my coffee table."

"We had a good time." In Bermuda, we'd laughed. The constant deep blue of sea and sky brought us together on the beach when our work was done. We delayed coming home for three days.

"A great time," he said. "What's this about not being available? You felt available to me in Bermuda."

"I've done the marriage thing."

"I'm not asking you to marry me."

"I know, but if we don't end up married, don't we end up breaking up?"

He shook his head. "You think too much."

As we ate, we talked about his upcoming gallery showing, his son in California, and my daughter Cassie's pregnancy. The risotto was rich, the salmon crispy on the outside.

"I forgot how worry-free your face looks in low light," he said while we were taking our first bites of crème brulee after dinner.

I didn't know how to answer that. "So, during the day it's a mask of worry?"

"Concern. I'd call it concern. There's a saying I like, 'You don't have to spend another day wondering and worrying.' I'll have to get it framed for you."

My spoon dipped into more of the caramel-crusted pudding. I hadn't spent any time wondering and worrying while I was in

Bermuda with him. "I wish I could embrace that," I said as I lifted my eyes to his.

"Hike with me." He lived near the Cuyahoga Valley National Park, which he hiked every moment he could.

"I'm too busy."

"You can't spend every moment working."

"I don't." I wanted to hike with him. I could feel my legs working the hills as we followed the bridle paths into the woods.

"What do you do when you're not working?"

"Drink wine, walk, read, sleep." It was sad.

He shook his head, paid the bill, took my hand. "I wish you'd lighten up."

"Come back to my place with me," I suggested on an impulse.

"That's a good start to lightening up. Let's go."

I lost myself in his arms, in his lips. I craved human contact, and he gave it to me. I felt him give up who he was and merge into me. When I fell asleep, I felt I'd been turned inside out. I loved him in that moment when sleep pulled me under.

We were sound asleep when the phone rang. The clock read 6:30. When I picked up the phone, Cassie said, "Hey, Mom . . ."

"Cassie?"

"Grandma's dying." She was choking back tears.

I sat up, not sure I'd heard. "Dying?"

"Yeah, you heard it right." Her voice was tense, terse, clipped.

"Are you sure?"

Robert stirred beside me. His skin was brown against the sheets.

"Would I call you to tell you this first thing in the morning if it wasn't true? I wanted to tell you as soon as I could."

"Okay." I tried to ignore her tone and the sudden cliff-hanging dread that welled up in my body and traveled to my heart's center. Mom was dying. "What's wrong?"

"Cancer. It's already advanced. She found out yesterday afternoon. She's taking it like a trooper. You'd think they told her she has a broken ankle that will heal in six weeks. But Ben's a basket case. Twice he said, in front of her, 'We've only had five years together.'"

I hated to hear that. Ben was too kind to feel this loss. "Is there no cure?"

"Apparently not." Cassie's voice broke. I knew she was having a hard time saying the words she had to say. She was close to Mom.

My mother the artist, the survivor, the balanced woman who raised me, was leaving, and I barely knew her any more. Knowing I couldn't, since it wasn't Sunday, I said, "I'll call Grandma later today." I hesitated, then asked, "How are you?"

"Oh . . . devastated," she said, as if that was enough. I knew it was more than that, could hear it in her voice. "I'm sure you'll leave us to deal with this on our own."

I took a deep breath and sighed. I had to keep myself from becoming defensive. "Take care of yourself." It was lame.

"You too." Her voice was empty of emotion, as if she'd smoothed over a disturbed surface, like footprints in the sand washed over by waves. The call to me had been obligatory.

I clicked the phone off and laid down flat on my back.

"What's going on?" Robert was propped up on his elbow.

"My mother's dying of cancer."

He pulled me to him and held me close. "That's deep."

Robert holding me made me want to cry. He was too caring, too loving, too possessive, too strong. I couldn't stop the tears from coming. I cried for Mom, for Cassie, for me. Robert didn't ask why I was crying.

When the tears were spent, I said, "I need to go."

We dressed in silence until he said, "Call me after you get out to the farm. I'm here for you."

I watched him walk down the hall. He reminded me of Tom, walking down the hallway of my dorm. I hadn't thought of Tom in a long while, and now I was watching him walk away and not doing anything about it, again.

I closed the door, leaned up against it, and sighed. Back to the grind. It was Friday. I had work to do.

"I made plane reservations for next Friday afternoon. A car and driver are set up to meet the two of you at the airport. You leave Athens on Thursday morning and arrive in Cleveland on Thanksgiving afternoon."

I scarcely heard what she said.

"Here's a printed copy." Mo paused at the door. She frowned and walked out.

All through getting dressed, the walk to work, listening to

messages, and checking e-mails, I was thinking about cancer. And my Mom. Mom and I only spoke with each other on Sundays after she got home from church. It wouldn't be enough to ask *How are you, Mom?* I wanted to ask Cassie what to do, but I wasn't willing to admit I didn't know.

The story on Jerusalem included a photo of the temple where Christ argued with the elders. People living a Hasidic life were shown shopping for food for the holidays. Me, a proclaimed Agnostic, had chosen Jerusalem because Jerusalem wasn't commercial and false. It was a place where religions met, collided, and intertwined, a place I could relate to because it didn't tell me what to think or feel about God. It gave me choices.

My religion began in a white-steepled 1840 clapboard church in Conneaut. I sang "Kum Ba Yah" during Vacation Bible School and shared potluck dinners after services, my plate piled high with scalloped corn, meatloaf, green Jell-O salads, and cherry cobbler. On my wedding day, as we stood near the altar crowded with vases of calla lilies, my husband Rick's eyes tried to help me believe it was the right thing to do.

God's not there for me. This truth came at me these days, evocative and hard to avoid. This was not just about winning a contest, I realized. I was looking for answers for me.

Rochelle's article about the ancient Middle Eastern city told stories. The rabbi priests maintained the temple and said Hanukkah was a nonreligious holiday. The Catholic priest struggled to keep art safe in a city where tourists disrespected the House of God. Prayers were unceasing at the Moslem mosque. The writer captured the lives of believers.

I wanted to believe in something, anything.

I didn't change a thing in the article, a rarity. They didn't call me "Dragon Lady" for laughs. I called Rochelle. "Great job on the story. I don't have any changes."

"Really?"

"I was drawn into it and the voice was compelling. If I stop thinking about the writing, you've done what was needed."

"Thank you," she said with great excitement. "I can't believe this."

"Don't expect a call like this every issue," I said coldly and hung up. I sighed. *Why do I have to be a bitch? How does that jive with perfection?*

I pulled my walking shoes from under the counter, put them on and turned out the light in my office. After pulling my collar up around my neck, I headed down East Fourth Street and out towards the baseball park on Ontario, away from the cold wind off the lake. At Carnegie, where empty parking lots seemed a symbol of life in Cleveland on a wintery night, I turned left and walked east towards the university district. Gradually, as I walked, I felt the tension subside.

I turned up E. 18th Street and then up Euclid. On my right, Trinity Cathedral, which had survived the downfall of the wealthy families who once lived on the grand avenue, was lit up. I was drawn to it, as I'd been drawn to the holy places in the story of Jerusalem—the supplicant prayer, the incense, the art and architecture meant to bring people closer to God.

I entered the sanctuary of light and shadow. The three-story timbered ceiling, great stone columns, and ornate stained glass created a place of beauty, and peace. People sat in the pews. The grand organ's brass pipes trembled with chamber music. I sat and felt the music flow through me. My face warmed up.

I bowed my head in prayer as I struggled to believe God would listen. *Dear God, help me.* It was all I could come up with. I listened with my eyes closed. The minutes multiplied. The organ trilled louder, coming to a crescendo. The musical denouement was soft and lovely. I lost patience.

Outside again, I walked past the bright lights of the theaters and people dressed up, chatty and excited about an evening on the town. I walked past E. 9th Street, through Public Square and its spooky street people asking for money, and down Superior to W. 9th Street.

Walking was what I did when I was trying to work things out, a lifelong habit picked up when I was a child. My mother sometimes walked into town even though the truck was sitting in the driveway. My grandmother used to say walking slowed down life and that was what we needed.

I watched a movie, drank some wine, fell asleep. I was wide awake at two in the morning. This waking-up-in-the-middle-of-the-night thing was getting old.

When my left hip hurt, I switched to my right until that hip hurt. I finally laid flat on my back and counted backwards from 100. I wouldn't be able to get my work done in the morning, I'd be so tired. Winifred walked across my chest, and I pushed her away. I finally got up and poured another half glass of wine, noticing I'd already had half a bottle that evening. I read James Joyce's *The Dubliners,* which made me sleepy enough to creep back to bed.

Saturday at the office went by in a fog. I was tired. Bits and pieces of Mom came back to me throughout the day, and some of her sayings as if she was with me. *No one said life was about having fun. God is there; it's you who moved away.* And the best one, the one that I'd clung to, *Follow your dreams.* I wasn't ready to lose Mom. When was the last time I saw her? Easter, no Mother's Day. I spent time with my mother like some people went to church, on the obligatory days.

Waiting until Sunday's call, I fidgeted. After work, I went on another walk, drank some more wine, and read.

On Sunday morning, I waited patiently for church to be over, and then I dialed Mom's phone number.

She answered the phone with cheer in her voice. "Hi, daughter."

"How was church?"

"Oh, it was wonderful, as it always is. You should come sometime."

I sighed. "I don't like church."

"Of course you do. You used to love everything about it, especially the shaking hands during Sharing the Peace. People ask about you all the time."

"They're asking because they care about you." I hesitated before I continued. "Cassie called me."

"Oh." Her voice lowered.

"How do you feel?"

"I'm tired. That's why I went to the doctor. That and there's blood in the toilet."

"Sounds scary."

"I feel okay. Really. I'm not in pain." I heard Ben's muffled voice. "He wants to talk to you."

"Hi, Betsy." He sounded old. "The doctors can't do anything. They say your mother will live only a few months. The cancer's bad."

"Geez. Cassie didn't tell me that." Months. I needed more time than that.

"Cassie's upset. It's not good for the baby."

Mom had only a few months and might not meet her great-grandchild. My mother who was dying said she was fine. Ben sounded afraid. My back ached, my eyes were scratchy. "You need me." I surprised myself the way I'd blurted that out. "We need each other."

"Don't you worry about us," Ben said.

They always said things like that to appease me. Or to keep me away. "How bad is she?"

"You know how she is. She'll go to work tomorrow. She was there yesterday. She smiles at everyone and doesn't tell them she's sick."

"I'm coming out there." The decision was final, coming from the place inside me that knew the right thing to do. There was religion in that moment.

"Today?" It almost sounded like he didn't want me to visit. "Well, all right. We'll see you in a bit."

Stunned, I hung up the phone. I'd decided to drive out to Windy Hill even though I had a week to create the most beautiful magazine of the year.

Mom was in the kitchen when I came through the back door. We held onto each other for a long time. Her usual robust body felt bony, frail. When we came apart, she said, "I love you, honey." I brushed her soft white hair away from her face. Her blue eyes were a reassurance that nothing that mattered had changed.

"I love you too, Mom." Overwhelmed, I covered my face, moved my hands up to my scalp, and pulled my hair up in fistfuls.

"You used to do that when you were fifteen. I didn't know you still did."

Hair still in my hands, I said, "Neither did I."

"Sit. Have some tea." She poured iced tea into tall elegant glasses, and I felt better as soon as I sipped it.

"I wanted to call as soon as I heard, but we don't do that."

"What?"

"Call each other. Unless it's Sunday."

She reached for my hand and sat down at the table with me. "How did we get there?"

"I don't know." My voice broke. "All that work, leaving Cassie with you, not coming back enough."

"You don't owe me any apologies."

"Yes, I do."

"I forgive you." She looked at me hard, eyes narrowed. "Now go on and forgive yourself."

I didn't understand. "What do you mean?"

"Your problem is not forgiving yourself. I should have said it a long time ago."

"For what?"

"For everything. For all the things you just said, and for the rest."

"Some of what I've done can't be forgiven." I took another sip of farmhouse-style sweet tea. "You don't know what I've done."

We were so close, I could smell her breath. "I wouldn't bet on that one, if I were you."

"But I don't deserve to be forgiven."

"You were hurting, and I didn't want you to hurt more, so we didn't talk about it."

We sat in the kitchen, not talking or moving, until I couldn't stand it anymore. "Need any driftwood?"

"No, not really. You want to go to the beach, though?"

I nodded.

"I'll get my jacket." She stood up with all the energy I had at my age.

We spent two hours at Willow Beach. We didn't say much. We walked, picked up driftwood, talked about the magazine and her latest painting. It felt good to just be together. When we were back in my car, I said, "I thought I was happy. But I drink too much and I don't sleep at night."

"You've been as happy as you know how to be. You'll figure it out." She stroked my back.

"I admire your faith."

"That's a good start."

Later, on my way home, I felt the wound of my mother's illness and the odd possibility that all would be well.

I put a lot of energy into the magazine over the next week, and at the end of it, when it was at the printer and done, I asked Rochelle if she wanted to go to Greece. Her eyes widened with anticipation. "You deserve it."

She stood up and came over to give me a hug. I looked up at her, surprised.

"Was that too forward?"

"I don't think anyone's ever hugged me in the office."

Her eyes told me that I was usually too unapproachable.

"You guys don't like me much."

"It's not that. You don't look like you want to be hugged."

I took that in. Then I said, "My mother is dying. I haven't spent enough time with her. I only have now."

She was quiet as she searched for the words and then said, "I'm sorry. I hope you find it to be healing."

I was left wondering why she thought I needed healing. Healing? Me? What was it a young woman like Rochelle knew that I didn't know?

Mom had no reason to complain about how I spent my Thanksgiving. Time just stopped. "I didn't know you had devotion in you," she commented.

I caught my willowy Cassie glancing our way. I was using the baster, trying not to get juice all over the stove, Mom was glazing sweet potatoes. I reached out to touch my daughter's belly, let my hand linger, felt the alien movement and remembered like it was yesterday what it felt like to have a child inside me. "I guess we were wrong."

Thanksgiving weekend, I peeled carrots in the kitchen while Mom napped in the living room. She had The Beatles on the CD player, and I had been thinking about her sudden nostalgic bent. It had been a quiet celebration, all of us knowing this would be Mom's last Thanksgiving with us, and Ben, Mom, and I holed up in the sitting room to watch old movies all weekend. Popcorn could be found in between the couch cushions and smashed into the rug.

My cell phone rang just as I was wiping off my hands, and I answered without looking at it. "Hey there." Robert's soft bedroom voice came through the receiver. I felt the shiver run through me. I felt his hands on me, caressing me, molding me into something new. I no longer felt like the Dragon Lady, and love had everything to do with it.

"Hi."

"Are you all right?"

"I'm missing you." I hadn't known it until I said it out loud.

"Really?"

"Yes, but I can't do anything about it right now."

The pause dragged out long. "The holiday issue is really nice. I saw a proof. Lots of heart and soul. I think you inspired your staff too."

I smiled. "Really?" Wow.

"Certainly seems like it. When can I see you?"

"I—"

"What? You're not available?"

I sighed. "Robert, I like you. A lot. But I'm here in Conneaut trying to find "me" again. I lost her along the way, and now I don't even know who she is."

"She's there. I see her once in a while." He was teasing me.

"I love that you notice." The Beatles was turned off. Mom walked into the room. "I have to get going." Mom shook her head vigorously. "I'm trying to get dinner in the oven. Pot roast." Mom made a face, screwing up her face and looking up at the ceiling, like "Oh lord."

"I'll call you. Promise."

He sighed. "Okay, I give. You didn't even ask how I am." He hung up.

Mom took the phone from me, looked at the name on it. "A man. And you're too busy for him? I'll never understand you."

"I don't understand either."

I was there every weekend. Wine and long walks and books before sleep were part of my routine, but sleeping through the night was a nice change. Mom and I talked and walked and caught up with an ease that took me back to childhood and Mom making me dandelion necklaces while we sat in the grass in our backyard, before the divorce.

And then it was Christmas. Mom twinkled at Dazzles, her art gallery, where she threw a holiday gala complete with party favors she hand painted. Cassie and her husband Mike brought a big Frazier fir into the living room at Windy Hill and Mom clapped from her winged back chair. Cassie's belly protruded into the tree as she reached up to hang ornaments.

Bittersweet. I watched Mom's face, saw her joy, knew she also knew this was the last time. That ability to look fear in the face, to live each day to its fullest, to know God would provide eluded me, but Mom had it in aces.

Cassie looked at me strangely when I went to church on New Year's Eve. I worried Mom thought I was a convert.

The day the email came out announcing the International Magazine Association Best Editing Award, I'd just come in from an errand in the cold. The lake had just frozen. From my building, past the Mall, out past the stadium and Shoreway, and out into the lake before the breakwall, the world was white.

"IMA announces the annual international awards for magazine writing, editing, photography, and layout. Although we found much talent out there, we had to choose." I scanned down the page until I found my name: "Elizabeth Kramer, best travel magazine editor, for her innovative monthly columns, hot "in every issue" clips, and well-thought features." I walked out into the hallway. "Did you see this?" I asked Mo, pointing toward the laptop in my hands.

She was genuinely happy. "Hey, everyone, guess who won the travel magazine editor of the year award." She caught everyone's attention with her speaker's voice, and then she turned to show me off to the world. "Betsy!"

I basked in the handshakes and pats on the back and a week of people mentioning it in the hallway and through e-mails, and then it was over, forgotten. It was a temporary recognition, in a way. The joy it gave lasted only a short week.

When the weather warmed in late February, Mom and I started going to the beach every Saturday, collecting driftwood like she had all the time in the world to make it into the art she sold at her gallery. "I'm living in the moment without trying," I said.

Mom smiled. "It's not something one tries to do, honey."

She was moving slower all the time and getting thinner every week. On our fourth Saturday, she stumbled and couldn't get up. I put my hands under her armpits and lifted her dead weight. We struggled to get to the car.

The next weekend, I found her in her bedroom when I arrived. "It's gorgeous out there, Mom. It's spring. Wanna go to the beach?"

"You go without me." She waved me off. "I'm too tired."

Ben shook his head from the doorway.

"Okay. If you're too tired, it can wait. There will be other beautiful days. Can I read to you?" I picked up the John Irving novel we'd been reading and opened it to the page where we left off.

She was asleep. I listened to her labored breathing. Her hand on top of the blanket looked like the hand of an eighty-year-old. She was lying on her back; she never laid on her back.

Outside her room, Ben had a stricken look in his eyes. "I called the doctor and he came out yesterday because I couldn't get her out of bed. She admitted she hurts. All over. The doctor said it's normal."

Despite witnessing it, I didn't believe it. But I could still feel how hard it had been to lift her to her feet, how weak she'd been the week before. "Can't she fight it?"

"She doesn't want to. Let her be, okay?"

Later, Mom opened her eyes while I sat near her. I'd been thinking about how she thought my return to Windy Hill meant my priorities had changed. I thought I'd only been seeing my mother through her final days. After she died, life would get back to normalcy again. But maybe Mom knew, as I was discovering, that I no longer knew what normal was.

"Hi, Mom."

She brushed my cheek with her finger. Mom would die, and I still had a father somewhere out there in the world. It was a great love story until he went back to Italy.

"Can I ask you something?"

She nodded weakly.

"Where's my father?"

Startled, she turned her head towards the window. There was a long pause before she said, "I don't want you to know."

Was this stubbornness to continue even though she was dying? "You know then?"

She didn't look at me. "Yes."

"Don't you think I should have a father?"

"Not that man. Ben can be your father."

"Mom . . . come on." My voice rose. I felt desperate. The words came out mean. I could be mean now—time was running out.

"You're being selfish."

She closed her eyes and turned away.

"Please tell me."

No answer.

I was exasperated. "I'll never understand why you would keep him from me."

The rift was still there, between us. Mom wouldn't tell me the truth. She didn't really forgive me. If she forgave me, she wouldn't be able to withhold the truth.

Mom only woke for short periods of time as spring brought longer days. She got round-the-clock care at the hospital and improved with intravenous feeding. Mom slept, hooked up to monitors. I sat and held her hand. Ben came in and held her hand. When we left the hospital, we asked the nurses to sit there with her, even though we knew they wouldn't.

"Hey, guess what?" Mike practically jumped into the room. Mom startled, I stood up.

"What?" He was acting very weird.

"You're going to be a grandmother, very soon."

Mom laughed. I hugged Mike. "Is she here?"

"Yep. She's in labor and delivery."

"Go," Mom said.

And I did. I visited Cassie, her face clenched in effort as she breathed through the contractions, and she let me hold her hand as her eyes held onto her husband's. Mike was a good labor coach, and as the contractions came faster and stronger, I spent more time with Cassie than with Mom. My granddaughter was a pink, curled up being who was trying to open her eyes. It was too bright in the world. I loved her instantly. I held the newborn and stroked my worn daughter's hair. "I'm sorry I haven't been around much. Can I be your mother, this baby's grandmother?"

Her eyes were still wet with tears of joy and relief. "I named her after you and grandma. Elizabeth Margaret. We'll call her Beth."

I must have been doing something right. It was the first kindness or acknowledgment from my daughter in years. "I'll be here for you guys, whatever you need."

"I just wish . . ." Cassie said.

I knew she wished things hadn't been the way they'd been, that we didn't have the coldness and disappointment between us. "We can't undo the past, but we can start over." I handed the baby back to her.

Back in my mother's room, I said, "Mom, it's incredible. She's perfect."

"Of course she is," Mom said. "I can't wait to see her little toes and teeny face."

"I remember when Cassie was born, how in love I was with the baby. I haven't been in love . . ."

"I know, darling."

"Mom?" We weren't talking about babies any more.

"You can pretend whatever you want to pretend, but I know you loved that man fiercely. You were so strange that summer. I couldn't figure out why you broke up with him. He called so many times . . ." Mom dismissed me with her hand and turned her head. "It was a bunch of ridiculousness."

I didn't know what to say. She'd never said anything like that to me, not even that summer when I was inconsolable over losing Tom. "I wasn't good enough for him."

She raised her voice and pointed a finger at me. "Jesus H Christ, and you know I don't swear. He thought you were his soul mate. You were soul mates, far as I could see. How could you not be good enough for him? Who made you the judge of that anyway?"

Me and my sins. Me and my inability to believe in love.

"Fuck, Jerry," she said as she laid back down. "I should be apologizing to you."

"Jerry?"

"You know what I mean." She drifted off to sleep again.

I was stunned. Mom knew about Jerry?

I remembered how his hands claimed my body. He used it how he needed to. He left me spent, almost unconscious, with no will of my own. No will to fight. I remembered how much I needed him, how obsessed I was about when I'd get my next fix.

A nurse came in to check on Mom's vitals, so I left to go to Cassie's room. As I stared into the eyes of my granddaughter, I knew God was part of the miracle.

Why wasn't God there to save me from Jerry?

We went into top-care mode in April when Mom came home and hospice got involved. I arrived at the house around five every afternoon to relieve the nurse, care for Mom, and make dinner. Ben ate dinner and went to bed. I kept watch until he got up at one in the morning. Then it was my turn to go to bed. I slept until seven, and Ben and I ate breakfast together before we headed off to work when the visiting nurse came. The days became one long unhappy fog.

We were united in our desire for Mom not to die alone.

During that time, Mom had wonderfully lucid moments. She would say to me, out of the blue, "Remember our trip to Niagara Falls when you were twelve and how beautiful the tulips were in the gardens near the falls? How about Niagara-on-the-Lake? They had such a nice Christmas shop on that street."

One tired evening, Ben told me Mom had awakened repeatedly the previous night. She said the fairies wouldn't let her sleep. She said the wood fairies were covered in green fern velvet with skin the color of acorns and the river fairies wore shapeless flowing gowns the color of the sun's reflection in water. He'd bought a fairy music box on his way home.

We put it next to Mom's bed. It played Tchaikovsky's "Dance of the Sugar Plum Fairy." Mom watched with contentment as the fairies danced. "It's like my dream, only they seem happy."

"I hope you dream happy dreams tonight," I said. Since when were Mom's dreams unhappy?

A week later, Mom was propped up in bed on a pile of pillows when I arrived.

"It's almost time," she said.

"Time?" I was confused until I saw her resigned face.

"Can you go get the teacup?"

I patted her arm, nodded, and followed the path of the Oriental rugs down the wooden stairs. "Almost time, almost time," my feet beat out. My hand shook as I reached around wine glasses in the gloomy light of the dining room to pick up the teacup Grandpa brought home from Japan. I steadied the cup in its saucer as I walked back up the steps.

Mom's eyes were closed. For a moment, I worried that she was gone, but she opened her eyes and said, "It's yours now." I wiped at the tears on my cheeks with the back of my hand but didn't try to hide them. "You're still a young woman. Live well. Notice the beauty. The roses have thorns, but they won't kill you. Have hope. Do what you need to do to move on to a better life."

"But . . ."

"Oh, I know what you do. You hook up with strangers in ship cabins, on the beach, in gondolas for all I know."

"It's not as bad as all that. It's not as though I sleep with them."

"No, I don't think you sleep with all of them, but you sleep with some. I know men and how they are with women they've slept with. I catch the clues, things like expensive jewelry bought in Bermuda where I know jewelry costs three times as much as it should. You tell me Robert, a friend, bought it for you while over there to write a story on spas. When the magazine came out, I read your romantic article and saw that the photographer's name was Robert. Out of sight, out of mind, and you move on."

I felt anger flare. My defensive instinct kicked in, but I banished it. I put my head down on the bed next to her shoulder. She stroked my hair, like when I was a girl. My mother was right, and I knew it.

When she was asleep again, I put the teacup back where it belonged. It might be mine, but it would stay in my grandparents' home. I went out the back door to sit on the stoop. The sun was an orange orb above the horizon leaving pink sky in its wake. I hugged my knees in close as I looked out at the farmland and thought about the seventy-acre farm with its frame farmhouse, Amish-built barn and silo, dairy processing plant, and keeper's cottage. The house Grandpa built when he came home from the war was going to be half mine.

The daffodils were closed up for the night. Their long slender stalks curled toward the moon. They grew in clumps all along the back of the house on either side of where I sat. *Why does she have to die during daffodil days?*

I don't know how long I sat there on the stoop. I eventually picked myself up and went back to her room. When she woke, her face was filled with concern and urgency as if she had something to tell me that she didn't know how to say. "I'll hold on to the teacup," I said. "But it will stay in this house."

She smiled blissfully. I'd said what she wanted to hear.

CHAPTER TWO – THE TREE HOUSE

Ben's urgent cry woke me from a light sleep in the middle of the night. My clock read two in the morning. By the time I reached their room, he was on his knees, withered and crumpled in the semi-darkness, holding her hand, and crying. The moon lit her smooth lank features to grayness, and her wispy hair fanned the pillow that cradled her head. I knelt on the other side of the bed and listened to her faint breath. I said her name and stroked her cheek.

My mother's husband and I waited. I tried not to think about what was happening and became part of the breathing, the darkness, the consuming moment. The slow rise and fall of her chest was reassuring even though the breaths were too far apart. Like God's voice whispering on the wind, she sighed, took a final brave inhale, then failed to exhale. Ben and I sat immobile, waiting. It was as if we were waiting for God to say, "It is done."

A slight movement, and then Ben and I felt more than heard a sigh like the wings of a dragonfly. Our eyes met over her body. Her spirit had flown away. Everything that had come between Mom and me flew away as well. It was an awesome moment.

I felt the old Christian resignation that "it was meant to be" in the way he gathered up his shoulders and rose onto the chair on the other side of the bed. I was afraid to see the despair on his face because it matched my own. We had no words. We were miserable, black-mooded, and melancholy. A life was over and the finality of it was incomprehensible. Now I was an orphan and all I had was my daughter and her family. I had little else in the way of relationships. Being with Mom had shown me how to care again, but it was too late.

We sat by her bedside until dawn lit the room and I looked out the window to see Pedro ambling towards the cow barn. It was time to make some coffee.

The grandfather clock struck six times as I creaked down the stairs past the oak door as I headed to the kitchen. I pulled the can of coffee from the refrigerator, filled a filter, added water. The coffee pot brewed fitfully. I leaned against the wall next to the telephone to gather my thoughts before I dialed Cassie's number.

Mike answered in a sleep-crusted voice, but perked up when I said his name. "She's gone," was all I could muster. He said he'd let Cassie know. I was thankful no other words were needed.

Half an hour later, long, dark hair wet from a shower, my tall, slim daughter came through the kitchen door, briefly looked at me, and said, "I should have been here."

"You didn't know."

"She said good-bye to me yesterday. She knew. I should have stayed last night."

I reached out to her, but she brushed past and left me sitting at the kitchen table with my tepid cup of coffee. Her footsteps on the stairs sounded too loud and urgent for something that was already done. When she came back into the room a few minutes later she went directly to the telephone.

"I don't want them to take her yet."

She looked at me in disbelief and shook her head. Her mouth was pinched. "They have to."

"She's not theirs." I wanted her to be with us longer. I thought that if she stayed in that room, she was still with us.

"Mom, they'll take her to the funeral home. She's not there in that body anyway. You show up here at the end and think you know the way, the right things to do?"

I looked down at the cup in my hands and started crying. Uncharacteristically, she stroked my shoulder, hesitation in her touch. Her muffled sobs surfaced as ugly cough-like hiccups louder than my moans. We wailed like Old Testament women. We sounded inhuman, or maybe too human. We were overwhelmed by Death's finality. I felt physically ill.

Mom, I thought, *how could you leave me when we scarcely began again?*

When the wailing stopped, Cassie moved over to the window above the sink. In the morning light, her drying hair shone with red highlights. We heard Ben's drumbeat sobs of loss streaming through the ceiling.

The flashing red lights of the ambulance disturbed the fragrant moist morning. I swept past Cassie, opened the back screen door, and walked out. Despite my expressed desire to leave her longer, the ambulance came to take her away from the only true home she'd ever known. I didn't want to witness that.

Anger mixed with grief, a heady concoction. I walked past the barn with the Ohio Bicentennial painting on its side and out through the greening pasture. I continued into the woods along the creek, and found the long country road into town. Walking hard took away the anger.

I slowed to a stroll on the sidewalk. The storefronts may as well have been empty for what I saw of them. I already knew that Mimi's Bakery had a couple of tiered wedding cakes in her window and Hardy's Hardware sported a small riding mower and a fistful of seed packs spread against bags of topsoil. I turned off Main onto Maple to avoid Dazzles and almost ran into Rick who was coming out of his townhouse.

"I'm sorry, Betsy," my ex-husband said when he read the expression on my face.

He wore jeans and a long-sleeved cotton shirt. The lines on his face and the longish gray hair surprised me. If I broke down here, I'd be in his alcoholic life again. I felt his eyes taking in the cropped pants and baggy sweater over a body that had become thin with stress. Our eyes met. "I need to go," I said.

He nodded and let me pass.

I walked blindly until I came to Willow Beach. As I strolled along the shoreline, the beach disappeared and my feet were in the water. Wild rambling vines scratched my legs as I walked through the brambles at water's edge. The sun was high and warmed me beneath my loose-knit cotton sweater. I kept walking, my sandals held high above the roiling surf that seemed angry that my mother had been taken away. I couldn't decide with whom I was most angry, God, Mom, or me.

Searching the horizon from the sandy cove, I sought Mom's presence, but all I found was emptiness. I stood in the spot where Rick and I used to meet almost thirty years ago. Mom, with her mocha-brown hair piled up high on her head flirted with the 21-year-old man who knew all the right things to say to a lady.

Memories of Mom came back to me. I thought about how happy she'd been when Rick and I were married, how much she cooed over the baby when Cassie was born, how she'd cried at night, and how she stubbornly refused to tell me anything about my father.

When the wave of anger came over me, I was angry with her, not me, and not God. She told me very little about my father. She pretended he didn't exist. She didn't care that the children at school felt sorry that I didn't have a father and that they taunted me with "bastard child" on the playground. She ignored my questions about what he looked like, what he meant to her, did she miss him, what was it that she loved most about him—truthfully, I'd never gotten around to asking some of those questions because she wouldn't even tell me how tall he was.

He was a mystery and her dirty secret. I screamed into the wind, "Mom! Where's my father? Did he try to find me? How can you leave me and not tell me where he is?"

Defeated, I sat down on the damp sand and stared out at the lake. I missed her even in her stubbornness. The waves crashed against the rocks angrily, then the water quieted until another slammed the shore. I was tired. I was drained. I was empty. I didn't know how to feel. I felt everything and nothing at once. I was hollowed out. My head and stomach ached, my knees twitched. I started shaking and couldn't get warm. I stood up and walked the shore. The sand stuck to the bottom of my feet. The water was cold, but I didn't care. My mother was gone.

Who's going to teach me to live now?

No answer came back to me. I felt more alone than I ever had in my life. I'd never had a father, but there had always been Mom. Now I wanted the father more than I ever had. I had to have at least one parent.

Where are you, the man who made me, the man who left my mother alone and pregnant when she was all of twenty? Where are you, you lousy Dago?

"Shit," I said out loud. "Why should I have a father?" My grandfather, even though he was angry with that lousy Dago, had been a good father, a faithful husband, despite his faults. Mom had at least had that.

I headed back home. In the shallow valley near our woods, I stopped at the Magical Pond. When Mom was a girl, she believed wood nymphs and pond fairies came out at night to sit on toad stools, climb the cattails, and ride on the backs of dragonflies. During the day, the woods, tall grasses, and clouds hovered over the smooth mirrored surface of the pond that was sheltered from the strong winds startled up by Lake Erie's shallow depth. I sat on the edge, in the shadow of a row of evergreens, my feet close to the mud at water's edge.

A balmy wind caressed my cheek. I felt my breath slow as the breeze calmed me and seemed to tell me I'd done my best in my mother's final days. My life no longer writhed but felt as still as the water of the pond. I was at peace. I sat and waited until I felt her presence. I looked for her in last year's tall brown grasses. "Mom," I said. "I'm sorry I was so caught up in my work. But I'm glad we had our time together these last six months. Did it make up for not being there when you were raising my daughter, when your parents died, and when you decided to live your dreams at sixty?"

I doubted it. Like the dying man asking for forgiveness and swearing he loves Jesus, I worried I had no right into heaven for owning up to my sins in the final moments. If I remembered the parable, the prodigal son came home to a warm greeting while his faithful brother faded into the walls. Neither the prodigal son nor the newly-saved deserved their rewards any more than I did. God was near.

A goose swooped to drag its feet against the surface of the water. It left a V-shaped wake as it pulled its wings in and glided across the dark reflective pond. The bird moved forward, then turned like a sailboat changing directions to come across the pond from the other direction. I picked up a pebble from the ground next to where I sat in the grassy reeds, raised my arm to toss it, and stopped. I decided against disturbing the peace of the lonely goose on our Magical Pond. A meditative calmness from above rested on my shoulders and drew them down, removed the tension from my neck, and calmed my breathing. I closed my eyes and let God in. My thoughts were replaced by wordless silence.

I felt drawn to the woods. The path I'd followed as a girl was freshly tramped down. Trespassers. I wondered who wandered into this part of the woods that led to my old hideout. Ten minutes along a meandering path that took me past vernal pools and skunk cabbage brought me to the foot of the old oak tree. The rough-hewn tree house my grandfather built when I was eight loomed above, its unpainted oak siding grayed by the elements, the windows gaping like wide cave openings. The ladder of boards hammered into the ancient oak was intact. I couldn't imagine how my grandfather thought it a good idea for a child to climb a ladder of nailed boards to a space floating in the air fifteen feet off the ground. But he had no fear, and I loved having a place of my own.

I shivered when I thought about how cold Cassie's eyes had been when she saw me sneaking out the back door when the ambulance came. My daughter had become my judge, and I didn't want to go back home.

Still feeling Mom with me, I asked aloud, "What is a good mother?" My voice was loud in the stillness of the woods where birds chirped. The air smelled green. Ferns were starting to uncurl on their stalks and violets covered the forest floor. My mother was the sort of woman who wore her hair long beyond the age of fifty and was never afraid of getting her good shoes dirty when she spied weeds in the garden. She danced and sang for no apparent reason. When I returned home for the night as a teenager, the sound of crickets was troubled by her robust soprano filling the air from the open window.

The last time I'd been in the tree house was during my sixteenth summer. After that, it had been too painful to visit again. And here I was, at the foot of this place that had been a solace and then a place to avoid. *Why am I here in this place of betrayal and sin and unforgiveness?*

I climbed the ladder.

Cars were parked outside when I arrived back at the house that afternoon. The living room was full of people. Lots of hugs, lots of kind words, lots of food spread out across our dining room table. Someone offered me a gin and tonic, and I sipped without thinking. Cassie asked if I was okay.

"I'm sorry," I said.

She looked startled. "About being gone?"

I nodded but said, "About everything."

Tears came to her eyes and she turned toward Mike, who guided her to the couch.

When Ben took my hand and tried to comfort me, it was more than I could stand. I gave him a hug and said, "Mom came to me at the pond."

He smiled and put his arm around me.

"I can't do this now," I said.

I pulled away, and he nodded with understanding. We seemed to have come to an agreement that everything was optional and careful. We didn't want to interrupt anyone's feelings or disturb any peace. If we said too much, there could be a breakdown, a banged door, or a screaming fit in response, so we gave each other space.

I slipped up the stairs to Mom's "salon," her private space carved from a spare bedroom waiting to be used. The sunny yellow walls bore long afternoon shadows. Her last watercolor sat on the easel by the window, and I felt the ache of knowing she would never add the brush strokes to "pink" the sky of the painting.

I walked to the shelves near her desk and ran my hands over the leather-bound journals until I found the last one on the right. The book felt solid and heavy in my hands, stiff and empty and ready for my scrawling long-hand.

I sank gingerly onto the edge of the cushioned armchair at the antique desk and looked out the window over the fields of Windy Hill. On the first page I wrote "A Meandering Creek Turning Up Muck." That was what my life was, and the muck was pretty much choking me now that Mom was gone. *How do I chronicle a life that feels so untidy and find a new, straighter path?* Winifred batted the paper, then settled onto the desk, her paw on top of mine, purring. I sat with the blank page under my hand.

Cassie's voice carried from the kitchen below as she tried to soothe my grandbaby Beth. Through the window, I saw Mandy Stephenson's old Ford pickup roll down the driveway and the unsteady woman stretched her legs to the gravel as she balanced a casserole in her arms. Over the murmuring voices below, the baby's cry broke the quiet.

Sitting with the blank journal in hand, I wanted to get the moment down, the grief, the emptiness, the anger, but I couldn't transcribe my feelings. I couldn't even describe how cold Lake Erie's water felt on my feet earlier in the day. I pulled Mom's last journal from the shelf and opened to the last journal page dated two weeks before she died, when she was too weak to do anything else and even a journal entry would have been difficult.

> My life was not all I wanted it to be, but it was enough. I hope the people I leave behind will think I lived it well. The key is in being truthful, with others, but especially with one's self.

How does it feel to know you are dying and to write something like that? How could she write that but not tell me about my father? What would I write today if I knew I was dying? Is my life enough? Have I lived well? Am I truthful, especially with myself?

I didn't like the answers I came up with. Good thing I wasn't about to die. I couldn't find it in me to write anything down.

I had to call my friend Maria, not only because I needed her but because she would want to be there for me. I hesitated because our phone calls were staccato starts and stops as she dealt with four kids and a husband. Even busy, she always had time for me. "Geez, Betsy," she said when I told her. "You must be crushed. I have to get dinner done, and then I'll come over."

"You don't need to do that," but in my heart I knew it was exactly what I needed.

"Yes, I do. You need me more than these guys do. Do you have food?" I hear the muffled tonal qualities of consternation and consolation, but not the actual words, like muffled radio from another room, in the background.

"Enough to feed us for a month."

"Okay, then I'll just come over. In the meantime, take care of Ben."

"How —"

She didn't let me finish. "If you take care of him, you'll be able to deal with what you're feeling."

Maria was right—staying in my head, being reflective, should wait for later. I didn't know what I thought about anything. It was raw emotion.

I also needed to call Linda, my childhood friend in California. The distance between us had grown over the last twenty years and when we spoke, silence stretched the void. All I said was, "Mom died early this morning."

It took a few seconds, as if she were gathering the courage to say the words that may not come out right. Then the voice that I'd known since we were seven said, "I'm sorry, Betsy. I can't imagine how it would feel to lose my mother. Would it be the same as what it's like to lose a father? And not as bad as losing a child, I suppose, oh, there we go again, I'm thinking about little Susie. When will I get over that one?"

I sighed and said, "You won't, Linda. But right now, today, I've lost my mother, and Susie died fifteen years ago."

"There you go again. You're unsympathetic. I remember when I lost my dog Rollo how you walked around with me calling, but you didn't sound like you were trying very hard."

"So, you're saying I wasn't sympathetic when Susie died."

"That's what I'm saying. You were getting ready to go on a trip for work and weren't even willing to delay things by a day or two."

"Christ," I said under my breath.

"Oh, this isn't about me, it's about you. My therapist tells me I have to understand that everything isn't about me. I'm trying. Am I trying enough, Betsy?"

I shook my head and spoke carefully into my cell phone. "No. You did it again, turned it all back in your direction."

"Oh, of course. You're right. Let's start over, shall we?" Her voice became fake and sugar-sweet. "Betsy, honey, I'm so sorry to hear about your mother. How are you doing?" She went on about how important mothers are and how Mom would still be there for me, in spirit. "Why, Mom's so much a part of my life, we almost don't have to talk to each other, sort of like a long marriage." She laughed nervously.

I realized she didn't want to listen to what I had to say. I knew she was a diarist, so I said, "I tried to write about it, and I can't. I walked for a long time and ended up at Willow Beach."

"Willow Beach? Betsy, that's, what, three miles from Windy Hill?"

"I know. Imagine how I felt when I realized I had to walk back."

"You're not yourself."

"I wouldn't say that. I think this is me."

"Maybe you should write about that."

I couldn't. "You know, I need to get going. I hate to cut you off, but . . ."

"Wait. When's the funeral?"

"It'll probably be on Friday." I hung up without saying good-bye, but Linda would understand why as soon as she disconnected her end of the call.

I reached my hand down to pet Winifred's rabbit-foot soft fur. She rubbed against my bare legs like she did when she was hungry.

Out the window, the comings and goings of people who knew us, people I didn't know anymore, took place against the scenery.

It was time to be with my family. In the kitchen, Ben was setting the table for dinner, Mike was feeding Beth a bottle, and Cassie was pulling a dish out of the oven. They all looked at me, and I waved my hand in greeting. After Cassie put the tuna noodle casserole on the table, we followed Ben's lead as he bowed his head to pray.

"Thank you for bringing Margaret into our lives. Keep her close, God. She was one of your best soldiers. Amen." He squeezed my hand and nodded to me when we looked up from the table.

"You were the best thing in Mom's life, you know that?" I said to Ben as we continued to hold hands.

He looked embarrassed. "I did what I had to do. I was her *husband.*"

"You were the best husband she could have had."

He looked at me as if I was someone other than me. "My, how you've changed. I don't think you would have said that a few months ago."

"What? I couldn't give a compliment?"

He scrunched up his face and looked at me sideways. "No, I don't think you could. I'm glad you gave up so much time to be here. You needed to be here as much as your Mom needed you to be here."

I looked at Cassie to see if she was agreeing with him, but she held up a hand. "Don't get me into this." She took a breath, then announced "Guess what? I spoke with the funeral home. We're all set for Friday." She looked as tired as I felt, and she must have thought the same thing because she said, "How you doing, Mom?"

"Fine" I answered. *She may love me after all.*

"You were gone a long time today. We weren't sure if you were coming back."

"I walked."

"That's what we figured, but you should have called us. Are you taking lessons from Dad?"

"God, no." Her accusation smarted but I understood it. Rick used to disappear for entire nights. Had Cassie known? She was so little when our marriage ended. "I've been thinking a lot about Mom and me. I wish she'd told me more about my father, if you want to know the truth. I guess a bad father isn't a good one to have, but . . . Cassie, do you remember your father being gone at night?"

"Oh, yeah," she said in a breathless tone with her eyebrows raised. "I remember those days more than I want to, you crying and standing by the window, putting me to bed with tears streaming down your face, me asking what was wrong, and you saying, 'nothing, honey' when I knew something was. Then in the morning the two of you would sit at the kitchen table not talking to each other but smiling at me as I ate my cereal."

"I didn't know. All these years I thought you didn't remember a thing."

"Did you bother to ask?" Her voice sounded accusatory. Mike

reached over and put his hand on hers.

"Did your walk make you feel better?" Ben asked.

"I spent some time by the Magical Pond after my walk. I felt like the pond was whispering that everything would be all right."

"God was there. He wants you to let go of your anger and give into his plan."

I waved him off. "That theory won't hold with me."

He smiled. I think he thought I was on the edge of conversion and it was a game to get me fully into his camp of fundamentalist theology. "You didn't get much sleep," Ben said. "I napped for three hours this morning."

"I'm glad you could."

"It's important to take care of ourselves."

"I know. Maria will be here soon."

"She'll liven up this place," Cassie said.

I took a bite of the tuna casserole that tasted like someone boiled noodles, added canned tuna and condensed mushroom soup and didn't bother to add spices. I pushed my plate away.

I tried to remember that people meant well. They did.

Maria embraced me warmly when I met her at the door a short while later. She insisted on sitting close enough on the loveseat to drape her arm around me, so I settled back into her like she was a lover. While Ben sat in the wing back chair and Cassie's small family filled the couch, Maria told us stories about growing up in Upper Michigan before her family moved to Conneaut. Moose looked in their windows, the family calendar hung on the outhouse wall with a pen on a string hanging from it, and her parents kicked their seven kids out of the house on Sunday afternoons so they could have sex alone in the house.

Ben said, "One of the best things about getting married after your children are gone is how much alone time there is. Our marriage was a joy and a blessing every day. We knew we would only have a decade or two together, so we soaked it all up." His voice became quieter and trailed off. "Turns out we didn't have as much time as we thought."

Tears welled in his eyes, and I felt the welling of my own. I liked the image of him and Mom getting up in the morning and moving about the kitchen together, making coffee and toast, sanctifying the day with their routine.

"Grandma had a way of bringing everyone around her into the moment. She treasured her moments," Cassie said.

"Those days on the beach," I said. "I thought of her when I was there today, about how she took me down there to pick out driftwood. I wonder if she was trying to convince me she'd be around long enough . . ."

"Stop," Cassie said. She covered her ears. I got up and took Beth from her and brought the baby back to the loveseat with me.

Maria changed the conversation back to stories from the Upper Peninsula. "A raccoon nested and gave birth under the sink in our kitchen when I was ten. When Dad couldn't coax her out, the game warden came and spent an hour enduring angry screeches until he got close enough to tranquilize her. We had to close up a hole in the floor of the cabin—that's how she got in."

I lost the ability to follow the thread of even the wildest of stories ("Dad knew you were supposed to stand up to a bear when you saw one, but he couldn't do it, he ran zig-zag through the woods and got to the house . . .") and nodded off. When Maria whispered "go to bed," I stumbled up the stairs to my room, flopped onto the bed, and pulled the bedspread over me.

I woke in the clothes I'd been wearing for twenty-four hours, went to Mom's salon and found the volume of Mom's journal from when I was fifteen. I looked for Jerry's name and read through entries about nice evenings they'd had, how she wasn't ready for sex with him, sections where she said she wasn't in love with him. I was relieved that she didn't love him.

Then I found an entry from September of that year. She wrote:

> Something's changed with Betsy. She's become a sexual being overnight. All of a sudden, she's wearing tighter, more provocative clothing, big-hooped earrings, and eyeliner.
>
> If it were merely that, I wouldn't worry. She's sixteen. But I've noticed she's attentive to Jerry when he comes to dinner. They giggle together, feet touching under the kitchen table. Yesterday, I caught Jerry with his arm around her in the kitchen, and it looked like he was close to kissing her neck, but I couldn't be sure. The way they jumped away from each other when I entered the room told me all I need to know. They have a secret relationship.

> I'm not going to say anything to Betsy. She would be ashamed. But Jerry . . . oh, my God. He's molested my daughter. I don't know how far it's gone, but I need to figure it out. I don't think he'd have sex with her. I hope he's not that stupid.
>
> I hope this doesn't hurt Betsy. She may be a willing participant, but that doesn't mean it's not harmful.

The next entry was written a week later:

> I told Jerry to stay away from us. I changed the locks. I told Betsy he and I broke up. I made it clear that she should be on my side and stay away from him.
>
> Whether he told me the truth or not is not possible to know. He denied anything was happening other than some heavy petting. He actually said he loved her, which made me so angry I shoved him out the door. Heavy petting! What does that mean?
>
> So I asked Betsy whether she had a boyfriend, what happened to Tom. She said she doesn't have a boyfriend and that Tom is too intense. He scared her with how much he liked her, she said. When I asked whether she liked Jerry, she gave me that look that said I'd lost my mind, so I backed off.

She didn't know everything. No one knew everything. Only Jerry and I knew the truth. I sat down at the desk where the blank journal page still waited, and then I wrote.

> I fell asleep in my clothes last night. The day started out with Ben calling to me and me going to Mom's bed for her final moments. I don't know if she knew we were there, but it was peaceful, just the three of us, and Mom's quiet breaths. I was holding her hand, listening and waiting, and it felt like a sacred moment, a time of total concentration on what was happening. Then she stopped breathing, and we felt her soul leave her body.
>
> I had to get away when Cassie came over and started putting things in order. I felt we needed to give it time. We could have gathered around, we could have talked and comforted each other, but she was calling 9-1-1 and when I left, she was going to the door to let in the EMS people. It felt at odds with what Ben and I

felt in the bedroom, which was a special moment of passing into the next world.

So I walked. Through town and to Willow Beach. I didn't stop until I came to the cove and there Mom's spirit's out there, fluttering, waiting for us to call to her, and then she'll come. But she didn't. I was crying as I walked back home. Like a kid, I walked through fields and backyards and along the creek until I came to the tree house. I climbed the ladder to the tree house, surprised by how easy it was. Inside I found the same table and benches surrounded by windows on four sides. The old green blanket I used to nap on had survived the moths and spiders and was lying in a corner where I left it. I could picture the table set with tea for my dolls.

Birds chattered in the trees. A robin sat on a branch outside the window, its beady eyes on me.

I can't believe how it came back to me. I felt his big hand on my thigh and how my desire rose with the first kiss, light and playful, as we sat on the floor knowing we were utterly alone and would never be found out. He was old enough to be my father, but we spent fervent afternoons having sex on the floor of the tree house, breaking to smoke his imported cigarettes until his tongue on my shoulder blade roused me again and we fell to the blanket and stayed.

I haven't thought about Jerry for a long time. Having sex with my mother's boyfriend made me grown up, and made me bad. It was also a kick in the face of anyone who ever felt I wasn't adult enough. I was a kid who wanted to be more than I was, more than a girl on a farm, more than the unwanted child of an Italian guy who left my mother, more than Margaret's daughter who talked to cows and liked baking cookies with her grandmother. I liked having a secret life.

I stopped going to the tree house when I stopped seeing Jerry. Was it because the tree house made me feel guilty or that I missed him? I suppose it was some of both. But it was mostly that feeling that came over me all over again when I was there yesterday, the feeling of doing something that was against what I believed in.

"Mom?" I said out loud. "What do I do now?" I waited like we're taught to wait after a prayer. But I didn't get an answer.

God didn't say anything out loud in a God voice, but I got lost in spending time with Mom's ghost at Windy Hill.

CHAPTER THREE – THE TEACUP

Mom married Ben on the very spot where the casket rested on her funeral day. Her closed casket was decorated with a spray of roses and calla lilies tied with lavender ribbons, Cassie's work. I was conferring with Reverend Kirby in the back of the small sanctuary when a tall, blond man in a European-cut black suit and slate gray tie entered the side door of the church. He blinked in the light coming through the stained-glass windows that bathed his face blue and yellow, then walked self-assuredly to the casket, bowed his head a moment, and turned to look around the room. He was the first mourner to arrive.

"I think people will have things to say about Mom," I continued to confer with the Reverend, even as I wondered who the other person in the room was. "I'll begin, Cassie will follow, and then we'll let the rest happen as it does. Mom would like the idea of just letting the words flow, like rain flowing into a stream."

The Reverend laughed. "I can tell you're her daughter. That's the way she would say it too."

I shook my head. "I'm sorry. I spend too much time with words. I forget myself."

"Your mother also had a way of painting a picture with words. She'll be missed at church services, rummage sales, and potlucks. She was part of the church family. But I think you . . ." He looked at me, then sighed heavily. "Never mind. Now is not the time . . . there should be lots of people here today."

"Yeah, we're finally no longer shunned.

He shrugged. "That your mother was an unwed mother is no longer important. Maybe we should talk about this some time. I think you have things misconstrued."

"Oh, I don't think so," I said, surprising even myself. What possessed me to say these things to a preacher I hardly knew? Reverend Kirby edged away from me as the blond man drew nearer. "We'll talk later."

When he was a few feet away, he smiled and held out both hands to me.

It was Tom. I held out my hands and he covered them with his. I felt the blush on my cheeks as I remembered our last telephone conversation and the angry words I spewed at him. His final words to me had been, "I wipe my hands of you," just before the phone clicked dead. I was astonished that he would give up on us. Despite our past, he now seemed glad to see me. "Hey, Betsy Kramer," he said in a soothing voice. "I'm sorry to hear about your mother."

I looked away. How was I going to keep the tears at bay? "I'm surprised to see you. Why would you come all the way out to Conneaut for Mom's funeral? The last I knew, you were angry with me." I stopped and took a breath. He was strikingly handsome with his angular features, the small-town boy whose childhood and youth still swathed him. I wasn't sure if I missed him or my childhood or living in this town, but I felt the pang of it. "I'm sorry, I'm forgetting my manners."

I wondered what he thought of my shorter haircut and how slender I was. I was wearing a black pantsuit with hand-hewn silver jewelry and a turquoise silk scarf, a different look from my T-shirt and jean days.

He squeezed my hands before letting them go. "I came yesterday afternoon because Dad needed me to help install new hardware in the bathrooms at his house. We were driving down Main Street past Dazzles, and Dad said what a shame it was the gallery had to close, with your mother's passing away. I didn't know. Then Linda called and said she'd spoken to you."

"So, Linda sent you?"

"Sort of. I guess I'm the family's ambassador." He paused. "I couldn't get Mom or Dad to come. They hate public places anymore. Don't think I didn't want to come. I would have anyway. I wanted to be here for you."

I was touched. The statement was so naked, the forgiveness unspoken but lying there between us. The white walls, the sterile gown, the screaming, the grief, all came rolling over me, memories from that awful day were vivid enough to cause me to shake. He looked at me, concern in his eyes, but I pulled myself up straighter and tried to smile.

I didn't deserve Tom's goodness. To me, he was an innocent, and I wasn't. "It's been difficult."

"It's okay, Elizabeth." His voice was gentle. That he called me Elizabeth made me smile. He loved that name—Elizabeth. Outside of the office, he was the only person who called me that.

"So, your two children are all grown up, and you're a lawyer, I hear." I'd already noticed he wasn't wearing a wedding band.

He nodded, absently, his eyes remaining on my face. "You haven't changed a bit."

"You're a liar. I look like hell."

He bit his lip. His warm hands touched the cold skin of my arm. "Actually, you look the same as you did in college. Small and perky and beautiful."

The way he bit his lip, the feel of his intimate touch, his name, took me back. "And you still bite your lip. I can see you studying in a pair of cut-offs, biting your lip."

"You're the same," he repeated. And there was an awkward pause, like he wanted to say more but stopped himself.

What would he see that's different about me? "Hair's shorter."

"It becomes you." He waited, watching my eyes.

"Nothing has worked out since you and I split up."

He reached up to smooth a stray hair from his forehead. I could never resist kissing his hands when we were lovers. "I've had that problem too. Do you think it has anything to do with what we had?"

'What we had' hung in the air as the front door of the church opened behind us. Cassie, Mike, and Beth entered the room in a whir of flapping suit coat and crisp dress. My daughter's lips skimmed my cheek, the baby between us, as she said, "Sorry we're late." Mike gave me a quick hug before they turned their interest to Tom.

"Cassie, Mike, I'd like you to meet Tom Madison, a friend from my childhood. He's Linda's older brother."

Cassie shifted her infant daughter to her left arm and reached out her right arm, the whiteness of her hand stark against her black sleeve. "Good to meet you." Her commanding voice lifted into the room.

Tom took in her long brown hair and blue eyes, and his mouth formed a slow smile. "I would know you as Elizabeth's daughter any place." He warmly took her hand. "You have the exact same color of eyes. I've always thought of it as autumn blue."

She raised an eyebrow, taken aback by the little speech, then turned to Mike, who reached out a hand and gave Tom's hand a hearty shake. Cassie said, "This is my husband Mike."

Mike, ever the friendly community banker, said, "Hi, Tom. How's your father doing? I haven't seen him in the bank lately."

"He's Dad. Getting older and needing more help. But he's okay."

"Is he thinking about selling some of the property out by the county line?"

"He should. I think he'll sell the back acres and keep the original twenty from the homestead land that's been in our family for generations."

"I was surprised they sold the house on Erie Street," I said.

Tom's eyes met mine and held. "They've been content out in the country, like they're hiding out. I'm not sure that's a good thing." Then he turned and peered under the blanket at my two-month old granddaughter.

"Her name is Beth," Cassie said.

"The baby's named after her grandmother—that's wonderful. I don't know why people can't leave that name alone—Betsy, Liz, Beth."

"We think it's too much for mere peasants," I said, joking.

No one laughed. "It IS a queenly name," Tom said, sounding serious. Then he turned to me, "Remember how we used to read Shakespeare out loud?"

I looked over at Cassie, whose face wore a wry curiosity. "Shakespeare, a poet and playwright supported by his Queen Elizabeth," I said, raising my voice to lofty declaration. "Too bad writers don't have sponsors these days. I could use one." The bitterness scared me like the poison it was. Softly, I said, "How could I forget?"

"Thank God for that." It was almost a whisper.

The opening door fractured the awkward pause that followed. Behind chattering church women, I recognized people from my office. "I'll find a seat," Tom said. "My prayers are with all of you." He touched my elbow and walked to the back of the sanctuary.

The last time I watched Tommy walk away was during my sophomore year in college. We had studied in my dorm room all day, moving from pillows on the floor to my bed, to the hard-backed chairs by the desk, our feet entwined, legs touching, hands together, sometimes taking a break for a kiss. We'd made love in the middle of the afternoon and fell asleep for a short while before he woke up and said, "We need to get back to Heidegger." We read out loud from our notes, traded interpretations, opened the text to confirm meaning, and quizzed each other. At seven, he asked if I wanted to

get something to eat, but I still had to study for my other final. He kissed me before he left, confident he'd see me the next day.
  I decided Tom and I wouldn't work out, and it didn't.

People floated in and out to give me a hug and ask if I needed anything. When it was my time to speak during the service, I told the crowd that we trimmed our Christmas tree with origami birds of many colors and sang Christmas carols around the piano after baking sugar cookies. I concluded by saying, "Mom once told me that daffodils are full of the promise of abundant life because they come up in the springtime. She wasn't always happy, but she found abundance in nature and art. She believed strongly that God was there for her. And then she met Ben, who made her happy. She had an amazing joy at being alive, a joy I only began to understand in the last months of her life."

  I made it through without tears, but Cassie wept when she spoke about the day Beth was born and how we all gathered in Mom's hospital room. "Grandma was frail but she sat in a chair next to my bed and held the baby. It was one of life's special moments. Grandma said life is made up of moments like when the dragonflies flit across the Magical Pond at Windy Hill. I felt like I floated from moment to moment whenever I was with Grandma. She lived in the moment." When she sat down, she looked straight ahead as Ben climbed the steps to the podium.

  "I met Margaret six years ago, at Dazzles. She was the most beautiful woman I'd ever seen. I think it was love at first sight." He paused and looked around. "People don't believe it happens, but it did for me. I asked her to go out for coffee with me after the store closed that night, and she did. Margaret and I kept up an easy conversation that led to a comfortable companionship, you know?" He caught my eye, and I nodded. "Now she's gone from the world but I know she's still here for me." The tears rolled down his face as he struggled on. "We had five good years of marriage. We'd both been married before, but ours was the love that was meant to be. I believe we'll be together in heaven, and my place beside her at the cemetery waits. I could say I don't know how I'll live without her, and that would be true, but Margaret wouldn't want me to look at that waiting grave. So I'll move forward."

  When he stepped down to take his seat again, he was more stooped than usual. I heard the familiar crack of his knees.

Others followed. Some knew her when she was a girl, others when she was a young mother, but most remembered her as the woman who made a sacred space for art and music and creative people to connect. Her best friend Holly talked about the day she and Mom walked past the space where Dazzles would be and Mom announced what she was going to do with the money she inherited from her parents.

Outside the church, while we were waiting for the car to take us to the cemetery, Robert looked handsome in his dark suit. He pulled me to him with a disconcerting familiarity and whispered, "You haven't returned my calls. I was worried about you." His lips grazed my ear.

I pulled away. "A lot was going on."

He shook his head. "I thought I could be there for you, but you didn't allow it."

I stepped away from him and into the black sedan without answering him.

The day took on a surreal feel as if we were watching other people go through the motions of burying their dead. Cassie and I stood at the gravesite, a foot apart from each other, with Mom's casket stretched out on the edge of the newly-dug grave. The world whirled around us, and the gray sky and unusual cold crept into my toes and my mood. A harsh wind flew through the budding trees. People I knew from high school, friends of Cassie's, old neighbors, and farm hands stood around the grave in homogenous shades of gray and black. My ex-husband leaned against a tree apart from everyone else, watching me. The man who was my true love kept his eyes on the ground, yet I wanted him to go. My ears heard voices, and my eyes saw lips moving, but I couldn't connect the sound into meaning. I was as exhausted as I'd been the morning after Cassie was born, when my mind couldn't comprehend what the nurse was telling me.

I closed my eyes. Following the "Amen" of the prayer, my eyes rested on Tom, straight and tall across from me. He raised a white rose to his nose before tossing it on the casket.

In the dining room at the house later, Tom waved good-bye from across the room while I sat on a cushioned wooden chair next to Holly. I nodded. It took too much energy to raise a hand. I felt a tinge of regret that we didn't have time to talk, and then Maria was asking if there were any paper napkins in the pantry.

I slept the sleep of one deprived of it for months. When I woke the next morning, the rose-papered walls and white woodwork were as cheery as they'd ever been, mocking me. Dolls dangled their legs from the wall shelf, happy faces looking down at my bed where I was wrapped in a Victorian crazy quilt bought at a county fair when I was about six. I needed more sleep. My body felt heavy, my mind drugged.

I lay still and moved my body against the sheets, waking myself up. I pushed one leg as far down the bed as I could, and then the other, my arms stretched above my head. My body was stiff, my hips hurting as they had in pregnancy. It was rare that I slept more than seven hours and I must have been in that bed for nine or ten. My feet found the rough hand-made rag rug and I grabbed the robe at the end of the bed. The light shafting through the wood-paned window was diffused as the sun struggled through the clouds.

Mom was gone but it wasn't going to be easy to know it. That would take a long time. My mind was full of confused thoughts about what life would look like from now on. Now that I'd become immersed in Mom's life, it would be hard to disentangle from it.

Ben rattled around in the kitchen, where surely he was making a weak coffee. When I entered the kitchen with its white cabinets and granite countertops, he was standing before the window, arms straight and hands firmly on either side of the sink, head bowed and shoulders shrunken forward. He looked shriveled, like a mountain climber who never reached the peak but was still left with the battle fatigue. The coffeepot was making such a gurgling, he didn't hear my footsteps on the tiled floor. The grief on his face was stark and difficult to witness.

Upon seeing Ben so sad, I held out my arms and he came into them like a child who had lost everything. He was undone. "How can we begin life again?" I asked, and then I hugged him closer. "Remember how happy Mom was when you brought her that music box?"

He pulled away and nodded. The skin around his eyes was deeply lined with happy, not gloomy, creases. His was a pleasant and open face. "Yep."

"You should keep it with you, to remember happy moments and how important she was to you."

He smiled at me. "She was more important to me than anything.

I ...I loved her." He looked at me sideways. "You remind me of her, you know, in your better moments."

"What do you mean?"

"You believe in life's goodness, at your core."

"But . . ." I stopped. Earlier he'd said I'd changed, couldn't give a compliment, and Cassie agreed. "But I don't."

"You do. You could be writing life stories rather than travel stories."

"You're saying I should write other stuff?"

"Yeah, I am. And stop doing those trips. I think they bring out the worst in you."

I stiffened. "I'm doing all right. I can live on my own advice."

Ben laughed. "None of us is above needing advice."

"Maybe I think more of myself than you know. Maybe I'm above needing advice."

"You do have a 'holier than thou' way about you, but it's a cover."

"A 'cover'? Really, I'm pretty happy with who I am."

"Are you now? And what about the fact that your daughter doesn't want to talk to you if she can help it?"

I left the kitchen. *What about my not loving Tom enough to tell him the truth? What about me being with my mother's boyfriend?* As I was walking through the dining room, my eyes came to rest on the deep-bowled ornate cup painted with red and pink roses connected by thorny vines and gold trim Grandpa purchased from a proud girl of about twelve whose work impressed my grandfather. He loved the story of the Japanese girl showing off her handiwork, full of the possibilities of dreams.

The light in the salon was different in late morning. I remembered Mom telling me her best painting was done mid-day, from ten until about two, because that was the time when the light was bright. I picked up her last journal and turned to an entry at the back.

> I gave the teacup to Betsy. My mother gave it to me on a hot summer afternoon on the porch of Windy Hill, probably close to twenty years ago now. Mom came through the door holding the teacup in both her hands and stood in front of me with it. She repeated Daddy's story about how the girl Emiko's proud brush strokes beautified a plain and functional cup, and he bought it

because of her fortitude. She told me we were passing it down to the oldest daughter, generation after generation, a symbol of how good life can be—fine and beautiful, a work of art—even in the midst of turmoil.

I don't think Betsy understands that the teacup is a symbol of a life of promise. I hope that one day Betsy will understand how good life can be, if we let it. It took me many years to understand life is beautiful when we embrace its blessings.

So the teacup was more than an heirloom. I knew its origin but didn't know that Mom had given it meaning higher than a receptacle for tea. She was right, I didn't know how beautiful life could be—it felt like I was trudging through it, like trudging through muck, just like I wrote yesterday. Opening my own journal, I tried to understand the teacup more.

When I was a girl, Mom and I used to walk after dinner, even when it was ten degrees outside or raining torrentially, and sometimes my shoes were still wet when I put them on the next morning. It was our time to talk.

What do I need to do besides notice the beauty of my surroundings? Mom hoped I would understand life is beautiful—that's what I'm looking for when I travel. But I'm struggling for it, reaching for it, feeling that the good life is just beyond my reach.

What Mom did with that teacup was explore her artistic life. She painted and made driftwood sculptures. She opened up Dazzles and invited artists to bring their art in to add to her collection. She opened her heart, and then Ben showed up.

Grandpa may have given Grandma a teacup, but he gave me my private getaway. When he took me into the woods and wouldn't let me look until I was standing below the tree house, he was giving me something he thought would help me notice the beauty, something that would help me experience my self. When I opened my eyes and saw the house with its blue shutters, I felt life was full of promise.

Mom thought that when I lost Tom, I gave up on love. And Mom thought love came down when all was right in the soul. So when I walked away from love, I walked away from the best part of me. I left my soul floundering.

What a nice little neat package I could tie up with that. Too bad it's more complicated than that. I loved Tom. I was able to talk to him. He supported me in my dreams, read my first short stories, and took me by the shoulders and proclaimed them wonderful. When my first novella was completed, he stayed up half the night, not able to put it down, and became my first fan.

Some things in life are worth fighting for, taking risks for. Love is one of them.

Mo called me on my cell phone. "Everyone wants to know when you're coming back."

"I don't know. I think I need some more time."

"I don't think they want you to take more time."

"I'll call you tomorrow," I said, sounding gruff.

"Talk to you then."

I closed my journal, opened my laptop, and checked e-mail. I went through three hundred e-mails over the next couple of hours and felt the adrenaline pick up. I was back in the game. I read some of the shorter travel pieces we weren't sure about using, sent off responsive e-mails, jotted notes, put dates on my calendar for the following week. I was feeling like life was returning to normal, and I was drawn to it.

The phone rang at 3:00 p.m. It was my boss.

"Hi, Henry."

"Betsy! How's it going?"

"Good."

"I saw your note to Sam telling him to start research on Sanibel Island. I like Sanibel, but haven't we visited it before?"

"I searched the archives and didn't see anything."

"Okay, good."

"Do you think I would forget to do that?"

"No, no, that's not it." He seemed defensive. "You're not here, you're there, and you've been dealing with a lot."

"I've been doing this job for ten years. I can't exactly do it with my eyes closed, but I know the tasks that need to be accomplished to put out a magazine."

"All right. No worries. I'm sure you're on top of things. I know there are lots of pieces, and you not being in the office . . . but it looks like you'll be back next week."

"I didn't say that." I was tired. I felt it in my eyes and shoulders.

It was a weariness I thought would take a long time to shed.

"Chris told me what you put on your calendar."

I sighed audibly. "I know I need to be back there next week. I'll be there."

"Do you need me to keep Tina in charge for a while?"

"No, I think I can handle it from now on. I can work from here until I get to the office."

"All right, Thanks. I know it's been a hard time for you."

For the first time in my career, I did not want to go to work.

CHAPTER FOUR – DAFFODILS

"Dazzles Art Gallery" was scripted in zazzy purple across a white sign above the storefront. Mom took out the curtained dressing rooms and high metal racks from the old bridal shop and transformed it into a place where mobiles strung with floating moons and drifting dragons hung above decorated driftwood sculptures. Standing outside the door with me, Ben reached into his pocket for the key. His red and brown flannel shirt and brown khakis were looser than before Mom became sick. He needed a haircut—his hair curled over his collar.

"We should have done this sooner," he said as the door opened. "This door hasn't been opened in months."

"We were busy with other things."

"You're right. We wouldn't have had the time before . . ." He let the words "she died" hang in the air.

The door closed to the tinkling of the bells above it, and we stood on the threshold and took it all in. Above our heads were kites and flying long-tailed unicorns, companions to drifting fireflies on golden threads. Track lighting lit shelves of cupid sculptures, artisan paper journals, sea shell decorated frames, and horsehair-fired vases. Local photography hung on the walls alongside Mom's watercolors. To the left of the front door, books by northeast Ohio writers filled a mahogany bookshelf.

Cobwebs and dust added more jazz to the entire dazzle. Mom's large secretarial was filled to its nooks with consignment contracts and bills; over the past couple of months we'd paid the bills but left the rest of it alone.

"I met her here." Ben's voice was so quiet I almost didn't hear him. "She was right where you are now, stylish with her short hair, and hers was one of the warmest smiles I've ever seen. How could God take her away after giving her to me?"

I ran my hand over the desk. Her handwriting filled the top page of a notepad. "God didn't take her away. Cancer did. Maybe cancer's made by the devil," I said, looking for an argument.

"The devil doesn't MAKE anything."

"Ask Reverend Kirby." I picked up the stack of consignment

contracts. "Anything can be made right, if only we believe blindly, unthinkingly, sure of God up there protecting each and every one of us, even His children in India and Africa and Appalachia who are starving . . ." I stacked the consignment contracts, and said, "I guess we'll have to take these with us since the phone service is out here."

"You don't think Reverend Kirby has any answers?"

"I think people can only make guesses."

"You can have some answers if you let God in."

"That's what I hear." I stood in the doorway and took a picture, went outside to capture the window display, stood by the backroom and took another photo.

"Stubborn." Ben turned to the wall behind him and pulled an oil painting off the wall.

I spent the next hour packing pricing tags, gift boxes, and tissue paper into shipping boxes to be gifted to Linda McClellan's gift shop. When I had a couple of stacked boxes, I emerged from the back to take them down the street.

Ben sorted all Mom's water colors and sculptures into boxes in one corner. Each artist's work was separated so they could be easily located and gathered up by their owners.

"This isn't taking long," I said.

"Nope."

"When are you going back to work?"

"Soon," Ben said. "I need to. How 'bout you?"

"I have this week off."

"That's good. What are you going to do with all that time?"

"Decide about Windy Hill."

He looked at me sharply. "What, about selling it?"

"Don't know." I was purposely nonchalant. "Maybe I will, maybe I won't."

"You're back to your old self, difficult."

We heard a sharp rap on the glass door. Cassie stood outside and looked like a forlorn four-year-old girl who'd lost her favorite doll in her cotton dress and flat shoes. When I opened the door, she said, "You could have told me! I would've liked to have seen Grandma's place before you wrecked it, you guys. You guys!"

"I'm sorry, honey, I didn't think." I showed her my digital camera. "Look, I took pictures."

"You never think, do you?" Her tone was accusatory and not unexpected. She flipped back through the pictures I'd taken. "Do you?" Then stood back from us and caught me looking like deer in headlights. "Well, what do you have to say for yourself, huh?"

"I really didn't think."

"You know what? You're thinking about getting this done so you can move on, back to your life in the city, to the all-important work you have going on there. It's worthwhile work, is it?"

"I think it is." My answer sounded weak, even to my ears. I looked away. "I try to have a good life. I do the best I can."

"Yeah, you do, if it has anything to do with the publishing world."

I refused to look at her and started packing again.

"Mom!"

I looked up. The anger in Cassie's eyes was dangerous. "What do you want, Cassie?"

For a moment, she looked for a response, then she said, "I want you to say you're sorry."

My own anger was stoked. "For what? I already apologized."

She shook her head. "There's no point talking to you. Forget it. You don't get it." She walked in a circle and wrung her hands.

Ben stepped toward her. "Now don't go blaming your Mom too much. I didn't say anything to you either."

The corners of Cassie's mouth came up. She loved Ben and his good cheer. "Well, you both should have thought of me. Why are you in such a hurry to wipe out her memory?"

I said, "The landlord says we have to be cleared out by the end of the month."

"Oh. You should have told me." Cassie picked up a tiny driftwood sculpture that I'd set aside. "I spent a lot of time sanding wood smooth in the back sunroom."

I remembered how much she enjoyed hanging out with Mom. "Sometimes I came home and you'd be wearing the most interesting hairpiece on the top of your head."

"I still have some of them."

"Good for you. You should wear them sometimes."

I hefted two boxes onto my knees and lifted them to my left hip. "I'm taking these down the street to Linda's."

"I'll help," Cassie said as she picked up some boxes. We walked in silence, dropped them off, and headed back to Dazzles. "You know what, Mom? Being with Beth, watching her nose scrunched up against my breast while she nurses, I know we had that, you and I.

And then when I was little, we had so much fun hiding in the hayloft when Dad was looking for us, giggling because we were right above him. And then all the laughter stopped."

"I was having a hard time."

She sighed. "I felt like I'd lost my Mom, like you gave up on me. Is that what happened?"

The idea that my daughter would think I gave up on her was tragic. I never meant that. "No, of course not. I loved you. I just didn't do all those 'Mom' things."

"I never saw you."

"It was hard for me to work and be a mother too."

"It was more than that. It was like you didn't want to be a mother."

I went on the defense. "Cassie! Of course I wanted to be a mother. I WAS a mother, and I was working to raise you."

"But we were staying with Grandma and Grandpa."

She was right. I purposely immersed myself in work. "I helped your grandparents through the lean years."

"You didn't get home until we were already eating dinner most of the time."

"When you were little, I wanted a nice quiet life in my hometown in a place where everyone knew who I was. Then it was all ruined. I didn't want to be here anymore where everyone knew what happened. But that didn't mean I didn't want you here."

"The way you yelled at me from the time you came in the door, I almost didn't want you to come home. You were always barking orders."

My blood rose. "Barking orders, huh? You know, I felt it. I felt your resentment. I thought it was normal mother-daughter stuff." My voice had risen. A few people turned to look at us as we stood in the middle of the sidewalk.

"You weren't even around for my high school prom, but whenever you came in that door, at night after work or home from a trip, you had something to complain about—my room was a disgrace, the "C" in Algebra wasn't acceptable, my hair was a fright, and then there were the threats of taking away my piano lessons, grounding me until I had nothing but As and Bs on my report card, refusing to give me allowance money until I picked up my room. I was glad when you moved to Cleveland. When I came back home during breaks from school, I didn't have to deal with you. You tried to parent me when you weren't REALLY parenting me." She was facing me, talking loudly, hurtfully, moving her hands, almost touching me. I wondered if she would hit me.

"Cassie..." I couldn't be angry with Cassie, it wasn't her fault. It was mine.

She put her hands over her face. "Don't talk to me. I don't want to hear it. Anything you have to say would be too late and not enough. I suppose you think you're going to sell the house and be done with Windy Hill. I suppose you don't care about all those sad-eyed cows and what will become of them. You're going to take the money and run, aren't you?"

She had good reasons to believe I'd do exactly that. "I'm thinking about things." She turned her back on me and kept walking down the sidewalk. "Cassie! I'm sorry I was a lousy mother. But I never claimed to be a good mother."

She stopped on the sidewalk and turned around to face me. "Do you think that matters? Do you think it matters whether you 'claimed' to be a good mother?" She rolled her eyes. "You should have been with me for the prom. You didn't help me with my dress or my hair or getting the boutonnière. Mike and I were all dressed up for pictures, and I looked and waited for you, but you didn't show. I had to have copies made of other people's pictures."

"I thought you weren't angry anymore."

"I try not to be, but it really can't be helped. It hurts too much."

She took off several paces ahead of me. As we walked past Toby's Grille, Cassie saw her father Rick before I did. He was sitting at the counter and waved widely at us. "There's Daddy."

Rick was sitting at the counter, a cup of coffee in front of him. He was dressed in a dark blue blazer, slate blue shirt, and black slacks. I said, "You can go in and say hello to him if you'd like."

"No. He didn't come to the house after Grandma's funeral. And why the hell is he acting so happy?"

"Your father has always had a weak grip on reality." It came out with more bitterness than I'd intended. Six years into our marriage, I caught my playboy husband making out with one of his female employees behind his unlocked office door. When I bombarded through the door to get to the parking lot after finding them, the guys smoking cigarettes outside laughed at me. The whole town knew about Rick's nights on the town, but instead of telling me, they waited for the storm to develop so they could watch the lightning show. No one told me—why would they?

"I could smell drink on his breath when he came up to tuck me in at night. He stumbled on the rugs."

I was surprised by her sourness. "I thought you were crazy about your father."

"He doesn't even go to work anymore."

"He doesn't?"

"No. I went to his office the day after Grandma died, and he wasn't there. His secretary Abby said she hadn't seen him in a week. He told her he's taking a break from work."

"I'm sure his father loves that."

"Grandpa Ed doesn't know about it." Cassie glanced into Toby's. "Oh, Lord, here he comes." She turned to greet her father, and then we were immersed in his presence. His hair was pulled into a ponytail. Always theatrical, he put his arms around both our shoulders, which brought our foreheads together.

"How are my girls? It looks like you're clearing out Dazzles. Margaret must be crying in heaven."

I pulled away by breaking his grasp. "That sounded sarcastic."

"Your mother loved the place, that's all I meant. I liked Margaret, but she stopped liking me," he said as Cassie disentangled herself from her father's arms only to have him kiss her noisily on the cheek.

"That could be because of how you treated Mom," Cassie said.

He looked at her, confounded. She had always forgiven him for the things he did when he was still drinking, like when he missed her award-winning artwork hanging in City Hall.

When he looked at me, I shrugged. "I guess you and your mom have been talking. That's what I get when the old lady dies, an ex-wife telling my daughter all the ills that befell her when she was married to me. I'm sure she told you I beat her every night."

Cassie took a step back. "Do you think I didn't hear her crying at night when you didn't come home? How about those times when you walked into the house at two in the morning singing songs at the top of your voice? How about those mornings when Mom begged you to get out of bed and go to work before you got fired?."

Anger rose red in Rick's face. "We should get going," I said. "I don't think we want to continue this conversation in the middle of Main Street."

"Okay," she said. "Maybe we can continue it in Dazzles."

Rick clenched and unclenched his fists. But he held his peace and looked down at the bubble-gum strewn sidewalk. "I didn't mean to hurt you, sweetheart." He brought a finger under Cassie's chin so he could look into his daughter's face. She had my eyes but his handsome nose and noble cheekbones. She was only a few inches shy of his six feet. "It was the drink. Not only the drink, but me with the drink. I let myself be controlled by it, and I wasn't the man I should have been. I wasn't the father you needed to have." He paused and looked at me as if waiting for me to give him direction, but the pause wasn't long enough for a response when he continued. "We've had some good times, right?"

The fire had gone out of her. "Why aren't you going to work?"

He was momentarily confused then looked like he'd been caught in a deception. "Life is short. I'm your grandfather's flunky, a forty-seven-year-old guy whose father still tells him what to do even though the son now owns the business. I could have been an actor. Right, Betsy?"

He had been good. Everyone loved him on stage. "You would have brought the crowds on Broadway to their feet."

Cassie looked from Rick to me and back again, and shook her head. "You both blew it. Everything's so F'd up."

Then Rick said, "It's your Grandma, isn't it?"

Cassie's face crumbled. Rick had hit the nail on the head.

"You miss her, don't you, Princess?" He hugged her, then looked at me. "I've got this," he said as he guided her into the nearby restaurant.

When I went back inside the gallery, Ben looked at me and said, "We shouldn't forget how much Cassie's going to miss Margaret."

I walked out to the mailbox by the road every day. It felt like I was in a different century, before the assassinations of the Kennedys and Martin Luther King Jr., in a time when women still made their own clothes and had their hair done at the beauty shop every Saturday morning while they gossiped. I was eight and Grandma told me to go out to the gravel road to get the mail because the mail truck had recently rolled by.

Cards of condolence kept the grief alive rather than helping me deal with it. But a few days after the funeral, I received a small envelope with a Vermilion postmark and Tom's neat script addressed to Elizabeth Kramer. Unable to wait, I opened the envelope as I walked down the driveway towards the house. I sat down on the porch swing.

>Elizabeth:
>
>If there was any way to take away your pain, I would. I know you and your mother were close—I saw you sometimes on the beach in pants rolled up to your knees and baggy sweatshirts, ponytails flying, scurrying around to pick up driftwood. Sometimes I wandered into your mother's gallery, and I'd see that driftwood painted and swaggered, looking like gay mementoes. I wonder at the joy within a woman who could create such crazy works of art. When her husband stood up at the funeral and talked about how much he loved her, I witnessed how joy spreads.
>
>It's too bad she had to die when the daffodils are blooming. Your favorite flower, and . . . now they'll remind you of your mother's death. Or they can remind you of her life, if you choose.
>
>You are still lovely, but sad. I hope you come to know your mother's kind of joy.
>
>Fondly,
>Thomas

I'd tried hard NOT to remember Tom over the years. And "joy"? It wasn't part of my armor, although I had to admit, Mom always made me smile. It was a nice note, a first try at reconnecting, and it didn't expect an answer. Yet I chose to think of it as conniving—like all those other men and their wily ways.

Tom caught me stealing a daffodil when we were fifteen.

I had stopped on the way home from school to admire the daffodils behind Mrs. Smith's white picket fence. On impulse, I reached over the fence and picked a bright yellow daffodil. When I turned around, Tommy Madison was standing a few steps behind me with his mouth wide open in surprise.

"I can't believe you did that," he'd said.

"Isn't it pretty?"

"Yeah, but I hope Mrs. Smith didn't see you."

We both looked across the garden to the white two-story house. It looked like the coast was clear. "I think we're safe." I turned to continue down the sidewalk, waiting to see if Tommy would catch up to me. When he did, he took my books from me—how strange and old-fashioned that seemed. He was smooth-faced handsome and wore his long hair shaggy. He played football, participated in 4-H, and went Christmas caroling with the church choir. I'd often been in their house, but I'd never had never had a conversation with him.

"How's your Mom?" he asked.

Overwhelmed by him, I lost my voice and mumbled that Mom was fine.

"And how are you? You haven't been over lately."

"I'm okay. I've been busy with papers."

"Papers?"

"Yeah, you know, papers about Beowulf and Chaucer." The truth was I'd been reading the Bronte sisters and couldn't wait to get home to find out what was going to happen next to Jane Eyre.

"Mrs. Angle didn't assign us papers about Beowulf and Chaucer."

"Well, she's doing that to our class," and he backed down. "So, what's going on with you?"

"I've been helping my father spray the fruit trees. I'm working on a 4-H project about fruit trees—it'll be at the county fair."

In Fulton Park, we walked amongst the trees toward the back of the park, past the duck pond. We sat down on a bench, and he put my books haphazardly on the ground with his and moved over closer to me. "That's cool. What kind of fruit trees?"

"Peach."

"I've never been to the farm. I guess that's because it's on the other side of town from my grandparents' farm."

"I've been to your grandparents' farm though."

"Fourth grade?"

"Yep."

"Everyone in town has been to my grandparents' farm to see how milk's made."

"It smells."

"It's milk."

"So, when you get home, your Mom won't be there, huh?"

I shook my head and kicked at a pine cone by my foot. "No,

Mom comes home around five." I looked across a greening meadow between the pines, almost golf-course perfect.

Tommy pointed up into a bare oak tree looming above us. "Look, a robin's building a nest."

"How do you know that's what she's doing?"

"She's putting all those twigs in one spot, there," and he pointed a little to the right of where he pointed before, "in the crook between those branches."

The red-breasted bird was flitting from branch to branch, mouth full, as she made her nest. She was busy. "Oh, yeah," I said, like it was a revelation to me, which it was.

"So what do you do when you're at home alone?"

"I read."

He cocked his head to one side and I decided he was pretty cute. Sitting there with him, he felt like someone else, not merely Linda's brother. "What do you read?"

"*Emma, Pride and Prejudice, Wuthering Heights, Jane Eyre.* I love those old books. My mom has an entire wall of books in our living room. She likes to read too."

"And write."

"She writes for the newspaper because they let her write about art. She should have been an artist."

He nodded, sat back. "Do you get the feeling a lot of adults should have been something else? My mom used to be in piano competitions in New York. Then she met my father."

"Yeah, you're right about adults."

His pinky finger caressed the side of my hand. He didn't look at me, just kept touching my hand with his finger.

I lowered my head. "I'm not sleeping much. I can hear Mom crying in her room. Once I asked her what was wrong and she looked confused, then cross, and said, 'nothing, why do you ask?' So I don't ask anymore. Sometimes I wonder if she wishes she were still with my father."

Tommy took my hand and squeezed it, there on the hard bench.

"Can she get back together with him?"

"No. They were in love and he went back to Italy and left her here."

"Then they weren't in love." He picked up our hands off the bench. It was like he'd already claimed my hands, and me, the way he picked them up. "Maybe he found out she was pregnant, and he got scared."

"Heathcliff wouldn't do that. He would stick by Catherine."

"Who's Heathcliff?"

"From *Wuthering Heights*."

"Oh, okay. True love, huh?" Tommy kept hold of my hand and moved closer, so our hips were touching and his leg fell against mine.

"It's just a book. Mom's going out with a guy, but I don't like him."

"Do they go out to dinner?"

"Yeah. He tries. But Mom isn't going to love him, I can tell."

He put his arm around me, and tilted his head towards mine. We looked up into the tree and watched the male robin fly into the nest, busy about in there, and fly out again. It was peaceful, sitting on a park bench with Tommy. Then he said, "My parents sleep in separate rooms."

Everything I thought about them as a couple was shattered when he told me that.

When I turned to look at him, he said, "Are your eyes really that color or is that the sky reflected in them?"

I shook my head. "The color's real."

"I wonder if they would change if I kissed you."

I was mesmerized. I wanted to be kissed.

Then he did. He kissed me lightly at first, until I felt his tongue tracing the line of my lips and I opened my mouth. I felt like I was lost in him and nothing else mattered. If someone walked past us, I wouldn't know it. His hands ran down my back and pulled me close to him. When he looked into my eyes, I could tell he was as entranced as I was.

The moment ended abruptly. He pulled away, picked up my books, and stood up. We walked home in silence. I wanted to ask what it meant, but didn't dare break the spell, didn't dare open up remorse, confusion, regret. Stupidity, that's what it was. I kept my eyes on the daffodil in my hand, even when he let the books fall into my arms and left me standing on the sidewalk outside my home.

I had understood that Tommy hadn't been quite ready, that he hadn't been there yet in his head. After putting the daffodil in a half-empty Coke can on my desk, I'd fallen onto the bed and thought about the kiss.

Every time I see a daffodil, I picture how it will look in a Coke can. I never forgot that first kiss. How could one have a kiss like that, then simply stop?

A couple of days later, I'd found an envelope on the bottom of my locker. It had been slipped through the grate at the top. The word "Elizabeth" was written in perfect slanting script. Elizabeth was my true name, but it was never used by anyone but my grandfather, who had died a few months before. The use of that name, rather than Betsy, raised a lump in my throat.

Betsy:

Daffodils are my favorite flower too. It was funny that you were afraid of getting caught stealing a flower. I'm glad I caught you because I was able to steal a kiss. I hope you're okay about it.

Tom

He caught me with the note in my hand. "I'm okay with it," I'd said.

He smiled. "Good. Can we go to the movies on Saturday night?"

"The rule is no dating until 16."

"There's always a way to get around rules." He casually threw out the words, watching for my reaction until his voice and attitude changed and he said, "Hey, are you saying you don't want to?"

"No."

"Never mind. It probably wasn't a good idea." He turned abruptly and walked away.

Even so, on Saturday at noon he had showed up at my door with a handful of daffodils. I laughed out loud. "Did you pick them from Mrs. Smith's garden?"

He looked down one side of the street and up the other and put a finger to his lips. I laughed again. Mom called out and asked what was going on, then she was at the door in her apron saying, "How lovely," the way Mom would. "Come on in, Tommy. I just finished making sandwiches for lunch. Why don't you join us?"

At the Formica table in our tiny kitchen, Mom and Tom talked through lunch. I watched my mother talking with her hands, the red polish on her nails adding color to the black and white kitchen with avocado green appliances.

"You know, I asked Betsy if she wanted to go to a movie with me and she didn't think you'd let her. I know she's only 15, but she's a friend of my sister's and you go to our church, and I just want to take her to a movie, nothing else. Can she go with me?"

Mom's hands were folded under her chin. She raised her eyebrows and cocked her head with a silly grin. "After a speech like that, I can hardly say no."

"So?"

"Okay. She can go, but I think you have to ask her. Maybe she doesn't want to go with you, ever think of that?" She winked at me before she stood up to put her plate next to the sink. Her unbuttoned chambray shirt over a white T-shirt billowed around her shapely body. The hair ribbon holding back her ponytail was the same color as her shirt, paler than her eyes. "I have to go finish folding the laundry," she said, looking over her shoulder. Then she was gone.

I felt the warmth of his hand as it took mine. "Well? Do you want to go with me to a movie tonight?"

His eyes wouldn't let me look away. I could hardly have said no.

Photos . . . boxes and boxes of them. A few years back, Grandma spent hours organizing her photo albums into years and spans of years. Stacks of unorganized photos were in a drawer in the living room. On the dining room table at Windy Hill, Cassie helped me sort pictures of family picnics, first days of school, and birthdays. We were together in many of the photos. Maybe I was there more than I remembered when Cassie was growing up.

"This wine is pretty good, Mom," Cassie said as she swirled the wine in its glass to look at its legs. "Mmmm. The second sip is even better. Are you sure this is an Ohio Cabernet Franc?"

I nodded. "Frank has a good nose and his taste buds are refined by Turkish hashish."

Cassie looked at me in astonishment. "Mom!"

"It's true." I laughed. "He tells tales of exotic spices and scarved women on the Turkish Adriatic. And caves . . . can you imagine that they build hotel rooms in caves right on the edge of the sea? He shows off his pictures while the smoke from his cigarette twirls above bottles of wine."

"He sounds Bohemian."

"Oh, he is. But he knows grapes and grows what he puts in his wine, no juice buying for him. He grafts hybrid grapes for soft deep reds with exotic names, like this one called Amberessence. One other thing . . . he has sensual gentle hands, the kind that can gently pluck a grape from its stem at exactly the right moment."

"Geez, Mom. You sound like you're half in love with him." Cassie took another sip of wine and studied me.

"I do find him attractive. All the guys I know are married though. I missed out not marrying again while I was young."

"Maybe not." Cassie continued to look at me straight on.

Was she trying to tell me something? She and Mike married as soon as they finished college, had the baby a year later. I thought they should have waited, but they were old enough to know, had been together two years. "What's that mean?"

"Oh, just that there are lots of people I know who are unhappy in their marriages. People get married because it seems like the right thing to do."

"You and Mike . . . ?"

"Oh, don't worry about that. Think about it—he's ten miles away baby sitting a ten-week-old baby while I'm here for the third night in a row."

"Not many men would do that without complaining."

"He doesn't complain. He goes with the flow. I'm grateful for that." She picked up a picture of me and Rick at our wedding. "Look at you two. You look so young and happy together."

"We were crazy in love for a while. When I saw your father on the beach after my sophomore year in college, I was vulnerable and lonely. Your father, he was, is, always will be, a charmer."

"I always thought you got together in high school, not while you were in college."

"We knew each other in high school and went out on a couple dates. Your grandmother was always saying, 'That Rick, now he's something.' Yes, he was something. He loved an audience. I didn't want to be one of his conquests, so I stayed away from him."

Cassie seemed distracted, like she was thinking about home.

"You don't have to stay. I won't be alone; Ben's here."

She looked relieved. "I miss being at home, honestly."

"Then go. We can't stop our lives forever. I need to get back to my condo too."

She sighed and turned over another photo. "I was angry at the two of you, you and Dad—I thought you should have tried harder."

"Your father had a drinking problem."

"That doesn't mean you discard him. For better or worse . . . ?"

"I suppose it works for some people." I sighed. "I haven't thought back to that time for a long while, but I can tell you this—your father wasn't there for me. He didn't help me take care of you, he didn't help out around the house, and he didn't care about me. I emptied bottles of vodka into the sink and dealt with his maniacal tirades when he couldn't find his fix. I turned my back on him when he called me names and tried not to take it personally when he didn't show up all night. Maybe I was too young to deal with it. But at that point in my life, I couldn't deal with it."

"We could've had a better life. Daddy has a good heart. We had a good talk yesterday. I guess . . . I'm angry but not angry, at both of you. You did the best you could."

"We were young."

"Not too young. You were only a few years older than me now."

After Cassie left, I sifted aimlessly through the pictures. Grandma and Grandpa handed out gifts on Christmas morning in front of the tree that stood in the corner of the living room. On my first day of kindergarten I stood in front of the house dressed in a plaid skirt and penny loafers, the sun in my eyes, face screwed up in a grimace. There I was sitting on the bed in my room reading a book, a young woman who didn't like her picture taken. Later, me in jeans and a T-shirt, hair long down my back, looking pretty and glad to be going off to college, I stood in front of the packed station wagon with my hand raised in a wave.

When I pulled the stack of pictures from the living room drawer toward me, a single black and white photo was left behind. A young man and woman appeared close up to the camera, grinning, their light olive complexions matching. They looked happy, and like they belonged together. I turned it over. The words "Margie and Rafe, happy together," were written in pencil in my mother's handwriting.

My father was gone before I was born—he was a moment in time, a figment. I knew he was a brawny Italian guy whom she met in a café on Little Italy's Murray Hill. She told me she loved the rich concoction of espresso, sweetened by bites of cannoli. She gradually became aware of the dark, cool barista's lingering gaze. Once they started talking, she discovered he was a southern Italian who went home during the harvest. What she liked most about him was that he was writing a novel.

She never saw that novel. He went to Italy the summer after her junior year and she went home. She wrote him three letters and received no answer. Pregnant and desperate that fall, a young woman who had never heard of Rafe Paglia answered my mother's knock on his old apartment door.

Grandpa referred to my father alternately as that dirty Italian who got his daughter pregnant or just "the Dago." A photo of Grandpa near the end of his life depicted a white-haired man with a bald spot on top, a thin face in a round head, eyes direct and serious. He knew the world—you can see it in his eyes.

Despite my grandfather's disappointment in my mother, he was fond of me. A German immigrant, he let me sip his Pilsner while I sat on his lap. I laid my ear against his chest so I could hear and feel his heartbeat and smell the warm tobacco lingering on his clothes. And then, one day, Grandpa's heart stopped beating while he was sleeping.

What did my mother think about my divorce? What did she write during the time when my marriage was falling apart? Presumably, one could be authentic and real in a diary, but could that be the case when you were the sort of diarist who labeled the years and set the books marching on a shelf? I walked the stairs to pick up the right volume. The day my divorce was final, she wrote:

> I know Betsy did what she thought she had to do, but marriage should be forever. They've failed, not only Betsy, but Rick too. Rick always drinks more than he can handle. And just like that, she's packing up all their belongings as if she's glad to be done with all the silver and china her guests brought to the wedding. She's turning away from her husband and doesn't know what she's bringing down upon her head—they have a child together. She's running away, and one day she may regret it.
>
> On the other hand, if the love is gone . . . But if it isn't, if she still loves him, God help her. Running away is never a good answer to anything.

But what do I know about relationships? I know that a man will say what he needs to say and words are cheap. I know that love doesn't last any longer than the time it takes to get the house in order. I dismissed Rafe's love for me even though he was offering it—it was too late. I hurt too much. The love was gone.

Mom and I were in agreement that words are cheap, but the rest . . . I was not running away when I left. I HAD to leave. My physical health was deteriorating as I stopped sleeping at night, and Rick and I did nothing but argue when he was home.

What was that about my father offering his love? That was curious. So maybe the story was different than the one Mom told me. I picked up the last volume, my volume, and wrote.

> As much as Mom tried to get me to believe in promises and happily ever after, in fairies and dragonflies, in the hope that fireflies bring to a summer evening, I didn't believe in them.
>
> From the beginning of my life, there were secrets. My father was gone but I didn't know if he knew about me or where he was or if he did know about me, if he wanted to know me. Promises are as flimsy as a layered cake with whipped cream frosting that sits on a table in summer heat waiting for the party to get started. Mom apparently thought my father was false, that he made promises he couldn't keep, that he was a fast talker who took advantage. She's bitter in her journal, and that was at the end of her life—why did she hold onto that belief? Why wasn't she open to his love when it was offered? Could the love really have been gone?
>
> Marriage taught me to take care of myself and not trust anyone else to do it for me. It had been a mistake to believe in that love. At least that's what I've always thought. Love is imperfect, but that's not what we learn from the Cinderella story.
>
> As for how it was when I was with Jerry, I didn't care whether I hurt Mom. It was as if she were a neighbor with whom I exchanged pleasantries without feeling. Mom did what a Mom would do and forgave her child who didn't know better. I have forever been regretting that year, the year I turned sixteen and became the person I was to become. I wonder if it would have been different if Mom and I talked about all this then.

I know very little about Mom's pain from losing my father. When I was twelve and heard Mom crying, I felt her pain, but when I was fifteen and heard her crying after Jerry broke up with her, I felt despair.

It was getting late when I went downstairs to make sure the house was shut tight for the night. Ben was in the kitchen drinking a glass of orange juice. He swallowed, then said, "I know I can live here as long as I want, and the place is half mine, but I don't want to without your mother. I'll find a place close to work for the next couple of years, until I retire, then I'm thinking about moving south. I don't feel like doing these winters anymore; weeks on end with two feet of snow last winter nearly did me in."

"You've made this your home."

He looked like a farmer. He'd been out in the orchards. He met the veterinarian when he came to check on the new calf. The farm *was* his home. But he was the type of guy who was good at making a home wherever he laid his hat. "Your mother left half of it for me because that was the right thing to do, but I'm deeding my half to you. It needs to be kept in the family. Your family. With you, and Cassie. Last thing you need is for me to die and my kids own part of it too."

That made sense. "So what do we do with this?" I raised my arms in all directions.

"That's for you to decide."

I raised my hand in protest and shook my head. "It's yours too. Look at you. You're a farmer. You have a farmer's soul."

He laughed. "No, I just have a farmer's clothes. And they don't look good on me."

I put my arm around him and felt his rough cheek against mine. "My mother was lucky to have you. No one else could have loved her as well as you did. I'm thankful for that, Ben."

He looked out the window across the pastureland. "You were a good daughter." He looked back over his shoulder at me. "You came around. This farm is yours. Your grandfather made this farm what it is and you were practically raised on it. I know you have your place in downtown Cleveland, but this place has to stay with you."

"Like the teacup."

"Yes. And that teacup . . ."

"Stays in this house."

"Yep." He nodded.

I moved over to the table and sat down. Looking up at him, I said, "I'm not sure I want to live all the way out here. It took effort to leave this town."

"Sometimes life comes back to where it began. Let the question be there for a while. You need to learn to love the questions themselves."

I smiled. "Mom used to say that."

"Yes. She taught me that lesson. It takes a lot of learning, that lesson."

He left the kitchen. His footsteps on the stairs and overhead in the bedroom echoed against the walls of the house. I couldn't see how he could sleep in their bed, the bed she died in, but he did.

Grandma and I used to sit on the couch while she entertained me with her dramatic reading of *Cinderella* and *Sleeping Beauty*. When the fairy tale ended, Grandma liked to ask, "Now what's your story?"

"I was born to be a princess who lives in Castlemara high up on a hill above the sea. My birthright was stolen from me. But some day, a man will come and solve the mystery and put me on the throne where I'll rule and have everything I ever dreamed of."

Grandma, dressed in draping smooth pajamas. looked pleased when I made up names for things like "Castlemara." The story was always better with made up words and places. "And what is it you want more than anything? What is it you dream of?"

"A man who loves me and cares about me and listens to me."

I believed it would happen for me. Rick wasn't my knight in shining armor, but he was good at acting like a prince. He owned the school with his popularity, and later, he owned the town. By the time Cassie was a toddler, he already had a seat on City Council. My prince didn't have a concubine, but my husband had his women.

I'd kept that first note Tommy wrote me in a stationery box with other pieces of my life—I wonder if he would be surprised that I still had that note.

DRIFTWOOD
At Willow Beach

Startled by a human voice, I open my eyes. In my remembering, I forgot that I was still sitting on a bench at Willow Beach. The cyclist is gone and my remaining companion nods his gray-haired head knowingly at a conversation in his head. But he'd said something out loud like he was drifting from his inner world to the outer one. Yes, that is how I feel as well—the inner world and outer world have no boundaries, nor does my sleeping and wakefulness, nor does reality and unreality. It's a place of peace and I know now that true madness resides in trying to be too much a part of the world.

Seagulls streak through the sky before landing on the break wall. An old black man wearing dungarees fishes off the pier, a mother and her school-aged children walk knee-high in the water, and an older couple scavenges the beach with metal detectors. My legs have become numb because they have been stretched too high on the fence railing in front of me. I let them drop to the ground and rub the circulation back into my legs.

If only life could beat with the steady firmness of the rising moon and falling sun, the rise and fall of the waves, the rise and fall of voices. The past rolls under and out again. Every now and again, in my forgetting, the need to be achieving out there in this world comes back. That's when I take the teacup from the dining room china cabinet to feel its frail lightness in my hands. As Sophocles said, "Look and you will find it—what is unsought will go undetected." I have only to look around me to find the things that anchor me to who I am. I often forget.

It took my mother's dying to find out that there was more to life than what I had. The lake, with its high waves and sandy shorelines, is every bit a part of who we are, from the grapes growing in the temperate micro-climates to the freighters that navigate the deep waters of the St. Lawrence Seaway. I'm drawn to the soothing rhythm of life and the promise of something better.

An eight-inch long brown-striated piece of wood, smoothed by the force of water, lies right above the water line. I can't resist. I shimmy between the fence and the dozing old man, then walk down the cement steps to the beach. The sand squishes and shifts beneath my feet as I approach the marooned wood and gather it to me.

Last March, Mom convinced me to drive her here to find driftwood. We parked as close as we could to the stairs and I steadied her with my hand on her frail arm as she gripped the metal railing. Rough rust clawed at her hands. It was a difficult descent, but we made it. Talking loudly because of the wind, I told Mom I would stay with her this time—we would look for a large, smooth, and mostly flat piece together. She frowned, not sure about me staying with her. It wasn't her way. Our eyes hunted ahead of our feet, searching, until she pointed to a spot fifty feet ahead of us where a piece of driftwood about a foot long by four inches wide lay on the sand. When I picked it up and handed it to her, I felt its surf-worn smoothness.

Her eyes confirmed what she was thinking: the universe had provided, again. This light piece of wood in my hand is a gift from the lake. Providence.

My story is a steady testament to grace and God's providence and things falling in place, but I didn't see it that way when I was living through last year. I had a teacup and a farm. My daughter wasn't as angry as she'd been, and Mom . . . I felt her with me every day.

It was the letters that pushed me closer to Mom's way of thinking. First I had Tom's gently nudging inquiries, then I had my father's hidden probes, and finally, I had Mom's side of the story, which helped me with my own. The secrets overwhelmed me.

As you will see as I continue to tell my story. I hope you won't hate me, or maybe you already do because I became so lost.

CHAPTER FIVE – LETTERS

For years I'd wondered what was in the hatbox on the closet shelf in Mom's salon. I pulled it down and put it on the desk. Under the lid were important papers—bank account statements, social security cards, the deed to the farm. Further down, like buried treasure, was a 2-inch stack of letters in envelopes tied with a green ribbon. The top envelope bore an Italian postmark on its tattered paper. I took a deep breath as I felt my heart take a dip and shivers flow through my midriff. Now there were letters from a man who supposedly never wrote.

"How could you?!" I yelled into the air, out into the universe where Mom was hovering. "You had letters from my father, and I didn't know it?"

I was pissed. My father HAD written back. He didn't desert her. He cared enough to write . . . I flipped through the stack . . . several dozen letters. Despite my disbelief, I was elated at the thought of being able to find out more about him.

I untied the green ribbon and flipped through the letters. Three were from Italy and about thirty were postmarked from Cleveland. All had been opened. Mom lied to me all my life, not just once but thousands of days of lies because the whole story of how my father left and didn't write was a lie.

I hated her in that moment. She was no longer a victim, but a witch. She had decided to create a fairy tale that wasn't true, a fairy tale of how a woman fell in love with a man who didn't care about her and never bothered to be in touch with her ever again, leaving her pregnant and having to raise a child of her own. She chose to be a victim.

I pulled the first letter from its Italian envelope and smoothed the opaque sheets of paper out on the table.

Dearest Margie,

Already I miss you. On my way over, I wondered if it was the right thing to do, to leave you there without me. I know you'll miss me too.

I love you. I hope you know that. I hope you'll remember it each and every time you walk past the cafe and each time you lay on the bed where we made love.

Life here in Sorrento is as it always is in the summer. The olive trees color the hills with the silver-green of their leaves. We grow Minucciola and Leccino olives at the Paglia fattoria d'oliva so we can make our fine olive oil. We also have Aglianico vineyards, the red grapes for the wine we produce. We predict an early harvest this year, in mid-September, but we shall see, it's so hard to tell.

La nostra casa sits on the top of a hill with a view of the Bay of Naples—I wish you could see it. It's 26 degrees today and sunny, and the tourists are filling up the town, which makes us stay away. We are glad that many of them find their way up the road to la nostra fattoria because those that do want to know how we make the olive oil and wine, and we show them our storerooms and production processes. People sit in our tasting room and try a bit of olive oil with Mama's bread and taste our wines blended with juice from our neighbors' harvests.

My uncle has asked me to become his partner at the café so he can retire in a few years. I haven't told my parents—they still want me to live in Italy. They think my sojourns to the US are fancies. I hope to be back to you by late September. I'm taking a class in comparative literature that begins mid-semester. I can't stop being a student, I guess. But being a student gives me that much more I can share with you.

I miss you day and night. You with your cute little walk in your skirt with the slit up the side, those high heels. No one has ever been my girl like you are. I feel we are one, we are in love, and all is well.

All my love,
Rafe

Rafe Paglia's family lived in Sorrento and sold wine and olive oil made from the fruit of their own soil. He was taking college courses. He had the opportunity to own a coffee shop in Cleveland. He wanted to return to Cleveland after that summer in Italy. He missed my mother. He wrote her back that summer. My mother lied to me for forty-six years.

I had always believed theirs was a special love. But she was bitter with anger every time she told me how he disappeared without a trace. That anger was real, but he wasn't lost like she said. Why make up a reason for him not being in her life anymore? What was the real reason?

I returned the letter to its hiding place. I was pretty sure that I wouldn't learn the reason by reading his letters to her. He probably didn't know her reason either.

I opened a photo album, one of my early adulthood. I found a picture of me and Tom taken on his father's boat the summer after my freshman year in college, tanned, good-looking people in bathing suits, Tom's hand on the rudder with me sitting next to him at the stern. Then there was me and Tom at Linda's wedding, Tom in a tux and me in a floor-length burgundy dress, my face turned up to his. A later photo showed Tom in a T-shirt and cutoffs leaning in the door of my dorm room with a hammer in his hand. His smile said that he was on top of the world.

I got up early the morning I ran away. Maria picked me up outside my dorm when the sky was becoming light. I called her at midnight the night before and told her to pack a bag for a two-day trip. Once I made up my mind, I had to get on with it in case I changed my mind.

Stupid girl.

I missed what he and I had. If I spent time with Tom, I risked falling in love with him again, and I didn't want to take that risk. I didn't want an all-consuming love and I didn't want to keep secrets from him. He didn't deserve that.

When I wrote my response to Tom, I just did it, the way beads fall to the floor when a necklace breaks. Once they hit, they bounce, and they're out there in the world, all those little words making up meaning, trickling across a piece of paper. The beads were all over, and I had trouble bringing my thoughts to paper. There was too much to say, but yet, there was little I was able to say to him.

Maybe I wasn't such a stupid girl when I ran away after all.

Dear Tom,

Thank you for coming to the funeral. I never would have thought you'd want to be in the same room with me again, yet you were kind to me. I'm not sure the passing years can wipe out how poorly I treated you. They say time heals all wounds. I hope that's true. I've been thinking about that since Mom's death—there were apologies at the end, but for me, some of the wounds remain, not what I've done to the people in my life but what I've done to myself.

I appreciate the note you sent me. You must get out to Conneaut often enough, to have seen Mom and me on the beach. Funny I never noticed you there, but I was busy keeping Mom from falling.

I live in a Warehouse District condo in Cleveland, and I love it. I work as an editor for a travel magazine, part of a huge publishing house; you wouldn't believe all the trade publications out there—think public works, business news, financial times, and dentistry. I also do some real writing once in a while when the magazine sends me somewhere to write a feature. The trips get me away from the monotony of real life.

I'm not sure what I'm going to do with Windy Hill. I can't sell it, but I can't live here either. Ben says I should let the question be. Mom always said the answer comes while the question simmers, like bubbles rising to the surface in a pot of boiling water. Do you believe the universe gives us answers in its own time? I guess I do—I'm waiting, but with impatience
.

Mom became happier the longer she lived. She was always singing as she went out to milk the cows or pick apples. Later, she made the driftwood stuff and painted. She became happier the more she created. For the longest time, she and I were distant, but her illness brought us together again. Cassie pointed out to me that if Mom had died suddenly, I would not have come home as I did.

It's hard for me to be happy. I'm letting go of my old ways of thinking, yet no new path has opened for me.

    Fondly,
    Betsy

I mailed the letter to the return address on the letter he sent me—Bryce Road, Vermilion. From Conneaut to Vermilion along the Lake was a drunken sailor's trip with the inlets and points receding and advancing. It's about 115 miles. Not so far—when Cassie was in college, I regularly drove to Ohio University in Athens, down by the Ohio River and 115 miles meant we were close to home.

During the next couple of days, Ben and I packed up most of my mother's clothes for Goodwill and threw her toiletries away. I confiscated a favorite cotton navy sweater, almost brand-new Keds, and several silk scarves. When Pedro showed me how to plow the fields, high on Grandpa's old tractor, I wore the Keds. In the evenings, I read through Mom's journals, picking out dates of significance, knowing I was avoiding reading the whole flow of her life, and especially the years right after I was born. The letters from my father stayed on the bottom of the box.

Journaling became a regular part of my routine. It helped me sort things out. I felt better after I wrote. In fact, there were days when that was the first thing I did, and I was surprised how much I needed to sit down at the desk, pull out a journal, and put pen to paper to write out my thoughts the old-fashioned way, in cursive. It was good soul work.

> I'm afraid of what I'll find in my father's letters. Mom must have been protecting me from something fragile by keeping my father's location from me all those years. Reading her journals, I get the feeling she was protecting herself from feeling what she felt for my father, that she was in resistance and denial of self. I hope her journals, and their letters, will tell me more.
>
> My father might still live in the Cleveland area, but maybe the secret was that he knew about me and didn't want to acknowledge it. Or maybe he wanted to know me but couldn't because of something going on with my mother.
>
> I cry a lot these days. It's grief but it's lots of other things. My emotions are all over the place, from the excitement of remembrance to the sorrow of loss. In that loss I regret breaking up with Tom, I regret my relationship with Jerry, and I hate what

I've done to men in my life like Robert. When I saw Tom in the sanctuary, memories rose into my consciousness and I had to put them aside to maintain my composure. But what would have happened if I had stood there and embraced the pain right then and there, right there in front of Tom? The truth would have been confronted and dealt with and we could have moved on. Holding onto a secret, pretending it didn't happen, hurts me. But it would be selfish to bring Tom into it just because I'm looking for forgiveness. I wanted Tom to have his dreams then, and now I want him to have his fallacies.

That probably isn't fair to Tom. As then, I don't think Tom has the strength to handle what life can dish out. Who put me in charge of protecting him? Does he even want to be protected?

A few days before I was to leave Windy Hill, when Ben and I were waiting for our farewell dinner to be done, I went to the mailbox. The only mail was a letter in a blue envelope from Vermilion. I sat down at the table with it, while Ben watched me curiously.

Dear Betsy:

When I had my first glimpse of you, standing below the cross at the front of the church, all the memories of our times together came rushing back. I had trouble speaking with you and your family because all I wanted to say was how beautiful you've become. I think the gray streaks in your hair become you. But I still see that girl you were, the one with thirst for knowledge, who liked to explore with me. You have a vibrancy and energy and grace that are a hard combination to find. I also see that you are in the midst of something big, something you've been waiting for all your life.

I don't know what the change is, and maybe you don't even know it's taking place. I find that we unfold in layers as we get older and we're getting closer to our true selves all the time. The way I see life now is not the way I saw it when I was twenty-one. We need to be careful to remember that—you are not who you were at twenty either.

There are big parts of your story that I want to know. How much did it hurt to deal with your husband's alcoholism? I think you bottled up and did what you had to do. You chose to go on, stoically and courageously. Now is the time to cry about that loss and let it go. Maybe you've done that, but maybe you haven't finished it.

I have been angry with you many of these years. I've also spent those years wondering about you and thinking about what we had. Seeing you on the beach, that was no accident. I came to know you and your mother went there on Saturday mornings, and so I went there as well, keeping a distance down the beach or up above you on one of the benches, sunglasses and age hiding who I was.

Don't we all struggle to be happy? Are any of us truly happy? And if we were, would we know it? It's part of human nature to be dissatisfied and seeking.

Fondly,
Tom

Wow, I thought. That was the loveliest letter I'd ever received. Ben caught me smiling. "Well?"
"It's a letter."
"From?"
"A guy I used to know who was at the funeral. We had some good times together when we were kids. I was thinking about how much he's changed, but the last time I saw him was twenty-seven years ago."
Ben looked at me thoughtfully. "I hope you're both different than you were twenty-seven years ago."
"Life's about the journey, isn't it?"
"Heck. That's basic. And I'm off on the next leg of it. Nice spread for my last night here. Thank you, Betsy." He surveyed the eggplant parmesan, capelliini, and roasted vegetables, then reached for the bread basket and butter. We ate silently, but in fellowship.
While we were eating cheesecake, I asked, "What did Mom tell you about my father?"
He sighed and sat back in his chair. He took a while to answer. "There's more to that story than I know, Betsy. She kept that one pretty close to her and I had to pry out of her what I know. She told me what she told you, that he went off to Italy and then she couldn't

find him again. But sometimes I had the sense that she wanted it that way, that she didn't try so hard to find him. I think he hurt her, but I think she was the reason they never saw each other again. I also think they were in touch with each other over the years."

"Why do you think so?"

He shrugged. "It's more of a hunch than anything else. She'd say things like he was a loser and probably unhappy in the vineyards of Italy, then she'd say something about him having a new family he cared about more than his first one, and when I asked her how she knew that she looked at me as if she'd been caught in a lie, but she shrugged it off."

"I had that same feeling a couple of times."

"My guess is she did speak to him at one point. I think he came back from Italy and she decided, for whatever reason, that it was over."

"And pride could never get her to admit that." My mother believed in telling the truth, but only when it wouldn't hurt; discussing a former lover with her husband was not worth the hurt.

"Let me show you something," I said and stood to go into the dining room. I came back with the bundle of letters. "I found this in the bottom of the hat box."

Ben looked at the first envelope and then flipped through them all the way to the bottom. "Have you looked at these?"

"I read the first one. He'd barely arrived in Italy and he wrote her a letter telling her he missed her."

"The most recent one is dated six months ago. The return addresses start in Italy and then move to Cleveland and finally to Cleveland Heights. Looks like there are thirty or more letters here, kiddo."

Mom was always lecturing us about sticking with the truth, with a big "T," yet she must have thought this was a little "t." She believed in living in tune with life's ups and downs, like Lake Erie in all her moods, smooth as glass one hour and fretful with eight-foot waves crashing over the pier the next. She sought authenticity, but in this one part of her life, she wasn't able to be true.

"Mom's truth wasn't so true," I said. "How could she lie to me like she did?"

He shook his head. "She was trying to protect you. Maybe she got so caught up in the lies, there was no going back to the truth. She never told me she wrote to him, or that he wrote to her, so she lied to me as well. But whatever the lies are about, she wanted them to be over after she died. She wanted you to find these letters."

"I don't want to read them."

"They aren't going anywhere. I suppose she knew that the choice was yours, in the end, whether you wanted to know or didn't. But maybe you want to believe the story she told you—that your father was a rascal. That was your grandfather's story and your mother allowed it because of him, perhaps. Stories take on a life of their own, you know."

"I'll have to read the letters."

"Of course you will." He gave me a short hug. "But they can stay right here until you're ready for them."

I nodded. "I have some things I thought you should have." I handed him the bag that had been next to my chair.

"What do we have here?" He reached into the bag and pulled out Mom's favorite silk nightgown, the straw hat she liked to wear when she was outside in the summer, a small sketch of children on the beach, and a driftwood boat bearing three small clay fairies with raised arms. He placed them one by one on the table and said, "I'm leaving the diamond pendant and earrings, the emerald ring, and the sapphire tennis bracelet for you. They're in her jewelry box."

"Thank you."

"Your mother stuck to the story of how some good-for-nothing guy got her pregnant, a good story for future marriage prospects, I suppose."

I turned the letters over in my hand, feeling the soft-worn paper, then put them back into the box. "I'm not looking forward to the steady deadlines and the publisher's crunching of numbers. I don't want to go back to work."

"I know. Life out there is rough. I'll be going to Mexico to open an office in Mazatlan instead of to the office, so the transition should be easier than it would be otherwise."

We'd lived so much life together over the last six months. We rarely talked about ourselves, just went through the motions of keeping up with what was required of each other. It would be strange not to have Ben in my life.

Ben helped me clean up the kitchen and gave me a hug before he went upstairs to finish packing. In the morning, a truck would come to take away the few pieces of furniture and boxes of personal items he brought with him to the marriage.

I sat on the stoop after dinner with a cup of tea. The daffodils were shriveled brown and scrawny, but their stalks stood defiantly straight and tall. I could be five or twenty or forty years old sitting here on the stoop. It was a place I'd sat my entire life.

My journal had begun to travel with me in large pockets or under my arm. I tore out a page and wrote to Tom.

>Tom,
>
>Your last letter was beautiful. I have trouble finding the girl I used to be but you make me believe she's still there, somewhere. Do you know they call me the Dragon at work? They're probably glad I'm not there making them work until eight every night and trying to make up for it by buying them pizza for dinner. The work is too hard for me now. I've lost my drive.
>
>I don't want to leave Windy Hill. I want to slip back to 1970 and stay there and never grow up. I grew up too soon. If I could grow up differently I would.
>
>I just found out my father's in Cleveland and has written to my mother for years, yet she kept that a secret from me. I used to pray for God to bring my father back to us from Italy so we could be a family and when it didn't happen, I was angry with God when I wasn't thinking about how there's a reason for everything and we can't know the mystery of God's way.
>
>Isn't it interesting how an object will trigger a memory, something you never thought you'd forget, but you did, and it comes back fresh? The daffodils have died in our backyard, but they took me back to kindergarten at Jenkins Elementary School where we made daffodils from construction paper, toilet paper tubes, and tissue paper. Daffodils remind me of the day you first kissed me. You were so bold and sure of yourself. I sense that old boldness of spirit in you.
>
>There's no way to explain Rick and me in a letter. I married him because getting married seemed the right thing to do at that point in my life. After about a year of marriage, I knew he didn't love me enough. I don't think I loved him enough either. That's when he started drinking. It was a mistake for both of us.

I was never happier than when I was with you, yet I didn't believe I was good enough for you. Leaving you wasn't a leaving, it was a giving to you. I wanted you to have something better than I could give. I didn't think I was the kind of woman who could be a senator's wife.

I'll be leaving Conneaut on Sunday. These letters have been a good way to reconnect. I look forward to hearing from you again soon.

Betsy

The next morning, I met with Pedro and told him about raising his salary and checking in every other week. When I finished, he asked urgently, "Miss Betsy, are you going to sell this place? Tell me. I need to know. I need money, can't be without job, you see? And we have a place to live, a place where we can be comfortable. We don't . . ."

"I know, Pedro. If I decide to sell it, you'll be the first to know. I don't think that's going to happen." I must have been making a decision on that without knowing it.

Pedro had been our caretaker for thirty years. He tipped his worn cowboy hat and said, "It's a deal. I keep the house, the cows, the gardens, and orchards. I send the milk away to the Heine's dairy like I always have. I have your number. And you'll keep the farm."

His familiar brown face wore the beginnings of a smile. When I was a girl he cared for a horse from the neighboring farm for a few weeks. He surprised me one day by taking me to the corral. He taught me how to put the heavy saddle up on the horse's back, the headpiece over the horse's head, and pull the reins through. He showed me how to adjust the stirrups. "Thank you for teaching me how to ride a horse," I said.

"You were a natural on the horse."

"It felt pretty good."

"You were busy back then, a teenager with things she had to do, places she had to go, people she had to meet." He looked at me knowingly and held my gaze. "You think I didn't know about the tree house?"

I didn't breathe. "I thought it was a secret."

He shrugged. "Maybe from some people, but not from me." He grinned and shook his head. "You were young and wild and it was natural for you to have a lover. Why do you feel it was so wrong?"

"He was a man."

Again he shrugged. "Good way to start to know things, huh?" He winked at me.

Yes, Jerry taught me a few things all right. "I thought it was wrong."

"Too hard on yourself, miss."

I looked out over the fields. "I'll be here through the weekend and will leave on Sunday night." I said. "I know you'll take good care of the place. You always have."

"Like my own."

"Yes."

"*Trato hecho*," he said as he gave my hand a squeeze.

I stood on the back step and watched him amble with a slight limp across the driveway and past the barn to the caretaker's cottage under the willow tree. Pedro had become the only person who had known me as a child, and he accepted me for who I was, like a father would. He seemed satisfied with what he had, even though his wife was limited to a wheelchair.

I walked into town to the post office to mail Tom's letter, then continued to Willow Beach. The weather was getting warm, and the air was humid from an earlier rain. My jeans were sticking to me by the time I reached the beach. I watched the seagulls dip into the surf to find their lunch.

Why was Tom back in my life?

Neither God nor the universe responded.

I let that question linger. I couldn't explain it. He should be angry with me, he WAS angry with me the last time we spoke, and now it was all gone, dispelled by time. I wrote in my journal.

> We've lived a lifetime since I went to Detroit without an explanation. But now we are both alone and we're teetering on the edge of middle age. We must have something to share even though we're not the same people we were. We grew up the same way, on farms and in a small town. We heard the same sermons and knew the same way of life.

Tom won't like the story of Jerry. He wouldn't like that I've had lovers on my trips. I'm afraid of his judgment, yet I'm not sure why I think he'll be judgmental.

What about those lovers? The last time I traveled, I met a man who could have been my next husband. We spent ten glorious days together and I felt the familiar infatuation, cloud nine craziness that made me throw caution to the wind. But when I got back home again, I refused to see him. Mom was right about me—I run away from relationships. I tried it with Robert again, but I feel no desire to call him back. I can't explain it, other than to acknowledge I'm just not open to it.

The ultimate running away was when I ran away from Tom. Maybe it's time to stop running. I need to figure out why I thought I couldn't talk to him. All I remember is that conversation in the restaurant. But before that, why didn't I tell him about Jerry?

It goes back to Mom and her shame for getting pregnant. That's where it started. And then there was me sneaking around with Jerry, a sin because Mom was dating him, and he preferred me.

I didn't want Tom to know how bad I was. I wanted him to see me as good, untouched. Does me not telling him about the baby mean I thought our relationship was lacking? I think so. If I thought Tom would think less of me because I was pregnant with his baby, that means I didn't treasure what we had, didn't see it as pure love.

I'd lost my way.

On Friday evening, the sun set in pink and orange, and long rays of light bathed the pastures stretching from behind the barn to the woods on the hill. Gnarly orchard trees, greening with small bright leaves, stood on the ridge to the left of the house, three stately rows of apple and peach trees marching along the south side of the property. Nearer to the house, between the barn and the orchards, Pedro had turned the soil of the one-acre vegetable garden. He was carrying on like nothing had changed.

And nothing had. Not for the farm. The earth would yield apples and peaches and vegetables, and the cows would graze in the pasture and produce milk. Two of our thirty cows had already calved and a third one would within the week. Windy Hill, my grandfather's closely-planned realm, his legacy, remained.

My quiet was broken when Cassie and her family drove up the gravel driveway in their Jeep. I'd made lasagna primavera. Cassie hugged me and handed Beth to me. We'd arrived at this at last. This family was a true thing even though a bit of resentment separated us.

"The place looks great, Mom. The kitchen floor hasn't shined like this in a year."

I showed her my raw-skinned, dry hands. "I have hands that show it."

She smiled. "I bet that was good for your soul."

I chuckled. "Yes, it was the perfect way to end my time here."

"And you made your lasagna, didn't you?" Mike kissed my cheek and walked over to open the oven.

"Sure did."

We sat in the living room with our wine and talked while the lasagna browned in the oven, then ate at the big farmhouse table.

"I'll try to get back here every couple of weeks," I said to Cassie. "Pedro will take good care of things."

"I can stop by sometimes too."

"It's a shame to leave the place empty," Mike said. "Maybe we should sell our place . . ."

Cassie shot him a warning look but didn't say anything.

"I think we should love that question for a while. An answer will come."

I was on the porch when the mailman came the next morning. I waved to cranky old Mr. Flynn as he rolled by on the wrong side of his vehicle. I wasn't surprised when I pulled out an envelope with a return address in Vermilion.

Dear Elizabeth:

What a joy it was to read your letter, and to see that you're thinking through some things about your life. I was right about you growing, about being on the edge of things.

That your father is alive and nearby is quite a discovery. I'm sure you have mixed feelings about finding him and getting to know him, and the question itself is an interesting one. If you got to know him, you'd have to tell him how much it hurt not to have a father. You'd have to confront him on why he hurt your mom. You'd have to find out why they never got together again. If you don't reconnect, you'll be wondering all those things forever, but I guess you could stick with the story your mother gave you.

Suffice it to say that daffodils have always reminded me of you. As have fireflies. You don't mention them, but remember how we used to catch them in back of our house in Conneaut and then later when we went to church camp? Other kids were involved in hide-n-seek and you and I were reaching out for those floating lights and trying to figure out where the next one was. You are my daffodil and firefly girl. Hmmm. I've never expressed that before.

Rick and you were always an unlikely match. You need to let go of that. I know it hurt because we always expect the best when we marry someone. The vows are meant to unite us forever and we believe in the possibility of a love that lasts forever. I'm sorry you had to go through that.

I imagine you're now packing up your things to return to your real life soon. I had to write you quick, before you left Conneaut, because you haven't given me your new address and I feared we'd lose connection with each other. Soon you'll be trudging to the office again to work hard and going home to . . . what? To write? To cook? To dance? I try to imagine the life you have, and I can't. It's been way too long. You'll have to let me get a glimpse of that.

We built a house on the lake fifteen years ago. My children seem to be happy—Rob manages a retail store in Seattle and Elena is a junior in graphic design at Bowling Green. Miriam and I kept the semblance of a marriage for a long time, but now she's living in Santa Fe and learning how to dye yarns and weave scarves and blankets. The divorce was final in January.

I have my own law practice specializing in real estate and

environmental law. I enjoy it. I like to take photos, sail, and sit on my back deck to watch the waves. I read a lot, recently read Ken Follett's *Pillars of the Earth*, a tome of a book, but worth reading just to witness the effort that went into it.

What trips have you been on lately? Where are you going next? I suppose I should do some traveling too, but doing it alone is a lonely thing. It gets lonely around here on the weekends and that feeling keeps me from doing things.

I was happy when I was with you. I don't think it was the dream state of youth, I think it was meant to be, me and you, even though you ran away. I'm speaking from a lifetime of experience, now, and I still feel, after all these years, that we let go of something fine when we broke up. You were worthy of me in every way and you would have made a fine senator's wife. But I'm not a senator, and even if I was, I was always just me, you know.

I think you ran away from me because you didn't want to love that much. It saddens me to think you didn't believe that our happiness, or our love, could last.

Tell me why you left me. Come on, Betsy, I deserve to know how this all turned out the way it did. I've spent years thinking about it. And what do you mean when you say you grew up too soon?

If you want to call me, my number's 440-555-6980.

Fondly,
Thomas

Calling Tom, hearing his voice, connecting in a way we hadn't in years, sounded painful to me. "Tell me why you left me," was a challenge and I didn't like that. We both needed the answer to that question. I tried to work it out in the letter I wrote back to him.

Dear Thomas:

I just finished reading your letter.

The next time I open one of your letters, I'll be sitting on my balcony overlooking the Cuyahoga River and drinking a glass of Chardonnay. That's what I usually do when I get home from work. I drink a glass of wine and read one of the books stacked on my end table in the living room or next to my bed. Sometimes I go to a movie or out for drinks with old friends (Lord knows I have no new ones), but mostly I sit by myself and read. I might rent a movie. I like to cook good meals just for me. I don't dance much, but maybe I should.

I was touched by you calling me your "daffodil and firefly girl." I was dancing when I was catching those fireflies—we were both dancing with them. And the daffodils . . . they've always held promise beyond that they were a beautiful brightness in the winter landscape.

Not wanting to go back to work, spending time at Windy Hill, repairing relationships, reading and writing journals, and getting your letters—it's been a fine time. I think the next thing I'll do is apologize to Rick, and then some of my life will be tidied up. But as you sense, that's only the beginning—I intend to read the letters my father sent my mother and keep reading her journal.

I keep thinking about why I left you, and I'm still trying to figure out the answer. I didn't want to leave you. Maybe I loved you too much. It had nothing to do with you and everything to do with me. There were so many things I should have told you, but I didn't, and that was a mistake. I was afraid that if I told you too much, you wouldn't love me like you did. I didn't trust that your love was big enough to accept all that I was. I guess the challenge of being with you permanently was too much, and that's where we were headed. Does that help you understand better? It doesn't really help me.

My mother told me I need to get on with my life, which meant I should settle down. She always thought having a man was important, but I've grown accustomed to solitude. The great thing about being single is not worrying about what your spouse needs or thinks or wants. Being at Windy Hill for a few weeks, I think I've discovered that I'm lonely.

I try to picture your house on the lake, and you sailing from a dock right outside your window. I like my view of the river, the jutting points of land along the shoreline, but I'd like living directly on the lake more.

I haven't been on a trip in a while. Mom's diagnosis was made six months ago, so I've been going to Conneaut a lot. Before she became too ill, we went places together, trying to make the most of the time we had left. She liked the wineries and covered bridges. Sometimes we drove over to Presque Isle in Erie or over to Mentor Headlands State Park. Sometimes she spent the night with me at my place.

Life changed so much when Mom became ill, I feel as if I'm starting over again. My life is divided into before illness, illness, and after death. The time of caring for her has left me tired and unsure.

I'm glad for these letters that travel along the lake. You take me back. It feels like my two worlds, which used to be separate, are coming together, and it's wonderful, but unsettling. I'm not sure where I belong, but your letters help my perspective. From now on, you'll want to write me at: 1510 W. 9th Street, Cleveland, Ohio 44114.

Looking forward to our next correspondence,
Elizabeth

When I was finished, I wrote in my journal.

Letters along the lake . . . do they pick up the scent of soot and salt or whisper to the Lady of the Lake and her lover, waiting for her on the shore? What can the meaning of letters be in this time of internet communications?

I just wrote another letter to Tom. We slow down and think when we write with pens on paper, making sure our bad handwriting is legible again. Because we allow the words to settle in more, the time to be fluid and lingering, we dig a little deeper, say a little more, but only after thinking it through. It's not so instantaneous.

But why write to this guy I once loved? The answer lies in the fact that the love didn't halt because I chose to run away from him and hide my dirty secret, a secret that did not have to be dirty, yet I made it so. I reacted from a childhood of being called a bastard child. When I left without explanation, I was protecting my unborn child from the pain I knew. I was too young to know how big a mistake I was making.

When I knew how much Tom loved me it was too late. I couldn't break his heart by telling him the truth. He would've grieved the child's death and hated me. I didn't want our lives to be broken by the secret between us. It was easiest to break up without explanation.

Today we are available to each other in a way we have never been. Why not see what comes of it, you who are so free with yourself in other ways? Can I tell him the truth about having an abortion? If not, I should end this budding relationship now.

CHAPTER SIX – A BLANK PAGE

I made several trips to the car with my suitcases and personal belongings. For the first time since 1944, the house at Windy Hill was vacant.

Tom was on my mind. I kept going over what I could remember of our shared childhood, the awkward high school years, and the "us" time when we were in love. Once I stood on a ladder to paint the house of a shut-in and caught Tom looking at me. During a football game, when he was on the field, Tom searched the stands and caught my eye. Another time, he almost stopped when I was reading on the park bench where he'd first kissed me.

I pulled into the parking garage of my building, and took Winifred into my arms to walk down to the lobby. The college-aged guy behind the desk looked up from the textbook he was reading when Winifred meowed as she squirmed in my arms. "I'm going to take the cat up to my unit. When I come down, can I borrow a moving cart to move some things out of my car?"

"Sure," he said. He turned his attention from the book to look at the squirming cat. "Hi kitty," he said, and reached out a hand to pet her. That caused her to wriggle more. "Which unit are you in?"

"312."

He whistled softly. "What do you do for a living?"

"Managing Editor of *Leisure Travel.*"

"A writer?"

"Sometimes. I mostly tell other people what to write."

"Do you like that?"

"Sometimes, sometimes not."

"Sounds like something you're working on."

"You're right." I smiled to myself. *Grow, Betsy, grow.*

When Tom and I walked together, we always developed a pace that suited us, a rhythm that felt like we'd been doing it for years, and so it was with everything we did during the time we were together in college. How could I now even begin to tell him how dismayed I was to realize an unplanned pregnancy would ruin his life? The weeks after, when I felt the early bloating of pregnancy, were agonizing. I kept my secret from Tom, and every time I was with him, when I opened my mouth to tell him, I couldn't say it. Even when I refused to see him, I knew he still believed that our love was greater than anything the world could throw our way. It broke my heart because I believed it too. Back then I believed in true love.

I'd let him go even though our love was powerful. I didn't trust our love to survive the challenges of life. I was like my mother who somehow couldn't trust the love she had for Rafe to be true enough, and she walked away from it. What made us not trust the people who loved us? Mom may have thought she had faith in God, but she didn't if she couldn't believe love conquers all.

I didn't allow God to take care of things back then any more than I allowed Him to do that now. I thought that Sunday-school religion was all there was, and how else would I know differently when all I'd had was my small-town church to go to learn about God? God was narrow in that space. God is bigger than that.

The river flowed by gently and the pleasure boats with their sunbathers on deck floated on its surface. The sun shone down as if it were anointing me. I sipped the wine and remembered how those daffodils looked in the Coke can in my room.

Our letters were a new beginning, much as I wasn't sure I wanted someone to love me.

Later, I went down to street level. On my poplar-lined street in the Warehouse District, flower pots hung from Victorian-era lampposts, and potted plants stood next to doorways. Tables and chairs filled the sidewalks outside cafes and restaurants. The ghosts of Rockefeller and other early 20th- century industrialists lingered in the alleyways and the sub-floor stairwells. I walked the block down to Costanza's Market. I bought strawberries, yogurt, granola, romaine, tomatoes, and onions, and a calzone for dinner. Mary, who worked behind the prepared foods counter, asked me how my time away was. "You know," I said, "it's like it never happened, now that I'm home again."

She looked puzzled. "How do you mean?"

I thought a moment before saying, "I think I compartmentalize my life."

That admission disturbed me enough that I thought about it while eating my dinner and couldn't let go of it. I picked up my journal and wrote:

When I'm not at the farm, it almost doesn't exist. How can that be, when I've been so immersed in it? Mom used to say that living on the farm forced her to live in the moment because each day was filled with everyday chores. With Mom dying and all that went along with that, I didn't have a chance to give into the cadence of living full time at Windy Hill. I'll have to figure out how to explore that—-it might help me figure out how to let go of this frenzied lifestyle.

The questions that kept me awake that night was why I should spend time at the farm or get to know Tom again and complicate my life. The answers frightened and excited me. The two o'clock freighter came around the bend with a warning toot.

The March, April, and May issues of the magazine had hardly been mine. I'd tried to work on the content while I was away, but I knew it hadn't been enough. When I returned to the office the next day, I was surprised by the stares and whispers from the cubicles and hallways, and I couldn't help but notice Mo's worried look.

She slipped into my office behind me. "All ready for the June issue?"

"Yes, but we're behind the eight ball now. I've been following e-mails but I haven't been here for three weeks. What's going on around here?"

"People feel like they haven't had enough direction from you."

That made sense. "Then we'll start with an e-mail to the staff." I turned on my computer and typed in "Cleveland All" on the "To" line and "Back to Normal" in the "Subject" line. "How do you think 'Back to Normal' sounds in the subject line?"

"Yeah, that works."

"Are people angry with me?"

"No."

"Sure?"

"I don't think anyone's angry."

"Okay, here we go." I typed:

> Dear colleagues:
>
> Thank you for your support and hard work while I was

gone. I know I didn't keep up as well as I could have and many of you had to step in to help out. I appreciate your ability to be flexible.

It's time for the June issue to be completed. I know you all have your projects, but we haven't touched base in person in quite a while. Over the next couple of days, I would like to meet with each of you personally to make sure you know what you need to do and so I can check on your progress.

Please make appointments with Mo.

I'm glad to be back.
Elizabeth

"It sounds fine to me," Mo said, "But be prepared for some drama from Jamie and Tina."

Jamie had been doing my writing, and Tina the editing. "Okay. Thanks for letting me know."

Five minutes later, Tina, who stood eight inches taller than me, came into my office. She looked angry. She didn't knock, and she closed the door loudly. "You're not the editor anymore. I'm handling the June issue."

"I don't think so. That was temporary while I was gone."

"Well, you can't have people doing what you told them to do because I designed this issue and decided on content."

"That's impossible. I sent out e-mails with assignments. They take assignments from me, not you."

"Not anymore."

"Who says?"

"I do."

I stood up. I couldn't conceive how she thought she was now in charge. My voice rose when I said, "Damn it! You're out of line. Insubordinate. You have no authority around here. I'm the managing editor. Get out of my office. Now." I held myself back from walking around the desk to shove her through the door. I'd already gone beyond professional.

She ambled over to my desk in her hip-skimming skirt and high heels and pointed her finger at me. "This is my magazine."

"Jesus H Christ. Are you kidding me? I was out because my

mother died and this is what I come back to? Do you have any heart?"

"You're the one who's a bitch. People around here don't like you, never have. You may as well go back to cow country right now."

I couldn't stop the anger that rose within me. I slammed my hands down on the desk. "Get out of here," I said firmly, trying to keep my temper in control. "Before I call security. And unless you can come up with a good reason why I should let you stay, you'd better start looking for a new job. You have 30 days."

"Fine," she said and hightailed it out of my office. I was forced to walk over to the door to close it.

Why do I care so much? Why the hell does this even matter? It's just a job.

"It's my job," I said out loud. I was confounded. One thing I had learned over the last six months was to take control when Life threw the punches. Before I changed my mind, I sent a follow-up e-mail:

> To all my co-workers here at Leisure Travel:
>
> The assignments I gave you stand, but if you have been working on Tina's orders and your project is underway, we can talk about it.
>
> By the way, I know you call me the Dragon. I hope you will begin to see me as some creature that doesn't breathe fire. My time away has given me the chance to reassess my life.
>
> Elizabeth

Somehow, I got through the day. People came into my office and showed me what Tina gave them to do and we talked about my ideas. I had it straightened out by quitting time. I felt the pressure of careful political conversations, short tempers, and unreasonable expectations, and my shoulders were up near my ears. I was very unhappy.

That evening, before going home, I stepped inside the Old Stone Church on Public Square and made my way to the sanctuary. In the shadowy light filtered through the Tiffany stained-glass windows, I was in another world, one with soft edges and gentle memories, one where I didn't have to explain myself to anyone. It was a place of peace, a sanctuary from the world, and it was empty. The cross in the center of a blue gold-studded frontal piece behind the altar stripped away all pretense. I couldn't pretend to love God with all my heart, because God knew what was in my heart. I lowered my head and prayed for God to be with me. I waited. My breathing quieted, my shoulders relaxed.

As I let myself give into serenity, the weary demands of work were left behind. "Dear Lord," I said out loud, my hands folded near my heart, "Remember when all I wanted was to write so well I would get the feature articles?" I felt my slow breath in the back of my throat and the pressure of how hard I was pressing my hands together. My hands fell to my lap and I looked up at the cross. God was pure love. "Being able to travel and write about it was a fringe benefit I valued, but I'm tired, even of that."

It was still light outside at 6:30, so I walked down past the Old Courthouse, over the railroad tracks for the lakefront line, and under the Shoreway towards the lake. While I walked around Browns stadium with its steep rows of empty orange seats, my energy picked up, a nervous energy that I knew was growing because there was no answer. The steps near the Firefighters Monument took me, finally, down to the water. Only there, at water's edge, did I feel a bit of the answer. Lake Erie was sun-tipped pink, glorious in its rippled surface, a great lake as vast as the ocean. I felt peaceful, happy, and content. I walked down the Marginal Road between the Shoreway and Burke Lakefront Airport until I was tired. Then I headed to my city home.

Another letter from Tom was in my mail slot. I opened it on my balcony.

Dear Elizabeth:

I like that we're writing to each other during these days of e-mail and cell phones, with the ability to have ready conversations in cyberspace or over the cell waves any time we'd like. We can be more thoughtful in the space of a letter.

You know, with the weather changing, I have to tell you how much I love to sail. I spend hours out there on the lake, feeling the swell of water gathering below me, and I'm at one with it. I can walk off the deck, across the lawn, and down the stairs to the dock, where my boat waits. I sailed today and felt the water and wind take me along. Sailing is such a luscious, wonderful, harmonious experience for me.

Like you, I read a lot, just as I always have. It has always been one of our shared interests, and I'm glad neither one of us stopped. I finished Tracy Kidder's *Mountains Beyond Mountains,* which was some book. Have you read it? How about the *Kite Runner*? I read that book before Kidder's.

I spent lots of time in Conneaut, before Miriam moved out, trying to sort things out. Willow Beach is good for that, better than my place on the lake. Something about the way the waves hit the shore at an angle and fly up at the rocks . . . it's a powerful sound that clears my head. And Conneaut draws me more into who I am. The end of my marriage caused me to turn inward more. I think that's what's happening to you.

I don't know you daily anymore, but I know you. You are still the girl I loved all those years ago. Those twenty-one months we had together were quite possibly the best I ever had. We had breakfast together, went to classes, came together again, made love, did homework, watched movies, and ate dinner, together. I slept at your place or you slept at mine. Then, with no warning, you ran away. We didn't know where you were for two days, and when you came back you stayed away from me like I meant nothing to you.

You still haven't given me an adequate explanation. What you said about it having everything to do with you, you got that right. I knew I wasn't responsible for what happened to us. I was very angry with you when you didn't allow us to even try to work things out. Are you trying to say the reason you left was because I deserved better than you? How could that be when I felt like it was the end of the world after you were gone? What can I trust if I can't trust the love we had for each other?

I'm sorry for lashing out. You said the thought of being with me permanently was too much, and there were things you kept from me that kept us apart. I agree that keeping secrets is no way to have a relationship. I'll let you take your time with those things you didn't tell me because I sense they're big hurts for you. We shouldn't lose sight of the fact that all this happened a long time ago.

I look forward to your next letter.
Affectionately, Thomas

"In pain." Those words hit me in the gut. Happiness depended on being free of pain. I'd been in pain for years. Those words went into my journal that night and stayed with me as I slept.

When I went back into my bedroom to get ready for work the next morning, my eyes fell upon Mom's journals lined up on a low shelf next to my bed. I picked up the first volume and got back into bed with my coffee. I took a deep breath and started reading Mom's journals from the beginning. Tom had written that we can be more thoughtful in the space of a letter. Mom could be more thoughtful here.

The first thing she wrote on the first page of her first journal was "I can't believe I'm pregnant." *I don't want to know this,* I thought. But she went on to say, "It'll be fine because Rafe loves me. When he gets home and finds out, he'll be happy. We'll be happy." The next paragraph began with "I can't tell my parents. How do I keep this from them? How will they feel about this? I don't even know how I feel." She never mentioned having an abortion. That choice didn't seem to be an option she considered. Was it because of her belief system? Was it because she knew Rafe would love the baby? Or was it simply that abortions weren't readily available then?

I had briefly gone in that direction. My Mom would have flipped out because she'd spent many words of warning about teenaged pregnancy.

For Mom, the first month went by with fretting and the third month spawned panic when she realized she was showing. She felt like she was all alone but was hopeful. "I told the baby today that we would one day move to Italy and live amongst the grape vines and olive trees. I felt the butterfly flittering the baby makes." She had trouble keeping up with school. "Rafe told me he moves faster in the harvest so he can get back here. He misses me bunches deep in his heart, the place where he and I are joined."

She didn't write at all during her fifth month of pregnancy. When she wrote again, she said "What awful craziness I caused with Daddy-o, but things have settled down. He doesn't talk to me much but every so often looks at me with pity and gives me a hug. I know that everything will turn out because despite this mess I've made. Dad still loves me. He forgives me my mistake now that I made what he thinks is the right decision." Her voice became stronger the further I read. She dismissed the idea that my father wouldn't come home "because the way we fit together . . . he couldn't have that with any other woman."

My coffee was gone and the sun was high by the time I finished half the journal. I felt the same way when I was with Tom. Mom had the faith that love would survive back then. Theirs WAS a fairy tale romance after all.

I went to work with thoughts of my parents and Tom on my mind. I had trouble sorting out what material to include in the summer getaways issue. In the middle of an e-mail I recalled how my love relationship with Tom began.

One day during my freshman year at Kent State, I had looked up from putting my books away and there was Tom, tanned and wearing jeans and a navy T-shirt. As if he saw me every day, he said hello. I mumbled a response as I stood up to leave. He followed me down the steps and outside, then walked with me in the shadows of the formidable brick buildings strung together along front campus.

The conversation picked up an easy rhythm. "How do you like your classes?" he asked.

"Oh, I love them. I feel like I haven't been thinking my whole life. In World History we're learning about tribal migrations thousands of years before Christ. In English, we spent an hour writing about a blank wall."

He laughed. "It's a lot different that high school, isn't it?"

"Yeah. I thought you were different when you came home from college last Christmas—grown up. Maybe college did that to you."

"Could be I finally decided I wasn't going to ask you out anymore."

I glanced sideways at him. "It took you that long, huh?" There was no reason to be mean, and so I asked, "Did you know I was in the class before today?"

"Yeah, I did. I finally decided it was time to say hello."

By the time we reached my doorway, we were comfortable with each other. He asked if I'd be interested in going to a movie sometime. "It might be a date, it might not. I guess it depends on whether you've gotten over your weird phase."

"Weird phase?"

"Yeah, you know, the I-don't-date and I'm-done-with-guys phase. The other half of the universe is guys and we can be interesting sometimes."

I needed a friend, and he made me smile. "What kind of movie?"

"Something worthy of winning film competitions."

That was a new one for me. We went to the Kiva on campus that weekend, and again the following weekend. Tom was a foreign film junkie and knew the work of the writer, the director, and the actors. He kissed me good night on the second "date." We fell into a routine of going to the Kiva on Fridays and afternoon walks followed by beer and burgers at Ray's Place on Saturdays.

At the end of October, we kissed in his kitchen on a Sunday afternoon, and I found my body arching towards his. His hands were in my hair and then under my shirt. He swooped me up and carried me to his bedroom. Everything about making love with Tom was a surprise for me. He spent ten minutes undressing me as he kissed each newly bared part of my body. He let himself be led from one thing to the next, like he was a traveler in a new land trying to capture every nook and cranny of the landscape. By the time he entered me, I was aching for him, but he took his time, lingering, as he kissed my forehead, my eyelids, my neck, and my breasts. His lips never left mine as he moved inside me. I felt the shudder of his body, and I shuddered into my own climax before he gently fell to his side. His skin remained on mine, the length of his body against me. He had held me close and I felt protected and safe for the first time in my life.

It was different than it had been with Jerry. With Jerry it felt dangerous; with Tom it felt safe.

Distracted by these old memories, I escaped to the Cleveland Public Library's Eastman Reading Garden with pen and journal in mid-afternoon. I settled into a wire mesh chair in the northeast corner where tendrils of ivy twined the bricks near my feet. New leaves shaded the sun from my eyes on the first summer-like day of the year, and I watched passers-by meandering along the bricks engraved with names of supporters.

Birds twittered in the trees. I smelled the sweetness of green and felt the touch of a soft breeze on my cheek. I reached down for my water bottle and tasted the mountain spring water in my mouth. I picked up my journal and wrote.

> Relationships are about what's said and not said, about mutual giving and accepting, or it feels like a taking. Tom, with his ambitions and his love of decorum, was somewhat judgmental and didn't accept me for who I was even though I felt safe with him and knew he loved me. It's weird to think that someone can love you with their whole being but have expectations that show they don't know what's in your soul. Can another person ever know what's inside our soul? Did I even know that Tom was being judgmental?
>
> Now, I have nothing to lose by being myself. It's not even a risk, because I have no intention of ever being in a romantic relationship with Tom. I write that, but I'm lying to myself, aren't I? At work today I was even remembering what it was like to make love to him.
>
> Should I start my life story at the beginning or journal like Mom did, capturing moments on blank pages, trying to capture the innate goodness Rousseau insisted is there? We all begin as blank pages that become layered with meaning and words and eventually, a voice, our own voice, emerges, as my mother's did when she wrote. For her, that voice was transferred to the paintings she created on canvas.
>
> Having a voice, my own original voice, and being honest, at least in a journal, cultivates an inner life that sometimes shines to the outside, the layers being revealed like pulling petals from a rose. I hope to do my best to not just write what I'm feeling and exploring, but to find myself in a way that others can relate to.
> I want the people important to me, and possibly Tom is one of those, to know what's in my soul. To do that, I need to know myself.

In the garden, people ate sandwiches while reading or sitting knee to knee talking to friends. Women took off their shoes, stretched out their legs and turned their faces to the sun. It was time to stop being a time traveler reminiscing in the Eastman Garden and get back to work. I'd recently read a book by Linda Olsson called *Astrid & Veronika*. In it Astrid said, "My life's memories take up space with no regard to when they happened, or to their actual time-span. The memories of brief incidents occupy almost all my time, while years of my life have left no trace." Most of my life was unremembered but now I had ways of remembering, through my mother's journal, corresponding with Tom, spending time at Windy Hill, and writing in my own journal.

On Thursday morning, Henry Weatherby, a vice president of the publishing house, appeared in my office doorway. His wavy brown hair made him look like the medieval enthusiast he was. His face was grim.

I smiled at him. "Hey there, Shakespeare. Where're the tights?"

He usually laughed at the long-standing joke, but this time he walked gingerly across the carpet towards my desk and sat in one of the satin-upholstered guest chairs. His broad shoulders were silhouetted against the blue sky above the gray horizon in the window behind him. He cleared his throat, crossed his legs, and brought his hands together under his chin. He studied my face. "We have a problem. The board reviewed the current issue of the magazine this morning, and given that Tina functioned as the editor of this issue, the board feels she should be listed as Managing Editor on the masthead."

I blinked. I knew Henry well. We'd been working together for twenty years. "But my title doesn't change because I'm out of commission. I AM the Managing Editor of the magazine."

"But Tina chose who would write the stories and coordinated the layout. I know you were available by e-mail, but Tina pulled it together."

"I conceived the focus. I chose which travel service projects to feature, which side stories would compliment the features, came up with some companion history pieces. I wrote the editor's letter."

"It's only for one issue."

"If I'm not listed as Managing Editor, where will my name appear on the masthead?"

When I saw the look on his face, it was obvious he intended to leave me off altogether. Anger welled up in me, but I checked it by swallowing and counting to ten.

"How about being listed as emeritus or something like that and show Tina as the temporary Managing Editor?" His voice was tinged with hope.

"What? There's no such thing as a temporary Managing Editor or an emeritus Managing Editor. Tina's a senior editor and she stepped up to the plate when I couldn't be here, and that's that."

I didn't think he supported me before the board, but I could tell he agreed with me. "Okay, okay. You're right, of course. You've already acknowledged her in your letter, so we'll add a separate letter from me, on behalf of the Board, acknowledging her efforts as well. How's that?"

I looked beyond him at a lone sailboat inside the break wall where the water was glass. I didn't really care, not that much. "That works. But I shouldn't have to fight for this, it shouldn't even have come up. Should I be worried? Who on the board made the suggestion?"

He was reluctant to reveal the inner workings of the board, with good reason. "The board likes this issue. The quality of the writing and the feel of a history of mission work make it a wonderful human values issue with a message we all need to hear."

"It sounds like I no longer have the Board's full support."

Henry looked uncomfortable. "I wouldn't worry about it, not yet. Keep doing a good job, and this sentiment will pass."

"Did Tina tell you I fired her?"

"Yes. We didn't think that was an appropriate move on your part. She's not fired."

"Sentiment." A sentiment could be the beginning of an overarching belief, I thought later, as I sat on a concrete bench on Mall B looking at the fiery glow of the lowering sun in the windows of the Cleveland Convention Center. I had heard of editors being ousted when they reached middle age, but I'd never thought it would happen to me. Between being worried about my job and thinking about Tom's last letter, the afternoon had been unproductive. I kept thinking about the time Tom had taken down the sails and dropped anchor a mile from shore off Willow Beach, and we lay in each other's arms on the boat's wooden floor and planned our wedding.

The letters on the pages of the book I was reading started to blur around the edges with the darkening sky. I walked the ten blocks home. The long dimly-lit, door-lined hallway of the old warehouse seemed sinister. The floors were bare wood, the walls the color of red clay, and the wall sconces looked like lanterns on the end of river boats. Large windows let in dim light at either end of the hall. There was nowhere for anyone to hide, but I felt afraid. I'd never felt afraid in those hallways before.

I let myself into the condo unit and turned on all the lights. Safe in the kitchen, I put a frozen pizza in the oven, then walked around to turn on the lights. I poured myself a glass of wine and looked out the window. I could avoid a confrontation with Tom for a while, couldn't I? I could ease into the truth with him, after he trusted me, after I felt comfortable with him. I remembered how I could tell him about pre-test jitters, unwarranted paranoia that people were talking about me, and worries about the way my hair looked. If I could talk to Tom, I felt I would have some answers to questions I hadn't yet formed. I hesitated to call Tom only because I was afraid it wouldn't go well, and I wanted it desperately to go well.

I found the number in the letter he wrote and dialed it. His "Hello," was distant, disengaged.

"Tom, it's Betsy."

"Elizabeth!" My name was a melody. His voice warmed and perked up as he said it. It was how I remembered it. "I'm delighted that you've called."

"I'm sorry to call you unexpectedly."

"Unexpected, but not a bad unexpected. What's going on?"

"You asked about books, about reading, in your last letter."

"Yeah, I remember." Water was running in the background.

"I've read the same books you've read. With wars in Afghanistan and Iraq, I guess it makes sense that we're both reading Hossein."

"Writers change the way the world sees things by telling about their lives. It's what writing's all about."

"In *The Shadow of the Wind*, I can't think of who wrote it, there's a building where forgotten books are kept like in a museum, so neither the book nor the writer will be forgotten."

"The writer's name is Carlos Ruiz Zafon."

Our book connection remained. I mentioned some of the other books I'd read recently, he mentioned the ones he read. I told him about reading John Irving to Mom, whose favorite book by him remained *A Widow For One Year*, while mine was *Cider House Rules*. We compared Irving's earlier books to his later ones and noted it didn't matter that they were long, they were that good. "Tone, the resonance of words well chosen, is what makes the writing come alive. In the book by Zafon, the never ending love and devotion blew me away."

"You liked that part, the part about never ending love?" His voice carried a pinch of accusation.

We'd both believed in never ending love. We'd said our love would never end.

"I'm sorry," he said before I could figure out how to respond. "That was a long time ago. Marriages ago."

I didn't respond. What was there to say?

His voice softened to bedroom level, a whisper in my ear, the caress of a word on my soul. "Remember reading Zola's *Germinal* at the same time? You were always crying."

Tom and I would sit on a recliner on the front porch of the house he rented in Kent, legs entwined, each with our own copy of the book. I read faster than he did, and I had to wait for him to finish before we talked about it. When the heroine died in her lover's arms I started sobbing into his shoulder and couldn't stop. He had to catch up to where I was to find out why I was crying. "You probably wanted to cry too, but you had to comfort me."

"Miriam didn't read much."

He was comparing us. During the years Rick and I were married I brainwashed myself into thinking Rick was a better choice, my better half. Why did I do that? "Neither did Rick. But you probably figured that out. You knew him."

"Know him. I actually ran into him the evening of your Mom's funeral, at Toby's Grill, having dinner by himself. He waved me over and I had a Coke with him. I asked him why he didn't go to Windy Hill after the funeral, and he said no one would want to see him there. I thought that was a copout."

"Of course it was. He knows he should go to his ex-mother-in-law's funeral."

"He has always run away from his responsibilities. He's a hapless drunk, even though he holds a city council seat and runs a construction business. I can't believe you married him after you left me."

"I didn't leave you."

"Yes you did. You ran away and I couldn't find you and then you wouldn't take my calls. All summer. The following fall I heard you were with him."

"You left me."

"How?"

"You weren't listening to me. I couldn't be myself with you anymore."

"You could have talked to me about it."

"At the time, I didn't think I could."

"So you married Rick."

"You sound angry."

"I think we're kind of pitiful, reading books, eating dinner alone, trying to make sense of wrong-choice marriages. There could have been a better way."

I took the sizzling pizza out of the oven while I cradled the phone under my chin. "Sometimes I know I made a mistake in marrying him, and other times I wonder if I could have made the marriage work. He tried to get me to read *The Big Book* with him. It sounded so fake, so untrue, that I couldn't. By that time I hated him too much to even try. I tried too hard for too long, and I got to the point where I couldn't do it anymore."

"It doesn't sound like you gave up too soon."

I changed the subject and said, "I'm having a pizza. What are you eating?"

He laughed. "I thought I was doing a good job hiding my eating from you. I'm eating the second half of a sub sandwich left over from lunch."

"Reading the same things, eating at the same time, working . . . "

"I know. I've never felt totally disconnected from you. You say I wasn't listening, that you couldn't talk to me; I guess I missed some clues."

I exhaled heavily. "It was so much more than that. Does anyone ever fall in love and live happily ever after? I used to think that when people love each other there's no line between where one person ends and the other begins. No effort would be required."

"I used to think that, but marriage taught me that love requires more work than that. Life tugs on us, pulls us down, and a marriage, the union of two lives, either flexes like a rubber band or breaks with a snap that makes it profoundly clear there's nothing left."

"A marriage slowly dying is about the saddest thing there is," I said quietly. "Listen, I was thinking about you because I'm in a bit of a jam and I could always talk to you."

"That's cool. What's up?"

"I'm worried about my job," I started, and then I told him the whole conversation with Shakespeare, about the time I'd taken off, and about my attitude.

"It sounds to me like you're adjusting to life being different after doing the best you could for your mother. If you lose your job, it's probably the right thing to happen. You'll figure it out. Just be in the waiting time."

"I wish I felt that easygoing about it."

"The worst thing that would happen is you'd have to move back to Windy Hill and be a farmer."

And lose everything I'd worked for—the lifestyle, the credits, the money, and the benefits. "It would be different."

"Maybe you need to shake it up a bit."

Why was I afraid of losing those things? "I knew you'd be helpful. I'm going to take a nice hot shower and settle down with my Mom's journals. I'm reading them front to back."

"That's great."

"I'll write to you again soon."

"I'll write you back."

"Promise?"

I could hear his smile in his voice. And then he laughed at our memory, the way we always said that to each other. "Promise. Good-bye, Elizabeth."

When I hung up the telephone, the sound of his voice remained with me. I could hear the low tenor, the intimacy, the words that came without forethought, and the silences in which the last thing he said remained with me. And that "Elizabeth" at the end told me he was different, he wasn't like any other. He was Tom.

I wondered what I'd started and whether we should have left it in letters. How easily the way we used to say "Promise?" came back. It came to my lips as if our lives over the last twenty-some years had not been lived.

The Travel Channel was showing Alaska. I watched the polar bears trudging through the tundra looking for a place to birth and I was struck by how sad that was. The world was irrevocably changing, but Mom's journals anchored me. I was learning about how she raised me.

Morning brought a stiff and fuzzy-headed walk to the office after a quick towel dry and clothes that clung to my damp body. I drank three cups of coffee to feel normal and kept up the coffee into the afternoon as I reviewed copy, encouraged the writers to riff write, found personal essays to fill space, and tried to respond to a couple hundred e-mails a day. My staff and I needed every minute we had to put out the July issue featuring America's National Parks. My editorial profiled Teddy Roosevelt and John Muir and the other pioneers who had the vision of public lands against the backdrop of my own experiences in Yosemite and Yellowstone. I gave instructions to people in a tired way, and I caught some of the junior editors glancing at me oddly, as if they didn't know me.

Yanci, a young intern who reminded me of my younger self, came into my office on Wednesday afternoon with her backpack slung across her shoulder and asked if we could talk. I nodded, and she shut the door and sat down across from me. "We're all sorry for your loss, and we're glad you're back. We'll do the best we can while you're going through your grief."

I blinked. "The others put you up to this, huh?"

"Yes," she said with a sheepish grin.

I smiled at her. "No one else was comfortable saying anything to me. I'm glad you are. And you know what?"

"What?"

"Spread the word that when you talked to me, I've noticed how dedicated you all are. But I can put in the required time. Knowing you're there for me gives me more energy."

She nodded, satisfied. "I'll see you tomorrow. Almost done!" Her bag sagged against her hip as she opened the door. She stopped at desks to talk with people and eyes turned furtively in my direction on the other side of the glass wall. I looked down at the copy in front of me to avoid mutual embarrassment.

I stayed at the office late on Thursday night. Most of the writers, designers, and photographers were there as late as I was, and at 10 p.m., I walked out of my office and announced, "Time to go to bed everyone. I'll see you at 8 a.m.. We're almost there."

The group clapped. I'd never caused clapping before. It made me smile, and the smile was returned as people packed up their desks, turned off their computers, and headed for the door. Bleary-eyed photographers emerged from the dark room and closed the door behind them. Our local editor, Sandy, came to my doorway and asked if she could drop me off at the condo. I took her up on it.

The last thing I did before leaving the office, after everyone else cleared out, was send an e-mail invitation for them to come to my place for pizza the next evening. That had never happened either.

I made the decision to be real with Tom. I wrote as easily as I wrote in my journal.

> Dear Tom:
>
> Mom was overly cheerful in the morning, walking through the house saying "Good morning, Betsy" in a singsong voice. Maybe I've learned to put on a good show.

How many times did I write things that sounded like what needed to be said, even these words, here, these words that I was writing down for Tom. If what I was doing was putting on a good show, what was going on underneath? Nights of wine and books, days of harried busyness, weekends the same as my workdays, walks and more walks. Here I was, back in my regular life, and I was going right back to the routines that felt flat and uninvolved.

> I did something different this week—I had my staff over for pizza. I handed out beer, let them hang out wherever they congregated, in groups, me floating around with plates of brownies bought from the market downstairs. It was different. It didn't feel like a show.
>
> That summer when we broke up, what I mostly felt was the loss of you in my life. I didn't have the courage to tell you what I was feeling, I didn't want you to love me less than you did. I wanted to freeze what we had in time, hold it there forever in a glass jar like how we collected fireflies when we were kids. I thought I could put our love away like that. Mom was beside herself, took me on vacation for an entire month, and when I came home, you wouldn't answer the phone.
>
> Why I thought Rick could save me . . . now that was a stretch. After we were married, I often went to sleep before he came

home and woke to feel his weight on the edge of the bed and his finger stroking my face. When he had too much to drink, he bought flowers or took me out to dinner with a promise he'd never do it again. He was no help with the baby, and one week he didn't bring home a paycheck. A couple of weeks later, he came home with plane tickets to Cancun even though we hadn't had any new money going into our bank account in a month. There were times when he didn't even know who I was when I helped him up the stairs.

He always bought me roses. He didn't even try to know what my favorite flower is. He wasn't in love with me, not like you were. I knew that.

We can say all the right things, we can allow time to pass, we can allow wounds to heal, but underneath, the deep-rooted anger and secrets will fester. I loved you, Tom, and I'm sorry for what I did to you. But even if you forgive me, I don't think we could ever be what we were before. There's pain from when you and I broke up, pain from our marriages, all kinds of things we've lived through.

Isn't it easier to just continue on in our solitary lives?

Even though I say that, I have to admit that the conversation we had on the phone felt like no years had passed by. And it made me happy.

Love, Betsy

I wondered if I was editing my life even as I thought I was being honest. Why was it so hard?

It was high summer. And I had a farm out in the country. I left the factories and warehouses behind and the highway went from eight lanes to four lanes hedged by vineyards as I headed out to Windy Hill for the weekend. After Cassie dropped her off, I tucked Beth into her papoose and carried her with me as I surveyed the fruit trees and the barn. I relished the sour-tang smell of fresh milk. While Beth was sleeping, I helped Pedro check the cow hooves for cracking and their coats for spots before we let them out into the fields for the day.

Alone with Beth, I strolled the pastures and headed into the woods and down to the Magical Pond and out by the tree house. I enjoyed the soft warmness of my granddaughter next to me as I walked.

After all these years, I had trouble believing that I snuck off to the tree house to have sex with my mother's boyfriend. I was in a phase of wearing frilly blouses and short skirts and high platform shoes around the house when Jerry came to pick Mom up for their first date. Jerry looked me up and down with interest. "Well, hello there," I remember him saying jovially. "You must be Betsy." He stepped up the stairs to the open door and put out his hand. "Good to meet you."

The following week, Jerry offered to help me with dishes in the kitchen while Mom watched cartoons with his two young sons. While we were standing at the sink, my hands in and out of the soapy water, he asked me whether I wanted to have a boyfriend. I shook my head and laughed, as if it was a joke. All of a sudden, Jerry leaned over and kissed me on the mouth. When I tried to pull away, he put the towel down on the counter and looped an arm around my waist to pull me towards him. Breathless, I said, "Stop!" and pulled away. He laughed and said, "One day you'll have a boyfriend. And I'll be jealous."

Three months into the relationship, my mother looked confused when Jerry knew what class I had during tenth period, and Jerry made up a story about how he knew. Jerry told her he couldn't take her out on dates anymore because he didn't love her. She told him not to bother coming over to eat dinner with us anymore.

I felt terribly guilty. I worried we would be found together. I had trouble sleeping, and I couldn't look Mom in the eye. In church, during silent prayer, I prayed for God to still love me.

Jerry had me under his spell, but there was always a dangerous edge when he was around. He was like a stray dog whose background was unknown. I managed to avoid him only for a day or two until he sought me out, sitting outside the school in his car, waiting for me. If I told him I wanted to go out to see my grandparents, he offered to give me a ride and we ended up in the tree house, his finger tracing a steady trail from my nose to my navel while my breath became ragged and my eyes closed.

In the meantime, Tom continued to try to get my attention. His notebook-paper notes and origami packages floated to the bottom of my locker. They all said the same thing in different ways—would I go out with him one more time? When I was at his house playing "Chop Sticks" on the piano with his sister, he sat close by, waiting to catch my eye, and if he did, he casually walked out of the room as if he expected me to follow him. Later, he sat down and ate corn chips with us in the kitchen and looked at me like he was trying to figure me out.

After five months of craziness, I was desperate to have Jerry out of my life. He found me everywhere I went, even at the library where he forced me to kiss him behind the stacks of books when all I wanted was to find a book of poems by Wordsworth. One day I fainted while trying to run away from him and I woke to see his face hovering above mine. I couldn't remember the last time I'd eaten, so he took me to McDonald's and when I told him I wanted him to leave me alone, he looked like a wounded animal, and said, "It isn't working anyway."

Just like that, he was gone. I tried to bury the memory of Jerry, but that image of me with my head thrown back, the feel of the rough wall against my back, his body on mine, my moans . . . the pleasure and sweetness of it haunted me. I woke up thinking about him in the morning and thought about him when I went to sleep at night.

Over time, I convinced myself that I didn't miss him at all. I never loved him at all. Until one day it was like it never happened.

Tom's origami cranes and peace notes stopped showing up in my locker, yet he came into Bunion's Coffee Shop to watch me dress cake donuts with chocolate and cinnamon. When he or anyone asked me if I was seeing anyone, I said I was done with men, which always caused confusion because no one had ever known me to date.

Windy Hill stirred memories on the wings of fairies. The old place was telling me to take a look at my life. I was still confused as I listened to the frogs' melody at the edges of the Magical Pond with my granddaughter snuggled up against me. This place seemed a million miles away from what happened with Jerry, yet it was very close, very much a part of what Jerry and I had. It was quiet, by the pond. I could feel the baby's breathing under my hand. I settled down by the tall grasses and tried to become one with the scene. I concentrated on the moment.

Back at the house, I caught part of a movie on television while I was making soup. The main character was raped by an older man when she was seventeen and the scene was amazingly like the first time I was with Jerry. It was rape, not love-making.

Why this never occurred to me before, I don't know. While Beth napped, I wrote:

> I'd been an innocent. I am still an innocent, in a way. I didn't want to be with Jerry. I didn't want to be with Rick. I wanted to have loving relationships, but I didn't know what that looked like, didn't know that what I had with Tom had been a loving relationship. All these years I've been unable to look at the tree house, but I didn't really look at why until Mom died. I knew Jerry was the cause of distance between Mom and me, and I blamed myself. I always thought I was a bad girl for wanting to have sex with him, for craving it, for making it so central in my life. It felt wrong because I HAD to keep it a secret, whether it was from Mom, from Tom, or from the world. It felt wrong because it could never go anywhere—it would always be a secret no matter how much I pretended it was a real relationship.
>
> And I convinced myself it was. It was sort of like playing at tea—I was playing at an adult relationship. I was all grown up and having sex with a grown man who thought I was a woman, who treated me like a woman, and I was interesting to him and appealing even though I was a girl.
>
> I made Jerry inconsequential in the scheme of things by not thinking about him. I avoided the tree house.
>
> But it was rape. It was molestation. I was in a situation that I couldn't handle and didn't know my way out of. Rape is a big word. It's a word that means I wasn't given a choice to have sex. I'm not sure when it moved from rape to consensual, but maybe that never did happen. My thinking was warped. I didn't know my own mind.
>
> Why had I held onto guilt about a relationship that ended thirty years ago? About a relationship that started with rape? Mom would say that I was just a girl who didn't know any better.
>
> I couldn't see it that way because I'd ignored the most basic fact—that I'd been raped. Instead, I thought I was a harlot, a conniving and selfish person who cared only about herself. I had

been a victim yet I felt that I was a bad person because of it. And as the relationship continued, I confused sex with love. And I was very good at keeping secrets from those I love, even if it wasn't necessary.

Over the years, I never knew what the rules were about sex. I could try to explain to Tom how Jerry confused me, took my soul with him each time he came to our house to be with me, causing me to betray my own mother and know a shame deeper than the one that caused me to be called "bastard." I could tell him about that trip to Detroit, the sterile white room with too bright lights, how Maria held me all night long as I cried in that horrid Super 8 on the highway, and how I knew I should have told him, should have let him in—I made the decision alone with cutting certainty.

Perhaps that is why this man who I once loved and once opened my heart to, the guy who listened to my stories of cows escaping into the neighbors fields and bringing them home, of watching Grandpa build the tree house, and of how I found Jesus sitting on the floor next to a cross made of legless tables at a youth retreat in Geneva, is in my life again. It's serendipity. I've been given a life boat.

What is it inside me that told me I needed to be rescued? The answers come as I write Virginia Woolf-style stream of consciousness sentences filling up the pages, seemingly meaning nothing, but meaning everything. A glimpse into my unveiled heart without my brain getting into it will help me figure it out.

Beth woke up. Feeding her was a nourishing time for both of us. She was trusting. I was adoring. I made faces and baby sounds, while I thought about life's pain, choices, and problems. I left her in her playpen while I made sandwiches and lemonade for the field hands and started mixing up a batch of chocolate chip cookies.

Later, she sat on my lap on the front porch swing while I rocked. She fell asleep, her mouth slack. While my daughter in her infancy had felt like an imposition, an albatross keeping me in a false marriage, my granddaughter was a blessing. And when I thought about my mother, I wondered which way it had been for her—had I been an imposition or a blessing?

When Cassie opened the door, she found us on the couch, the

baby snuggled on one arm and the journal open and next to me. I touched my finger to my lips, and she put her bags quietly down on the table and came over to sit down, moving everything aside.

She whispered, "What do you have there, Mom?" She held the leather book beside me.

"My journal."

"It looks like one of Grandma's."

"It is. She never started this one. It was blank when I found it."

"I'd rather talk about things."

"You've always been more of a talker."

"And you assume everyone should write." She examined my face. "You have a dreamy look on your face."

"Hmmm. I've been thinking about a man I once loved. I never told you about Tom, and now it's hard to know how to begin. He came to the funeral and then he started writing me letters. And now I'm thinking about the mess I've made of my life."

Cassie frowned. Then she reached over and took the warm bundle of softness that was her daughter from me, leaving me cold. I stood up and glanced at the clock. It was 4 o'clock, late enough for a glass of wine.

"Would you like a glass?"

Cassie stood as well. She was wearing black slacks with a black sweater, artisan silver at her ears and her wrists. She was the personnel manager at an accounting firm and had gone to work on a Saturday to prepare a video presentation to show in group meetings next week. I watched her put Beth into her baby seat. When she stood, she smoothed her sweater down, pushed her hair away from her face, and looked at me. "Sure, Mom. That sounds good, especially if you're going to tell me about this guy Tom."

My back was to her. I was at the dining room table opening a bottle of Trinity from South River Winery, which is housed in a church. Cassie and Mike were married there. "All right, we're having your favorite wine."

I poured the wine and joined her again on the couch. "We were in love with each other in college. It was the kind of love that leaves you dizzy and disoriented and needy, craving the next moment together. When I broke up with him, he made it clear he wanted nothing else to do with me, ever."

I sighed and sipped some wine. "I don't know about you, Cassie, but sometimes a woman finds the right guy and lets him go and thinks about that the rest of her life, with regret. You and Mike have been together a long time, so maybe he's the one, and if so, you're very lucky."

She was nodding. "I think he is. I am lucky."

"I've never had that. Anyway, Tom's the same age as your father. We went out on a date when I was fifteen. He asked me out again, and I said no. Over the next couple of years, I went out with some guys, including your father, but nothing became serious. When I met up with Tom again at Kent, he was the first guy I'd ever been able to talk to about anything and everything. It was so . . . exhilarating and exciting and totally wonderful to be able to talk to someone about philosophy and ethical issues and pretty much everything from food to books to the imagination and ecstasy. We connected on a deep level, and we became a couple.

"I did something wrong, and then I was too ashamed to tell him, so I broke up with him. He started dating someone else and got married. Then your father was there, being who he was."

Cassie narrowed her eyes. "Whatever it was you did, it can't matter any more."

"It matters that I lied to him."

Cassie shook her head impatiently. "Then come clean. Unless you murdered someone, nothing can be that bad. Really, Mom? You and Grandma always told me the truth was the best course."

"Yeah, but your Grandma had some secrets too—there's a box of letters from my father, your grandfather from Sorrento, in the hatbox. He wrote to her for years."

"You know," she said as she got up from the couch. "I can't help thinking that if you'd known your father was writing your mother and if Tom knew why you went to Detroit, your lives would have come out the way they were supposed to be. Because you weren't truthful, your lives have been disjointed"

"You don't know that."

"The truth is always best. I believe it, even if you don't." She tossed her hair as she said it.

I recognized the gesture as my own. Jerry told me it was the way I tossed my hair that attracted him to me.

CHAPTER SEVEN – STORIES

The Beaux Arts statue of a man reached for the sky, and at its base the names of dead Cleveland servicemen were engraved in stone. The blue water of the Lake could be seen beyond the green expanse of land surrounded by public buildings on Mall C, part of Cleveland's Burnham Plan. Each of those fallen officers had a story, as did the architects behind city planning and their dreams.

I sat on a bench on the Mall and opened Tom's latest letter.

> Dear Betsy,
>
> I'm not expecting anything here, nothing more than two old friends talking with each other. We haven't picked up exactly where we left off, but it's comfortable. I knew it would be.
>
> I'm sailing a lot and thinking about what happened to my marriage. Meeting you again has started me thinking about what I've been avoiding. I purposely sabotaged the marriage. I think Miriam was able to watch it happen and that's why she became shrill with me. She wanted me to stop missing dinner and taking private calls at midnight. She wanted a say in what was going to happen but I was on a course that left her behind, that negated her altogether. I was hurtful toward her.
>
> The other day I called her and started the conversation like I was calling about one of the kids, and then I told her I'd been thinking and I knew that the divorce was my fault and I was sorry. She didn't answer right away, just listened, and thanked me for calling. For her there's nothing else to be said.
>
> Sometimes I think about you when I'm out there on the lake. I know you're not sure you want to wake up our feelings for each other, and I'm not sure either.
>
> As far as the pain— jump right into it. That's where the healing will take place. We both made mistakes back then, when we were young. What happened to you with Rick was painful. What happened to us was painful. We need the pain to be gone.

Of course it's easier to just continue on in our solitary lives, but it's pretty sad. We shared so much then, and we have much to share now. I think we can find some happiness by spending time together and trading thoughts about things. I already feel like I'm working through things that I've chosen to ignore, simply because I know you again.

I don't want to stop the conversation. I don't think you do either.

Fondly,
Tom

    I missed those sun-filled summer days of being on Tom's father's boat gliding across the water like a swan. It was thrilling to have the wind propelling us on with the boat listing to one side and me afraid we'd tip over into the water. I remembered the grin on Tom's face as he kept the jib sail taut.
    I put his letter in my pocket and walked down into the Flats on St. Clair and up again onto Superior, past the places that used to be places—Fagan's, the Watermark, and the Beach Club—and I felt energized. I continued up Huron to Prospect and down to East Fourth's pedestrian walkway and back to the Warehouse District again to let myself into my building in the bright light from the parking lot.
    Once I settled on the couch with my stationery, it took me a while to know where to start. I wanted Tom to know some of my stories, the things in life we hadn't shared.

Dear Tom:

I want to hear all your stories. Why did you marry Miriam? What did she have to offer you? How much did you love her? How did what you had with her compare with what you had with me?

A couple years after my marriage to Rick ended, I fell in love with a man named Max. When I think about Max I think about fireflies because we often went to the tree-rimmed shores of the Rocky River and spread out a blanket. There we'd lay and talk on our backs until we became comfortable with the privacy afforded by the shrubs, and we made love. Fireflies came out of the trees and floated in the air above the blanket. The other reason is the reason you gave in one of your letters—fireflies are about reaching out and following our dreams and not caring who saw us dancing.

I loved him enough to spend the rest of my life with him, but I didn't want any more children, and he did. He didn't love me enough to accept that I was done having children, and I loved him enough to know that if he didn't have children, he'd regret it. Months later, I called him at his office on a lark, from Rome. I simply missed him. He was overjoyed, but he sounded unwell. He said he didn't sleep, his stomach was messed up, and the doctors had no idea what was wrong. But it didn't matter—when was I coming home? He missed me.

Weeks later I spoke with him and he told me that he'd been diagnosed with cancer. He was slowly dying. I wept when he said he'd see me soon, when he got better, but I heard in his voice that he wasn't going to get any better. That was when I truly understood the depth of how much I loved him. It was too late. That was the hardest telephone conversation I've ever had.

I caused his death. The love I withdrew ate a hole in his cells and tore him up from the inside because of the unhappiness I wrought.

Just one of my stories . . . one that you need to know.

Betsy

When I was writing the letter, I didn't think of this—maybe I was causing my own death by denying Tom's love. I could be shortening his life too. I put down my pen and folded the letter in thirds, aware that I'd written the letter to tell him a story about how I hurt someone and felt hurt by losing someone. The major point of the story was that by not opening up my heart, I let death come in.

I met Maria at the Cleveland Art Museum the following Saturday. The Monet exhibit detailed the artist's life and showed how his life influenced his art. We moved from painting to painting, orbiting the same earth, but apart in our separate experiences of the art, until it was over and we removed our headphones.

"That was great!" Maria grinned. Her enthusiasm for the exhibit created a bright aura about her. "I don't see how he married his benefactor's wife and how he worked with all those kids around."

"I think she made it so he didn't have to worry about a thing. She coddled him so he could work." We walked past the gardens and gift shop, headed for the café where we took in the menu selections and checked out the salads and quiches.

"How are your plans for the Montreal trip going?" she asked.

"Great," I said as I picked up a pre-packaged chicken Caesar salad and filtered water into a glass. "I'm staying in Vieux Montreal by the Basilica."

"You need to meet a guy who's about 40 years old, wears a deep tan all year round, is the owner of a resort, and makes love in French. Then I hope you marry him and stay there."

I looked at her to see if she was serious, and she looked like she was. "Maria?"

"God, Betsy. When are you going to find the right guy? Aren't you tired of all this weird philandering you do? What the F do you think you're doing, meeting guys all over the world then ignoring them as soon as you get home again?" When we reached the table, she was shaking her head. I watched her struggle out of her red rain jacket. She took a sip of her soda, then said, "I mean it, Betsy. I'm getting tired of hearing all about this guy and that one, a guy you went parachuting with over Cancun, another who shared a plane ride over a volcano in Hawaii. Good, eligible guys who you sleep with, then it's over. And not by their choice, by yours. You're attractive as hell for someone your age, in good shape thanks to all that walking you do, and you're all alone."

"Maybe I like it that way. And I don't sleep with them."

"Yeah, right. They go all gaga over you because you're a good conversationalist."

"I can't believe you said that."

"Okay, you are fun to be with. That wasn't fair. I was trying to make a point about your behavior. Oh, I'm sure you tell yourself that you like being alone. Like being in that condo by the river."

"I DO like the condo by the river!"

"Bullshit. Your heart is on that farm and you know it." She looked at me pointedly. "So, how did it feel to be there last weekend?"

"It felt good. Everything's taken care of, and I did some farm stuff, you know, checked the cows out, made lunch for the farmhands, paid some bills. I had Beth with me, sleeping in her sack on my chest as I walked the property."

"You could live like the rich in Europe, a house in the country and a house in the city."

"I already do that."

She nodded. "So you do. It'll get tiring after a while."

"I don't think so. I could go out there every weekend now that I've cut back on my hours at work."

"You have?" She seemed astonished.

"I haven't told anyone that. We'll see how it goes. You know, one thing Mom's death brought home for me is that life's too short." I paused, gathered my thoughts. "I've been working too much, and it hasn't been necessary."

"You're sounding healthier to me."

"I'm finding that journaling helps me bring my life in focus."

"Like?"

"How guilty I felt about Jerry and still do. How I still care about Tom. The secrets aren't good either. Look what happened with Tom and me, and my mother and father. The secrets destroyed what could have been good things."

"What are you going to do about your father? Are you going to try to contact him?"

"In a way, I have no choice. I think Mom wanted me to find him."

She sighed and pushed her empty plate over to the side. "There had to be a reason for continuing to lie to you, and there has to be a reason why she thought you needed to know now."

"So now my mother has died, and I have a farm, a father who is no longer lost, and an ex-boyfriend who's writing me letters."

"What's going on with Tom?"

"If we're going to keep going like this, I need to tell him about Detroit. What should I tell him?"

"I don't think you should. It's a big deal, Betsy, what you did. And you didn't think enough of Tom to think he could deal with the truth."

"If it was a big deal for me, it will be for him as well."

"Follow your heart, your true heart, not the false one that tells you not to get close to anyone. Then decide."

I looked out the window at the blooming courtyard garden. The fountain was joyously spraying its plumes and the metal chairs and tables decorated the terraced sandstone. Ivy dripped over the stones that circled the trees. Violets lingered, their yellow centers glowing from the blue-purple and forest green. "Life's short."

She smiled coyly. "And that's why you should act on this thing with Tom. Remember, you're talking to someone who saw you two together. He worshipped you, which was, admittedly, a bit much, but having a guy love you like that is most of the battle. In fact, that kind of love isn't a battle at all, it just is. I'm not saying he loves you like that now, but I think if you leave yourself open to the possibility of whatever happens, you'll find something genuine."

"He thinks I don't believe I deserve happiness."

"Betsy, think about this: John doesn't say things like that to me; he doesn't even try to figure me out. Most men don't say those things to women, even when they think it."

"I know. That's always been Tom's way."

"I told you then to return his calls, not to let him go. But I admit I was surprised when he lost patience and basically told you to go to hell. God, Betsy, the guy was expressing an undying love for you, wanting to know what was wrong, and you were so stubborn, you turned away. And then you let Rick in? That was crazy. I stood next to you on your wedding day, but I didn't like it."

"I didn't mail the letter I wrote to Tom yesterday. It's here in my pocket. In the letter I told him how I killed Max."

She wrinkled up her nose. "How'd that come up?"

"I wanted to show Tom that I'm not who he thinks I am. I'm not an innocent."

"You didn't kill Max. And of course you're not innocent—you're too old for that. Honestly, Betsy, sometimes you act like you're twenty and have been behaving badly. That's not the case. You seem to be stuck."

I put my tray on the table behind me, brought my hands together in front of me. "I think I did kill him."

"You can turn a story in any direction you want, I suppose." She stood up and pulled her coat back on. "Don't send that letter, Betsy. He already thinks you're half crazy."

We stood and walked down the hallway, past the gift shop and over to the elevators. When we stopped, Maria gave me a hug and said, "It was good spending time together today."

"Yeah, it was. Thanks for the advice." She was looking at me evocatively when the elevator doors closed.

I walked along Martin Luther King Boulevard in Rockefeller Park. Cultures of Romania, Ireland, Russia, Scotland, Poland, and other parts of the world were kept alive in the Cultural Gardens. Climbing the hill near the Greenhouse, close to the top, I spied a mailbox. Without hesitation, I mailed Tom's letter.

I let it go, like fireflies taking flight, their soft wings delicately catching the wind. How long would it be before I had to tell him the whole truth?

I was watching an old movie, curled up infant-like on the couch, drapes pulled closed to darken the room, when the telephone rang. It was three days after I'd mailed the letter. The caller ID said the call was from a restricted number. I let the answering machine pick it up.

"Betsy, it's Tom. I was hoping to talk to you . . . "

I touched the button, and said, "Hi Tom. I'm here."

"Screening your calls, huh?"

"Guilty as charged."

"What are you up to?"

"Watching *The Last Emperor*."

"Splendid movie. I liked it. Is this your first time watching it?"

"Oh, no, I've seen it before. I own it. I only buy movies that are partly historical and take place in foreign lands."

He didn't miss a beat. "Like *Ghandi* and *Memoirs of a Geisha*."

"Yep." I pointed the remote at the screen and paused the movie. "You've been a big influence on my taste in films."

"I'll take credit for that. Hey, I'm worried about you. It seems like you're trying to scare me off. Is that what's going on with you?"

I sighed. "I don't know. I think I wanted to tell you I loved someone else and I let him go too. I can't love men."

"You loved me pretty well for a while."

"I left you even though I loved you."

"But there are some things you've said to me in your letters that give me pause. You haven't said I hurt you, but I think I did."

"Does it matter anymore?"

"I think so. Doesn't your head ever go to the place where it asks, 'if you love someone, you stick with them, no matter what'?"

"If you love someone you don't keep secrets."

He let that go. In the silence, I understood that was what he was doing. "Can we have lunch tomorrow?"

I had meetings all over my Outlook calendar, but lunch was free. "Okay, we can do that. Do you want me to meet you somewhere?"

"How about meeting at 1890 in the Arcade at noon?"

"It's a date."

"I'll see you at noon then." Memories of Tom floated through scenes of China as I finished the movie. When it was over, I picked up my trusty journal.

> Memories are always connected with moments in time. I'll always think about Tom when I see a daffodil. I'll always think about Jerry when I'm near the tree house. I'll always think of Mom when I see driftwood. I'll always think about Max when I see fireflies.
>
> Tom's right that Mom dying during daffodil days is a potential problem, but it's not because even though I miss her, and there's an ache when I thought about her being gone forever, I feel hope that life's going to get better now. Mom has moved my thinking along, and I feel like I'm no longer stuck. I have no idea where I'm going with the property, with work, with Tom, but the possibilities excite me.
>
> When we talk to each other, it's as if the years never passed. The best part of what we had was the friendship. And it's happening again, the talking, the listening, the wanting to spend time together. We're moving forward and I don't want to stop it. It's been too long since I've had someone who understands me.
>
> We have only promised to share our stories, and maybe our stories will set us free to just be ourselves. Maybe our stories will help us discover ourselves.
>
> I'll stick with only the good ones.

Built in 1890, The Arcade is a four-story Victorian shopping mall. The domed glass-paned roof lets in the sunlight. I was walking up the divided stairs when I looked up and saw Tom smiling down at me. He stood at the top of the stairs in a suit with an overcoat and holding a briefcase, his hair well-controlled and professional. I stepped up to him and he leaned down to brush my cheek with his lips.

"Hi," he said softly. "It feels like I just saw you yesterday. Maybe it's because I think about you so much."

Not being able to resist, I said, "You haven't been spying on me, have you?"

He let the mild accusation go and said, "I noticed Dazzles is closed. When did you work on that?" We stood at the podium waiting to be seated.

"I took a couple weeks off after the funeral. Ben, Cassie, and I worked on it for a couple of days—that's all it took. Mom stopped working six months before that, so some people had already claimed their stuff."

"That must have been hard, to close that down." We followed the maître'd to a booth at the back of the dimly-lit room with windows that looked out on the Arcade.

"Not so hard. Mom told me everything I needed to know about running a farm and everything I needed to know about shutting down her shop before she died."

"What I meant was, it must have been hard emotionally."

"Yeah, I guess it was. It was harder to deal with her physical decline those last weeks. Ben called to me in the middle of the night. It was so quiet in the room when I walked into it I thought she'd already died, but she waited for me. We sat with her, and when she died, we could feel her spirit lift. Have you ever felt that?"

"Yes, actually." The waiter poured our water, placed my napkin in my lap, handed us the menus, then left, as Tom paused. "Our daughter Angela died an hour after she was born." He said it so quietly I almost didn't catch it.

"Oh, Tom. I'm sorry. When was that?"

"She was our first child. If she were alive, she'd be twenty-four now, the same age as your daughter. She was born eight weeks early. We knew she wasn't going to make it the moment she was born. The doctor took her away, wrapped her up, and brought her back She weighed 40 ounces, was so tiny she almost didn't look real. But she had tiny little hands and eyelashes and a mouth that sought to suck but couldn't, and lungs that weren't fully formed. We held her quiet body, taking turns, until she stopped breathing. Miriam pushed her at me and turned away. I watched that little face turn blue, saw the stillness of her white chest, and felt her give up life. I felt the life lift right out of her. I was totally confronted by God's existence, and I was angry because the God I'd known wouldn't have taken her."

We aren't the same people we were when we were young. "That must have been hard for you and Miriam to get through."

He ran his hands through his hair. "For months we slept in separate rooms. She didn't want anything to do with me, and I didn't have the strength to try to make it better. We had our work, so we dove into it full throttle. But all that time, all I could think of was why would God do that to us."

"I haven't been sure about God for a long, long time, but Mom's spirit lifting, the feeling that she was in the room with us, made me think there is an afterlife. Our spirits survive somehow, with all our one-of-a-kind uniqueness. For me, feeling that lifting of the spirit was a confirmation that God exists and dying is part of the plan."

"When we were kids, it just was, you know, you soaked it in and believed. I'd been going along like that for years, going to church pretty much every Sunday, and I'd never questioned things like I did when Angela died."

"And now?"

"My religion has nothing to do with the church anymore. A walk in the park, sailing on the water, those things keep me more connected to God."

"I know what you mean. But I've lately discovered I like being in church. It feels more sacred to me than sitting by the Magical Pond or at Willow Beach. And then somehow . . ." I stopped because I didn't want our lunch to become a discussion about a religion set up for people to lean on instead of facing life. He waited for me to finish. I glanced at him and shook my head.

"Let's have us a toast." He held up his glass of water and I did the same. "To a new beginning for us." Although I wasn't sure of his meaning, we clinked glasses and drank.

"I'm going to have the halibut," he announced to the waiter a few minutes later, closing his menu.

"And I'll have the chicken." I turned back to Tom and asked, "How did you come to terms with the baby dying?"

"Miriam and I discovered we needed each other more than we thought. We needed to let each other in, know what I mean?"

I nodded. "I think so." I looked down at my hands on my lap. I was wearing my navy blue suit and it pulled tightly over my thighs as I sat. *Have I ever let anyone in?* "With Rick, I tried to be beautiful and interesting so I could keep him, then I was sad that it was falling apart, angry for making the choice to marry him, miserable because what I wanted was to be loved. I never suspected we could let each other in"

Tom reached his left across the table and sat it down palm side up next to my glass. I placed my hand in his. "There are times when marriage can be the loneliest place to be in the world. With us, after Angela died, we were miserable and we wanted to stay in our misery and we couldn't conjure up any love for each other."

"So what happened then?"

"One day we gave up trying, and then everything opened up for us. We talked. We cried. We emptied ourselves of the sadness and decided to make a brave attempt to be there for each other."

The salads the waiter put in front of us were almost too pretty to eat.

"I get it. In *The Mermaid Chair* by Sue Monk Kidd, the couple struggles to love each other after loss and the wife becomes infatuated with someone else, and they go awry and come back together, and I suppose it's always about an acceptance of the situation and allowing intimacy to happen, not just physical intimacy, but soul-to-soul togetherness. And losing a child like that, it takes chunks out of the relationship, digs pieces out of the soul."

As it would if Tom knew what I'd done. This complicates things.

"It's amazing people stay married, isn't it?"

"Yeah, it is." The food arrived as soon as our salads were removed. "Thank you for suggesting lunch, Tom."

He nodded. "I hope, if nothing else, that we can be friends again. We were friends first. Sometimes I wonder if I messed up by asking you to go to a movie with me before you were ready for that."

"I knew you well enough. I was over at your house at least twice a month, hanging out with Linda. We used to spy on you."

He laughed. "I know. I would be studying in my room with the door open and hear the ruffling sound of the knees of jeans on the wood floor in the hallway. When I looked up from my book, I'd hear giggling and the quick shuffle as you scooted back to my sister's room."

"We had some crazy ideas that you were doing something you

shouldn't have been, who knows what."

"I always liked you," he said with a grin.

I liked that he was flirting with me.

After the waiter stopped by to see if we wanted anything else, Tom took a deep breath and said, "I have to tell you something sensitive." He paused and looked at me.

"Go on, I'm listening."

"I had an affair with another woman for the last five years of my marriage. Alicia has a small house on a country road in southern Lorain county out by a place called Mill Hollow, where she lives alone. She paints landscapes. If I had a difficult day, all I had to do was go see Alicia, and she'd stop everything she'd been doing, and sit and listen to me."

I listened in disbelief. "But you were the 4-H and church choir kind of guy."

"It's not that I'm proud of this indiscretion. I'm not. But it changed what I want out of life. Does that make sense?"

"Like your marriage wasn't enough?"

"Not only marriage, but life in general. I needed something beyond the everyday monotony." He looked thoughtful.

"What happened between you and Alicia?"

"The day I told her we'd made the decision to divorce, Alicia told me she couldn't see me anymore. She wanted me to get on with my life without her as a crutch, and she wanted me to be sure I wasn't leaving Miriam for her."

"Were you?"

"No. But when Alicia told me that, I wasn't so sure. It was what I'd struggled with for years, and she knew it." He shook his head like he was trying to get something out of his head, then he looked back at me. "I miss her more than I miss Miriam."

His eyes had softened when he spoke of Alicia. I could see he loved her.

"Is there a chance you'll get back together?"

"No. I think she WAS a crutch." He stood up. Lunch was over. "I'm glad we had lunch together."

"Me too."

Over the next few days, I kept thinking about how it felt to lay my head upon his shoulder when I went to sleep, and how his arm held me firmly close to him. We'd slept heart to heart, my right cheek near his neck. I felt his heart beat all night long.

When Tom and I had sat at the Rusty Nail with his boss at the law firm in Kent and Tom agreed with what his boss said about girls who got pregnant, my heart sank because I was already pretty sure I was pregnant. I didn't tell Tom the antibiotic I took when I had a sinus infection had diminished the effectiveness of my birth control pills. I couldn't tell him I'd been foolish enough to get pregnant.

Maria and I checked into a Super 8 and when it was over, Maria let me sleep while she went to the pool. We left Conneaut on Friday and returned on a Monday. Afterwards, I slept until noon every day, read novels on the porch swing, and escaped to the Magical Pond. I ignored the telephone when it rang, and if Tom had called, they were supposed to say I wasn't there.

If I had the baby and gave it up for adoption, I was just like all those stupid girls they helped in their practice. It wasn't that I couldn't talk to him. It was that I didn't want him to be involved in the choice because I knew that would be hard for him. I didn't give him a choice.

To get up my nerve, I had to pretend that I wasn't aborting a baby, that I was aborting an unformed group of cells that wasn't really alive yet. Afterwards, I felt I'd killed our child. I had. I knew I couldn't look Tom in the eye and make up a story. I knew I would never feel comfortable making love to him again. I knew I couldn't live a lie.

Yes, I missed Tom, but I stoically finished school, got a job, became a wife. I tried to make the most of it, but I never loved Rick enough to want to help him. That's why I gave up.

And all this happened because I didn't want to bear a child who would be a bastard like me. *Oh, Mom, look what I did.* Look at what a mess I made of things. I wish I had sought your advice. But I messed that up too—we weren't friends because of Jerry. Did your secret lead to my secret, which lead to your secret, a sickness that became an epidemic?

The epidemic is continuing.

Work was more stable, more routine, now that I'd been back for a while. The staff was helpful, and we now had an easy-going creative team. I was enjoying the writing and design process. I loved the photography. I added more short pieces to give more writers the chance to get their names in print.

The Friday after we had lunch, Tom called me as I was walking in the door. After the usual pleasantries, he jumped on me. "Why didn't you see me that summer?"

"You wanted to change the world. And there I was, an unsophisticated girl from Conneaut, Ohio, who had no idea what she wanted to do with her life other than read Dostoevsky and Voltaire. You needed one of those trophy wives who could cook a gourmet meal and know all the right things to say, the art of proper conversation."

He groaned. "That's not a good enough reason. I picked you. You were that woman for me. How the hell did you conclude you couldn't be a "trophy" wife? You were all of twenty, and I had no idea where I was going. I talked big. Am I a senator living in DC? I'm a plaintiff's attorney living in Vermilion with a practice in Rocky River."

"I wanted you to grow up to be who you wanted to be. I didn't want to be in your way."

The silence was almost menacing. Then he said, quietly, after a long sigh, "Did I give you the impression you would be in my way?"

"You know, we talked about this exact same thing twenty-seven years ago. I remember this exact conversation. Do we have to do it again?"

"Yes!" He was emphatic. "I need the answer. When in desperation I called you one last time, you said you weren't good enough for me and that's when I told you we were done. That's all the conversation we had."

"You're still angry with me."

"You're right about that. I've been thinking about how nice it was to see you again and it makes me angry that it ended."

"Maybe I needed to sort out who I was."

"What do you mean?"

"I didn't know what I wanted. How can you hold me to the decisions I made when I was a girl? When I went back to school, without you, I became studious and moved into the Honors dorm and studied at the desk against the wall. I did what I needed to do—I hibernated. I really just wanted to be left alone."

He let out a big sigh. He was giving up the fight. Then he cleared his throat but didn't say anything. I wondered if he was crying.

"Tom? Listen, I'm making a life that works for me. I don't know if I can make you understand everything about me, and at this point . . . I'm not even sure I want you to."

He again cleared his throat. If I could see his face, it would register a frown. "I think I want this too much."

"What is it you want?"

"I want to be with you."

"Why? You don't know me. I'm not who I was. I'm stumbling along the rocks of the meandering creek of life, mired in muck, looking for answers in journals and letters, trying to be authentic."

"So, what are you trying to tell me?"

If he wanted a relationship with me before he knew me, this might be more about the chase than anything else. "I'm just saying . . . I guess I'm trying to say I need to be allowed to be myself, and if we get to know each other again, our journeys will coincide for awhile, but right now, you can't want it that bad. If you want it that much, you don't want me, you want the idea of me."

He was quiet, then he said, "Wow. You're so right." He let the idea sink in. "I'm being disrespectful of you and who you are by expecting things from you when I have no right to those expectations. Did I do that to you before? When we were together before?"

"Uh huh. I knew you loved me and the next step was marriage. I felt I'd have to reinvent myself to marry you. We were headed straight in that direction and it wasn't going to be interrupted. There would be no reason for it to derail."

"So you derailed it."

"I didn't know that's what I was doing then, but now, yeah, I think that's partly what happened"

He sighed. "Thank you for being honest."

I was trying to be honest with him and with me. It hadn't occurred to me until then that there was more to the end of our relationship than an abortion that had to be kept secret. The abortion was a result of other things that were going on between us. "Listen. We've been making this too complicated. I'm doing the same thing you are, rushing it." I sighed. In the silence, I was thinking thoughts without form, without words to describe them, the foggy thinking where you know something should become clear and you wait for the fog to dissipate. There was so much I needed to know.

Into the white blankness, he asked, "Do you like antiques?"

"I do."

"Let's do this—meet me tomorrow to go antiquing."

"I was going to go to Windy Hill."

"We'll buy something old-new for the farm, how's that? You can be in Conneaut by mid-afternoon. I'm thinking about a place in Ashtabula."

It sounded fun. "Okay."

"There's this place called the Teahouse. I can meet you there at eleven, okay?"

"Sure. And hey, Tom?"

"Yes, Betsy?"

"No expectations, okay?"

"I think we've lived lives full of expectation, and that's been part of why things haven't gone well. We just need to be."

"Agreed."

I wrote in my journal.

> We've been shaped by our homes, by our questions, by our mistakes, by the paths we've chosen. This journey with Tom is one I need to make, without expectation. It's not just a matter of being open to each other, it's about accepting ourselves and being true to ourselves.
>
> What a large charge that is! But isn't this why we're here on this Earth, to become better, more true, more honest, more connected, with each other and with God?
>
> Writing "God" brings to mind all the stories of *The Bible*, the Old Testament stories of Jonah trying to run from his calling, of Ruth doing what she needed to do with Naomi, of Mary choosing one path and Martha another, are all about people trying to find the path, the story, that is true to who they were. As much as I question Jesus as the Messiah, I see God at work. I feel His tug on me by the God connection that's in me. It's a yearning to become a unique part of the whole.
>
> If I listen to the God within me and connect with what He wants me to do, I will be on the path chosen for me. Or is it a path I choose for myself with God's direction being that little bit of God within me?

For now, the goal is to embrace the stories of the past and let them go like fireflies floating above a blanket next to the Rocky River. That means letting go of the heartbreak of not having a father to love, letting go of the fact my mother had secrets, letting go of Jerry's molestation, letting go of how I may or may not have failed Rick, letting go of making a bad decision about Tom's baby, and letting go of missing out on love with Max. When I made mistakes, there was a reason for them, and in most cases, I know the reasons. When I catch myself in a lie or holding back, I'm going to stop and pay attention.

That means I'll have to tell Tom about the abortion.

DANGLING ROOTS
At Willow Beach

I still have difficulty living in the moment, but the driftwood in my hands strengthens my faith. The driftwood ignited possibilities for Mom. If Tom were here, I would tell him how the driftwood washed up on the beach so I could find it, because we both know that nothing happens by accident. The water-smoothed driftwood I've gathered feels warm, as if it contains energy from the Earth. I plan to hang the wood from the ceiling of Mom's old salon and adorn it with beach glass tied to the ends of blue ribbons. The ribbons will dangle like my roots.

Tom will like that I'm claiming that room and making it sacred. He'll like that I'm letting the roots dangle, letting the painful things of life, the untidiness, be there for all to see. He knows I need to see the difference between me now and me then.

The ebb and flow of Mom's last days taught me how to pay attention to what was inside of me and inside of others. The bit of whimsy that will come from the mobile will remind me not to be so serious about it all. God wants us to relax with the lessons through which we need to live and accept what comes our way.

Tom and I share our stories, split wide open and exposed, without secrets. Like the books we share and discuss until they're raw, our stories can be rough, but telling them smoothes the edges as the waves smooth pieces of wood that are torn from trees along the shore. I've let go of my secrets now, like fireflies let out into the world, like daffodils opening to the sun. Freedom comes from being who I am.

I still don't believe I'm good at love, but I'm open to it, which is a good place to be. I wonder if our love will fade like the misty dawn over the lake? Or is our love the true kind, the kind that sustains and expands? How would I know?

We're working on that together. Tom has the same questions.

I suppose the search for love is part of my journey. The whimsy of the driftwood will dangle while I search for love. No secrets now. I wrote in my journal how important it is to let go of pain, to love, but I think it's more that we need to embrace it. Life was never meant to be a string of only happy moments.

I wasn't happy, but I wasn't sad, the summer after Mom died. I was confused. I felt like life was waiting for me to do something and I wasn't doing it. I was frustrated with myself for not moving on, but I didn't know what I was supposed to move on to. Tom was my most consistent friend. I wonder what would have happened if he hadn't been there?

The day we went antiquing brought us closer to each other. I started to remember more about how we were together as a couple. At that point in the story, I wasn't ready to love anyone yet; I didn't love myself.

CHAPTER EIGHT – FIREFLIES

When I spied the white-brick century house with the wall of windows on the west side, I turned into the drive and drove behind to find a parking space. I pulled in next to the tree behind the house.

Tom stood on the walkway, a smile on his face. He wore jeans and a long-sleeved white shirt with the sleeves rolled up, the top two buttons open.

He cocked his head to one side as he sized me up in my jeans, low-heeled boots and long-sleeved tie-dyed T-shirt. I laughed. "A lot can be said without words," I said softly.

"Maybe we should try that experiment. No words." He leaned in and kissed my nose like he used to do. Then he pressed his nose against mine. When he pulled away, his eyes were alive with amusement. He turned my hands over and tickled my palms with a soft stroke from his index finger. I remembered the way he used to trace my spine with the same soft stroke. I could feel how it felt when he stroked the spot right above my tailbone, circling slowly in the spot right below the small of my back as I sprawled on his bed on lazy Sunday mornings when we were barely awake.

I looked away from our hands and up to his face. His eyes were on mine, watching for my reaction. Our eyes held long after he took my hands in his again and held them firmly. We saw acceptance in each others' eyes.

We walked to the doorway, hands entwined. Inside the Teahouse, he said, "This farmhouse was built in 1850, and has stood on this site the entire time, before the Civil War. There's a little tea room here on the glass porch side of the house." Inside the doorway, pastries and quiches were displayed in the glass bakery case. "The apple fritters are really good." He pointed out crispy brown and freshly glazed pastries. "I can smell the apples . . . Remember when we picked apples off that tree on Summit Street in Kent and took them back to your place and baked an apple pie?"

I nodded. "I had to call Grandma for the exact amount of the ingredients for the crust."

"She was thrilled you called for a recipe."

"She liked that I wanted to make you a pie. But I wasn't making that pie for you."

"You weren't?"

I shook my head. "I wanted an apple pie."

He feigned hurt and I squeezed his hand. We stopped before a watercolor painting of a gabled Victorian house. "It looks like your grandparents' house," Tom said.

"No it doesn't."

He studied me then. "It does, Betsy. Look at it. You're drawn to it because it reminds you of the house."

"Our house doesn't have a full wraparound porch. It doesn't have gables."

"The style, the farmland behind it, the porch. It reminds me of the house even if it isn't exact. The feel is the same. I think that was the style your grandfather was shooting for when he planned it."

At Windy Hill, the house stood at the end of a long driveway, a large willow tree on one side and the oak trees that followed the driveway on the right. The barn and keeper's cottage sat beyond the house and past the oak trees. Fields climbed up a slight hill behind the house and ended in a line of trees at the back of the property. The porch graced the front and part of the side of the first floor. The house in the painting stood all alone in the midst of the land and the trees lined the drive, just like Windy Hill. "You're right." We stood and looked at it for a while.

He followed me down the hallway to the back porch, which was filled with wicker. "I've always loved this stuff."

"It's generally not very comfortable." To prove it, he sat down on a settee. He patted it, and I sat down with him. "Are you okay with this? With another date?"

"I'm going to see what happens." I squeezed his knee and left my hand there. We could easily slip back to where we'd been years before.

Eventually, Tom said, "This wicker's poking into my back," and got up.

The house held an eclectic mix of old china and washboards, spinning wheels and dry sinks, framed photos and postcards sent from places like Atlantic City and Hawaii during the 1950s. Amongst the antiques were hand-made stained glass ornaments, rough-hewn clay pots, and dried flower arrangements. We chatted comfortably as we walked amongst the wallpapered rooms, teasing each other about things the other one would like.

We both noticed a hand-blown glass bowl on a maple table at the same time. It had a dewy quality to it, like it was made to reflect water.

"I bet it would look good at your place," I said.

He looked at me with a strange expression. "You know, you're right, and you haven't even seen my place. It would look great at my place. I could use some art."

I picked it up and examined the bottom of the 15-inch flattened bowl and said, "I'll buy it for you."

"No, that's okay, Betsy. You don't have to do that for me."

But I could tell he was pleased. As we walked downstairs to the cash register, he went back to examine the farmhouse picture. "Those are vineyards in the background." He pulled it off the wall. "I'm buying this for you, whether it reminds you of your house or not."

We paid for our gifts and a couple apple fritters, then went outside. We wandered to a gift shop and a weaving studio where someone was weaving on a loom before running to the door of a train caboose in a sudden downpour. Inside, we heard the noise of toy trains on tracks before we saw them. Six trains ran on tracks in a large display along the far wall. I remembered the train set he'd had when he was a boy. "Ah, the train shop," I said.

He winked at me, a boy's mischievous look on his face. He grabbed an engineer's cap by the front door and put it on his head. "I still have my train set, and we set it up around the Christmas tree every year. Or we did. I don't know what I'll do this year."

He was trying to make sense of his life as much as I was. Only I'd had just me for a long time and he'd had a wife and a home and a family that had been intact until recently. He watched the trains go around the tracks, each one different and going at its own speed.

"You're having a hard time with the divorce, aren't you?" I asked.

I felt the loss in his eyes. "It's not the divorce that's hard, it's the way the house is so empty when I come home, how super-quiet the nights are. Half our belongings are somewhere else."

I leaned into him and put my arm around him, my head on his shoulder. "I guess it takes some getting used to."

"And how about the farm? Could you ever feel right, being in the house alone?"

"When I'm there, it feels like I'm home. More so than the condo these days."

He turned back to the trains, and I kept my arm around him. It felt good to be close to him. I didn't let go until he moved toward the door. "I'm glad I already have my train," he said as we left the shop.

In the Davis House gift shop I couldn't resist buying hand towels for the bathroom at the condo. "You must be so torn," Tom said as we walked back towards the cars.

I looked at my watch and it was nearing one o'clock. Time had slipped by quickly. "What do you mean?" I shifted my weight to my car. My chin was raised and my face was within inches of his.

"About the house, about your condo. You know, where you should live."

I felt the prick of anxiety lance the good cheer I'd been feeling. "I'm trying not to think about it, yet. My initial reaction, right after the funeral, was to run away as far as I could from Windy Hill, but I find I'm drawn to it. I have time to think about it."

"That's a good plan, to just wait," he whispered. He reached up and pushed a strand of my hair away from my cheek.

It was such an intimate gesture. "I'm trying to live in the moment." I said, not wanting our time together to end.

"I can stay at my parents' house tonight, so I don't have to spend so much time driving back to Vermilion."

He wanted to ask to come to Windy Hill. He didn't. Instead, he bent down and kissed me good-bye, a brief and light kiss, one that told me he liked me, one that made me feel like I was fifteen again and was being kissed by a boy on the football team who helped repair the houses of shut-ins during the summer. I was taken so far back that when I pulled away from him I didn't feel like me anymore. I felt young and unsure and afraid.

He looked down and when he reached for my hands, I dropped the bag of hand-embroidered towels. "No matter whom you've been with or what things you've done, you'll always be Betsy pure and simple, a girl who liked to bake cookies and take them to all her neighbors. You're still the girl who brought books to our house and sat and read while Linda watched television, and the girl who helped her grandparents sell vegetables at the vegetable stand. I liked how you were, my daffodils and fireflies girl."

"You're the most romantic man I've ever known."

He smiled and squeezed my hands.

"I don't want our time together to end," I said.
"We said we would just go for it, right?"
I nodded. We were going to Windy Hill.

We walked into the house after taking the mail out of the mailbox. It still came, junk mail for my mother or Ben. Nothing had changed since my last visit two weeks ago, except for Cassie's note on the kitchen table. While Tom watched me, I read,

> Hi Mom. Welcome home again. I arranged for the cable and telephone to be turned off last week. I'll pay the other utility bills, but if you could send me $220 to cover them, I'd appreciate it. Things seem to be going smoothly, but the peaches are ripe and will start to fall if we don't get some workers in here. We need to think about that. It's Saturday, and we just finished picking the peaches you'll find behind the house. We should get some to the market. Call me if you need to. Love, Cassie.

When I looked up into Tom's face, I said, "Do you feel like picking peaches?"

Without hesitation, he said, "Sure. I'd love to."

We were in the groves for four hours, up and down the ladders, filling baskets hanging to our hips. When they become heavy, we unloaded them and started again. I wasn't used to the work, but it was mindless, methodical, somehow spiritual. We didn't talk much as we got involved in it. At one point Tom pointed out that it reminded him of painting houses when we were kids, the rhythm of the work taking over, each person in their own head. And I agreed.

We stopped at six-thirty, sat in the grass and ate peaches. The sky was the hazy blue of a summer day after a torrential rain. I waved to Pedro as he led the cows home. Pedro's face lit up as he heartily waved back.

"I don't think he knew we were here."

"Doesn't look like it." Tom watched the slow progress of the cows with their haunches and udders swinging, trailing each other.

"I had a favorite cow when I was a girl."

"And why was she your favorite?"

"I felt like she listened to me. I called her Sam. I would sit beside her on the milking stool and talk to her. Grandma always told me I could stay with her on the farm anytime I wanted, and I sometimes walked the couple miles to get here, showed up without a phone call. When I did that, Grandma waited for me to talk, but if I didn't, she gave me a hug, then went into the kitchen to call my mother. Sam was sometimes out in the fields, so I would go looking for her."

"Sounds like she was pretty important to you."

"I talked to her like I talk when I write in my journal. I let my heart rise to the top and my pen write the truth."

He nodded. "I know that. Journaling is soulful, beautiful, a connection to the universe . . ."

"A wire tautly drawn and true."

"One could walk on that wire." He held a blade of grass tight between his thumbs and blew the boastful sound through the reed.

"An acrobat with a clear head," I said. "You journal?"

"Sort of, off and on. I write about things that happen. I'm not sure how soulful it really is most of the time."

I was sitting cross-legged next to him. "It's so peaceful out here."

"I like it. Too bad we don't have a blanket."

"I don't mind the grass." I laid down on my back and looked up into the green-red leaves of a Maple tree above my head. We were on the edge of the grove and the house and barn were a thousand feet away. Between our spot and the barn was the well-worn path trod by the cows. We could hear the noises of getting the cows settled and fed, metal against metal, scraping equipment, then the whir of the milk churner. "One of the things I told Sam about was Jerry."

Tom was quiet beside me. Waiting. I felt an intense urge to put my arm around him and pull him close, but I didn't. I think he knew I was about to confess something hinted at before. He hadn't pushed me to tell, but I needed to tell him.

"I was sitting in the living room watching television after school. It was only a couple of days after you first kissed me. Remember how you kissed me in the park?"

"I remember."

"That was my very first kiss. It made me feel special. I wasn't sure what to make of it, but I thought it would lead to something more between us. I guess it did, eventually, but not then.

"I was sitting in the semi-light of a rainy day, happy to be watching an old movie. I could hear the rain dripping from the gutter, the flow of it over the window behind the couch. I was watching a Cary Grant movie in black and white. My feet were on the coffee table, and I was eating popcorn. I'd been thinking about that kiss ever since it happened, had seen how you looked at me in the hallways at school, your eyes watching me."

"You glided down the halls and your hair cascaded down your back, your cute body in a T-shirt and cut-off jeans."

"And that's what I was wearing, sitting there watching the movie." *Nothing to lose, nothing to lose.* "All of a sudden, someone was at the door, with a key. It was too early for Mom to be home. A man's figure was outlined in the window. It had to be Mr. Frank, Mom's boyfriend, so I walked over to open it, just as he succeeded in opening it himself. He smiled at me, but it wasn't a fatherly smile, more like 'I hoped you would be here, and I hoped you'd be here alone.' He had this sneaky attitude about him, and when he turned to close the door as if he were invading the house, I knew something was about to happen. I told myself it was okay.

He brought out icy cold drinks and sat with me on the couch, but when he sat down again, he sat so close our bodies were touching. When the couple in the movie started to kiss, he touched my knee and looked over at me to see my reaction. I was simply surprised. He pulled my face to his and started kissing me, running his lips all over my face and down my neck, his arm going under me as he let go of my hand, and I was confused. He told me he'd been watching me and had been waiting for a time when we could be alone and then he told me he thought we were meant to be together and I was beautiful and sexy."

I'd been looking up into the tree, watching the leaves moving, and now I looked into Tommy's face. "He said the same things I thought you wanted to say. And I was those things, wasn't I?"

Tom nodded. He was absorbing what I said, taking it in. I felt he wanted to know, but he was afraid for me. There was anguish behind the encouraging look.

I continued. "I thought, during those kisses, about what we'd said, and then I felt like I wanted him, that yes, he'd been funny at dinner the night before, charming, actually, and he was a sophisticated man who traveled for work and studied for a year in Cambridge on a scholarship, in international business. My mother was so proud of this man she'd found, a good one, and he seemed to really like her. But now I knew it wasn't Mom he wanted, but me. Mom was beautiful, but I was even more beautiful. He told me he loved me, and it seemed right and natural and real, and I believed him, this guy I'd spent maybe a dozen hours with.

"Things got out of control. His hands were on my breasts, then under my shirt and he was on top of me taking off my jeans. I was scared. I told him to stop. His face was rough against my cheek. It hurt. His weight was hurting my back. He straddled me and sat up straight to remove his shirt. In a small voice I told him 'No, I mean it,' but he stayed where he was. He smiled and said, 'that's what you think now, but once we get going, you'll be glad.' I turned away from him, the tears streaming from my eyes now. I'd tried to squirm away, but he held my hands above my head as he rubbed himself against me, his hairy chest harsh against my bare breasts. His fingers fumbled with his fly and he pushed his jeans down, one hand still holding my wrists, and then he let go but I was under him and I felt him rubbing against me. He said, 'see, you do want me' in a super-pleased way and I wondered if I did. Maybe I did want him. But I said, again, 'please stop.'

"He laughed, like it was all in good fun, a joke." I looked up at the tree branches forming their umbrella to block out the sun. Tommy's fingers were playing with my hair, winding in it, lost in it. He was watching his fingers, not my face. He waited to hear the rest of the story, the story I wasn't sure I should tell, but I did.

"He started kissing me, and I told him to stop. I just wanted to be kissed. I thought maybe that would be all, we'd just be naked together. But he reached down and was inside me, and it hurt. I actually screamed and tried to push him off me. His thrusts became frenzied and I no longer felt beautiful and certainly not pure. I felt the pain, but mostly I felt shame. I was ashamed for letting this happen and that I had somehow encouraged it. I laid there, unresponsive as he continued to pound into me until he was done.

"He didn't think he'd done anything wrong," It was a revelation as I said it. "He moved to lay with me and cradled me to him and kissed my neck and ears like a lover would do and told me I was his. I wanted to believe it. I wanted to think that he was right, we were meant to be together and the only reason it felt wrong and painful was because it was the first time."

When I looked back at Tommy he looked serious. He asked, "So did you have sex with him after that?"

"Yes. When he came over, he'd catch me in the kitchen to sneak a kiss. I was the other woman with my mother's man. But interestingly, that furtive love affair, it felt like real love, the true thing. It was like the love of Lady Chatterley or Anna Karenina. Forbidden love was real love. I became so confused about what love was."

"So when I asked you to go out with me, is this the reason you didn't want to?"

"Yes. I thought Jerry loved me. I was Jerry's girl. I wanted to go out with you, but I felt that going out with you was a betrayal of Jerry. And also, I was afraid."

"Afraid of getting to that place with me?"

"Of becoming intimate with someone else and feeling that shame again. I didn't want to be a bad girl. I simply wanted to be loved. I didn't really want the sex, but if that's what Jerry wanted, I'd give it to him if it meant he'd love me."

"How long did it go on?"

"For months. When I tried to end things, he wouldn't let them end. I started staying away from the house. I got that job at the coffee shop."

"You were at our house a lot more. I remember because it was hard for me, having you there hanging out with Linda, but yet you wouldn't go out with me again."

"I'm sorry, Tom."

He stretched his arm out under his head and traced his finger along my inner arm and I turned toward him, our bodies touching full length. He pulled me close and I nuzzled my face into his neck. "Don't be sorry. It wasn't your fault. I can't imagine what a fifteen-year-old girl in that situation might have done differently. Of course you were confused. And every one of us wants to be loved."

"I thought I was a slut. Was it love or just sex? When I was with you, I had the same questions, was it love or sex and did you love me for who I was or was I being used? I didn't trust our love. And I think I couldn't trust our love because of Jerry. Does that make sense?"

He nodded. "Yes." He bowed his head and was quiet for a few moments. "For a long time I was glad I didn't end up with you and I didn't think about what we had. In the last couple of years, I decided something had been wrong. I went to the funeral because I was wanted to solve the problem."

I wanted to cry, seeing his welled-up eyes. I continued with my story. "Grandpa died that winter. I missed him. And Mom was always working. Grandma was at the farm, and I could go there on the weekends, but not during the week. But when I went there on the weekends, I didn't talk to Grandma, I talked to a cow."

It came out funny, and I laughed. Tom laughed too. Quietly, he said, "If I'd known, things could have been different."

"I know, I've thought about that."

"Simple choices . . ."

"Can make all the difference in the direction of our lives."

"Yep." He pulled away then and looked hard into my eyes, "I loved you, you know that, don't you?"

"Yes. I know."

"Do you know how much?"

"I think so."

"I don't think you do. I thought we were going to be married. I had a ring."

That was news to me. I suddenly understood how much I'd hurt him. I stammered, "I . . ."

"When you left and wouldn't talk to me, it was like you knew I was going to ask and you didn't want to allow yourself to get that close to someone, so you backed off. You ran away from a guy who loved you more than . . ." He searched for the words, then said, "More than I thought it was possible to love someone. When we talked, we could guess what the other had to say, and it flowed naturally, and true. When our bodies came together, the love we shared was special and more intimate than I could have imagined. We rarely argued, and we agreed on everything from how to study and what to study to the tyranny of American imperialism and Jimmy Carter's philanthropic deeds."

"And that trip over spring break . . ."

". . . Was heaven. I was at the beach in Florida with the love of my life in a string bikini lying in the sun, our first beer and taco stand burrito at noon, dancing in the clubs at night, listening to Joe Walsh and the Eagles as we made love with our window open at that old-fashioned place that's no longer there in Fort Lauderdale. We were in love with each other. For me, going home to visit our parents before returning to school, you having dinner at our house and me having dinner with your mother and grandmother here, at the farm, pot roast with potatoes and carrots and onions, fresh baked bread, a rhubarb pie for dessert, was great."

"You remember what we had to eat?"

"Jesus, Betsy. You don't get it, do you?" He pulled away then and sat up. I felt a cold breeze along the side of my body where his arm had been.

"You're saying because you loved me so much, you remembered every detail."

"Yes! And for you not to know that . . . it's irksome."

"I knew it. But I didn't deserve it."

"So because you 'thought' you didn't deserve it, you made the decision for the both of us?! Is that fair? Was that fair?"

I felt chastised. He was right, of course. But I didn't know how to reply in a way that he would really understand.

I sat up too, grabbed a peach, turned it in my hand looking for blemishes. Not one of the peaches we'd picked had a blemish. They were perfect.

Suddenly, Tom picked up a peach and threw it at the trunk of the tree. We heard its sickening split, the splat of innards smashing, and the thud following its downward fall.

I was stunned. "It makes me angry as well. If we'd stayed together. I wouldn't have had to go through those lonely and unhappy years with Rick. We could have had our own children. If it had been you and me together, we probably would have stayed here, in Conneaut, helped out on the farm weekends, and our kids would have too, and maybe you would have set up a practice here in town and I could have written more because I wouldn't have felt I had to work as I did. I would have been more content. I wouldn't have started the walking."

"The walking?" He looked confused.

"Sometimes I start walking and I can't stop. I once walked over the Detroit-Superior Bridge, down Detroit, to Edgewater Park—I think that's about 60 blocks—then walked back to the condo. Another time I didn't get home until 2 in the morning after one of those walks."

He stood up and pulled me up to show me he was done with the conversation.

Back at the house, we ate bread and cheese and trail sausage on the front porch. Across the road, waist-high corn was in the forefront and beyond that a row of townhouses a developer threw up last year. "If you sell the farm," Tom said, mouth full of bread, "someone's going to put in a housing development."

"I know."

Later, Tom sat in the kitchen while I talked to Pedro about the milk products and the costs that were coming out of the Estate. Pedro asked again what was going to happen with the farm, and I said I didn't know yet. Pedro tipped his hat and told me he'd be there as long as the farm was. He was happy working on the farm.

"Don't you get lonely out here?"

"I have my Miranda."

I'd forgotten about his wife. "I haven't seen her in years. How's she doing?"

He smiled shyly. "Miranda has diabetes and she don't walk no more. Your mother, she used to collect her in her wheelchair and bring her over to see the garden here at the house. Miranda's gotten much worse since your mother became ill. I try. We talk, remember the good times." He turned to Tom to explain, "We had four children, back in California, but they stayed there when we moved here. We came here as migrant workers, but we were tired, you know, tired of moving all the time, back and forth across the country, lookin' for the next work. When Miss Betsy's grandfather offered me a job, I took it."

I sat back and looked at Pedro. He was probably around sixty-five. His face was brown and furrowed, a face whose life was spent outdoors in the sun. My grandfather and my mother trusted him, took him into their lives, and me, I didn't even know what was going on with his wife.

"I'm sorry I haven't visited Miranda. Are you two doing okay?"

"We're fine. In fact, she'll be expecting me now. I should go. It's a busy time."

"Do you have migrant workers coming in to help you?"

"Tomorrow they come from the Job Corps. I'll go pick them up in the truck."

"I'll come back next week." After he left, I said, "I feel like such a heel, not being out here more."

"It's only a little over three months since your Mom died."

"And I've only been here four times. He had to deal with the peaches starting to fall off the trees by himself. Maybe I should come out here one night during the week too. It's not that far."

"Don't beat yourself up trying to make a point. It will backfire if you try too hard and don't have your heart in it."

"Following one's heart is one of the hardest things to do."

"It should be as simple as following a firefly."

I laughed and looked over at him. "That's not so easy."

"It meanders and rolls and turns and falters and then it lights up again, true and real and easy to find, then it's gone again. What's so hard about that?"

"It's worse than a meandering creek turning up muck, which is kind of how I see my life."

"But when it does light up, it's worth it, to see the light and to have made the journey, like the creek with its muck and stones and water bugs, sometimes overflowing with water, sometimes low, but making its way nonetheless."

"You always were a poet."

"All I'm saying is you need to follow the path that makes the most sense, and it may meander, but it needs to be true."

"Alone."

"Alone and fine with the decisions. For me, Alicia ending things is okay. It was meant to be, and I'm not angry with her."

"So my aloneness is a good thing because I've chosen it and it's made me who I am."

"I don't think you quite get the point," he said, his arm over his eyes to keep out the sun that insisted on low horizon brightness despite our sunglasses.

"Yes, I do. I think you're trying to tell me I haven't chosen my aloneness."

"I think you've forced it."

"Why is being with someone so important to everyone? Mom was always saying stuff like that too. I don't need anyone. I'm fine with my life."

He changed the subject. "What are you writing now?"

I turned and looked at him.

"Seriously. What are you writing?"

"I'm writing in my journal. I'm going to do a story on Montreal."

"When was the last time you wrote, really wrote?"

I sighed. An unfinished novel sat in the drawer of my bedside table. I'd had things to say in that book, a reason for starting it, and I stopped before the climax, the central moment of decision. "I think the journaling's good."

"Maybe you walk instead of writing. It's good to be immersed in something—a few years back I took photography classes and joined the photography club in the Metroparks."

"I have a novel I've worked on now and then over the years. I can't get back into it."

"You should."

We sat in silence for a while, and then he said, "I can't believe you never told me about Jerry."

Gathering my face together, I'm sure he saw enough on my face to tell him I still remembered too much of what happened then. "I'm not accustomed to wearing my heart on my sleeve."

He nodded. "That affair with Jerry . . . it made you not true to who you were, not true to your mother, not true to me. It changed you."

"I made a wrong decision."

"We all do that. We get past them and try to make our lives as good and complete as we can, if we have the heart for it. As for your writing for the magazine, I've followed it, and the writing is wonderful. If you only do travel writing, you've done something, but I think you're destined for something else."

"I had no idea you read my writing."

We stood up at the same time. "I was your first fan." He smiled.

"Yep. You were. Ready to go?" The sun was falling low in the sky.

"Yes, but . . ."

"It's getting late, Tom."

We'd fallen, already, into the rhythm of our college days, just hanging out together. It felt natural.

I kept Tom's car in my rearview mirror as I drove I-90 west to downtown Cleveland. His home, his life, my home, my life, our relationships—it was all a big puzzle whose pieces I was putting together to make sense of who we were today—at the heart it was just us. I suspected that happiness was enjoying the moments as they unfold.

When I got home, I dialed Rick's number. I'd been thinking about him off and on all day.

"Hello?" I could tell by the roughness of his voice that I'd caught him asleep.

"Hi, Rick, it's me," I said.

"Betsy?" He sounded incredulous.

"Yeah, you're right. It's weird that I'm calling you. I need to tell you I'm sorry that I wasn't there for you like I should have been."

Silence. Then he sighed. "You did the best you could with a husband who was a jerk. I never blamed you for anything."

I hadn't thought he did. But I'd never been a friend. "I hurt you more than I helped you."

"I needed to help myself. There was nothing you could have done for me. You know that. You went to Al Anon. Your job was to keep your distance and let me make my mistakes."

"But if I'd loved you . . ."

"How could you love me? I don't blame you for that either. Remember when I called you after the divorce and apologized to you?"

"Sure."

"I needed to do that to move on. But I meant it. I hear what you're saying now, and I'm glad you're moving on. You held onto this for too many years."

I let that sink in. "Thank you, Rick."

"You're welcome, sweetie. I'm always here if you need to talk."

A week later, Tom visited my condo. He studied pictures of my family on the hallway walls. He admired Mom's oil painting of the Cuyahoga and her driftwood mobiles whose crazy colored ribbons trailed like kite strings against the high white walls. In the kitchen, he ran his fingers over the Tuscan-style wood cabinets and the marble countertops, and tapped a fingernail against one of the shining pots hanging above the stove.

"This is so different from the farm, from the house you lived in with your mother when you were a teenager. It's kind of like you're dressing up," he said while he stood in the middle of the great room.

I laughed.

"You're just a small town girl and here, you're a sophisticated woman of the world." He looked toward the view of the river, then went to the French doors that opened to the balcony. When he stepped out onto the balcony, he whistled low and thrust his hands into his pockets while he took it in. He was rooted at the railing. He stood and looked until I gave him a glass of wine. He tapped his glass against mine. "To industry."

I looked to the west, and there it was, the industrial heart of Cleveland with its dusky windowless buildings and smokestacks and crawling muddy roads leading to mammoth doors and conveyors, and drawbridges for the railroad tracks. Above the valley, high-rise Gold Coast condos and trees on the curve where Cleveland became Lakewood were reminders of the good life wrought by steel. "To the good life," I replied.

"Remember when you and I bought a bottle of wine for Valentine's Day and we took that first sip and we both thought it was awful, but we didn't say anything, kept drinking it, and it wasn't until the next day we both admitted to each other we hated the wine?"

"We almost decided we didn't want to drink wine anymore. Do you think I've gotten better at choosing good wine?" I inhaled the aroma of cherry and took another sip of the deep grape smoothness.

"Much better. What is this?"

"It's a Pinot Noir from St. Joseph winery in Geneva."

"It's really good."

"Ohio wines are underrated. This one competes against the big boys in Sonoma and Napa and brings home the gold. I always buy a case to hold me over into the winter months, opening a bottle every few weeks."

Tom turned to sit on the Carolina wicker rocking chair behind him. "Where'd you get these?" He rocked.

"The Outer Banks. There's a furniture store by the sound that sells low country furniture."

We sipped our wine. Finally, he said, "Is this where your heart is?"

"It's my retreat."

"When I stopped by Alicia's place on my way home after work, and I did that most evenings, she provided me the space I needed to unwind."

"She provided your retreat."

"Not that home wasn't, but Miriam's tense negative energy was felt as soon as I entered the house. It made me not want to be there. Miriam didn't seem to care, so I didn't provide an explanation for why I came home late."

"Are you sure she wasn't upset and she just didn't show you?"

He gave me a steady look. "Miriam and I had grown apart."

"The widening emotional gap of a stale marriage can fool you into thinking what you're doing is right because you've been betrayed. Because you feel betrayed, it's okay to betray."

"I didn't tell myself it was all right. I knew it was wrong, and I did it anyway. I knew the marriage was over. We weren't emotionally involved with each other."

I lifted my glass to see the color in the dying light. The river below was now reflecting the lights from Shooters on the boardwalk on the other side, and the sky was turning the bright blue that preceded brilliant sunsets. "Did your children find out?"

"Yes. Miriam was angry enough to let them know their father was a cheater. They just know we had a 'thing' that was inappropriate. I've handled it by not saying much."

"I never would have thought you capable of such deceit."

"What is the greater deceit? Having an affair or living a lie?"

He was asking me whether his choice was better than mine. "That's a subject always open to debate, isn't it?"

When we'd had enough wine, we walked down and crossed the railroad tracks to Old River Road and went around the bend of the Cuyahoga and under the Detroit-Superior Bridge. The air was summer-moist but chilled with the wind off the Lake. I pulled my sweater tighter around me. Tom walked next to me, keeping pace.

"I love to walk."

"You always did."

"If I don't walk every day at a good, brisk pace, for long distances, I'm not myself."

"Meaning?"

"I'm like a drunk without a drink."

"Not really. You don't mean that . . . but do you want to walk longer? We can walk north towards Shooters along the boardwalk then come back this way."

"Okay," I said, and we headed that way. "It IS like that, Tom. I need to walk."

"I suppose there're worse things."

"I don't think you understand."

He put his arm around me and drew me close as our pace slowed. "It's the wanderer in you. You're looking for something while consoling yourself."

Back at my place, I found the ingredients for an omelet and salad and we ate at the counter before settling down to watch a movie. We fell asleep, spooning, while *Atonement* went on without us.

I woke some hours later. Tom was still wrapped around me, but my neck hurt. When I tried to straighten out, he woke and kissed my neck. "I need to get up," I whispered.

"Go on. Go to bed."

I turned off the television, then went back to the couch to take his hand. "Come with me."

He sleepily got up and followed me. In my room, he stripped to his underwear and curled up in bed. In the dark, I took off my clothes and slipped on the short cotton nightgown from the back of the bathroom door. I joined him in bed, snuggling into his shoulder. Tom and me, in bed together again. I sighed. It felt luxurious and tender. I smiled in the dark.

When I woke, Tom's face wore the shadow of a beard. He was lying on his side with his left arm bent and under his head. His breath was so light, I couldn't hear it, even though I was lying on my side a foot away from him on the bed. I could smell the scent of lavender on the pillows from the sachet I placed between the pillow and the cover. I leaned over and kissed Tom on the forehead, sat up, and smoothed down my nightgown when I got out of bed.

It was a gloomy Sunday morning. Dark cumulus clouds billowed above the steel-colored surface of the Lake. While I was waiting for the coffee to complete its brewing cycle, tempted by the rich smell of fresh-ground Columbian beans, lightening lit the sky to the northwest.

"What do you have planned for today?"

I turned around and saw my old rumple-haired Tom standing behind the kitchen counter in boxers but nothing else. "Not sure," I said as I stepped behind the counter. I filled two big Starbucks Cleveland mugs to the brim and took them over to the coffee table.

"Thank you," he said, taking a sip of the hot coffee. "Good sleeping last night, huh?"

"I haven't slept that well in years."

"There must be something to that. Your body against mine feels like it did when we were kids. It's like we have this body memory."

"I was surprised to wake up so refreshed. I only woke that one time."

"I woke several times when we were on the couch. Foghorns, tugboats, revelers. The bedroom's a lot quieter."

The coffee was good. Outside, the rain started. We sat and watched it, drowsy from the pattering. He finally stood, walking about with his coffee cup and opening kitchen cabinets. He went through the spice collection, checked out the granola and pastas, picked up a bottle of Spanish olive oil. When he opened the refrigerator, he asked, "Why do you have Kalamata olives—do you eat them plain or put them in a tapenade or bread?"

"It's a staple, like capers and mustard, fresh mozzarella and Roma tomatoes. I wouldn't be without whole wheat penne or raisin granola or pine nuts."

"I have to have sundried tomatoes and almonds."

"I generally have those too. My refrigerator is always stocked with romaine and plain yogurt."

"Plain yogurt? I have to have fruit in it."

"I put blueberries in it, stay away from the fruit syrup." I stood to come close to him in the kitchen. "So what would you like for breakfast?"

"Pancakes?"

"That sounds good."

He walked toward the bedrooms and dining room while I pulled out the syrup and butter. "Don't look in my underwear drawer," I called.

I wasn't sure how I felt about him being in my place. After a cozy night, the morning made me feel exposed, unlike myself, an actress in a play. The outdoor gloominess dampened my spirits.

When he came back into the kitchen, I was dropping batter onto the griddle. He held a picture of Rick and me, the only one I kept. "Does this mean you haven't quite let go?"

"Rick was part of my life, so I honor him by keeping a picture of him"

"Do you think Cassie would care whether or not there was a picture of her father here?"

"I thought so when I put the picture on the sideboard of the dining room. But she recently told me she doesn't like the framed photo of the three of us displayed at Windy Hill because we look happy and it's a lie."

We looked out at the pouring rain in the lighting sky. He was still rumpled, and I liked his longish uncombed blond hair and the way his cheeks dimpled when he smiled.

"Life's been good to you," I said.

"And to you. You still look like you're twenty."

"Humph, maybe it's because I have so much denial."

"There's something to that. You think you're not old, so you're not. Are you reading Jack Kerouac now?"

My eyes followed his gaze to the table next to the couch. "I'm on a travel memoir binge. I read *A Year in Provence* recently as well. I didn't much like *Travels with Charlie*."

"No, neither did I. Steinbeck wasn't at his best."

"We always did agree on books."

"I recall we agreed on everything."

When I walked back to the window, he followed me. We could see the wind blowing along the water, the imprint of the rain on the surface of the river. But the clouds were white instead of steel colored. Tom was so close that I touched his fingers without moving my arm. I leaned into him, and put my head playfully on his shoulder. "It was good."

"Except it ended." He moved away from me. "Why?"

"Because I was stupid and young and didn't know a good thing when I had it." I reached out and took his hand and pulled it to my lips and kissed his fingers one at a time, then closed them into a fist and took his closed hand between two of mine and brought it against my chest, looking up at him with affection.

He wrapped his arms around me and pulled me to him. The warmth of his body against mine while we slept was a recent memory, so it felt natural to be close to him, about to receive a kiss.

I'd kissed many men. Some were slow to kiss deeply. Others went right for an open-mouthed, tongue-throttling, aggressive thrashing. If I could choose a kiss, I would choose the way Tom kissed. He kissed my nose, he kissed my cheeks, he brushed my eyelashes with his. His body melded with mine—there was no open space between us. I felt his upper-body strength, the breadth of his chest feeling much larger than when he wasn't so close. I reached my arms up to lace my hands behind his neck, and I leaned into him. Our heads turned as he kissed my lips so gently I could almost not feel it. He continued to only slightly touch my lips, then applied more pressure, until our mouths opened, and I was out of breath. I felt bare, wide open. With other men, I would have looked away, started talking, or begun kissing anew, but with Tom, I allowed my eyes to linger with his.

I said, "What are we doing?" It was not a rhetorical question.

"We're allowing ourselves to tell each other how we feel."

"I feel like a girl again."

He smiled and nodded. "I feel like we're who we were then and who we are now and everything I have been since I kissed you in the park that day means nothing."

"Me too." I didn't want things to go further, not yet, so I pulled away. "Do you want to go to church with me?"

He raised an eyebrow. "Can I wear what I had on yesterday?"

"Sure. Let's get going, the service at the Cathedral is at ten."

We parked in the back lot of Trinity Cathedral and lingered in the art gallery before the service. Next to me in the pew, Tom gazed upward towards the cross and his face relaxed. The cross gave me comfort in a wordless, nameless way. The recitations, the music, the choir, and the message that we were to love each other crept into my soul. The music's vibrations pulsated at my feet. Tom's body heat was felt through the fabric on my arm. My soul was still.

It felt right that Tom was there with me. We were looking for the same thing.

"I'm getting what I hoped for with the weather." The skies had become blue to the west.

Tom looked thoughtful. His eyes were on the tall corner bookcase between the two sets of windows. "You've made this place your own. When I sit here, I understand how you've changed and grown over the years." Paintings, including some of Mom's work, hung beneath track lighting. A tall cabinet on another wall was filled with memorabilia from my travels. His eyes fell on the Quebec Province materials next to the couch. "Are you going to Montreal?"

I sat down next to him. "Yes. In a couple of weeks. I haven't gone anywhere in a long time . . . and I'm looking forward to this trip. I need it."

"Doesn't it get lonely to travel by yourself?"

"No. I rather like it. I meet people. I kind of feel like a different person when I'm being a tourist and writing about it. It's like I'm an explorer and anything goes because no one knows me or is likely to see me again. It's total and complete fun."

He laughed. "You're funny . . . and I get it." He moved closer to me and put his arm around me and I leaned into him. "It feels like no time passed at all, but then you surprise me. You never would have done something like that when you were young."

"I'm not a kid anymore. But when we sit like this and my head finds your shoulder and then you reach for my hand like you just did, I'm still who I was then. We're still the same."

"Yes, we are."

"I've never been to Montreal."

He wanted to join me. I could tell. "Do you know Quebec City is the only city in North America that's walled?"

"Are you going there too? I'm jealous. I like the walled cities in Europe. The summer after law school we spent time in Germany and Austria and visited a lot of medieval cities. It's . . ."

"I'm sorry I missed those times with you."

He pulled me to him, gave me a hug. "I regret that too." He stood up. "Okay, I'm going to get going."

I sat outside in the sun and read all afternoon. Time went by without notice. That was exactly right. In the evening, I listened to Eric Clapton's *Unplugged* album, hearing "Layla, you have me on my knees." Eric loved her despite her being married to someone else; he loved her enough that he was brought to his knees.

I sat on my bed in that quiet room and in my trusty journal and wrote.

> When I kept Jerry a secret, it was the first time I struggled with sin. God's been there through it all with me, that all-inventive higher being that started life, the seed of God within everything, keeping the children being born and continuing to grow, lifting the fireflies from the ground into the night, starting the peach tree buds in the spring and the fruit to ripen in the summer, keeping Windy Hill productive, keeping it my home. God will take care of things until I make up my mind how I want to live, where I want home to be, but I have to let Him do it. That's where my absolution takes place.
>
> Part of the reason I don't want to tell Tom about the baby is the process of going through this all over again. I'm not sure I want

to look at what I did full on. As long as I keep it distant and don't really focus on it, I'm safe from it. I'm not able to tell Tom yet. I don't want to show him what I'm capable of, how deep my sin goes. That I was able to do what I did is a sign of just how sick I was.

And if home is where the heart is, my heart is opened at Windy Hill. I wouldn't have told Tom about Jerry if we hadn't been there. A different part of my heart is in Cleveland.

Wednesday night I stopped on the Mall to read. The light withered. I barely had time to say a prayer or complete a thought as the windows withdraw into grayness and the Mall become blanketed with shadows. Then fireflies filled the air. It was as if they were born of the dark air. They just appeared. Could they have been in the air all along and I didn't see them?

Impossible.

I reached out my hand and caught the one closest to me. When I opened my hand, it was almost still but crawling slowly toward my thumb, seeking a way out. That slowness was what made it easy prey. When the light lit, every 20 seconds or so, orange and white marks, like tattoos, surfaced on its wings. It reached the end of the world, the end of my hand, opened its wings and was off in its limpid flight.

I sat still and watched. I tried to count, then realized the way to experience this was to sit and let them be. I needed to just be. So we were, the fireflies and me, just being for a while.

When darkness came down in a cloak, the air chilled, and the fireflies vanished.

Like magic.

Max. He and I watched the fireflies hovering above our blanket. He was striving for the things he needed in life just like everyone else was, and he became sick. Cancer can be brought on my stress and grief, as any kind of death can, but I did what I had to do so he could continue through his life. He wasn't happy to see me go, but life doesn't always give us what we want.

Once, at night at the farm, when Cassie was twelve or thirteen, she twirled around and around in the backyard as her nightgown billowed around her, laughing out loud. Her waist-long hair twirled out around her and she was a fairy in the midst of a twinkling shower of fireflies. It made me want to cry to watch her, and I never understood why, until now, when I think about it. Fireflies reminded me of my girlhood, and it seemed impossible to grasp that feeling of being young and unencumbered.

    Windy Hill made me angry. It reminded me of a father who was not there, who was non-existent, a father who left my mother high and dry, who wasn't there for my mother, a woman who deserved so much more. I'd been angry for a long time. It was an anger that was ever–present and had always been. A part of me didn't want to know what my no-good Dago father had to say.

CHAPTER NINE – TRIPTIKS

Tom showed up at my office at noon ten days later when he came home from a business trip. We walked down E. Ninth Street and felt the strong cold wind from Canada on our faces. The city-made path wound along the water as if it was natural to end up under the eaves of the Rock and Roll Hall of Fame and Museum. Janis Joplin's flower-child car was behind the glass. We sat and looked out on the lake and he took my hand.

"There's something about the lake that takes me home," I said.

"I agree." He put his arm around me and we watched a ship make its way between the two lighthouses that stood watch at the mouth of the Cuyahoga.

My Montreal plans were complete, and I would be leaving soon. I felt guilty about going without him "I'm leaving tomorrow morning and returning on Wednesday afternoon. I feel like I should be asking you to go with me."

He hugged me closer. "I know. That's why I insisted on coming here today. I'm not going to let you run this time. It's okay. You need to take your notes and make discoveries and get it down on paper. It takes presence."

I was surprised that he understood the process so well, that he understood why I needed to go alone. "You're right, that's what I need. Yes, it takes a great deal of presence to get it right."

He took my hand and pulled me to my feet. We walked around the perimeter of Voinovich Park at the end of the E. Ninth Street Pier, then headed back up Ninth Street past the Science Center to the Stadium and back up the hill into downtown again.

"I really enjoy spending time with you," he said when we were standing outside my building. "I can't wait to see you again. We can't let what's holding you back keep us apart, all these years later."

I felt the baby between us. Like the elephant in the bedroom, the bull in the china cabinet, the lump in the breast, the ugliness in the midst of something that could be good.

"I'll still care about you, no matter what."

He made me feel hopeful. I kissed him on the mouth. Our faces close, I said, "Will you pick me up at the airport?"

"Yep." Then he kissed me deeply, right there on the street where anyone could see. I felt him watching me walk away.

I started my visit to Montreal, which I had just learned was on an island in the St. Lawrence River, by renting a car at the airport and driving up to Mount Royal, high above the City. It was a good climb in the Toyota Camry. I walked a path uphill to a 1923 chateau and the breathtaking view of the closely-built metropolis in all its glory with its bridges, churches, winding medieval streets and tall buildings.

My room was in Old Montreal, where the Basilique Notre-Dame de Montreal, built in the early 1800s, dominates. After settling into the French provincial room of blue and yellow stripes and florals against a white background, I put on a sturdy pair of walking shoes, slung a camera over my shoulder, packed a map, a guidebook, and a small notebook in my purse, and got lost in the city.

Although the city was distinctly French-influenced, its colonial and native past was acknowledged in its monuments and sites. When I came around the corner to find the imposing Basilique with its iron-wrought fence in the heart of the city, I could have been in Europe, yet I wasn't fooled into a feeling of being in France. It wasn't provincial enough.

I went through the big wooden doors and into the basilica. Like its namesake, the Basilique Notre-Dame de Montreal's ceilings were high, its pillars strong, the light dim, but the carved banisters and pillars were warmed by yellow light. The statues and woodwork, lit to full effect, were stunning. I walked the majestic blue floor up the middle aisle to the nave and stood at the foot of the steps that led up to the altar. Christ was strung above it all, crucified and spent. His mother wept at his feet and the women who supported him were dismayed. He was surrounded by saints, all of them carved from warm wood and enthroned by arches against a blue background. Figures filled naves, winged beings posed at the top of a winding staircase, angels wept, and the Lord's Supper solemnly took place.

I took pictures, wrote down inscriptions on my tablet, smelled the mustiness of age. Then I found a bench and prayed for a sign that it was time to get on with life, that Tom would be okay about me telling him the truth. A voice inside asked, *What do you need? A miracle? A sign from heaven?*

It was late in the day when I lost myself in the narrow and winding streets of Vieux Montreal. A walk down Rue Saint-Paul was a trip into the 17th century and an odd mix of oriental, Native American, Italian, French, Middle Eastern, and Mexican establishments. Along the Place de Jacques-Cartier, outside patios and displayed menu boards and street musicians provided amusement. I ate dinner while being entertained by a mime.

On the first floor of my hotel, I found a small pub that was founded over two hundred years ago. The old stucco walls and wood beamed ceiling, the low lighting provided by electric sconces along the walls and votive candles on the tabletops, and the long unadorned bar wooed me in for a cup of coffee. I sat down at the bar several stools away from a man reading a newspaper and asked for a cappuccino.

The bartender-barista was in his early thirties and wore a white collared shirt with the sleeves rolled up. His hair was short with a boyish colic above his forehead. He turned his back to me and poured dark coffee beans into the machine.

"What can you tell me about this place?" I said, notebook in hand.

"This was originally a storefront establishment with the owner's living quarters above, run by a ship captain from Britain," he began as he worked. "The first wing of the hotel opened in 1835. The rest of the hotel was added in the 1890s, and by then it changed ownership to a different Montreal family, which still owns it."

"That's amazing."

"It's the way a lot of things around here are. It's an old city with old families. The monastery down the street is ancient. This is a port city at heart."

I took notes as he went on about Montreal's role on the St. Lawrence Seaway and said, "It's so Lewis and Clark," which made the bartender laugh. He held out his hand, "I'm Jim."

"Betsy," I said and shook his hand.

The guy with the newspaper folded it in half on the bar and moved his glass toward the edge of the bar for another round. "Need anything else?" Jim asked as he poured the scotch.

The guy shook his head. He was dressed in a business suit but his tie was loosened and his dark styled hair was rumpled as if he'd been frustrated and ran his hands through it and it stuck. "No, I'm good. So you're new to Montreal?" he asked me.

His eyes were brown pools with lashes too long for a man. He was in his fifties but age had been kind to him, the creases at the corners of his eyes and his mouth only enhancing his dignity. There were a few strands of gray, but I had that much gray when I was thirty. "Yes, I am."

He moved over a seat, leaving one between us. "You need to go to a shopping menagerie in a converted warehouse and see the beautiful painted walls on some of the buildings. And check out the marketplace. Very old world." He spoke with an accent that sounded like hot summer days. "Are you a reporter?"

I looked at my notebook. "I don't think of myself that way. I'm writing a story for a travel magazine."

"Good for you. I like writers. There's no lying to them, if they're good, and they can't tell a lie either. "Manuel." He held out his hand.

I took it and said, "Betsy. Are you here on business?"

"Yes. I work for a company in my home country of Spain, and I come here six times a year."

"I've never been to Spain."

He raised his eyebrows. "Really? Well, you should go. The Spanish are not as welcoming as the Italians, but we're close." He went on to tell me about the places I should visit beyond Barcelona and Madrid, and I was glad I had my notebook. "So tell me," he said, "what magazine will this article you're writing about this wonderful city be in?"

"*Leisure Travel.* It's published in Cleveland, but is international in scope. I've been writing a couple articles a year for them over the last ten years. I'm the managing editor."

"Wonderful. I'll have to look up this magazine. Can you send me a copy of the Montreal article when it's completed?" He fished a business card out of his jacket pocket and handed it to me.

"Of course."

His hands were artistic. I'd always been attracted to romance-language accents, but Manuel's appeal was mostly due to his friendly sensitivity to the world and its people and places. "So, do you ever bring your wife with you on these trips?"

He laughed. "I am not married."

I shrugged. "I didn't see a wedding band, but that doesn't mean a person is single."

"Unfortunately, no, it does not," he said as he downed his drink. "Too many people make that commitment and do not stick to it. Such is an age-old problem." He looked at his watch, then at me. "It's midnight. That is late. I take it you are not married, right?"

"No, I'm not."

He fished some Canadian bills from a well-worn wallet and put them on the counter. "Coffee's on me."

"Thank you."

"Oh, you're very welcome. I asked if you were married because I was wondering if you'll be my companion for some exploration tomorrow."

"That would be fun."

Jim, who was overhearing the conversation, presented us with a list of places written on a cocktail napkin. "You should really check out the gardens in the atrium of the Sphinx and go out to the site of the Olympics to visit the Geodome's rain forests and arctic displays."

"That sounds interesting," I said, turning to Manuel to see if he agreed.

"It does." He picked up the napkin and thanked Jim. "Will you be here tomorrow evening?"

"Sure," Jim said.

"Then we'll come back and tell you all about our day," Manuel said.

We agreed to meet for breakfast. I spent a happy night in my well-appointed room and appeared in the dining room for the continental breakfast with damp hair. He stood up when I approached his table and pulled out my chair. I felt a bit embarrassed by the gesture, but after I had a cup of coffee and sat with him to go over his plans for the day, I relaxed. This was going to be easy—I would follow Manuel's itinerary.

We strolled along the waterfront at the Old Port, then headed into the streets of Vieux Montreal, winding down St. Paul through 17th century streets, on Rue de la Commune after a tour of the monastery. Our feet became tired as the sun set. We'd discovered parks and underground malls and streets much like those in any other large city, filled with people and cars and neon signs and big-name designers. Old Montreal felt much more welcoming after a day in the busy city. It was an enclave.

Jim was glad to hear how much we saw. Our discussion added more information to my notes. I showed Jim and Manuel the pictures I'd taken, the three of us leaning in close to each other.

Over the course of the day, I'd found Manuel to be an intelligent explorer. He appeared bookish with his wire rimmed glasses and 1970s hair, and his body had softened into middle age. He told me he didn't believe in working out—our forefathers never worked out!—he only believed in being active. We didn't really talk about anything personal, and that was a good thing. We enjoyed each other's company.

We ate sandwiches at the bar. "We must do this again tomorrow," he said.

"We must go to other places."

"I have tickets for Chekov tomorrow night."

"Chekhov! Do you want company?"

"Yes, of course. Will you come?"

I nodded with excitement, then left him to retire to our room. I wrote late into the night, and the next day, we covered the rest of the city before eating Italian food for dinner.

I had my favorite silk dress and jacket ensemble with me—it was perfect for any evening event—with high black heels with a strap over the ankle. It was cold enough that I left the leather jacket I'd worn over a sweater throughout the day in the hotel room and wore my long wool coat.

He kissed me on the cheek as we settled into our seats in the dark theater. Later, he gave my knee a squeeze--when this sort of thing happens, the relationship moves into a different orbit. Maybe I let it, I don't know. But in my head it was no longer a friendship but a sex thing. And I somehow can't meld them. It's ruined for me.

Back at the hotel, I allowed him to buy me a glass of wine at the bar. Outside the doorway to my room, he leaned in to give me a quick kiss.

I moved my body close to his and opened my mouth when I kissed him.

He stiffened and pulled away from me quickly. His eyes were pleading.

"What is it?" I said.

"What are you doing? I'm not a one-night-stand kind of guy."

I'd been leading this expedition, not him. "I'm sorry, I . . ."

"I like you. We had a great couple of days. But I do not want to sleep with you."

"That's not what I meant," I said. But I felt foolish.

"I'll meet you for breakfast at 9, okay? We can still hang out together."

I nodded and opened the door. He'd never meant to go in that direction with me and I had gotten there mostly on my own volition. "See you in the morning then." I saw his kind face looking at me as I closed the door.

I had been leading the show. No one was taking advantage of me. How many times in my life had I been the one moving things toward a sexual encounter and blaming it on the guy later when I felt it was all wrong?

I was glad to hear Tom's voice the next morning when I called him. The night had been harrowing. I was awake half the night wondering whether I'd really intended to let things go where they would, even if it wasn't what either he or I wanted. And how many times did I convince myself that there was a real connection and attraction when there wasn't?

I didn't know myself anymore. At least I felt like I didn't until Tom said "How's my girl?"

"Your best friend, I hope."

"That's what I like to hear. How's the trip going?"

"I met a man at the bar on Friday night and he and the bartender had all kinds of ideas, and this guy, from Spain, he'd been to Montreal before, so he showed me around the city. And he had tickets for a play last night, so we went together. It's been nice to have him around." As I told this to Tom, I knew I sounded guilty, and that he would catch it in my voice.

He did. "Did anything happen between the two of you?"

"Almost . . ."

He groaned. "What does that mean?" Then, when I didn't answer right away, he said, "It's none of my business, is it?"

"I think it is. That's why I felt I had to tell you instead of telling you a lie. These trips . . . this kind of thing always happen. I start out thinking the guy's company, but with the traipsing about, talking and walking, I sometimes think there's more between us than at first. Despite everything I tell people, I'm looking for meaningful relationships."

"It's what we all want."

"But for me, I'm looking for it anywhere but near home."

"You're looking for it knowing you won't find it. Doesn't that mean you don't really want it?"

"I don't want to do it anymore. It's funny to think it, but I think this is partly a result of Mom's harping on me to have a man in my life. And it's also . . . my confusion about what a meaningful relationship is—it's not built on sex."

"You got it. This is kind of a milestone for you, isn't it?"

"It's a revelation. What I don't get is that I didn't see it before. It was pretty obvious."

"Have you and this Spanish guy said good-bye for good?"

"No, but I'm not sure I want to see him. What do I do now? Do I meet him for breakfast?"

He hesitated for half a minute. "You should meet him and change the flow of things."

"How would you feel if I spent the day with him again?"

"I would hope that you would remember that I love you. And I think of you as my girl."

He loved me—he'd said it.

I knew it before he said it, yet I wasn't prepared for it to be said yet. It was right that he should love me. There was no reason for me to keep looking for someone, because I loved Tom. "I love you too."

If a smile could be in a voice, I heard it when he said, "We've always loved each other. It never stopped. And I'm not just talking about Eros love."

My stomach fluttered with butterfly wings. Now that our feelings for each other were out in the open, I felt the reality of my feelings for him welling up within me. It was enormous. "I don't feel so lonely knowing you love me."

"A great love will sustain you."

I felt like a boulder had been lifted off my heart. He loved me and it felt unconditional. I was astonished. I don't think I'd ever trusted the caring that keeps a couple honest. But here it was. Tom thought I was capable of being trusted.

Manuel rose from his chair to kiss my cheek when I met him for breakfast. We started talking right away about the day before and the day ahead of us, and I didn't feel the need to say anything about the evening before. We enjoyed our last day together. When I said good-bye, I felt I was saying good-bye to a friend, not running away from a lover who I was ashamed of. I felt we had a relationship. I felt whole.

I was in the shadow of the basilica when Manuel left in a taxi. Turning into the church, the air felt chilly. The sanctuary felt haunted, as if the suffering of Christ happened right within its walls. I looked up at Christ on the cross. There, in that magnificent cathedral, where mere men created art from wood and stone and gold, I felt an overwhelming need to cry. I fell to the lowest step that led to the cross, covered my eyes, and let the tears come. My chest was filled with aching loss and shame and guilt, but as I cried, the ache was replaced by lightness and clarity. When I looked up and pushed the hair away from my wet face, the beneficent Christ looked down at me, with pity. I'd been acting like a child, putting off what needed to be done, like an exam with no deadline. The deadline had arrived. It was time to do what needed to be done, once I found the words.

Cameras snapped around me, voices murmured, footsteps fell on the tiled floor. I was a stranger in Montreal, just some middle-aged woman crying for no reason at all.

I made my way to a pew and sat down. The way a wooden pew felt on my bottom came back to me, and I was at church next to my mother and grandmother, looking up at the plain wooden cross at the front of the sanctuary. I remembered the welling emotion brought on by prayers of hope and redemption, the promise of an afterlife, of Jesus' guiding light.

Restoration and clarity replaced the tears, and I felt stronger than I ever had. I let God enter me, and I entered Him. We were one.

I prayed. I thanked God for all I had—my homes, my family, my job, my talent, my healthy body, my friends. I prayed for forgiveness—for betraying Mom, for having an abortion, for leaving Tom, for giving up on my marriage too soon, for not being the mother I could have been, for giving too much to work. I prayed for new ways of looking at relationships—with men, with Tom, with my father, with Cassie, with friends. I prayed for direction and guidance—my home, my work, my life. Then I listened. I listened for God in what had become a silent and sacred space, and I felt His comforting touch. He was with me, and the tears came again. I'd been waiting a long time.

It had been years since I'd felt God's presence like that. I hadn't allowed Him to touch me, to come close, in a long time. The world felt more friendly when I went back into it.

Tom was waiting for me in baggage claim at Cleveland Hopkins International Airport when I got back from the trip. He held me close for a long moment then kissed me tenderly. I was glad to be home.

While we drove to my place in his car, he asked me how it had worked out with Manuel. I told him I'd gained a friend.

"Tell me," Tom said, squeezing my hand as he maneuvered out onto Route 237 heading north to I-71 toward Cleveland past car rental and car storage lots, "how does it feel to have things work out differently than usual?"

I hesitated. He looked over at me as if to say it was all right but his jaw was tense. I wanted him to know that it was only once in a while, sharing time with strangers who were fun to be with. "Good. It feels good."

He reached toward the radio and turned the channel. Dylan's "Lay Lady Lay" was playing and that always tore me up. I looked out the window at the streets of bungalows. I wiped at the tears on my face with the back of my left hand and when I laid it in my lap, Tom took it and caressed it. He had to feel my tears.

"You're not losing a part of yourself by changing your behavior."

I didn't care that wet black lines were streaming down my face when I looked over at him. I knew Tommy wouldn't care. My lower lip stretched over my top lip when I nodded. Looking out the front window at the highway and Cleveland's landscape rising from the riverbed, I said, "I liked that they thought I was someone they wanted to be with, even if only for a short while. That I could have these men, that it was possible, I wanted to know that. I needed to know it. It makes me feel beautiful and interesting."

He held onto my hand a little harder.

I let out a small sob, choking on my tears. "But I always knew, at least I thought it was the case, that they wanted me in make believe, but not in real, at least that's what I thought. They were not real, and what we did together wasn't real. It was easy to simply write about my time in whatever place I was as if I was all alone. But I always had this secret, that I'd spent time with someone who found me enticing, who made it seem like there was a possibility of more. I liked the secrecy of it."

"Just like with Jerry."

I nodded when he looked over at me. "Isn't it weird that I wanted to have these secret relationships that no one else could touch, that no one else could know, except for me and the guy I'd been with?" I didn't give him time to answer. "Once, I think it was my second travel writing trip, when I went to the Yucatan Peninsula, I was with a guy who was a few years younger than me, a guy who'd never been married before. When I said good-bye to Carlos, he wouldn't let me walk to the gate in the airport until I promised to call him as soon as I got home. He wanted to visit me in a couple of weeks, and was already trying to figure out if he could live in Cleveland. I told him I wasn't planning to call him, not ever again. It had been just for that week. He was astonished. Then he was angry. He called me a whore so loudly that people turned to look. I felt their eyes on me, and I felt his hot anger. It shook me up.

"That should have been a wake up call. But it wasn't. My mother used to say I did it because I make the assumption that all men are bad, not worth pursuing a long relationship with, I'd only get hurt. She said I had to let down my guard and let love in. I listened, but I have never really believed that love would be there for me."

"Only you know what's in your heart," Tom said when I was done with that speech. "But I think your mother was probably right. You were protecting yourself from being hurt."

We were entering downtown. I reached into my purse for my keys. "You know, unless one's married to someone for the rest of their life, isn't it true that every relationship they've had has turned out badly?" I was overwhelmed. "How come everything's so mucked up? Why did I marry Rick who wasn't right for me and then meet Max when he wasn't available?"

"Why does a young woman who appears to be in love with her boyfriend all of a sudden end it at the end of the spring semester?"

That was mean. I turned away from him.

"Why does a middle-aged man decide he wants to have sex with a mere girl? That's the main question here, don't you think? As far as your sex life is concerned?"

"That first sexual experience taught me that when a man wanted me, that meant I was beautiful."

"Yep, it does, but that's only a small part of beautiful."

"I know that."

"Do you?" There was a challenge in his voice.

I sighed. He parked the car in the visitor's lot, popped the trunk, and opened up his door. He was already standing on the curb with my suitcase when I got out of the car. The sky was an early-winter gray and it was starting to get cold outside with the onset of evening. I was still surprised by how early darkness fell.

I came up next to him and put my arm around him to give him a hug. "How can you love me?"

He shook his head. "Why do you ask such questions? Come to think of it, you've always asked me questions like that. I remember having a pretty good argument about it."

It had been a few months into our relationship, and we were in the pattern of sleeping together either at his place or mine, together every night. We were happy in love. I loved every single thing about Thomas Edward Madison, right down to the way the hairs curled on his forearms. His kisses were a balm, his hands calmed me. I fell asleep with my head on his shoulder and woke with his body spooning around mine, his arms holding me tight. One morning I'd woken up feeling totally glad I had him, but it didn't feel like it could be real. How could this man who was so good to me be mine? So I asked him how he could possibly love me. He flipped out. He was so angry that I really did think I was mistaken to think I was his, that he loved me. He couldn't love me if he could get that angry with me.

"I remember. I thought you couldn't love me if you could get that angry with me."

We were standing on the sidewalk on West 9th Street and he put his hands on my shoulders and his forehead against mine and looked into my eyes in the dusky light and said, "It was the opposite, of course. I loved you so much it made me angry that you thought I didn't."

I wanted to say he wasn't thinking straight because look at how I'd left him and gone to Rick, how I wouldn't go out on a second date when we were kids, how I'd slept with a couple dozen strangers. That wasn't a person he could love. Why would he love that person that was me?

Somewhere on my life's journey I'd learned that there are times when it's best to keep one's mouth shut.

He still had his head against mine and it was starting to hurt. I realized he was waiting, so I said, "I love you, just because. I just love you."

"Love doesn't need to be explained. It's not cerebral. It's emotional. This time, let me love you. Please."

My smile was his answer. He kissed me lightly on the lips and picked up the suitcase.

"Would you like to stay here tonight?"

He smiled at me, put the suitcase on the sidewalk, and opened up the trunk once more. His overnight bag was inside. "Not that I was planning on this . . ."

"Yeah, right," I said, as I took his bag from him and took his hand in mine. We walked with our bags to the door of my building and once we were in the elevator, I said, "I can't wait to make love to you again."

"When we're ready, we'll know."

"We're not ready yet," I said when I hit the button for the third floor.

"You know we aren't. We have some things to work out."

He knew about the baby. What else could I be keeping from him? He was waiting for it to all evolve like it needed to. He was waiting for the universe's plan to unfold. I fell asleep with my head on his shoulder and woke with his body spooning mine. It felt like it had years before. Almost.

I returned to work the next day, and it felt like I'd been gone for weeks. Every person in my group had a problem that needed to be resolved. I worked quite late, until ten. It was always like this when I was gone for a few days; I was overwhelmed by work when I got back. Rather than eating, because it was too late to eat, I started to write my article about Montreal. We decided the photos I took would work out well enough. My newfound friend was in every sentence because he was in every place I went. He was part of my story of Montreal. I couldn't use "we" without him.

> We walk down Rue Saint-Paul, a trip into the 17tth century where Mexican sweaters, Arabian rugs, European leather, and Native American pottery vie for shoppers' attention. The eclectic mix of shops is eye candy for shoppers and a bottomless cash register for tourists. I cover my face with a Mardi Gras mask and become new while my companion sniffs fresh basil at the Italian market. Maitre d' from the restaurants spill onto the streets, luring some hungry people into restaurants open to the street. The sound of tambourines and kettle drums fills the air on one block while an accordion player makes German love songs on the next. We continue our stroll to the Old Port, then head into the streets of Vieux Montreal, winding down narrow Saint Paul to Rue de la Commune. Above Vieux Montreal, the Basilique Notre-Dame de Montreal stands as a sentinel, a reminder that God is in the details and provides guidance to those who care to acknowledge Him.

I put a copy of the story, which included crisp pictures of the sites we'd visited, in an 8-1/2 by 11-inch envelope to the address outside Barcelona I found on Manuel's business card.

CHAPTER TEN – GREEN RIBBONS

I was doing some work at home and there were papers all over the desk when Tom called me a couple evenings later.

"Well, that's a voice I love to hear!" His jolly voice boomed in.

I laughed. "You're in a good mood."

"Oh, I guess I am. It's funny how the people on the board of the preservation society affect me. They're interesting people who know a lot about history and architecture and all the goings-on about town, things I wouldn't know because I live there without children in the school system or attending church."

"It's great that you have that."

"It gets me out. Hey, are we still going out to Conneaut this weekend?"

"Sure. I haven't changed my mind. I've spent the week wondering why I work in downtown Cleveland when my family's homestead is sixty miles east of it."

I could almost hear him smile. "I'm glad we're going out there."

"My father's letters to my mother are sitting here on the table. I think I'll take them with me tomorrow."

"Oh, you're going tomorrow?"

"Yes."

"Then I'm not going with you? I thought we had a plan for Sunday."

I felt a rising excitement within me. I wanted to have him with me, but I knew I needed time alone. "Yes, we do have a plan for Sunday, but I want to go earlier."

"I like the idea of going together, the drive out there. And I want to be there with you when you're there."

I didn't respond at first. "You wouldn't be taking me for granted, would you?"

His voice was serious when he said, "I'd never do that. I'm glad you're back in my life and I want to keep it that way."

I needed to hear that. "Why in the world did you make a move with me at Kent when I'd been so mean to you before?"

"I couldn't help myself. I decided you were worth the pain of rejection."

"I'm glad I didn't reject you."

"Me too. I'm not sure that second rejection was worth it, though."

I heard pain in his voice. It was unexpected.

"When your mother took you away on vacation that summer, for a whole month, which was kind of weird, I started hanging out at your pond. Your grandparent's pond, the one your mother called the Magical Pond, and you know what?"

"What?"

"I set up camp there. My father didn't know where I was spending nights. He thought I had a girl. My mom worried about me. I . . . I stayed there for about six weeks. I stopped going to work, grew a beard, didn't change my clothes, missed the start of Fall semester, just sat and felt the dragonflies whir around me, heard the frogs plop into the water, watched the fish swim in their circular paths, and waited for the fairies. I remember your mother talking about those fairies as if they were real.

"I had some books. I read all the works of Shakespeare I hadn't already read, then *Beowulf* and Spencer's *The Faerie Queen* and for some reason, much of Proust, which I never finished. Who could finish Proust? And I walked some, baseball cap on my head, jeans rolled up, along the beach. Later, closer to the time I went back to school, I saw you and Rick. I saw you wrapped around each other on a blanket. You were happy without me. You laughed. I didn't remember that you ever laughed when you were me. Did you?"

It was painful to hear him talk about this, but I didn't want him to know it. "I'm sorry. I didn't know. I was dealing with my grief."

"Grief about me?"

The truth is that there was a baby. And the baby is gone. Tom has already lost one baby.

A car door closed and there was rustling on his end of the telephone. How had I been able to get rid of a baby and not tell him? I liked to think that wasn't me, but it was. And that thing I said about not being good enough . . . that was an excuse I was holding onto, the rape a reason for my behavior. I was trying to sort out how I thought about myself, whether I still thought that I was not good enough for Tom but just right for Rick. I still thought that way, that I wasn't good enough for anyone, that I was nothing but a whore. I couldn't answer him.

"I . . . was a whore," I said quietly. "And now I need to go. I'll talk to you tomorrow, okay?" I didn't wait for his answer, simply hung up.

I walked to the window and looked at the lights along the River, blue and yellow lights reflected in the water. I took a deep breath and stepped back onto my yoga mat to do my version of Tree. My focus point was the smokestack of the Powerhouse, high above the rest of the rooftops of the Flats, and I stood on my right foot, arms spread on either side of my head, for at least ten minutes. Breathe in, breathe out, my breath came slow and deep and by the time I shifted my weight to my left foot, the painful discussion was behind me. "I'm not a whore," I chanted before pulling out my journal to write.

> What is a place called Home? Is a home a place where secrets reside, where relationships falter, where Truth is raw? Or is it a place wrapped up in bows and ribbons, driftwood sculptures, stories read in a porch swinging at the edge of a farmhouse porch? Better yet, is it a place one calls one's own, where windows look out on a crooked river from a place that used to be a place of commerce? Or is Home within the heart, a place that travels along when one walks through the weeping branches of a willow, along the railroad tracks leading to an abandoned factory, or past the windows of a gay toy store?
>
> These things I write are pebbles along the road, a glimpse of a journey, but what are they worth, to me, to anyone? My life will mean little if I leave it without leaving a trace, for someone who cares.
>
> Questions . . . am I learning to love the questions themselves? Maybe. Home was with me as I traveled, on my journey, and home is the place of truth.
>
> Talking to Tom about why I married Rick, I now know that I made a judgment that I was good enough for Rick but not good enough for Tom. I was a lowly no-good not worthy of Tom's love. I was a whore. What a strong word that is, and why did it come to me today, so perfect for the situation that I said it out loud?
>
> Not only do I not believe in adultery, I don't believe in sleeping

around. Yet I do.

Tom's car was in the driveway at Windy Hill when Pedro and I returned from the milk plant on Saturday afternoon. He sat on the front porch drinking a beer and wearing a T-shirt and jean shorts. He raised the bottle to me as I climbed out of the pickup.

I paused on the top step of the stairs that led to the porch. "What do you think you're doing?"

"Waiting for you." He patted the seat next to him on the swing.

I walked over and sat next to him. "I told you I wanted to be here without you today."

"I know. But I sensed you needed me." He pulled me to him and kissed the top of my head.

"I have some things I want to do, alone." My voice rose in anger, not what I intended. "I have my father's letters."

He pulled away from me. "You really don't want me here, huh?"

I sighed. "You said you would never take me for granted."

He took a last swig of his beer. "It's easy to fall into the rhythm of being together."

"We're not kids anymore."

"Should I leave?" The bottle hit the porch hard when he put it down. He stood up and walked to the other side of the porch. "I can leave." He turned around with his arms crossed.

Irritation tickled my skin. "I need some time."

"You weren't a whore then, and you're not a whore now."

I shrugged, and looked away.

"You have to forgive yourself. You can't let regret and anger get in the way of who you are today. I'm sorry the conversation turned out the way it did the other night."

"Me too."

"I needed you to know what I went through that summer."

"There's a selfishness to that."

"I admit that."

"I didn't like who you were."

"I'm not sure I like you when you feel bad about yourself."

"Maybe you should leave." I looked up into his face to see his reaction. I was so undone by him being there, I didn't know what to say.

"If that's what you want."

"I don't really want that. Let's pick apples," I stood up from the swing. He followed me out to the orchards. Eventually he took my hand. We passed a dozen workers, a couple men, a couple women, and some teenagers, families with brown skin and warm eyes.

"Hola," I greeted a young woman near the southern end of the orchard who was up on a ladder carefully picking apples. She was in her early thirties, her hair wound up in a scarf, wearing jeans and a T-shirt that said "Smile!" on it. *"Como estas?"*

"Muy bien," she said. She had a timid, shy way of responding to me, as she looked down from her ladder. *"Y tu?"*

"Mucho bueno. How long have you been coming to the States?"

"Two years."

"Where are you from?"

"Guatemala."

"That's a long way away."

"Si," she replied. "But we're happy here."

"I'm glad," I replied, thinking about the hard trip through Mexico and across the Rio Grande. The journey was probably a painful, dangerous, and desperate one. "I'm glad you're here."

"We'll get our money tomorrow, Pedro say."

I nodded. "If I don't see you again, good luck."

I felt Tom squeeze my hand. "The journey. Isn't it amazing how different the journey through life can be? And we have no control over how it starts."

"Or even, sometimes, over how it ends." I nodded to the men in the other trees, held out a hand to one of the young boys. Turning back to Tom, I said, "When Pedro and I drove to the dairy, we saw some new vineyards. It seems like there are more all the time."

"I'm glad the winery business has picked up in Ohio."

"I hear that if you can grow peaches, you can grow grapes," We started picking apples toward the back of the orchard. "Growing grapes would take a lot of effort," I said, after a while. I was up on a ladder while Tom held it for me.

"I thought you weren't going to keep the place." Tom eyed me with a smile.

"You'd have to learn where to plant the vines, how to space them, how to trellis them—"

"How to prune them, how to keep them from the frost." I handed him a basket and he emptied it into the crate on the ground and handed it back. "These apples are going to start falling to the ground. You'll need to harvest them all this weekend."

"We need to set up the stand by the road tomorrow."

"'We'? You're being awfully presumptuous." He took a sip of water. "I could get into this, living on the land."

I shook my head. "My grandparents struggled to make a profit, and it was easier then than it is now. I'm lucky we're making any money now."

"I wonder what it takes to just farm."

"It takes more attention than I give to Windy Hill."

He nodded. "Good thing you have a faithful caretaker.

"We can't keep up like this for long. It's not going to work over the long run. I'm actually thinking about selling the cows and keeping the orchards and fields."

"But this is a dairy farm."

"It doesn't have to stay that way."

I caught his eyes on me. What was he thinking with that grin? "What?"

"It doesn't sound like you're planning to sell the place."

"I'm just letting the question sit."

"And ripen. Before you know it you'll have a full-blown plan for what to do with this property. Ready to get back to it?"

"Yep." We walked over to the tree where we left off and I climbed the ladder. "I already don't spend time with friends much. What would I be like if I was out here on the farm?"

"Maybe your neighbors would become friends. I don't have many friends because I've been too busy with work and the family. I feel I've gotten to the point where it's the people and connections that matter. I don't have any guys I can call and say, 'hey, come over and watch the football game with me.' I wish I did."

He sure was different from Rick, who couldn't stay home. "I feel the same way. I feel like I can't keep living this way."

"Things are livelier when there's someone else in your life." He looked thoughtful, and then anger flashed in his eyes. "I was never bored when I was with you." The sun was getting low on the horizon to the west. I counted to ten to keep myself from screaming. When I looked back at him, he had a strange look on his face. "I know. I was complete when I was with you. I destroyed it."

He didn't have time to answer. "Yoo hoo," my daughter's voice carried on the wind up the lane.

"Yoo hoo!" I responded. As I started down the ladder, Cassie walked towards us with Beth on her hip. I held out my arms to hug them. Cassie looked Tom's way, so I went over to stand next to him and reintroduced them to each other.

"Are y'all having fun?" Cassie asked with a country twang to her voice. "Ya know, these guys out here, they have their dirt bikes and snowmobiles and chewing tobacco and 'spect their women to be good, else they git a beatin'."

Tom laughed heartily, then shook his head. "Where'd you get that sense of humor?"

Cassie laughed. "Oh, I don't know. I try to lighten things up. I think it caught up to me in motherhood but I learned to talk like a hick when I was in college."

"Not only did she come home with a bit of a West Virginia hillbilly accent but with tales of tipping cows on the weekends in the Appalachian hills," I said as I took the baby into my arms. I ran my hand through Beth's wispy white-blond hair. She was wearing a pair of blue-jean overalls with a long-sleeved T-shirt and little red sneakers. She turned to look at me, her eyes inquisitive.

"Wow," Tom said under his breath. "The baby's adorable. So—"

"Interested." I could tell he meant to say something like that too. "So," I turned to Cassie. "What's up?"

"I needed more apples for some pies I'm baking for the women's group at church."

"Cassie lives only about ten minutes away," I explained to Tom. He moved closer to me and put his arm around me. Cassie noticed—how could she miss it? Everything was going to be all right. "I thought we'd look through the letters from my father."

"Interesting," Cassie responded.

"I'm a little nervous about it."

"You might have to let go of some of your anger to get through the letters," Tom said.

Cassie smiled. "We should be angry. She lied to us all those years."

"She was angry he was gone, but she never seemed to look for him," I said. "Well there's a reason for that. He was right here, writing to her all along." Tom took Beth from me, held her out in front of him and made her dance. She chortled, and we all laughed.

"You would think she would have written about that in her journals," Tom said.

"I'm getting hints."

"Well I hope you two solve the mystery. I need to get going." Cassie took Beth from me and I gave the baby a kiss. She turned to Tom. "I have a feeling I'll see you again."

"If your Mom will settle down enough to consider it."

Cassie smiled as if she knew exactly what he meant, turned, and waved a hand good-bye.

He watched my daughter walk away. "She's beautiful. Did you ever wonder what our children might have looked like?"

I felt like I'd been picked up by that funnel cloud and blown away. I wanted to turn away from that question that held more pain than Tom could know. "Yes, I wonder that all the time." *I wonder what the baby we had conceived looked like, the baby who would have been his first born, and mine.*

"Are you okay?" He looked concerned.

"Yes, of course. I'm here at home, the apples are ripe, the weather's great, and Cassie's being nice to me."

The trees and baskets turned to muted gray in the darkening evening. The air took on a quality of cool wetness after a humid day. The apples were stacked in crates on the back of the flatbed trailer hooked up to the tractor. Pedro walked through the orchard declaring the days' work done, and the workers dispersed. I approached Pedro when he got close. "So how's it going?"

"Almost done. I think we'll be finished up by noon tomorrow."

"Good job."

"I will sell the apples to WayFarer's Grocers on Monday. You should make some money. It is a good crop."

"I don't know what I'd do without you."

He smiled shyly and tipped his hat to me. *"Hasta la vista."*

At the house, I rummaged through the pantry and refrigerator and found the staples of dry fettuccini and jarred pasta sauce, even some parmesan. We opened a bottle of Sangiovese with dinner. Afterwards, I put the bundle of letters on the table. "We start with the first one and read all the way through."

He nodded. "Are you sure you want to share this with me?"

"Seeing as I can't get rid of you . . ." I was only half joking.

He put his hand on mine. "I think I'll go into the other room, read a book." He half rose, but I stopped him by holding on tight. I wanted him to share this with me. I couldn't do it alone. "I'm afraid to do this alone."

I undid the green ribbon, gave Tom the top envelope, and opened the second envelope in the stack. I began to read.

My love,

How are you today? Are you thinking about me?

I love the way you look at me when I'm getting ready to kiss you. Your eyes get moist like something special's going to happen and you can hardly contain yourself. I feel the same way when I look at you, and that's why I can't help myself—I have to kiss you, again and again, a hundred kisses until you tell me to stop.

I miss you. I can hardly stand it, I miss you so much.

Life is so normal here but so different. In Cleveland, I was in the city, here the neighbors are down the road. In the city, people were always about doing things, here the afternoon meals go on and on until we almost fall asleep with the food and wine, our bellies full for the work to come in the late afternoon. It's a slower pace, more gentle, but harder too.

I'm not sure this was a good idea to come here. You should have come with me. The harvest will go slowly, I'm afraid. It already is—when will those grapes ripen, already? I need to get back to you.

This is written while my mother calls me to dinner, and I cannot leave her waiting. I hope that when I post this tomorrow, one from you will have arrived.

Take care, my Margie. Until we feel each others' souls again, remember I am with you, always.

Your Rafe.

I gave it to Tom to read. Tom read the letter all the way through, then looked up at me. "He loved her, he missed her. He shared his life with her in these letters. He's planning to come back, maybe mostly for her."

I nodded. "I know, that's what I thought too."

"I don't hear any deception here."

"Me neither. Something must have happened."

"Well, let's find out," he said, and he picked up the next letter as I put the first two in their envelopes and turned them down on the table. I took the letter from his hand and scooted my chair next to his and I read the next one out loud.

Margie:

My father has become ill. Mi familia expects me to stay here in Italy after the summer ends. The olive trees are full of fruit, the vineyards are full of grapes and soon we will all be in the orchards and vineyards doing the work my family has done for generations. We will sing as we press the oil from the olives and the juice from the grapes and we will be glad for the Lord's bounty. I love this land, this work, more than I love making coffee for the Americanos, but I cannot forget that you are waiting for me. You have stolen my heart, bella. I wonder if you would like this life here in a place where it never snows and summer is eight months long. I wonder if I could convince you to come here, to be with me. I miss you.

In your letter you seemed anxious for my arrival and I am not leaving for two months. You must be patient, my love. This may be a test for our love—is it real or is it not?

We know the answer to that, of course. Never has my body known such delight, my mind such solace, as when I am with you. My heart stops a beat when I see your lovely face. And you are not like most American women; you are without prejudice. And you are a student and will be your whole life. These are the things I love about you. I love those things, but I also love you.

We're having trouble with my father being sick and it's a worry that he is going to die and in need of a head of household. This is the Italian way, the next generation taking over as the last one ends. I am a man of tradition as well, but here my life is limited by the traditions that make the son's life a mirror copy of his father's. Here in Italy, they love to talk.

Do not worry that I will not return. I will. For you, if not for a new way of life.

With the greatest of love, your Rafe.

When I finished reading the letter, Tom was looking at me. I shook my head and picked up the next letter and handed it to him to read. The letter contained more information about living in Italy. My father wrote about walking along a Roman wall, accompanying his brother to Florence to see an art exhibit, and making the family wine.

"It sounds like he was pretty connected with his roots," I said.

"But yet he professes his love for your mother every chance he gets."

"I'd like to know what she had to say. He tells her not to worry about him not coming back. Was she worried? He reassures her he loves her, but does she love him?"

"It's weird to read only one side of things."

The fifth letter was short. He had been to Umbria with his mother, and his father was doing better.

The sixth letter, which Tom read, was long and winding, with details of his father's relapse, his family's needs, the homestead's harvest, the hard work that his brother and he had to take over, and his sister's upcoming marriage. At the end of the letter, Rafe Paglia said, "I love you, you know that. But I must stay here through my sister's wedding. Please come to me and meet the family and be part of the wedding. Otherwise, I fear I will not see you until the new year."

"There we are. Mom definitely knew she was pregnant by now. And she's not traveling to Italy. I wonder when she told him?"

Tom handed me the next letter, dated a month later. There was anger and recrimination, questions about why she didn't come and whether she still loved him. There was selfishness, too, an assumption that Mom would have had the means to make a long trip like that. She was a student and daughter of a farmer, and she would not have had the money. "She didn't tell him," I said.

"Doesn't sound like it."

That was the last letter from Italy. I poured us some more wine. "It's six months later when he sent her this letter, from Cleveland. I was already born," I said as I picked up the next one. In it, he tried to get her to meet him. He was back in Little Italy working at his uncle's place. He still didn't know I had been born.

"Why didn't she tell him?" I asked.

"She must have decided she didn't want to be with him."

"Then why not tell me she decided she didn't love him rather than making me believe he deserted us? Why make him look bad?"

"I think she was angry with him," Tom said. "Look, this next letter is another six months later." He opened it and read through it. "Here you go. He says,

> We had a baby together, Margie. A baby. A cute little girl you named Elizabeth. If I hadn't run into you at the market, would you ever have told me? How could you keep this from me?
>
> I loved you so much, more than I thought I could love anyone, and you have decided it's over, that we can't be a family. Why? Why not try to be a family? Why not let me spend time with my daughter? I could love you again, Margie. You could love me, I know you could, if you'd just stop being so angry with me.

"She was angry with him for staying in Italy so long," I said. "She would have taken that to be a sign that he cared more about his family than about her. And then she decided to punish him."

"Didn't she tell you she had been totally in love with the guy?"

"All I can think is that she was so angry with him, the love went away. You know how that goes, the thin line between love and hate. She had to deal with her parents, and she was forced to drop out of school, stay at home, and be a mother. Her whole life changed. Gone were her hopes and dreams. So, in her mind, my father DID abandon her."

"I can't understand why she didn't allow you to know him."

I picked up the rest of the letters. They were from Cleveland and Cleveland Heights, a batch of four within three months of the last one, then strung out to once a year until I was about twenty. He kept up the correspondence. "I think she was also angry with him that she got pregnant in the first place, that he put her in that position. It makes me feel like she never wanted me to be born," I stood up to pace.

"We know that's not true," Tom said. "Your mother doted on you."

"She hated that she was a single mother."

"If she hated it that much, why didn't she allow your father to make it legitimate?"

"You know Mom—she was stubborn."

We read a few more that went on in the same way. As I got older, my father asked more about the details of me growing up and told her about his own family; he eventually got married and had children. "She was selfish," I said. "I have brothers." I let that sink in. Brothers who knew my father, who grew up with him. "My brothers had both a mother and a father."

"That doesn't mean they've had a happy life. Maybe that was part of why she didn't want you to know—you had brothers that she knew you'd be curious about, would be jealous of, would want to meet. It was simpler this way. And your grandparents were pillars of the community and had a daughter who'd done what she'd done—it was easier to make every one think your mother was a victim."

"I suppose that makes more sense than that she was selfish. I've never thought of her as selfish."

"It was pretty unselfish of her to make sure the letters were all together and give you a chance to find them and find out who your father is."

"That was cowardly."

Tom looked at me over the top of his glasses. "To Truth." Tom raised his glass.

"To Truth," I touched his glass with mine and we sipped. I used to believe the truth will set you free. Now I believed the truth will get you in trouble. The truth will destroy your future. The truth will imprison you. "To only telling the truth when it won't hurt someone."

"That's hedging. And it's not the truth."

I let it go. My mother was angry, my father was mollifying. He was angry, but it was a calm anger, a resigned tone underwriting every word he put on paper.

"Do you think it would have been better if you'd known the truth?"

"I think the truth was in the fireflies we chased in the backyard, in the kittens that mewed around the barn, in the color of the sunset, and the way the daffodils came up every spring. I think Mom felt that creating a truth of goodness and fine living was more important than a truth that hurt."

"How was the truth going to hurt?"

"She thought it would be better if I believed my father was in Italy and unknown than if he were in our backyard so to speak, and not with us. Like you said—she kept up appearances."

"That's crap, and you know it."

I took the dirty glasses into the kitchen. While I stood at the sink rinsing them, he came up behind me, put his hands on my shoulders, then ran them down my arms before looping his arms around me in a big hug. His face was next to my neck. "You smell good." He paused. "Do you know you smell the same as you did when you were a girl?"

"What do I smell like?"

"Faintly sweet but musky, warm and perfumed, clean."

"I smell musky and clean?"

"Yep." He kissed my ear and pulled away. "I don't want to rush things."

I turned around. He was close. I stepped up to him and put my arms around his neck. I think I surprised him with the kiss. If I'd wanted to get laid, that was a kiss that would do it. But that's not what I wanted, so I pulled away too.

"That was something." He smiled.

The next day, we drove up to Tom's parents' home so we could take them to church with us. People greeted us like prodigal children. It felt like I'd never left home. This time, instead of Tommy, Linda, and his parents sitting in pews behind me, I was sitting with them. Cassie came in and sat with us too. I missed Mom and Ben. People I didn't know told me how glad they were that I was home again and how much Mom was missed.

We drove the highway along the lakeshore from Conneaut to Cleveland in our separate cars and I waved to him as he continued on to Vermilion. Tom was leaving in the morning for a trial in Milwaukee.

My cat doesn't like it when I go away, but she really doesn't like to be in the car either. When I let myself into the condo, she was against my legs in the doorway, threatening to trip me, and followed me down the hallway to the kitchen, wrapping herself around my legs the whole way. Her bowls were empty, which was part of her enthusiasm.

I did what I'd been wanting to do since Tom and I finished reading the letters. I pulled out a Cleveland-area residential phone book and looked up Raphael Paglia. There he was, the only Paglia in the phone book, at the address in Cleveland Heights I recognized from his later letters. My father was not far away. I stared at his phone number for a long time. I wondered if he knew Mom had died. I wondered what I would say if I called him. I wondered whether it would be an intrusion.

A father. How does one begin a relationship with the man who made you, the man who your mother was angry with and didn't want you to know? How does one begin to ask all the questions, like why didn't he insist on being in my life?

When I was six or seven I asked my mother if she'd tried to reach my father. She said she hadn't, there was no point. He was dead to her, and in the thirty seconds from when she said that to her next breath, she said I didn't have a father. Her voice escalated as she asked me why I would want a father anyway. She gave me that mean, piercing look she had sometimes, times when I crossed the line into something I didn't know. I didn't ask again.

I unpacked my bags from the weekend, started some laundry, sorted the mail from Friday and Saturday. It was a cloudy evening, and the sun came through the windows with dullness. There was no sunset. I picked up the book I was reading, *You Remind Me of Me*, by local writer Dan Chaon, and put my feet up on the footstool as I sat in my leather chair. The cool water I'd poured for myself tasted of lemon. A breeze came through the window off the Lake.

An hour later, restless, I put on my shoes, grabbed a jacket, and left the apartment. The wind was picking up, gathering for rain. I walked down my street, past the bars that spilled out onto the sidewalks, quieter than usual on a Sunday evening. When I got to Superior, I girded myself for a walk over the double-layered bridge over the river. I felt the pull on my legs, the wind in my lungs and my hair, and the energy my body picked up as I walked. At the end of the bridge, I turned to walk onto the Superior Viaduct, passing Spaces gallery, the county engineer's building, and Ponte Vecchio restaurant. I was standing on the opposite side of the river, looking across at the building I lived in, and darkness had settled in. The wind picked up and I felt the spray of the first drops of rain.

Done walking, I took a deep breath. I wanted to meet my father. I wanted to find out what was going on in my mother's head. I knew I wanted those things even as I knew I wanted to be right where I was, hanging above the river and looking out past the train bridge to the roiling lake whose white-capped waves I could see even in the gathering darkness. *It's sort of like hiding out, being here where no one in the world knows where I am. I need the magical pond and the barn with the cows, but instead I have this. I can be at home here.*

I turned to pass the restaurant and condos. At W. 25th Street, I looked up at the rising bridge and climbed it again. At the top, I stopped and looked again out to the lake and my face became wet with the rain that was gathering volume. Lights from warehouses and a few cars lit the river, and it twinkled. I could be at home anywhere, really. But the home I was looking for was a place of peace within. Finding Rafe Paglia would help with that.

He was a teacher, a writer, a dreamer. He was a lover with family in Italy, whom he probably still loved. He would be a good person to know, even if it felt distant between us. I wasn't sure I wanted to find out if that awkwardness would be between us, but it was worth the risk. I didn't really think it was a risk at all—his letters told me enough to know he was a good person. I would call him, soon.

I was almost running by the time I got to the bottom of the bridge. I slowed to a walk and turned back onto my street. Chairs had been folded and stacked against the tables of the Warehouse District eateries and bars. Doors were closed now, shuttered against the rain.

In my condo, Winifred was every bit as loving as she'd been the first time I'd returned that evening. I bent down to pick her up and held her tight, rubbing my thumb against the top of her head. I soon felt her purr against my chest. I set her down on my bed and stripped off my clothes. For the first time in many years, I looked at myself naked in the mirror. My hips were developing bulges just behind my hip bones and my breasts were lower but still firm. I held them in my hands and brought them up higher, looking at my wide eyes while I felt their weight.

My nakedness had always embarrassed me. Although I lived alone, I never walked around naked. Quickly, I slipped between the sheets and picked up my journal from the nightstand.

> I still want to wander when I need to work something out. The wandering is also a hiding out, I now know. I think the reason it bothers me is it feels driven like when a person needs a drink or needs to get out of the room before she explodes. It's not just "I feel like going for a walk and it's a nice evening." It's more like "I have to get out of here right now and I don't care where I go, I just have to go."

I walked across the bridge to the other side of the river tonight. When I stood at the end of the Superior Viaduct, I thought about the father I've never known whose name I found in the phone book tonight. He is a good man, based on his letters, and finding him and talking with him, even if that's as far as our reunion goes, is worth the risk of it going badly.

His green-ribboned letters tell only part of the story, but I think the story is all there—Mom was all alone and pregnant and he took too long to get back to the States, leaving her alone to deal with her parents and neighbors and their opinions, that she was done with him. She decided it was better to go it alone, even if it meant keeping secrets from me and if he was a scoundrel, I wouldn't want to find him.

Secrets are devil riders. They cling to us like leeches, and try as we might, we can't shake them. They draw our lifeblood from us. And that's what's going on with me. I can't love Tom, or myself for that matter, with this secret gnawing at me. It's Tom or flinging off the secret.

The baby came between Tom and me. The secret was a dark hole between us, and we could no longer talk. We stopped making love. I hated that hole, the hole left when I kept my pregnancy from it. It gaped wide when I took the life of our unborn child. I ruined one of the few things in my life that was beautiful—what Tom and I had.

I have always felt that I was on the outside, not part of what other people have. Because I have no father, I don't deserve more.

I'd denied Tom the opportunity to be a father just as my mother had denied my father. How different my life would have been if my mother had chosen to tell my father about me before I was born, if she'd given him the chance to be a father when it was so crucial. How different my own life would have been had I decided to tell Tom I was pregnant and given him a chance to be a father.

In my little hideout, my modern-day tree house, I closed my journal and wept. The painful ache in my heart subsided as I cried out into the darkness. Tension and fear and regret left with the tears.

My heart felt less burdened. As the tears became breath-filled sobs, I calmed enough to think about why I was crying. I was crying because I lost my father. I was crying because I lost my first lover. I was crying because I lost a child I'd never known. I was crying because I lost my mother.

But mostly I was crying over the loss of the innocent and true, the essence of me.

CHAPTER ELEVEN – WAVES

Up against a deadline on Tuesday for the October issue of the magazine. I was wound so tight I didn't sleep for two nights. I walked to relieve tension, but it wasn't helping because I was carrying my father's phone number in my pocket and wavering between wanting and not wanting to call him. I was exhausted when I finally settled down to call Tom.

"Hey," he said when he answered.

"Hey?"

"Yeah, why not?"

I laughed. "It just didn't seem like you."

"I'm trying to change my style. So, how are you?"

"I'm well. I've been carrying my father's phone number around in my pocket."

"Like a keepsake?"

"Could be. I'm not sure if I'm going to call him or not. No, that's not true. I'm not sure when I'm going to call him."

"It'll be all right. You should pick up the phone and call him. By the way, I enjoyed being with you over the weekend. I'm glad you were okay with me helping to go through the letters."

"You have good instincts. You knew I needed you there to do it."

"I do pride myself on instinct."

In all my adult years I can't say there has ever been a man who would sit and read my father's letters with me and be able to feel what I was feeling, the agony of not knowing him, the anger of being kept from him all those years. I loved Tom because he was genuine and willing to help me work things out. If I compared him and Rick, only on that point, there was a clear contrast.

He should have been allowed to know about the pregnancy and give into the life that we'd been dealt. I should have allowed the pregnancy to be a giving in and celebration of life. Instead I chose death. Not just the death of a new life that we'd made, but the death of our spirits. Tom's spirit had been deadened as well. He hadn't been happy either.

How would we approach this together? How would he understand any of this? He still had a happy little life with his house on the lake and all the other things his career success had bought him. On the surface, I had a happy little life too.

Of things. Not soul things, stuff things. Material stuff—I was sick of it.

I loved Tom. My heart swelled when I thought about Tom being part of my life. Over the years, I'd pushed love away, but I was craving it now.

"Come to my place this weekend," he said softly.

"When?"

"On Friday, after work."

"I will go to the place of reflective waters."

The sun was still high above the horizon as I drove west towards Vermilion. The natural beauty of the bluff above the rocky shore and the house silhouetted against the turquoise blue sky in the fading light blew me away. I knew he loved this place, and now I knew why. The builder had even left a few trees on the property, so the house's precarious weakness, its openness to the harsh wind and water, was softened.

Tom was wearing a white chef's apron when he greeted me at the door. He looked pleased with himself, and he was still holding a wooden spoon in his right hand. He kissed me, then passed his left arm around me to guide me to the back of the house. "I'm glad you came. We have all the time in the world to find our way to what's going to happen next."

"It won't be like it was."

"We were kids living on the surface of life."

Exactly. If we saw that as the past and our way to the future as being different, there was a chance for something authentic to happen between us.

"I'm so glad you get that."

"Is that why you hold back? Is that why when I reach for you sometimes, I feel like you're untouchable and don't want me?" He pulled me to him and I moved into his body.

"Is that what I do?"

We were nose to nose. I felt like he wanted to be joined with me.

"Yes. Sometimes. Part of me feels I should leave you alone in the life you have, let you go on with it. I might lose you again, and the way things are going, it won't matter at this point. Not much. But if you let me in, let me get to know you, things could be delicious."

"I've never been happier than when I spent the night in your arms."

He smiled. "I hope that's what we have to look forward to tonight."

His lips touched mine. He was watching, waiting for a reaction. I kissed him back, looking in his eyes, my lips more forceful, my tongue searching his mouth. His mouth opened, and his arms pulled me closer.

Lord, is this your answer? Is this what should happen?

He pulled away. "Let me show you around my showplace on the lake."

He was being sarcastic. I had to know, "Do you regret having this wonderful place?"

"No. But to me, with it empty and just me here, there are cracks in the façade."

"Like the cracks in my little hideaway on the river."

He squeezed my hand and we walked the house together. The open floor plan highlighted the natural light that streamed through the tall windows throughout the first floor. Where some homes have no side windows and traditional-sized windows in the front, Tom's house was built with floor to ceiling windows in the foyer and along the side walls of the great room and dining room. The entire back of the house was windowed.

Outside, the waves were six feet high. The sun reflected on the turbulent water, which reflected back on the walls of Tom's great room and kitchen. The wavering light reminded me of an aquarium, especially the light that was reflected off the bowl I'd purchased, which now sat on his glass coffee table. The sound of the surf made me feel like I was on an 18th century skiff trying to cross the Atlantic. I felt all the fear and trembling a cross sea voyage would churn up—alone with Tom at his house, I was vulnerable and he was in charge.

Lord, grant me the strength to be real here, to let Tom in, to allow him to know what I'd done and to understand it. He's the only one who could understand my decision, the only one who could really appreciate what I'd done, yet I'm still unable to tell him.

I stood next to Tom as he finished poaching salmon with capers, something I'd never done. He wasn't following a recipe and was adept at knowing what spices to add and adjusting the oven temperature. I sliced red-skin potatoes and he sprinkled them with rosemary, and put drizzled olive oil over asparagus before putting it in the oven to roast.

"How do you like my place?" he asked and gestured with his glass.

"I feel like we're on a boat, the water is so much a part of this place. What's it like in a storm?"

He smiled. "It's pretty wild."

"And Miriam didn't like the water, huh?" She didn't like being on a boat, yet she lived in this place that was alive with the energetic pulse of the Earth. "This is a place where you could never forget about the water and its power. It's sort of scary."

"It makes me feel like I'm at the helm." His eyes met mine. "She liked the idea of being on the lake until we moved in, but once we did, this place made her feel restless."

"I can see that. It pulls at the soul, at all the emotions underneath." I took a deep breath. "I have to admit, I'm feeling a bit jarred."

He filled glasses with Spanish Rioja and we took sliced baguettes with olive oil and olives outside to a glass table on the patio. It was windy, but the patio was in an alcove between two wings of the house, with an unobstructed view.

"It was my idea to build the back of the house with a shelter from the wind," he said. "The builder didn't think of it, can you imagine he didn't?" He indicated the other back yards along the beach—the other houses were modeled after Tom's. "He should have given me a kickback or something."

The wind blew through my hair and lifted my spirits. Outside, the sinister aspect of the place left me. I enjoyed the pull of the waves as I always did. It was decadent to sit on the patio and relax. But I was uneasy, unsure of whether this was the time to tell Tom what I'd done, not sure I wanted to ruin the moment.

I was glad for the small details—the candle lit in the hurricane lamp, the cloth napkins, and the soft classical guitar music wafting through the speakers set on either side of the French doors. Tom was timid about setting our plates down in front of us. He seemed comfortable with his cooking, but I could tell he was waiting for my reaction. "This looks great!" I was suddenly ravenous.

When he sat down next to me, he leaned over to kiss me on the lips, as if he sensed I needed reassuring. "You know what I've been wondering? I wonder if you're walking has to do with something that's hidden inside you that wants to come out."

I stabbed a piece of red potato, and looked at him. He was sitting so close, I could smell his aftershave and feel the warmth of his body. Our arms were almost touching, leaning on the glass-topped table. Carefully, I said, "I think it does. I've always worked out problems through walking."

"Do you have a sense of what it is you're trying to work out?'

"There's not really a sense of trying to work something out as much as me trying to calm myself. I usually don't know what the unease is."

"Are you trying to work out things about us?" He threw it out casually, but I sensed it was a big question for him."

"You know there's something there."

"I could guess what it is. In fact, I bet I could guess it right, if I tried."

My heart ached. There were only a few options on what my big secret could be. "I know."

He cut a piece of salmon and looked towards the Lake when he put it in his mouth. "I want you to be comfortable with me. I'm willing to give you some time, to come to terms with things on your own time."

"I hadn't thought of 'us' in years. And then you showed up out of the blue."

He nodded. "It's been interesting for me. Your voice is the same, your eyes are the same, but you aren't the same, outside or inside."

"Do people change entirely or is there some nucleus, like the soul, that is untouchable, unwavering, always the same?"

"You know the answer to that."

I followed his gaze out to the horizon. White caps rolled, one after another towards the shore. The water threatened to take over. "I feel comfortable with you. But with us, there's baggage. We both gave up on dreams along the way."

Still gazing out at the water, he said, "At certain points in time, we went about our lives without having love in our lives."

"I loved Max more than I knew, but I almost liked him less for how much he loved me. I'm not sure I loved him back as he deserved to be loved."

"And Alicia loved me, loves me, and always will, I know, but she thought it time to part, which may be, come to think of it, what you felt, what your mother felt. Maybe love is something we shouldn't analyze so much."

"That I agree with. It's easier not to look at things too closely, but we need to. I have been untruthful with you, Tom. I . . ." I struggled to go on, and the waves made me feel like I wouldn't be heard.

He put his finger to my lips. "It's okay. If we push admissions and regrets, we lose the moments that we could have together."

I shook my head. "Tom, I did something terrible to you, to us."

He nodded.

"Loving you was different than anything I've ever experienced. I became part of you, you became part of me. "

"How do we get back there?"

I didn't know. Here we were having a great meal by the water, and I hurt. I felt raw and open and exposed and I missed what Tom and I had. I wanted it back, but I was holding back. I'd become so used to not letting love in, I couldn't do it now. "I'm not used to letting myself love."

"I know."

"I want love that goes beyond the physical and emotional. I want to be grounded, I want meaning, and that's why I walk, that's why I travel, that's why I have one-night stands. It's all about searching for meaning. I'm looking for something bigger than me, than what we have, than what I find in being in love, sometimes in the wrong places."

"Maybe you're just trying to figure out what makes you happy, what makes you who you're meant to be." He turned to me then, his elbow on the table, facing me. "God is easier on us, and so are other people, than we are on ourselves." He started picking up things from the table, and when I got up to help, he stopped me. "Relax."

I met his kiss when he bent down. "I don't think I'll ever tire of kissing you."

"I hope not."

I meant it, about the kissing. It woke something deep and forgiving and true. And I gave into it like it was a balm for sore lips. I didn't care about anything else that was going on in my life, outside or inside, when he kissed me. If I could hold onto that feeling . . . we held onto it that night as he wrapped me in his arms and held me as tight as he could because that's what I asked him for. I fell asleep with my head on his shoulder and our breaths matched, in and out to the rhythm of the waves.

On the way out to Ashtabula County the following weekend, I looked for the vineyards and corn, I noticed the barns and silos and wide open spaces between the buildings. The traffic became lighter, the cars more leisurely. *Dear Lord, let me learn to love home again. Let me come home again.*

It was always your home. It was always there for you. It was there for you like God was there for you, like Tom was there for you, like I was there for you. It was you who walked away. It was Mom's voice, or was it God's? Or was it what was inside me, me talking to me? Was it my soul? Was this the nucleus, the remembering and wanting and seeking and desire to have something more than I had, was this the soul that Tom and I talked about, the real me, the me that knew where home was and was waiting for me to get back to it?

Now it was the vegetables . . . zucchini and yellow squash and tomatoes. The vegetable stand stood, waiting for the harvest. Pedro and a couple of the workers were pounding the last nails into the side posts when I pulled my car into the gravel drive. "This hasn't been here in years."

Pedro squinted at me in the sun. *"Hola,* Miss Betsy. I didn't know you were coming."

"Sorry, I should have called. I didn't know you were putting up this stand."

"It's a surprise for you. I think about you and how you liked to come here when you were young and sit and sell vegetables."

I was overwhelmed. Of course. This was what I needed to do. I needed to sit and wait. I smiled. "Pedro, you're so smart." I put my arm around his small waist and kissed his cheek.

He grinned. I'd never kissed him before. "You must like the idea."

"I'm going to unpack and then start picking some vegetables to bring over. Right now."

And I did. I sat at the vegetable stand, with Pedro spotting me a couple times. Customers drove up in their pick-ups or convertibles, on their way to town to pick up supplies or touring wine country. They were my vegetables, from my land.

I felt Tom behind what I was doing. I resisted the urge to call him and ask him to join me. I needed space. I felt like I was starting on a whole new life. I needed to do it alone. I felt all at once a child and a new-formed adult. I felt both innocent and wise. I felt like I belonged. I felt accepted, by whom I didn't know. Was it God? Was it my mother? Was it Cassie? Was it Tom?

It was me. I was starting to accept who I was, the good and the bad, the girl who loved to read and write and explore and was open to possibilities, and the girl who sometimes did things she was ashamed of, not even understanding why she did them. I was human, and I made mistakes. All was well.

The old house at Windy Hill wrapped around me and hugged me. I was me then and me now and me as a woman who had been places and felt like her journey and waiting were about to end.

At the end of the day on Saturday, right after a young couple with two small children stopped to buy a weeks' supply of vegetables and a bushel of apples headed off back to town in their old Jeep, Pedro came by the stand.

"Miranda's glad you're back home, Miss Betsy."

Curious. How did she know I was here? "Has she seen me?"

"Yes. Her favorite place is by the window. She happy to just sit and watch the shadows move, the daily things I do."

"She must be lonely."

"She talks to our kids on the phone."

"Well, let's load up and pay her a visit," I said as I rose to pack up the vegetables in crates.

Pedro helped me and we put it all on the tractor bed and parked by the house. Inside the cottage, it was small and warm. Brightly-covered rugs and blankets hung from rails around the walls, covered the wooden floor and the furniture. Miranda was wrinkled and brown and shrunken in her chair, yet wide in the hips. When she looked up at me, I could see the pain in her brown eyes. She took my hand and held it with both of hers, and I was surprised by their softness and warmth, and by her affection.

"I remember you when you was a girl. Always running around, hair flying about, wearing boys' jeans your mama bought at the JC Penney in town. You were a good girl, loved your mama and grandparents. You like cows, yes?" She smiled at me knowingly.

That she could know me so well and I didn't even know it, that I was liked with affection by a non-relative, a woman whose life was reduced to a small cottage and a window, touched me.

"I remember. You used to feed them. You pretended you didn't know I was in the stall with Sam even when you were giving her more food."

"I sometimes needed to be here, away from town and the people, away from my mother and all that was going on with her."

She nodded. "When I was a girl in Mexico, we lived en la hacienda Pacifica and no *es verde.*" Her talk ran into Spanish and I had trouble picking it all up. She spoke of making tortillas by roasting them on a stone. I could see remnants of her youthful beauty in her olive skin and shiny black hair. Her husband was always smoothing her hair, stroking her hand. His devotion touched me. I hugged her and told them both I would visit again.

Back at the house, I re-read a few of the letters my father sent to Mom when I was growing up. When I was ten, he wrote:

Dear Margie,

The photos of Betsy are not enough, but thank you for sending them to me.

I'm going to go out on a limb and say that I've stopped loving you. I still think about how much fun we had experimenting with poetry together. I remember that day when you tried to operate the cappuccino machine at the café, thinking you were helping, and how we laughed when it didn't turn out and my uncle never found out you'd touched his precious machine. You were beautiful when you laughed.

It's been eleven years. I had to get on with my life, but in doing so, I had to forget about what we had. Those memories had to be shut away. I've been married for seven years, and it's a good marriage, but when you give up something that was passionate and life-fulfilling, life CHANGING, for something that's adequate and what you need, every once in a while regret enters in.

But I don't love you any more.

It's so sad. I allow myself to think what we could have had. I waited for you to change your mind, and I waited in vain. Maybe I should have gone to your house, walked right past your father and flung you over my shoulder. I should have kidnapped you and Betsy. But it's like the old saying about how you have to let the bird fly away if that's what they want to do—you can't keep them if they want to fly away.

The problem is that if I'd done that, if I'd claimed you, you may not have wanted to fly away. You may have wanted to love me. It was fear that you'd reject me that kept me back. Damn it! It's my own damned fault.

But the girl shouldn't suffer. She thinks her father's a good for nothing. Is that fair to me? Is it fair to her?

I know you intercepted her birthday gift, but a father should send something to his daughter on her birthday. I should be able to see her. Can we meet somewhere? Can I finally see my daughter?

Please, Margie. I need this, you need it, Betsy needs it. You know it's true.

Waiting, Rafe

She left the life she'd known with him so she could move forward, and once she made up her mind there was no going back. Then the truth hit me—I left that before abortion girl behind and became a different person. The Betsy Tom knew no longer existed because I'd buried her. The part of me who was capable of love no longer existed. I didn't know where she was any more either, but my longing was tied up in that question.

Back at home on Sunday night, I called Tom. As soon as he answered, I said, "I should have allowed us a chance. I didn't trust it, like I didn't trust other guys and broke up with them before they had a chance to. What I did wrong was to treat you like all those other guys and make the assumption that you didn't love me for who I was.

Silence. I was about to ask if he was still on the line when Tom took a deep breath and said, "It doesn't matter any more, does it? Isn't it important to move past it and begin again?" Then he said in a terse and impatient voice. "We've talked about this before." He sounded angry. "I want us to move on."

I didn't know how to respond. I wanted us to move on, but he was angry with me. Inside, I told myself, *I need to look at who I was then and who I am now and assimilate it all into the me who is, the me who's living out her days and sometimes not knowing why she's doing what she's doing.* I picked up Winifred and stroked her fur, the phone under my chin. What I thought he wanted to hear was what I said, "I'm sorry."

He sighed. "I know you are."

"I wanted to call you and tell you all this because I think everything's going to be okay."

"I hope so. It offends me that you lumped me with everyone else. I would never throw you into a category with other women."

"I'm not the girl you used to know."

"You left her behind when you said good night to me in Kent, knowing you would betray me."

"I . . ." My immediate reaction was denial, but I'd admitted to myself that what he said was exactly the case. "Maybe the person I was can't be found anymore. Maybe you're wasting your time."

"I'm hoping you'll find her again. I see glimpses of her. I see her right now."

"At Windy Hill this weekend, I sort of felt like it was all coming back to me. I sold vegetables at the vegetable stand like I used to do."

"What's inside a person can go away, I suppose, but the essence of the person is still there even if the surface looks different. I see my Betsy, the Betsy I've always liked best, in your eyes."

"I feel so torn. All I want to do is stay here at the farm. It's like a drug. But I have work to do at the office."

"Follow your heart."

"I need to make a living."

"Yes, there's that. I know what you mean. But you can put your heart into your work because you love it too. You can look at your work as part of the journey too. Your work has made you who you are today."

"I can be who I was and who I am at the same time."

"It's kind of like that," he said.

"Why do I look at things so black and white? I can be who I am today or who I was before. I can love or not love. I can work or not work. There are no grays in there."

"Maybe you don't need to love the questions. Maybe you need to stop asking them." I laughed. "I always think too much too."

"When I do that, I'm usually seeing the glass half empty instead of half full. You need to just live."

"I know. Yesterday I spent some time in the keeper's cottage with Pedro and Miranda. They live simply. Even though Miranda's crippled, what they have is precious. I am awed by Pedro's devotion to his wife." I thought of the scene in Zola's *Germinal* where the young woman is dying and her lover sits beside her and she's going to die and they know it, but they face their waning time together and make the most of it. They were so focused on their world they know nothing else but each other's spirit. "Remember *Germinal*?"

"I've been wanting a love like that. It's time we had that secret out."

I knew he was right. "I feel like we'll get there some day." It was all I could offer him.

The next day I felt myself sinking into need for him. I walked over the Detroit-Superior Bridge and down 25th Street. Street sweepers were outside the Westside Market cleaning up the debris of wasted fruits and vegetables from the previous day. Some of the vendors were unloading their boxes and setting up their stands of cascading lettuce and tomatoes, and they waved to me as I passed them to go up and over the Lorain-Carnegie Bridge.

Tom said it's time the secret was out. He would hate me but he would probably love me despite it. He was my guy, and he respected me. He didn't like things I'd done, decisions I'd made. He didn't really own up to his affair being something bad, and his lack of remorse bothered me. I felt like he had different rules for me than for him, but maybe it was that I had different rules for me than he had for him. I was deflecting.

I didn't really think about what it would be like to make love to him again. I didn't feel sexual at all, which was sort of weird, out of character. I liked the intensity of physical desire, the need to be with someone, the waiting expectantly thing that sort of drove me nuts. That wasn't happening with Tom. It was more of a friendship, more platonic.

I could drive out to his place and tell him I was ready for anything. I made a mistake, I did something I wasn't proud of, but that was a long time ago, and I was sorry.

If I'd had the child . . .

Why did that intrude, the "if" stuff? It just didn't matter. I made myself crazy by going through it all in my head, over and over again. What I wanted was to be close to him, to put my arms around his solid, strong body and let him hug me, kiss me, make love to me.

Making love to Tom . . . it would be gentle and drawn out and lingering. It would make me feel good about life. I could believe in love again. I would fall in love again.

There would be no turning back.

"There would be no turning back," I said when he answered the phone later that morning."

"Huh?"

"If we made love."

Caught off guard, he didn't respond right away. "Why do you think that?"

"I'd fall in love with you."

"Do you have to make love to me to fall in love with me?"

It was a good question. "I'm not sure, but if we did, that would be it, I'd fall. I was thinking about that on my walk this morning. You know, walks are the best way to have time to think. My grandmother always said they slow life down."

"I walked on the beach in Lorain this morning. It was beautiful. The air's crisp, like it's warning us of winter."

I shivered. "I'm trying not to think about that. Cautiously, I continued, "Last night you said it's time to let the secret out. You'll hate me, Tom."

"Every time we open our mouths, we're making a choice. When love's true and real, it remains, even when it's over, like with me and Alicia."

I didn't like hearing about her. To Tom, who needed to know his mistakes didn't make me think less of him, and who really had no regrets at all, and didn't consider Alicia to be a mistake, I said, "I believe you loved her and still do. I can tell by the way you talk about it. But have you considered how that made Miriam feel, you having an affair?"

"Of course."

I let him think about that a little longer. "You have? And you're still okay with it?"

He was confused. Of course he'd thought I was on his side. "What I had with Alicia was good."

"It was tinged with sin." I couldn't help saying it.

He sighed long and hard. I imagined his mouth in the hard line it formed when he was being tested and didn't really want to be put in that position. "It was different for me."

"Was it? Didn't you have to do a certain amount of disengaging from Miriam in order to give of yourself with Alicia? You checked out of the marriage long before it ended. You say you and Miriam were no longer connected . . . no, you weren't, because you weren't in the marriage anymore."

He was quiet. Then he said, "You're right about the marriage being over, but I was checked out because it was. I've looked at this, Betsy, I have. I've looked at my motives, at what love meant to me, at what the love was with the women in my life. I knew I was committing adultery, and I went into it with my eyes open."

"I couldn't do that."

"Because you don't believe in love." It was a challenge. "It was wrong, but love was more important, what I needed, what she needed, the soul work was more important than what society thinks is right and wrong. I knew what I needed, and I just did it."

We were in silence for a while. "I knew what I needed and did the opposite when I ran away to Detroit and away from you," Admitting it made me feel tired. What I needed was to tell Tom the truth, and it didn't seem like I could. As much as I wanted to love him, I couldn't. If I told him about the baby, it would only hurt him again. This being-open-to-love thing was beyond my capabilities. "This is why I wasn't sure we should see each other. I knew at some point we'd care too much that the other one would love us. And I knew we'd reach the point where that love would mean I'd have to make the same choice all over again, whether to just walk away."

"Is that what's going to happen?" The anger in his voice reminded me of the way Rick used to talk to me.

"This is making me tired. It's too much work."

He hung up.

FAIRIES
At Willow Beach

Willow Beach is still my place of solace. When I walked away from Windy Hill on the day my mother died, I was selfishly holding onto my grief. Neither Ben nor Cassie said anything, but I could see it in their eyes. Is it selfishness that made me hold onto my secret, that caused me to run away?

I started a novel years ago and never finished it because it seemed to be a flight of fancy, a silly thing. But it's no more fanciful than my mother's gallery, a place of possibility for local artists that she called Dazzles. We can all dazzle, if only we try. Not all of us dare.

I call my novel *Faerie Mists* because fairies rise from their hiding places in the mist of their mystique. I spent hours looking at the fairies sitting on top of my mother's music box and trying to discover their essence when Mom was waning, wondering what Mom got from them. Fairies are every bit as magical as the Magical Pond, which is always surrounded by mist in its low valley, and they only come out at night. When they do, they're so tiny they can barely be seen on a blade of grass or an equally hard-to-find toad.

The fairies have become real to me. There's Immogene the Innocent and Clara the True and Fawn the Faithful. As I write about them I discover innocence and truth and faith. I find the place within me that is all those things. Writing is therapeutic, and I'm finally able to write the things I need to write in order to grow. I journal every morning about what's going on at the farm, throughout the day I jot down memories of the past year, and I sometimes sit on the porch swing and play with poetry. I'm reading everything I can get my hands on during long afternoons when the air becomes warm and after the farm work is done.

This morning I am whole and sinless. Sin has a meaning beyond what I thought of as denial of truth when I started. Being sinless is a way of living in the world. I talk with God as I go through my day. Faith is that bit of holiness in me that keeps me on the straight path because I know exactly what is right and what is wrong, and I can trust it. As I write this, I'm talking with God, and He's talking through me.

The fairy Lily the Lover loves everyone and makes huge sacrifices that make the love come back to her again. Heloise the Centered knows that balance brings happiness and peace.

I sometimes think the book is trite, but it's also fun and beguiling and interesting, even to me, the writer, who follows the muse where she may go and writes it all down as best I know how.

I had no choice but to write it. I found the fairies in the waters of the Magical Pond, their faces clear as could be. If I hadn't seen them, *Faerie Mists* would never have become real.

Mom would have liked that I was inspired by the farm, by the place she eventually embraced when grandpa died and grandma was alone. She was a woman who could have gone to Italy or become a great artist, but she chose to stay home and open a consignment shop for artists who wanted people to see their work. I wonder how many of her paintings, sculptures, and mobiles are in people's homes?

There were some months when I didn't feel Mom much, when my heart was closed. But then, one day, I was surprised by angels in a historic cemetery.

CHAPTER TWELVE – ANGELS

Angels watched me while I walked through Little Italy's Lakeview Cemetery. Sentries of the dead, they seemed to be everywhere. Behind a leaf that hung too low from a nearby tree, an angel appeared, like a messenger. I snapped photos of cupid-like beings whose eyes were cast down over praying hands. I focused my camera on a headstone adorned with angels with flowing gowns. Another angel stood as a guardian on top of one of the stones, arms wide like those of a mother wanting to claim her child.

I stopped dead in my tracks, and the camera fell to my hip. *Why was I taking pictures of angels? Angels forewarned of the virgin birth and told of Jesus' resurrection. Angels forewarn, and they tell the truth. They're supernatural creatures like the fairies at Windy Hill. They wouldn't appear if they didn't have a mission.* My camera was full of angel pictures when I was supposed to be writing a story about the history of the cemetery and the important dignitaries buried there.

Not heeding the angels' insistent need for my attention, I continued walking, eyes to the ground. At the crossroad, I pulled the map out of my pocket and walked toward the place where Rockefeller was buried. I shot the picture of the monument, then dutifully jotted down the years of his birth and death and tried to connect who he was as a person with the type of memorial left for him.

Why the angels? *Because they protect, watch over people.* Why not just God? *They are God's messengers, His helpers.*

God was watching over me through his angels. No, He was just watching over me. My God was a personal God and not someone who sent someone on his behalf. *Yes, I am here for you.*

The angels were trying to get my attention.

Back home at my condo later that afternoon, I continued reading Mom's journals. The year when Cassie was ten, Mom wrote,

Betsy came home from work early today and took Cassie to swing from the rafters in the barn. I have to admit, the first thing I thought when she came in the door was that she must have been ill. She never comes home early, for no reason at all. Her focus on work is complete. Except for today. I hoped God paid her a visit and brought her home to her daughter who needs her." She went on about a sermon she'd heard that week, and how she felt God's presence more when she was in church. I wonder if she keeps her distance from her daughter because I didn't let her have a father. I know I made the right decision for me, but maybe not for Betsy.

I remembered the day I came home from work early. At work I'd been dealing with constant interrupting phone calls from Ernesto, a man I met in Rio to whom I'd mistakenly given my work phone number. I went home early to get away from his incessant calls and the noise of the outside world. Cassie's squeals as the swing went up toward the hayloft had been a balm for the soul, a better reason to live. Sometimes angels, messengers from God, come in the form of people, like Ernesto, who unknowingly caused me to change my day and spend time at home with my daughter.

In my own journal, I wrote.

> All the blessings in my life, my mother and daughter, and all the other people I've known and loved, are a balm for my soul. They give me solace, if I let them in. Over and over again, like that day when Cassie and I swung in the barn on an afternoon when I should have been at work, God tried to tell me to be open to possibility. I thought possibility meant being open to going places in the world and being a great writer, but I should have been paying attention to the little things, and to my life at home.
>
> Mom used to make the best tart lemonade out of fresh lemons. The tree house that Grandpa built is still the best place to read in the whole world. The farmhouse has stained glass windows that reflect rainbows onto the hardwood floors.
>
> Mom decided to let me live, even if it meant me not having a father. She never once thought about an abortion. Mom keeping me was a blessing, and me having a child with Tom would have been a blessing. I assumed Tom's love wasn't big enough to deal with our mistake, as Mom assumed with my father. It's almost as

if I knew that about Mom, and I took my clue from her even though she never said it.

When Mom talks to me, I know she's watching over me. I feel like Tom is God's messenger, sent to show me who I am because I was lost.

At the vegetable stand by the road at Windy Hill the following weekend, I read an Alice Hoffman novel with Beth sleeping in her stroller next to me. My hair was pulled back in a pony tail, and I wore a pair of Mom's old overalls over a tank top. I was happy, content. Beth slept well in the afternoon warmth. I didn't try to flag down cars to stop and buy the tomatoes, zucchini, pumpkins, or corn. Customers came in groups, pulling into the end of the driveway and churning up the gravel. When the car door closed, I looked up from my book.

The man who pulled up in a Buick had eyes the color of Robin's eggs under thick black lashes. He wore a worn denim jacket and an open collared shirt. A man of seventy, he had the look of knowing what he was doing and what he was about. He glanced at the vegetables and when he looked up to see my eyes on him, he stood up straighter. He looked startled, as if he was expecting someone else. A breeze blew across my shoulders and I shivered, despite the 90-degree day.

"Elizabeth?" His voice was hoarse with age. The name sounded foreign and melodious rolling off his tongue.

"Yes. May I help you?"

He looked down at the tomatoes in front of him, grimaced, and then looked me squarely in the eye and said, "I'm Rafe Paglia." He braced himself, let out a breath, and kept his eyes on me to see my reaction. He looked like he'd said the hardest thing he'd ever said. It probably was the hardest thing he'd ever said.

That he was my father, the dirty Dago who got my mother pregnant and left the country, the man who left me without a full set of parents, hit me in the gut. My mouth opened, but I was speechless. He wasn't what I expected but he wasn't not what I expected. I don't think I ever thought I'd really see him in person, ever. I felt an ache in my chest, an almost-impossible-to-breathe sensation. There were no rules for that moment, and when, in response to his patient stare, I finally said, "My father? Oh my . . . God."

"I know this is hard."

"That doesn't begin to cover it." *Am I ready to become a daughter who is loved, a daughter whose father missed her every bit as much as she missed him? And what if I am the daughter he's trying to forget, the daughter who was lost to him, the daughter who caused him pain because not having her meant not having the woman he had loved when he was young?*

"I know." He held my eyes and stayed where he was.

I didn't want him any closer. "You left my mother."

"No."

"You aren't my father. I think you need to go away." I was surprised by my own anger. I stood up and turned my back to him and rearranged the vegetables. I pulled more tomatoes out of the big basket and started putting them in the smaller ones. Icily and with control, I said, "I don't need a father." I'd gotten along fine without a father for my almost 50 years of life. I'd learned how to live with only part of a family and it was too late to undo all that learning.

"Your mother asked me to come," he said. He took a step toward me.

I whirled around and pointed a finger at him. "You have no business being on my land."

"Please, Betsy. Listen to me." His voice was humble and steady. "Before she died, your mother asked me to try to connect with you. All those years, she wouldn't let me. I wanted to see you, but she . . ."

"She couldn't have been that mean." I said it even though I knew it wasn't true.

Our eyes met. "Yes, she could."

I took him in—he was an old man but I could see how he may have looked as a young man. I nodded.

He smiled in relief. "I'm glad she told you my name. I wouldn't have thought she had."

I was beside myself. "I'm reading her journals and I have your letters to her. I don't understand why it was okay for me to have the truth after she died but not while she was alive. I have your phone number in my pocket." I pulled it out like it was a seaside souvenir.

He took his hands out of his pockets and held them open. "I would have come without her telling me to, Bella."

"Until a few days after she died, I didn't know she even knew where you were."

"I haven't moved in forty years. I sent letters and child support. Your mother sent me pictures."

"I know all about her lies." It felt vicious to admit that.

The word "lies" hung between us. I ran my hand through my hair. How to begin? How was I to talk to a father I'd never known?

"Bellissimo," he said. "You're more beautiful than I thought you'd be."

Without thinking, I said something I'd never admitted, even to myself. "Beauty is not always a good thing."

"You've suffered."

I could see he understood. I'd never said that to anyone, how I thought my beauty was a detriment to being able to live fully. I shook that thought away, for later. "I saw a picture of you and Mom when you were together. You look like the picture."

"I had a lot of pictures of your mother, and some of both of us. I only kept one."

"She only had one too, as far as I know. You looked happy in the picture."

"We were happy together."

"Mom said you disappeared."

"She was angry with me."

I nodded because he confirmed what I already knew. I indicated the stroller. "Meet your great-granddaughter."

He followed my eyes to the sleeping seven-month-old child, and he sighed loudly. Then he looked out over the property. "It's the way Margie said it was. She told me about her home, about her father coming home from the war and taking to farming, and how lonely she sometimes was in this house full of antiques. She always wished she had a sister or brother . . . a boisterous familia."

"Yeah, me too."

"I wonder if Margie and I would have more children if we'd been together. If we'd been together, everything would have been different."

"Mom may have had enough love for other children if she'd had you to love. Somehow love spawns more love."

"That's something to think about, my daughter."

The word "daughter" stilled my heart. This was my father. *It's okay, Betsy. You can let him into your world. You can open your heart.*

He came over to sit on my side of the long wooden table, a couple feet away from me on the wooden bench, and touched Beth's cheek.

"I was afraid of my daughter though," I said.

"Was that it?"

"I didn't want to love my daughter so much it hurt her. But I ended up hurting her because I didn't love her enough."

"You have time to make that right. And look, you can love this little one as much as you want." His voice was soft and held a gentle tenderness from affection and love. He was right about how I could love Beth, I thought, as I reached for her. I picked up the child, who was limp and heavy. "Do you want to hold her?"

He held out his arms. She startled a bit at first but when she sunk into his arms, she went back to sleep immediately. "You and your mother had difficulties. I know that. It's normal for mothers and daughters to resent each other, but you probably sensed there were things you didn't know." He was watching Beth's face, not meeting my eyes. We became quiet as we watched her together. Beth's eyelids were the petals of a flower, her mouth a bud.

I couldn't believe I was sitting next to my own father. He had broad shoulders, and wore his belt below his old man belly. He smelled like fresh basil. He held Beth like she was the most precious thing in the world. "I missed so much. I should have been more insistent about seeing you. I went back to Italy for almost a year, and I told your mother I'd only be gone the summer. By the time I came back, she wanted nothing to do with me. Margie didn't tell me she was pregnant."

"I don't think she knew until you were gone." In her journal she'd written that she should tell him but she was too angry to do it. It was easier to hide. I knew that impulse to hide, to keep secrets. "How did you meet again?"

"About a year after you were born, your Mom was shopping at the West Side Market and she walked right by me. She was laughing about somethin', and when her face turned my way, she froze at the sight of me. The pain of what she'd undergone darkened her face."

"She wrote in her journal that she didn't want to see you, that she hated you for leaving her, yet the summer before you'd promised to come home and she believed you. She loved getting your letters."

He turned back to the baby, and when his eyes met mine, he was struggling to remember. "I don't know what I said. Something like 'Hi, Margie,' and she had all kinds of anger in her. I was amazed at how angry she was; no one had ever been that angry with me. She started yelling at me. I didn't know she had it in her. I don't think she knew it either. Afterwards she stomped away and didn't turn back, all the other people looking from me to her."

"It's unbelievable to me that she didn't tell me any of this all these years."

He shrugged. "The year she thought I'd abandoned her must have been tough. She never forgave me. Not until the end."

"I would rather think you cared about me than that you abandoned us and never knew I existed."

"Well, your Mom, she didn't know what to do."

"You don't know how hard it was for me. For us."

"I can imagine. But you had grandparents."

The anger came rolling over me again as I looked at him. My hands became fists. "You should have forced it," I said with menace. "You should have come and told my grandfather that you had a right to your family and to living your life the way you thought it should be lived."

"I should have, yes." He gave me a hug. "Please don't be angry with me. Like all of us, I did the best I could. I can't be here long, and I need to get going to get somewhere by five." He handed me the baby, and I put her back in her stroller. She rolled onto her stomach and put her thumb into her mouth. His voice changed, became tender and guarded. "How was she at the end? Did she suffer much?"

"Sick. She slept a lot."

He nodded. "I have a thousand regrets, some of them one multiplied by a hundred. The one multiplied the most is the way I left things with your mother. I think she was grateful for the money, but I wasn't there when she needed me. She was so young."

"She never finished college, never realized her dreams."

His slow wistful nod told me he understood the impact he'd had on Mom's life, and mine. I sighed with a small measure of relief.

"Can I call you? Can we talk things through more? It's about time I got to know my daughter. I can't believe I'm seeing you, the real you, not your image."

"I have your eyes." I avoided his question.

"Yes, you surely do." He stood. "I'm glad you knew about me

before I showed up completely unexpected."

"Your letters . . . she left them for me. They were tied up in a green ribbon and I read them all, one by one."

He shook his head. "Then you know me better than I know you right now. What must you think?"

"You loved her. And that makes me happy."

I stood and walked with him toward the road. He made a slight bow towards me, and, as he started to get in his car, he turned back and said, "You're every bit as beautiful as your mother."

"I have her high cheekbones."

"Yes. And there's the way your mouth smoothes out into a line when you smile with your mouth closed." I gave him that smile, and he nodded. "That's it."

"Yes," I finally said. "You can call me." Wanting to say something for him to hold on to about Mom, I found kindness when I said, "She DID realize her dreams in the end—she became an artist who opened up her heart and a gallery for other artists."

He nodded. "We can find our way even with all the baggage we carry pulling us down. We learn to make our loads lighter, so we can fly."

I watched him get behind the wheel of his Buick, and turn around to drive onto the road. His progress was slow and steady.

I crossed my arms and sat back down on the bench. I could see Mom's eyes squinting at me, waiting for a battle. I felt confused, but I wasn't angry. "Mom," I said as if she was there with me. "I'm not angry, I'm disappointed. I thought we were close. It's like . . ." I knew my next words would hurt, but she needed to hear them. "It's like when I was with Rick and I poured myself into a relationship that was important to me, only to find out it wasn't so important to him. I could've had a father that I could share with—maybe I wouldn't have ended up with Rick if I'd had a father. I felt like I had to find someone and hold on tight." I paused, flung my arms in exasperation. *Oh, what am I saying?* "I have no idea if things would have been different." I stood up and started pacing, my back to my mother and her squinting defensiveness.

A small voice said, *I didn't know what to do, Betsy. I just didn't know.*

I turned and said, "Just some words, Mom. You could have said, 'Honey, I was angry with your father, but he's still there for you.' "

Weakly, I heard her voice again, *I didn't mean to hurt you.* I could hear her voice so well I thought I was having a conversation with a live woman. I was so tired, I couldn't say anything else. Besides, I felt sorry for her. Into the warm summer's heat, I said, "So you want us to know each other now?"

I didn't hear the answer, but I felt her say yes.

"I'll try, Mom."

I told Ben the story over the telephone when he returned from Mexico. I said, "That's all that was said between us. There's no reason for me to berate her for not sharing him with me earlier in my life. It would serve no purpose."

"He was at the funeral," Ben said.

"He was?"

"He slipped into the very last pew of the church right before the funeral began, and he left as soon as it was over. He showed up at the cemetery as we were leaving, and then I had no doubt it was him. He sent me a note that he would be contacting you because it was Margie's wish. The way he called her 'Margie' hit me, because I've never called her that and he seemed so personal about her, as if he knew her still. I decided not to say anything, to let it happen as it would between you, and I'm surprised it took this long. When she was alive, I kept telling your mother she had to tell you about your father. You know what I think? I think she listened too much to her father who called the guy a dirty no-good Dago, and she'd been watching too many Elvis movies where the guys treated the girls like they were nothing. For all we know, he was a good guy."

"I don't think Mom figured out good guys were out there until she met you."

My father called me a couple of days later. He said, "Hello, daughter," when I answered the telephone, and then he told me about his day. "I'm teaching inner-city kids how to grow vegetables. Maybe if it becomes a lifestyle, they'll do it as adults. Maybe they'll teach their parents to live off the land. You should see their faces when we're at the community garden and they pull a cabbage from the ground, a cabbage that they planted from a seed and watered. It's beautiful."

I listened to him go on about the kids in the garden on Cleveland's east side. There was a black boy who'd been in and out of juvenile court who he'd kind of taken under his wing. Another boy from a broken home showed up high on his mother's drugs. "I loved teaching, and I'm glad I could find something to do with myself in retirement. It keeps me busy, and I feel like I'm giving back.

"I also spend time with my grandchildren. My son Lyle has two sons, and my son Matt has a daughter. They're in high school and at college, but they like to help me in the community garden. I can't believe how lucky I am that those young people like hanging out with me so much."

I felt a pang of regret when he mentioned his sons. Not only did I have brothers, but I had nephews and a niece, people who were close to Cassie's age. She could have family too. "Cassie likes to work in the orchards, and when I'm not around, she helps Pedro run the farm. I have to admit, I haven't spent much time doing that."

"You had to work, provide."

I could have found the time. *You missed out. You lost your way. You turned your back on what you had. You loved the idea of the farm but not the farm itself.* Aloud, I said, "Cassie and I talked about that recently. She accused me of staying away on purpose. I think she's right."

"You know regret's bad for you, don't you?"

"I do. But knowing it and living what I know are two different things."

"It's the human condition."

As I grew to know my father, I learned he was clever and philosophical. He taught History in the Lyndhurst School District for thirty years and he'd written four novels, a mystery series that did better in Europe than it did in the States, and when I Googled his name, the books came up easily.

"I would like to publish fiction," I said.

"As you should. Your writing is colorful and clever, and you tell stories as you write, even if they are journalistic. I loved the way you told the story of the prince locked in a castle in Ireland in the magazine last year—you told a fairy tale in the midst of a travel piece."

There was so much to share about me, I didn't know how to start, so I started from there. "I love to write. I love the way the words flow and the way I find the thread that connects things and ties the story together. It's a bit of an adventure."

"That trance-like feeling."

"It's a drug."

He laughed, and we promised to talk a couple of days later.

During our next call, I told him about our life at Windy Hill, and how hard Mom worked. She dated a lot of guys, but none of them worked out until Ben. I told him about trying to figure out what I wanted to do with my life, about moving to Cleveland and about Mom being sick.

"We became close at the end. I loved her shop, her excitement for life, her playful way of looking at things."

"Do you regret how you've lived?"

I was proud of creating something just for me. "Some things, yes, but most of it I have not regretted. I guess I see the bad things more than the good."

"We do that."

"There's so much more to know and so much more I could tell. I want Mom to know, and you, too, I guess, that I'm starting to like who I am."

"Why haven't you liked yourself?"

"I wish I knew," then I stopped. "I know bits and pieces of it. But the heart of it all, I don't get. I'm still trying to figure it out."

"You will, I can feel it."

"Having you here to talk to, that will help."

"I'm glad you feel that way."

"It doesn't make sense, given her faith, that Mom wouldn't give you a chance. Come to think of it, she softened at the end like she finally let God in, let God be God. She stopped fighting Him."

"That's interesting. How did she soften?"

"She wasn't as headstrong. The change started when she bought Dazzles and continued when she met Ben. In fact, Ben was a possibility for her because she'd changed. It probably helped that Cassie grew up and she didn't have to care for her anymore. She lived better during her later years."

I expected Father to show up at the vegetable stand on the weekends, but he didn't. I'd been looking forward to seeing him again, so my heart leapt when he asked, during one of our evening phone calls, "Are you up for a walk next Tuesday night after work? I have to be downtown in the afternoon."

"Sure. I can do that. There's something about walking . . ."

"It opens people up to each other."

"Yes. Exactly."

The conversation seemed to dry up momentarily, until he asked, "What are you thinking about?"

"I was thinking about how much you've missed. The day my granddaughter was born was beautiful; the sun was bright and the branches of the trees were iced with snow. Mom was in the hospital and when she saw that baby . . . oh, it was the perfect moment. Mom may as well have been looking at an angel."

He didn't say anything for a while, but I knew he was thinking. "The only way I knew to celebrate your birthday was to raise a toast to you and say a prayer that God would keep you safe. Your mother sent me pictures of your parties. I remember one year, you had a cake shaped like a teddy bear. Another year you had a cake with a Barbie doll standing on top. Some birthday parties were kind of disastrous, like the time you planned an outdoor party and it rained in sheets and you had to have a scavenger hunt indoors. But your mother always made it happen."

"Yeah, she did, but sometimes it was only after she ranted for an hour, beside herself at our ill luck. She always wanted things to go her way."

"I think she was a bit of a control freak that way. She expected life to go according to her plans."

"I used to be that way. I try not to do that now, and the people at work actually ask me to go to lunch now and again."

He laughed. "It's hard to have friends when you're a control freak. So what else did I miss?"

"Vacations. First days of school. My wedding. How I looked when I was pregnant. My graduations."

He was quiet for a moment, then he cleared his throat. "I kept up the best I could. It got to the point where I didn't want you to know about me almost as much as your mother did, because if you knew about me, you would have to adjust, and it may have turned out badly."

That made some sense to me. "So, I'll see you on Tuesday then."

"Yep. I'm bringing something for you, something your Mom would want you to have."

"Really? What is it? A crazy-art mobile? I already have three of those in my condo."

"No. You'll just have to wait and see."

When Dad arrived at my office, he looked larger than he had at the farm stand. He was inside now, filling up the space. He smiled when Angela left us alone, came behind my desk and kissed me on my cheek. He felt like a stranger to me, but the scent of basil that seemed to be part of his skin had been lingering with me for days. My father was alive and well in Cleveland and was in my office and part of my life. I was still getting used to the idea. He was unknown.

"Nice office," he said when he stepped back. The khakis and polo shirt made him seem less like an Italian living off the land and more like a suburban school teacher.

"Thank you," I returned his grin. "It's a good job."

"But is it your life work?" He asked in a casual way as he sauntered to the wall of pictures across from my desk. He walked from one framed photo to the next, slowly, like he was in a gallery.

Learn to love the questions themselves.

He let the last question go. "Did you like your ride on the gondola in Venice?"

I looked past him at the framed photo from Venice. "It was a novelty. It was short. I did it by myself."

"That's not the way, of course, the alone part."

"I know."

He'd moved on to the next framed picture. "You let her braid your hair? What beach was that?"

"It was Jamaica." I remembered the poverty more than the blue waters. My tour driver didn't want me to be in the shanty town areas, but I insisted. The best pictures were of the huts, women carrying water jars, and children playing street hockey with sticks. He was looking at a picture of me in a one-piece black bathing suit sitting in front of a brown-skinned girl with corn-rowed hair while she braided my hair. "The girl was precious. She tucked the ten dollars I gave her into a pocket inside her shorts. She told me her mother sewed on the inside pocket to keep the money safe."

Dad nodded. "Good for the soul . . . beautiful pictures. I'm proud of you. You let yourself live in moments such as these."

"Not always." Could he hear the sadness in my voice? "The trips are good but here at home, life hasn't been what I want it to be. I'm not even sure why."

He did. "One thing—you're too much alone."

"What?"

He found a seat in one of the guest chairs and crossed his legs comfortably, like he was going to sit a while. "In Italy, we like to spend long Sundays together eating and enjoying our families. My family still owns the house my ancestors bought in the 17th century, a stucco house of many levels with a red tiled roof and porticos on two floors. The umbrella pine and cypress are an interesting contrast to the olive trees planted in trellised rows at the back of the property, up the hill that faces south."

"I wish I could see it."

"Maybe you will some day." He looked thoughtful. "Well, we'll have to figure out a life together, won't we?"

I'd been thinking about those brothers I didn't know. "I'm not sure I want to know them."

"My sons?"

I nodded and leaned over to change into my sneakers. "No, I'm not sure. They've lived without me for years, and I've lived without them. Why shake it up?"

My face must have told more than I'd meant it to. He said, "It's okay. I won't have you to dinner with my wife. I don't think that would be a comfortable time for either of you. Not yet. I'm waiting and praying for time to make that happen. At some point, you may want to know your brothers."

There would never be those moments remembered, of playing games, sitting knee to knee in the back seat, blowing out the candles, and being the big sister who watched out for them. Big sister . . . it was foreign to me. *But think about it. Think about what it could mean,* Mom's voice said.

Outside, the humidity that had been weighing the air was gone, washed away by an afternoon rain. The air was crisp and fresh. My father was wearing black tennis shoes. He kept up with me as I walked east down Superior toward Chester Commons and the Greyhound bus station. We headed up E. 17th through CSU property and towards Euclid Avenue.

As we walked, he talked. "Your Uncle Dino has a jewelry shop on the Ponte Vecchio. His father, my great-uncle Julius, won the shop in a card game with a wealthy Florentine who didn't know how to hold his liquor."

"Does he live in Florence?"

"Yeah, he still lives there, but it's expensive and his son isn't interested in the jewelry shop. Your Grandma Juliet, our mother, died a few years ago. She never cut her hair, not her entire life, and her braids were so long and thick by the time she died, they could hardly be kept wound around the top and back of her head. You have another Uncle, Michael, a medic. He married a woman from Pompeii he rescued from the wreckage of an earthquake. We all worked in your Grandpa Joe's vineyards. My father created the best wines in Tuscany because the vines had been grafted from those in Vatican City in the eighth century."

"Those are great stories."

"America, it doesn't have the stories, the history, the color, of the people I knew when I was growing up, you know? It's all about love, you know, no matter where you go, people being in the way of Cupid's arrow."

"Or believing in a magical pond."

He stopped and turned to me. "Your mother. She was a dreamer. But not such a good dreamer that she believed in a love that was true even though mistakes were made. Her dreams were untouchable, unrealistic."

She'd expected too much of him. "She didn't believe you were really needed back in Italy. She assumed you didn't love her." I took his hand and squeezed it before we walked on. We reached Euclid and turned left to walk east towards Fenn Tower and Trinity Cathedral.

"Yes. Assumptions always get you in trouble."

"And expectations."

He drew a deep breath. "My wife and me, we had to get through some tough times, you know? Marriages are never perfect. Oftentimes we compare who we're with to who we used to be with, and that gets us in trouble."

"When I was married to Rick I compared him to Tom . . . Tom

did things like buying flowers on his way home from classes or wrote love poems on notebook paper when he was in class. He cooked, Rick didn't. He was romantic, Rick wasn't. It made things all that much worse when Rick botched it up."

My father looked over at me as we stood ready to cross the street from Trinity Cathedral. "Your mother told me how things ended with you and Rick. I knew how much pain you were going through with a husband who was a drinker. And this Tom . . . I didn't hear about him."

"He came to the funeral. We were a couple in college, and we've become reacquainted. I'm not sure whether it will continue."

"Why not?"

I sighed and shook my head. I wasn't ready for this. "I don't want to talk about it." It had been weeks since I'd had any contact with Tom. The light changed and we forged ahead. Trinity's Gothic stone front with its pointed steeples was in front of us. The placard sign outside announced vespers, and I turned to look at him before I placed my foot on the stair. "Have you been here before?"

"Oh, yeah. This church is special."

"I feel God there in the high ceilings and echoing walls, the elegant simplicity and splendor of a space meant for God. It's a holy place, a place where I can feel God. Not all churches feel that way to me."

"Maybe you'll meet me here sometimes. You know, when your work isn't so busy."

"Maybe." I liked the idea but had the feeling it would be hard to get away during lunch hours. Instead of turning left to go back toward Public Square and beyond to the Warehouse District or even towards my father's car, we turned right. "You really want a long walk tonight, huh?"

"Soon we won't be able to walk much. It's getting to be winter." He put an arm around my shoulders and gave me a hug. "Now tell me about Tom."

"The last time we spoke I told him it was too much work."

He raised an eyebrow. "And that would be, why?"

"He's . . . he's a really nice guy, an attorney with a practice in Rocky River, divorced. We were good as a couple. But he's the kind of guy I would want to be with and there's so much that's complicated about that."

"Did you break up with him to marry Rick?"

"No. I ended the relationship because I didn't trust him with the truth."

"You didn't think he'd love you if he knew the truth?"

"No. All these wasted years. I've been alone for a long time and . . ."

"Not wasted years. Have you read *Zen and the Art of Motorcycle Maintenance*?"

"Yes. Pirsig, right? It explored the idea of journeying to find the answers."

"It's about journeying to find the truth. If we get lost in life a bit, we're living well when we allow the truth to unfold."

"So you're saying that if I'm fully engaged in life, it's not wasted."

"Like living in the moment."

"You're right about Tom. I didn't trust the love he had for me."

"Would you trust it now?"

"Too early to tell." Then we were standing at the corner, waiting for the light to change so we could cross Euclid. It was dark, and I was cold. "Where are we going?"

"Do you know that house over there?" He pointed towards the University Club.

I'd been there for meetings at times, an old Euclid Avenue mansion. "Yeah, a couple of times. Think about this street, from here all the way down to the Square, lined with beautiful homes surrounded by iron gates, with ponds and gardens. People could wander past on their Sunday walks."

"And feel the vast chasm between rich and poor."

I looked over at him. "It was a lavish display. Too much perhaps."

We stood at the iron fence and admired the house standing high up at the height of the property. "Anson Stager built this mansion in 1866. It's 10,000 square feet."

"It looks more like an old-fashioned civic building, like a courthouse, with its tower up the middle and red brick." I shivered and I pulled the collar of my coat closed. "I didn't know you would want to walk all the way to 38th today. You're as much a walker as I am."

"Weird, huh? I do it all the time. Maybe it's the European in me."

I noticed he picked up the pace, and I was glad. It warmed me to walk faster. "So do you think it's best to let bygones be bygones, or should I allow things to develop as they may between Tom and me?"

He sighed. "I don't know why you're asking me that question. I allowed your mother to stew and didn't stir things up for forty-some years. I let bygones be bygones and got on with my life. Except for this," and he reached into the inside of his coat and pulled out a cloth satchel. "These are her letters to me. There's probably thirty in here. Your mother asked me to put them all together for you. So here they are."

My mouth opened. I didn't know what to say. "I have the letters you sent to her, too."

"And now you have a book. I'm not going to be here on this Earth forever, you know," my father was saying, hands moving. "So I thought I'd pass these on now before something happens."

"Why is it people are giving me things all of a sudden? A teacup, a set of journals, a fairy music box, dangling mobiles, driftwood, and now this?"

"The universe seems to be pouring gifts on you."

"At Lakeview Cemetery a few weeks ago, I kept seeing angels. They were trying to tell me something."

"Love the question and let the answer come."

"Mom used to say we should learn to love the questions."

"I said that to her. Margie was never doing that, she was always in a hurry. I couldn't get her to sit and have a cappuccino with me, you know?" Fenn Tower stood above us as I opened the satchel and flipped through the envelopes. "You should be able to find some answers in the letters."

"But I was just learning to love the questions themselves."

He laughed out loud. "We live and die and exist no matter what because we all impact the world in our living, somehow, but when we write things down, we touch on something that makes us real."

Later, deep into the comfort of my bed, I wrote about my father.

> Dad came up with the idea of loving the questions themselves, not Mom. How much more would I find out about how he influenced her, and me? I might find out that Dad has been part of my life all along the way. There's so much catching up to do,

and I feel like I want to know it all at once.

I feel like the crevices are being filled in, like life is taking a new turn, a turn toward the completeness I've been craving. His voice, his touch, his memories, the way he talks . . . I keep reliving our walk and what he had to say.

I try to get it all down in these journal pages, but it's more than that. This is where I sort it out. Mom knew that. She knew that a narrated life made it more significant, more permanent. She wanted her life to be not only narrated, but understood in a way that others would learn how important life could be.

I'm not saying enough here. What is it I need from my parents? What is the thing inside me I need when I walk?

"Maria. Guess what?" I said when she answered the phone a few days later from the stoop in back of the farmhouse. The back acres of Windy Hill were a blaze of yellow, red and orange leaves. "My father showed up at Windy Hill a couple of weeks ago. My father."

"Really? No way! Where'd he come from? How'd he just show up?"

"It turns out he's been getting letters and photos my entire life, knows all about me, and sent child support when I was growing up. And my mother never told me."

Maria took a breath. "Jesus, Betsy. All this time, you thought he'd gone back to Italy and deserted you."

"I guess I haven't talked to you since I started reading his letters. Tom and I read most of them together one night."

"So what's the deal? Did he go back to Italy?"

"He did. But then he came back. After I was born. Mom was so ticked off at him she wouldn't let him see me, didn't tell him about me. He found out accidentally. He wanted to be with her, but she flat out refused."

Maria gasped. "That's horrible. What was she thinking?"

"About how he left her alone and pregnant. Her parents, especially Grandpa, were angry with her, and she was angry that she had to be alone. She decided to pretend he no longer existed, that he was the one who left her, not the other way around."

"You must be so mad at her."

"Not really. I'm perplexed."

"Maybe she was just hiding out with the fairies in the magical pond."

"Probably. So, Dad and I've been talking on the phone, and when we went for a walk together, he gave me the letters my mother wrote to him. I can weave them together and make a story. I can find out what she had to say to him."

"So you can tell it's him from his pictures?"

"Yeah, he has a great smile. He looks Italian, like Grandpa used to say, a real Dago, but he's handsome, with dark hair tinged with gray, olive skin, and bright blue eyes. I have his eyes. He's not a big man, but he has broad shoulders for an old guy."

"No wonder I never hear from you anymore—you're busy with your dad."

"And the farm—right now I'm looking at our vegetable garden that's full of pumpkins and squash. We have bushels of apples too."

"It's growing on you, isn't it?"

"I'm totally open to everything these days. I think it has to do with letting go of the past and feeling like I'm starting all over again. It's like my father came into my life to show me the way after my mother's job was done."

She inhaled and said, "That's deep. I'm on the run. We need to get together. What's going on with you and Tom—are you sleeping together yet?"

"No."

"So nothing's changed there."

"I wouldn't say that . . . I haven't seen him in a month. Maria, I think it's too hard, to be with him. There's so much that needs to be said, and I don't think I have it in me to make it right."

"You're dodging life if you think Tom is too much to handle. Are you listening to your heart?"

"I'm hanging out at Windy Hill, talking to my Dad. All that feels right."

"Don't mess things up with Tom. I think he's good for you."

The wooden vegetable cart stood by the pumpkins tendriled in vines. I pulled the knife from inside and cut away the larger of the pumpkins and lifted them into the cart. Tom once carved me a pumpkin and brought it to my dorm room, early in our relationship. When I opened the door, all I saw was a big-faced orange grin on a pumpkin head. Then I looked down and saw his tennis shoes and pushed the pumpkin away from his face. He was grinning like that pumpkin when he kissed my nose.

I loved when he kissed my nose.

I let the waves wash up to my thighs and soak my jeans when I walked on Willow Beach the next day. The sweatshirt wasn't quite warm enough, and my feet were cold, but I kept on walking. Tom hadn't called me over the last weeks. He was waiting for me. He'd been angry when he hung up, but he understood. I was thinking about Tom when I turned to walk up the steps to the bench at the top of the cliff. There he was, sitting there and watching me like it was the most natural thing in the world.

I sat down next to him, and he took my hand. "Fancy meeting you here."

"You're not mad at me?"

"I'm unsettled. I'm surprised you haven't called me."

"I was afraid to. I told you I'm not good at love."

"I don't want it to be hard. It doesn't have to be hard."

"I know. I just needed to . . . be. I've been working, staying here on the weekends. I've been talking with my father . . ."

"What?" He twisted toward me.

At that moment I realized he didn't know. "Oh, I forgot you didn't know. My father showed up one day and we're talking on the phone, going for walks. It's really cool."

"And you didn't tell me?" He let go of my hand.

I couldn't believe it either.

"You know, this IS too much work. You don't even think I deserve to know what's going on, even though I read his letters with you, even though when you were a girl you told me how much you wished you had a father, even though you know you can talk to me about anything, any time. You just don't get what it's like to share a life with someone."

I shook my head. "No, I don't. I haven't done it in a long time." It was hopeless. I knew that, which was why I didn't call him. I didn't call him because I wasn't thinking about him at all. I'd totally checked out of whatever we'd had going on. "I'm sort of hopeless."

He folded his arms. "Aren't those wet jeans bothering you?"

"I need to get them off soon."

He surprised me by putting his arm around me and pulling me close. His warmth felt good. So did his strength. "You're a good egg."

"I am?"

"Yes, you are. You just don't know it yet."

I wasn't sure exactly what he meant but I didn't want to dwell on it. "It's weird having a father. I don't know him, yet I've known him all my life. I can't figure out if it's knowing he's my father that makes me want to believe I feel like he's part of me or if there's an innate karma that happens when a father and child meet after years of separation."

"Interesting. It changes who you are."

"Pardon me?"

"It changes how I see you, you having a father. Doesn't it do that to you? Change how you see yourself?"

"Yeah, sort of. I was thinking about that, actually. I'm still getting used to the whole idea of a father who's tangible and can be part of my life. He tells me about Italy."

"I'm glad you've been reunited. Are you ready for me to come out for a visit?"

No. I wasn't ready for that conversation. "Not yet," I whispered.

He took my hand again, and we watched the waves hit the shore and the sky above the horizon turn from blue to gray.

At the bottom of the stack of letters that Mom wrote to Dad, I found the letter my mother wrote a few weeks before she died.

Dear Rafe:

I know I've shut you out of Betsy's life, but I'm dying. The only parent she'll have is you. Ben is more of an uncle, and that's not enough. It was prideful what I did. And then I didn't know how to turn it around, until now. All the letters you sent to me are here, and I know you have mine as well. Please make sure she has them all, and please be the father she didn't have when she was growing up.

I'm sorry.
Margaret

I thought about my grandparents. To me, they'd always been loving and understanding, but with my mother, there was always this tense stillness between them. Mom was made to feel ashamed, and rather than lashing out at her parents, she lashed out at Dad. Now that I was finished with the letters, I had the complete picture. Even though my parents were apart, they were still part of each others' lives all those years. Parenthood didn't allow them to separate the pieces of our lives, like I was never able to be totally separate from Rick.

Mom wasn't in love with Dad. She never said it, but she wasn't. The truth was, once she had a chance to be left alone, she realized she'd made a mistake, and she was going to live with it, rather than living a lie. She was following her heart.

She knew enough about Tom and me to take me away so I could forget that summer after I went to Detroit. Mom had been hoping I would heal and go back to Tom, but it backfired. I remember her telling me how important love was, how unusual it was to find it. She was trying to tell me not to walk away.

I tell myself I have nothing to lose by spilling my secret, but knowing the story of my parents shows me I have everything to lose. I've been avoiding telling Tom anything, acting like there's nothing there to tell. I need to tell him, but how do I do that without tearing us apart?

Perhaps I have to be still and listen for the answers. Maybe that's what I've been doing, loving the question itself. It's possible I'm not just avoiding but trying to come up with an answer in a patient way. I don't want to ruin this.

Angel Mom, what do you have to say?

LADY OF THE LAKE
At Willow Beach

We are in a rhythm of life, me and my guys. I enjoy having two men in my life. They have come together to chase my demons away.

The Lady of the Lake whispers to me as I sit with my feet up on the bench at Willow Beach. Whether we are at his place in Vermilion, my condo in Cleveland, or Willow Beach in Conneaut, Tom and I feel her in our lives, like the letters we send along the Lake. She draws us to the water and calms us. Tom created her persona, because it wasn't just the lake, it was more, it was a being, a soul, a person, who drew us to the water and calmed us when we came. She is the Lady of the Lake.

The first time he said that, I thought of Malory's King Arthur. I remembered her in the water coming up to the surface, a watery but beautiful being who Merlin loved and who helped Sir Lancelot. Tom had never read *Le Morte d'Arthur*. His Lady of the Lake was simply a woman who walked along the water and went into it at random and encouraged us to walk with her as she provided guidance. He said she wore long flowing robes and her hair trailed to her waist. In the wind, her hair and skirts blew around her.

It's interesting that Tom has his fantasies just as I have mine. I like that about him.

The Lady of the Lake gives me permission to ask questions and just let them be. I wait for the answers from the goddess, a phantom of a wave against the shore, a footprint in the sand. Mom left behind some letters, a journal, a place called Windy Hill, and a daughter who is learning to listen and wonder and not just act.

"What are you whispering, you lady fair, full-height faerie-angel in watery shroud?" My words are taken away on the wind. I wait for an answer, as Tom and I have learned to do.

"*You have found your way*," she says clear and true. I imagine her then, her hair blowing as she stands on the shore, a beautiful phantom with a smile like the Madonna.

I know now that I am wrong when I think I know what I'm about. God takes us on journeys we cannot imagine we could take. Like how I loved Jerry more than my mother and now love the man I rejected twenty-seven years ago.

I search for wisdom more than adventure these days. I bought myself a small coffee-table journal and I use it to write favorite quotes from Mom's journals. Things like "Life is but a moment in time, a whisper of breath, breathed shallowly because we are but figments"; "God is in the blades of grass, the beetles in the hydrangea, the touch of a hand, and the words we utter, and through it all, He watches and waits"; and, "We love, but never as well as we could. Loving someone is one of the most imperfect things we do."

I found that it's wise to face our demons, however hard that is to do. I spent years running, starting with running off to Detroit. I ran away from my husband and then I deserted my family, and my home.

Tom made me climb up into the tree house. He showed me how to face my demons.

CHAPTER THIRTEEN – MAGICAL POND

The trees surrounding the house guarded it from marauding warriors, and the fairies in the trees whispered quiet promises of a world turned new, with hope.

"It's magical!" I said.

Tom looked over at me and shook his head in disbelief. He was grinning when he said, "You have surely lost it. But I'm glad you're being less serious about life."

I wanted to argue with that—I wasn't too serious, my life wasn't dull, I had an imaginative inner life—but I didn't. "Maybe," was all I said. Maybe I also had a tendency to be too defensive.

The fields behind the house were plowed down to dull, dry stalks of what used to be life-giving vegetables. The house itself was dark against the orange Halloween sky, and I said, "It looks a bit spooky."

"Good witches," he said as the car stopped next to the porch. "Let's walk about and see what's going on."

The apples were gone and the peach leaves were folding into themselves. I leaned against Tom as we walked, shoulder to shoulder, past the orchards to the fields beyond and admired the way Pedro turned over the soil so the vegetation could become the humus for next year's crop.

"Pedro knows what he's doing."

"He seems to." The exasperation in my voice was as surprising to me as it was to him.

"What's up?"

"The estate is paying for the farm expenses, and I'm living somewhere else. It's empty and a stranger's caring for it."

"He's not exactly a stranger . . ."

"But he's not family." We walked along the eastern edge of the property where the forest was. "The tree house is still there on the edge, the one my grandfather built, the one I wouldn't let Cassie play in."

"Yep." He grinned. "Whenever I'm unsure about my life, I retreat there."

"You are a trespasser."

"And no one's ever found me." Already he was heading through the brush flattened into the path that took us to the tree house. "I've seen Cassie there."

"Cassie?"

"Sure," he said, amused again.

"But I . . ."

"Do you really think she wouldn't know it was there? She lived here. Any kid would go into the woods to see what she could find. I saw her here a couple weeks ago. She said you were controlling when she was a teenager."

That Cassie shared this information with Tom was upsetting. Was it that much a part of who she was that it was at the nexus of her consciousness?

"Come on. Let's go up into the tree house." He started up the ladder. I hesitated. He looked down at me from the doorway, and said, "Are you coming?"

I started to climb. I wasn't sure I wanted to be inside the tree house. I continued, one rung after another, until I was climbing through the floor of the tree house and sitting next to Tom on the wood floor.

Tom put his arm around me. "It's nice here. How'd that go for you?"

I sighed. I thought about Jerry and me and our habit of coming here together. "It was so hard to let him go. I thought I loved him, but I didn't want to love him. I convinced myself we were a couple and were supposed to be together. I worried about what he was doing when we weren't together, afraid he'd find someone else. I couldn't make any sense of it, and then I wanted it to be over. And Mom . . . she saw the romance she had such high hopes for fall apart. I heard the bitterness growing in her like a cancer every time she spoke."

He sat back against the wall and crossed his legs, forcing me to move back too if I wanted to continue to hold his hand. He lowered his head and shook it slowly from side to side. "How important is any of this now?"

"This place makes reminds me of how short-term relationships end and the promise of possibility becomes a false prophecy. It makes me feel like a fool. What is the truth? Was Jerry a good thing—a man who loved me—or a bad thing—a man who molested me? I can't sort it out."

Quietly, still shaking his head like he was trying to shake off rain, he said, "You have the answer. You have to look into your heart."

I thought about all those men, all the stupidity. "I'm afraid sometimes when I feel like I need you. It feels the same as when I was with him, fearful and wanting him with me all the time. I need to know that the relationship is intact and that I'm the center of it, always. It's hard for me unless I'm in control of ending it or in control of how I let it affect me." I turned to him then. "I don't want to feel so dependent. That's not what I want. I'm afraid of that."

"It's okay. Feel the tree house, the bad and the good. Let go."

I thought about the hard wood, and I touched it. I looked up at the spider webs above my head. I sat back more into the place where the wall met the floor. I wallowed in it and became one with it. I felt the wood under my legs and thighs, hard beneath my buttocks. I smelled the woodsy mustiness of detritus. The air within the tree house felt damp, as if the house was holding in the moisture of the mud and leaves on the forest floor. The room we were in was eight by eight with shuttered windows on all four sides. I knew that if we opened them, it would feel like we were high among the trees, a part of them. I could hear the rustling of the few dried leaves hanging on and a woodpecker hammering away at a nearby tree. "It used to be a safe place. Grandma wanted it to be when he built it."

He stood and opened up the shutters. "This has been bugging me since we came in here."

"When they're open, we become one with the woods."

He sat back down and pulled me between his legs, my back against his chest. I rested my head on his shoulder and we listened and smelled, and felt the breeze come through the windows. "This is the way I remember it," he said. "With Cassie, was it really about safety or did you not want to share it with her?"

"It was a place where she could get in trouble."

"Does it feel dangerous now?"

"Not at all."

"I think your daughter was trying to warn me about you." He paused for several moments. "When you were a girl, did you come up here to read?" He hugged me close to him, hard.

"Linda and I used to trade Nancy Drew books and come here to read them. But I always liked it best when I was alone here."

"I was into the Tolkien series when I came here during high school. I kept hoping you would show up, that I'd see your pretty face looking in at me from the top of the ladder, but it never happened. You know, the difference in you after that first date was astonishing. You were shy and good-natured. Then you became bitchy."

I sat up and turned around. "Really?"

"Yeah, I couldn't believe I'd ever been with you. I hated you, but I mourned you."

It was so dark that I couldn't see his face anymore. I figured it was around seven o'clock. "Do you want to go back to the house?" We weren't having a good time.

"Let's go to the pond first."

We climbed down the ladder in silence and walked to the pond. It was cold, even through my sweatshirt. We could see our breath by the light of the moon.

He broke the silence by saying, "It feels more and more like winter."

"Yes, it's lurking."

The pond was dead silent. We didn't even hear a fish jump. The moon shone on its black flaccid surface. It didn't feel magical to be there, not that night.

The first snow of the season came in a mist followed by flurries until the entire city was blanketed in white. I thought about the dogs in Alaska and how they keep warm by getting under the snow. I remembered snow days at the farm when I stayed home from school and we stayed near the fireplace. We escaped the world for a day. I missed Mom.

Ben called, as if on cue. I hadn't spoken to him in a couple of weeks. He was in and out of town, I couldn't keep track, but he seemed like he was in high spirits. Hearing Ben's voice, I missed Mom even more. He wanted to know what I was planning to do for Thanksgiving, and without thinking about it twice, I said it would be at the house in Conneaut. "I hope you'll come."

"I always hope I'll find you settled in there, but you haven't done it yet." He paused, then said, "Karen and her family are flying in from Texas—can they come to dinner?"

"Oh, sure. They can stay at the house. We can set up some extra beds if we need to."

"The boys can sleep on the floor."

"Okay, that'll work. So what do you think of the snow?"

"I'm glad it came after my plane landed."

"How long were you away this time?"

"A couple weeks. That's enough for me. Everyone's so poor, and the country looks like the Badlands. Crooks around every corner and the cops dying to beat someone up and put them in their rickety jails. One of the guys I work with ended up in jail for driving too fast on a dirt road with no posted speed limits. They roughed him up and put him in the back of the cruiser. We had to bail him out. He has a cut on his cheek that'll leave a good scar."

"Whoa. I hope you don't have to go back."

"Probably will. We're doing more work down there now. And in South America. I could end up in Colombia of all places." He paused, then asked, "So what's new, girl?"

I always liked it when he called me 'girl'; it was an endearment. "I'm well. Do you know I've been wrong about men for years?"

He grunted. "Some people say men are dogs. Men say that about their own kind."

"I'm seeing someone."

"You are? Who?"

"Tom Madison. I don't know that you'd know him. He's a year older than me, grew up in Conneaut, took me out once in high school, and we got together at Kent. We were together almost two years during college."

"How'd you meet up again?"

"Mom's funeral."

"Your mother would like that."

"I think she does. I like to think of her more like an angel than a ghost, because she watches over me."

"I feel that way too, but they don't say that, you know."

"Screw them. They know only what they want to know, what they're looking for, and our whole society is built around what 'they' have to say about things."

"I sense a bitterness."

"I AM bitter." The force of my words surprised me. "I feel like we're handed a bunch of bull. I feel like I've handed myself a bunch of bull. I've had all these misconceptions and ways of looking at things, and they're all falling apart now, rolling down the hill in pieces, from the way I view men, to how I see my father, to who Mom was, to what I want out of life."

"I don't know why that bothers you. Isn't that how life works? We figure things out as we go along our way. How we view the world at twenty is different from twenty-five and vastly different at forty-five. You have to allow for that."

I sighed. "I haven't been doing that. I've chosen to see life exactly the same way. I've been going through life punishing men for trying to love me, showing them that I wasn't going to be drawn into their tricks. My heart was still, unmoved. And I even did that with Tom—I offended him and hurt him by lumping him in with everyone else. This way of thinking caused me to make the biggest mistake of my life."

"What mistake was that?"

"Having an abortion."

He didn't say anything. He waited.

"I had an abortion in college. I didn't tell Tom."

"Does he know?"

"No."

"What are you waiting for, girl? You may as well get it over with."

I was building up strength and resolve. That's what I told myself.

I woke up anxious in the middle of the night. My heart felt like it was beating twice as fast as it usually did. I was sweating. I sat up and tried to breathe slowly. I wanted to get up for a drink of water, but I was too afraid.

At noon Tom called. "Are you ready for lunch?"

"I had a nightmare. And then I had another one. I didn't want to leave the bed."

"You don't sound like yourself."

"I'm fine," I said as I fully woke up. The throbbing welled up from my uterus like labor pains and made me nauseous. I doubled over from the menstrual cramp pain. "Oh, my God."

"I'll be there in fifteen minutes," Tom said, and he hung up.

I looked between my legs and saw no blood. I walked to the bathroom and stuffed tissue between my legs, just in case. I took a long drink of water with an ibuprofen.

The bell rang, and I rang him up. When I opened the door, he looked worried.

"It's okay," I said. I remembered Maria's face looking the same way, in that scummy little room in Detroit. "I'm just getting my period. I don't get it every month, so when I do, it's really bad." I walked back to the bedroom and he helped me under the covers.

"Tell me about the dream."

I shook my head.

"It'll feel less evil if you tell me."

I couldn't. I'd have to tell him that these cramps reminded me of Detroit. I always stayed in bed for half a day until they went away. In sleep it all came back to me, the feeling of having a life sucked out of me, maimed and killed by the mother who knew no love, only selfishness.

"I was being chased by a devil with a trident ready to hurl at me."

By the look on his face, I knew he wasn't going to be patient with me. "Try again."

"I had a baby without a face. In another dream, I had a baby with no fingers. The baby couldn't breathe. I tried to breathe for it but when I put my mouth over the baby's, there were no lips. It was so small, as small as a scampi, with transparent skin."

He turned away and looked at the picture of my mother, me, Cassie, and Beth. He picked it up. "What's it mean?"

I shook my head. Maybe the cramps made me dream it. "I think the cramps convinced me I was miscarrying in my sleep."

Tom's face was ashen.

Then I remembered his daughter Angela. "But since I haven't had sex, I can't be miscarrying."

He brightened up. "Of course."

In my journal I wrote.

> Tom was upset today when I was having menstrual cramps and he thought I might possibly be miscarrying. The look on his face . . . it was like the loss of his still-born daughter Angela had come back to him with all the terrible sadness from twenty-five years ago. The loss of that child is still amazingly raw.

How can I ever tell Tom the truth? If I told him, he'd not only hate me, he'd mourn the loss right along with me. If I tell him, it would be a selfish act, not a confession to bring us closer together. I'm looking for the first step to possible redemption. Maybe Maria's right—I can't tell him the truth. But that truth holds us back. He knows something happened to me, he may even suspect what it was. He still wants me to fess up.

A baby missing arms, missing a face, without a mouth. Why do I still dream about that almost thirty years later? How can I make it stop?

By telling Tom. That's the only way. Haven't I promised God to tell him? Why am I defying God?

The following night I dreamt of a clinical room with metal stirrups for my feet and women who looked at me like I was a derelict from the streets. I started counting and woke up in another room and they told me I had to lie on the bed until the bleeding stopped. When I tried to get up from the bed, I felt stickiness on my legs that told me it was too early. I looked down and saw that all the sheets and blankets were stained by my brown-red blood.

I felt so lonely. I felt all alone in the world. The way I felt in that dream was the way I felt about my life. It wasn't the abortion that was the terrible thing, it was that I did it without Tom.

Tom stopped by the condo when I was on my way out for a walk on Sunday morning, so I met him at the door of the lobby and we took off. We walked through the Flats and it began to snow. Later we stopped in at Costanzas and bought some calzones and antipasti and some bottled water. In my living room, looking out at the lights dotting the rise above Edgewater Park, fat snowflakes danced close to the window.

"I want to have Thanksgiving at the farm."

Tom stopped and drew me to him so he could kiss my neck. He left his mouth there, and I felt the quivering start in my groin. "Good idea, sweetie. Who are you inviting?"

"You, of course. And Ben and his family, your parents and Cassie and her family."

"I like that idea. My kids will be with Miriam in New Mexico."

I woke up with night sweats. Tom pulled away when I moved to sit up. I put my feet on the floor and felt my pulse in the soles of my feet. My heart was beating fast. I didn't want to disturb him, so I pulled on my robe and walked out into the living room of the condo to watch the lights on the River. I thought about sipping some wine but thought better of it.

When I went back to bed, sweat dried on my skin, I lay on my side of the bed, not touching Tom. Uneasiness settled on me, but it didn't prevent my going to sleep. I dreamt of the baby with no face again. This time I screamed when I tried to breathe into its mouth.

I screamed into the dark cave of the bedroom in a warehouse building on the banks of the Cuyahoga River.

Tom startled from his sleep and swooped me up into his arms. He rocked me until my screams turned to sobs. In the morning, he said, "This has to stop. What are you going to do about it?"

I shook my head.

"You should make arrangements to see someone." He looked tired.

I went to see Dr. Morgan, a therapist I'd been seeing off and on over the years in times of crisis. I started by telling him about the dreams and night sweats while he sat calmly in the chair at his desk and took notes on a notepad with his Bic.

"Do you think it has anything to do with Tom?"

"Tom's the new element in my life."

"No, I wouldn't say that. You also told me you now have a father. Your mother died earlier this year."

I looked over at him. He waited coolly for me to continue, but I shook my head.

"What is it, Betsy? What is it you're keeping from him?"

I stared. "How do you know I'm keeping something from him?"

"It's common to lose sleep when you feel guilty."

I ran my hand along the arm of the chair. The nappy corduroy almost hurt my fingers to touch it.

"You and I both know what it is. Remember, I know about the abortion. Wasn't it his baby?" Dr. Morgan looked over his bifocals at me, his head tipped down to give me a good look of the thin sweeps of hair over his bald scalp.

"Yes."

"What's the cost of telling him?"

The question was one I'd pondered so much, I answered right away. "It'll be over. How could he trust me again? I not only broke off our relationship when I was twenty, I didn't come clean. And I haven't come clean now either."

"Lots of time has passed. One could argue it can't possibly matter anymore."

"We loved each other, and I knew the baby was his, but I did it anyway. Having that abortion was more important to me than what Tom and I had."

He let that sink in, wrote a few notes. I curled my legs under me and settled into the couch, prepared for a long wait. I shook my head.

"That's right, shake it out of your head, my dear. It's not going to work. Tell me about you and Tom."

"We had this awkward angst-tinged relationship in high school but when we were at college together, we hooked up. It was different than when we tried to date in high school. We were away from home and felt grown up. We fell in love. It was easy, because we'd always liked each other."

"Did you have a hard time trusting his love?"

I looked past his shoulder and out the window. "Yes."

"Why?"

"It's complicated." He knew the answer and was letting me voice it. I closed my eyes.

Jerry's hands were prying my legs open and I was saying "no" but he was kissing my neck and sucking on my earlobes and his weight was on top of me and I couldn't move and it hurt when he was grinding against my pelvis bone and then I felt flesh against flesh, a pressure and pain. Then it felt all right but it was sex and I didn't want it, not with Jerry. It was all wrong, and I looked up at the ceiling and watched a spider making its way to the overhead light that we never turned out in the living room until he stopped and all was quiet. Only then did I have control, and I writhed out from under him. A swell of emotion came into my throat as I remembered that day, and I had to turn away as the tears started to flow. The doctor handed me the Kleenex box, and I dabbed at my eyes.

"Betsy," he said. I looked at him. "Why do you have trouble trusting?"

"I don't trust myself. I stole my mother's boyfriend."

"How did you do that? You were a child."

I nodded. "Fifteen going on sixteen."

"Did you ask him to have sex? Did you try to get his attention?"

My knees were up against my chest, my stocking feet on the couch. I closed my eyes and took a long, deep breath. "No."

"So why is it you think YOU can't be trusted? Why are you blaming yourself?"

I kept my eyes closed. I searched for why that was so. "I started to like him. I wanted him all the time. I became obsessed with him."

Silence. I opened my eyes. "What were you thinking about earlier, before you closed your eyes?"

"The first time."

"The first time you had sex with him? Tell me about it."

"I can't."

"Try."

I told him about lying on my back and looking at that spider on the ceiling. "It hurt, but it was part of the plan, and I let it happen."

"Part of the plan?"

"God's plan."

He sat back and put his hands together. "That's interesting. I think you're getting somewhere. There was an inner voice that told you it was the right thing to do?"

"I thought God's plan was for me to be with Jerry. I thought Jerry loved me. I had this idea that everything happened for a reason."

"No wonder you decided you didn't need God anymore." He wrote on his pad.

"But I knew it was wrong. And I wanted it to stop."

"Did you say that?"

"Yes."

"So, you were raped by your mother's boyfriend when you were fifteen and home alone and then the two of you met, what, two, three times after that?"

"We met almost every day for six months." I took another deep breath and let it out slowly. I hugged my knees in closer.

"Remember when you told me about this before, a few years ago? You acted like it was consensual. You didn't tell me you'd said 'no.'"

Jerry was on top of me trying to undo my zipper. He said "shit," and crushed me with his weight. His elbow came down on the soft flesh of my arm. I cried out and he yelled at me to shut up. He stood up and the face looking down at me was anything but loving. He yanked my shorts off and I started crying. I turned my head away from him when he tried to kiss me, but he roughly turned my face towards his so he could put his tongue inside my mouth. I gagged.

"Do you want to tell me what you're thinking about?"

"It was awful. He was rough and I was crying. His elbow hurt me. When I felt him against me, trying to find me, I was gritting my teeth, waiting. I said 'Stop it' really loud. He put his hand over my mouth, and I tried to bite him. I tried to move out from under him. He grabbed my hands and pulled them above my head and forced himself into me and I said 'Please stop, please stop,' over and over again, crying because it hurt. He didn't stop, and he didn't let go of my wrists."

"You can't blame yourself for being raped."

"Afterwards, I thought I loved him. I thought he loved me. He acted like what we did was what needed to happen the first time I had sex."

"You can't blame yourself."

"But Mom really liked him."

"You were a child. You'd never experienced that kind of attention before."

"But I kept seeing him."

"And it stopped."

"I stopped it. I couldn't do it anymore. It was wrong."

"Good. You took charge."

"But I slept with my mother's boyfriend."

"Do you think it mattered to your mother ten years, twenty years, later? Don't you think it's about time you forgave yourself for something that wasn't your fault? Are you hearing me—it wasn't your fault."

"I can't count on myself to make the right decisions."

"Yes, you can. You did make the right decision, by ending it. Betsy, look at me now. Think about this—it wasn't your fault." He was sitting forward, close to me, his eyes fixed on mine.

"What do you mean?" I let go of my legs and sat up like an adult.

"Tell me about who you are now."

I didn't know how to answer that question either. "I like to write. I miss my mother and my grandparents. I just met my father, and it feels like he's filling a void. My old boyfriend is being a good friend. I have this old farmhouse, and I love it, but I don't know what to do with it."

"Do you trust yourself now?"

"No. I don't know whether I should spend a lot of time with my father. I'm not sure whether I should have a relationship with Tom again. I'm afraid to choose to stay in the house when I only made the decision to leave a few years ago."

"One thing at a time, Betsy. I have a book for you." He reached over to his bookshelf and presented me with a book of Mary Oliver poetry. "She works through her problems in words."

"I keep a journal." I opened it up and saw the neatly typed words in rows of varying length.

He nodded. "We all have our private lives and we need to be comfortable with them. There has to be a reason why you're holding on to the past. When you understand yourself, you'll trust yourself."

"Tell me, what is it you plan to do with your one wild and precious life?" I read aloud from the book.

"As far as your father, the farmhouse, and your friend-boyfriend, stop thinking with your head and feel with your heart."

"If I tell Tom about the abortion . . ."

"You need to be done with it, Betsy. You NEED to be done with it. If he loves you . . ."

"If he can't forgive me, we lose what we have."

"You learned not to trust anyone. Everything was a lie. No one could be trusted. You learned you can't trust your own gut feelings."

"I'm surprised by what I write in my journal sometimes."

"It's the best thing you can do for yourself, writing in that journal." He paused and folded his hands under his chin. He appeared to be thinking about whether to say something. "What's the price of not telling him?"

"I don't know." I stopped for a moment. "I think I'll live with it. It will fade into the background over time."

"I wouldn't be so sure. The price you're paying is sleepless nights and horrific nightmares. They could continue for the rest of your life. You'd be tortured."

"We made a pact that you wouldn't tell me what to do."

"We did, but you need to consider whether it's worth it to guard the silence. It's not fair to you that you're not allowed to say anything. You have his affection now, and he's a reasonable person. Tell him."

I pursed my lips and met his eyes. "I'll consider it."

As I drove home, I felt the weariness of keeping a secret hidden so deep the only one who knew about it for years was Maria, and she told me to let it go, forget about it.

Now that Tom and I were trying to figure out how our relationship derailed, the abortion was a piece to the puzzle that Tom deserved to have.

I parked my car in the parking lot under my building. I gave into the urge to walk even though I wasn't dressed for it. The snow started falling as I walked down into the Flats and along the roads without sidewalks past dark buildings where a few cars parked in the growing shadows. The sunset was magnificent, the pinks varied through the bare trees on the high banks above the river.

I rehearsed the words I'd tell Tom. *When I went to Detroit for the weekend, it wasn't just a girls' weekend, I had an abortion. I have to tell you something and it may hurt you, but when we were young, I aborted our child. Remember how you thought those unwed mothers were stupid because there's all this birth control available but still they get pregnant? I was one of those stupid girls.* In the end, I knew the various things I could say to him but the time and place and our moods would determine how I said what needed to be said.

I walked near the steelyard and down the Towpath Trail to Steelyard Commons. I was cold, but I didn't care. I was in the trance of the rhythmic walking. I started humming. I was going to tell Tom. I was glad about my decision. "It's a way of taking care of myself," I said into the gathering darkness. I only had to place one foot in front of the other.

The wind whipped into my eyes and made them water. Tears froze on my cheeks and chin. I dug my hands deeper into my pockets and picked up the pace to keep warm. It didn't do much good. It was past twilight and black. I couldn't keep walking, my toes were too cold. Home was too far away.

In the shelter of an industrial park building doorway, I pulled out my cell phone and called Tom.

"Betsy?"

"Hi, Tom."

"Where are you?"

My teeth chattered. "I went for a walk and went too far. I only have a sweater, no coat. Are you in Rocky River? Can you pick me up?"

"What street are you on?"

"I don't know. Near Canal, on the Towpath."

"How do I get there?"

"I don't know, but I'm south of Steelyard Commons."

"How long were you walking?"

I looked at the time on my phone. "Two hours."

"You must be freezing. I'm leaving now. You're going to have to talk to me about where you are so I can find you."

"Okay," I said.

"You're a little nuts these days. Ya know that?"

"Yes."

"Are you trying to hurt yourself?" I could hear his breath, the sound of his keys clanging, the door closing, the engine starting, and all the time, he kept talking to me. He didn't wait for my answer. "Blow on your hands, move around, walk north, toward me."

"I think I should stay in this doorway."

"How are your feet?"

"Frozen."

"Can you feel them?"

"No."

"Walk toward me, Betsy. Walk north, back in the direction from which you came."

"I need to put the cell phone down. I need to put my hand in my pocket."

"Okay. I'll look for you, and I'll call you if I need to. Do you know how much I love you?"

"Even though I'm a little crazy?" I blew on my hands and walked. "Do you know I always do what you tell me to do, that's how much I trust you?"

"Yes, and that's why you're going to tell me about your appointment with Dr. Morgan and why you're having these dreams. You're going to do it because you trust me. You're going to do it because you love me and you know I love you. I'm not Jerry or Rick who told you one thing and did something else the next day. I'm me, Tom."

All those wasted years. All the wandering. Just because I was pregnant didn't mean we couldn't have a good life together.

It was a baby I got rid of. It would have been our son or daughter. It would have been our first child. We would have loved that child. Tom would have felt as responsible for the pregnancy as I did. We would have had a child.

I knew it was his car by how tentative it was about going down the road. I could see Tom behind the wheel scanning the walkway as I neared Steelyard Commons. When he turned toward the berm, the headlights lit up the path to the car. I walked to it.

He got out of the car and came around to my side to help me into the car. He didn't look into my eyes. I felt he was angry. Inside the car, the warmth hurt my feet. When he was sitting in the driver's seat again, he turned to me and said, "What the hell did that doctor tell you?"

I didn't answer. It wasn't the right time. "I think we should go to the hospital."

In the emergency room, they declared my numbed, almost purple feet to be free of frostbite but susceptible to episodes of coldness if I didn't keep them warm.

The condo was not my own when we walked into it at two in the morning. The cave-like bedroom, the floor-to-ceiling windows, the stone countertop, they belonged to someone else, a frenzied woman who walked the streets in the cold of winter, who dreamt of dead babies, and who forgot to take showers on the weekend. That was the person I needed to leave behind. I'd been frenzied and alone my whole life, it seemed.

"Let me know when you're ready to talk," Tom said. He walked back out the door.

CHAPTER FOURTEEN - COCOON

I read Mary Oliver's poetry.
I didn't even try to assess the situation. I didn't try to figure it out. I was tired of going over the same things over and over again. I was a woman who spent as little time in the office as possible, who didn't care about office politics, who didn't even remember how to walk in a frenzy any more. I stopped journaling. I didn't answer the phone when it rang and I left the room when the answering machine started to record a voice message. I ate Cheerios for breakfast and grilled cheese for lunch and frozen meals with wine for dinner.

The stack of books included more Mary Oliver. It also included Gwendolyn Brooks' poetry and novels, Marianne Moore, Sue Monk Kidd's novels and memoir, and all the Bronte works. I read all of it. I devoured pages of words as if I was eating them, letting them soak on my tongue and in my brain, and chewing them as I went on to the next morsel.

Wuthering Heights suited my mood and the clear black coldness of oncoming winter. When I read Bronte's story of Heathcliff, I wondered if Emily discussed that great love with her sisters or if she alone knew what it was all about. And how had that pastor's daughter, kept in isolation, known the heart of men. My father told me not to mess this up, and I didn't want to.

I lived the abortion over and over again. I watched Tom walk away from me. I heard him tell me he was done with me. The look on his ex-wife's face, startled, when she opened that door and looked me over, was fierce.

I remembered all the men, and I wrote down their names. I wrote about where I met them and what we did. I remembered how I wanted to be loved and it never felt like the love I wanted to have. I remembered how some of them called for days and gave up, how some showed up at my door, and how some bought me gifts to try to win me over. I remembered the way they looked at me with adoration as they told me how beautiful I was and the looks on their faces when I didn't believe them and lashed out at them in anger.

I'd hated myself more than I'd hated anyone else in my life. I could understand Jerry's lust for me. I could understand Rick's wanting to settle down but not knowing how to do it. I could understand Max wanting a child and wanting a child with me. I could understand Tom staying away from me. They didn't want to get hurt by me, they didn't want to feel the hatred that I couldn't contain.

The hatred was hatred toward myself.

No wonder God left me alone.

I took long baths. I shaved my legs. I nourished my hair. I drank lots of water. I slathered my tummy and shoulders with moisturizer. I gave myself a pedicure. I looked at my face in the mirror and decided it was a good face, a strong face, with eyes that were questioning and even trusting.

I'd always enjoyed Sue Monk Kidd's books, but I discovered that she wrote essays on spirituality by searching her name on the internet. I was looking for a novel, and I found *When the Heart Waits*, a memoir. The book was written in her darkness, during the time when she wondered if her marriage was working for her, and there seemed to be no blame in that; she was trying to find out what she needed out of life. Kidd believes we must wait and not push life ahead so we can allow ourselves to be transformed while God enters into our waiting. We often push forward and strive and we're not sure why, exactly. The title of the book says it all—we must live every day in a dance with God, in our waiting, and He will show us the way, literally. The way we do this is by being mindful, by paying attention to every moment and how we feel about it so we know how to react to it. In our waiting, we turn within and actively let God work with our soul. Soul making takes place, and we become renewed without knowing it's happening because we're not actively making it happen, we're actively turned inward, waiting for God to work within us. We go into a cocoon, into the darkness, and our faith and hope, our God connection is making us into a butterfly—we are reborn. Sue Monk Kidd would say we must embrace the darkness to reach the light.

That's what I was doing even before I opened Kidd's book, and when I did open it, I found it spoke to where I was in my life. Life could be so much easier, if I gave into whatever was planned for me and let go of my expectations and needs. I was living wrong.

Tom didn't call. I didn't call him either. I wasn't really worried because I knew he was waiting, like he had before. On the tenth day of our silence, I sent him a letter.

Dear Tom:

I miss you. You have become everything to me. If you come back, I promise to tell you every single thing that hides within my heart, all you need to know. I have nothing to lose, with you down the Lake in the other house and me here missing your warm body against mine while I sleep.

I'm living the questions. I'm letting them become part of my soul. I'm listening to women's voices, and they all say the same thing—I need to be truthful, I need to accept my mistakes and go past them. Mom said I needed to learn to love the questions, but she didn't say that I had to take them inside of me. She left that part out.

I want you to be with me at Windy Hill for Thanksgiving, and by the time you get this letter, it will be time.

You know what I've discovered? That I hate myself. I'm trying to love again, starting with me.

All my love, and then some,
Betsy

    I didn't know what to expect. But I didn't believe things were over between Tom and me. I trusted the universe to make it all work out.
    If Mom's journals weren't so voluminous, maybe it wouldn't take me so long to get through them. She had many of the same thoughts I had, and one thing my soul began to understand was how much we were alike, how much all of us are alike. And how much we need God.
    When I went away to college, Mom missed me, like I'd missed my own daughter. Instead of accepting that loss, I turned away from it. I planned travel trips, worked long hours, bought the condo in the city, decided to get on with life. Mom did the opposite—she sent care packages, visited me in Kent, cajoled me into coming home on the weekends. She wrote that I'd grown up too fast. She hoped I would be okay. She worried about all the boys, and then she was happy about Tom because he was stabile and caring, a good guy.
    Tom was a good guy, and I didn't deserve him. Mom wrote.

Why is it women often choose the bad boys over the good guys? Why is it that when a man cares about us in an authentic and giving way, we run away like there's something wrong with him for loving us the way we deserve to be loved?

Rafe told me I meant more to him than life itself. Then he left me, but he had good reason to. Instead of seeing what he did as the way things were in Italy—the need to help with harvest, to support the family when his father died, to help his mother through her grief—I chose to think that he deserted me, that he left me all alone and pregnant. That wasn't fair because he didn't know I was pregnant. He trusted our love. He trusted I would love him.

I figured out my mistake too late. I hated him, even after he came back. Those months with Dad not talking to me, with Mom looking like someone died, me starting to show and not going out much because people were talking about me, they made me hate him more. I hated myself for getting into the situation. But I blamed Rafe.

Betsy can count on Tom not to make those mistakes. He knows right and wrong. He cares. And Betsy's in a place where she can believe that he'll take care of her. I hope.

    I could trust Tom. I knew that as I sat in the churches of my life. Day after day I found myself at Trinity, at the Old Stone Church, at the church in Conneaut. October went by, November came, and we drew closer to Thanksgiving. I read Thomas Merton and Mother Theresa and Sue Monk Kidd. I lived the questions themselves. I waited. My life became a prayer in my days of darkness.
    I'd deserted Tom because I didn't love myself and I couldn't love him because of it. One thing that was different between Mom and I was that I trusted Tom to be there, while she didn't trust my father.
    They didn't have the benefit of having known each other for a lifetime.

"I'm ready." I stood in my kitchen at the opaque whiteness that fogged the dark iron buildings of the Flats. "I can talk to you now."

Tom didn't answer right away. "I've been hoping you would call for days. I've been in waiting mode, pacing, reading, driving, checking the phone to see if I missed a call. I got your note, but I wasn't sure whether to respond."

"I'm sorry I've been so difficult. Walk with me."

"I'll meet you in forty minutes."

I pulled on a coat and went downstairs to wait on the street. The snow whirled in the wind. I stuck out my tongue to catch some, and Tom beeped his horn when he saw me.

"Silly," he said when he climbed out of his car.

"You'd do it if you were out there." I was in a good mood. I felt like a cloud had lifted, one that had been there for forty years. I leaned over and kissed his cheek. "Want to loop around downtown?"

He turned off the car. "Whatever you say. You seem to be calling the shots."

"Are you angry with me?"

"I haven't spoken to you in twelve days, but today you call me like everything's okay and I'm just going to drop everything and be here for you."

I took his hand. "That's selfish. I can't help it—I want to spread the joy. I feel like life is starting over."

"You found love."

"And now I can love you."

He squeezed my hand. "I hear hesitation in your voice."

I drew close to him, arms were entwined from our shoulders to our waists and leaned over to kiss his lips. "I'm really happy to have you in my life."

He drew me closer and folded me in his arms so he could kiss me fully on the lips. The feeling welled in me again. I was in love. I leaned into him, allowing him to pull me yet closer. People walked around us, trying to keep going along the sidewalk toward Tower City.

"Are you okay?" he asked.

"I am," I said into his shoulder. "Mom once told me that when she went within and became more spiritual and connected with her inner artist, she gave up wanting to have a lover. It wasn't necessary. She felt the glimmer of possibility, just the slightest, the day Ben walked into the store. When he came back in again, the next day, to say 'hello,' she wanted to love again. I haven't wanted to love, and part of me has now decided it's not necessary."

He pulled away so we could look at each other, "I know."

"I'm not sure I want to be in love. But there's that glimmer of possibility."

He grinned and shook his head. "You know what I've always said—we don't choose to be in love."

"I'm not sure I want this," I repeated.

"Are you going to run away from me again? Because if that's what you're planning, I'm not going to allow it to happen this time. My mistake last time was that I gave up too soon."

Our pace picked up. I felt like I was starting to run away, but his pace caused me to slow. "I kept hoping I'd fall in love somewhere along the way. By holding onto that need, that hope, for something that I didn't even know what it looked like, I kept myself from growing. And even though I thought I wanted to love, I didn't, not really. I didn't know myself. I was stupid."

"You're not stupid. You're a woman who lost her way. Slow down and stand still."

I stopped. He stopped. "Don't keep me waiting any longer." More quietly, he said, "Remember, we can't help loving each other."

I trusted his love, I reminded myself.

He squeezed my hand. We were facing each other.

"That summer, when I left, I was pregnant, and didn't want you to know."

His eyes flickered, but held firm on mine. The corners of his lips twitched. He kept steadfastly looking at me. "And?"

"I didn't want to keep you from your life, your ambitions," I offered. "I knew if I told you, you would've talked me out of it. I felt so stupid, getting pregnant, like Mom. I didn't want to be like Mom, having a baby I wasn't ready to raise."

He looked away and dropped my hand. I feared I'd lost him. I hadn't said the word "abortion," but he understood what I was saying. He looked distraught when he said, "You didn't trust me to help you. You didn't know how big my love was." His voice trembled.

When he looked back at me, I shook my head. "I assumed you wouldn't be able to handle it, which was unfair. My plan only went as far as getting to a clinic when I left, and once I made up my mind,

I just got on with it. I steeled myself for the task at hand. I couldn't tell you anything because if I said anything, if I even had contact with you, you might have guessed. I didn't want you to talk me out of it."

He looked at me with such disappointment, it seemed like all the love had drained out of him. I was destroying what we had. He would have been better off not knowing.

"I'm sorry." My heart reached out to him. I wanted to tell him it would be okay, but maybe it wouldn't be. This could be the end of us, of what we knew. *This is what I needed to do, it's what has been holding me back, and whatever happens, I'll still love him, he'll still love me, but that love may have to be kept on a shelf because of what I did and how he feels about it. Stay steady, say the right words. Be with me, God.* "I left because I loved you. I know that's crazy, but I've examined it, and it really is what I was after. I didn't want to be pregnant, but I would have had the child if things had been different. The timing was off. We were young and you had things you had to do and having an uneducated wife and baby weren't part of your plans. We would have been in the way."

His eyes were on the ground. I didn't know what else to say so I started pacing, down the sidewalk and back again. When he didn't say anything, I did it again. On my fourth round, he said, "Stop it!" with such force in his voice, I stopped. I stood a ways away from him, and waited to see what he had to say. "I suspected this," he said. "I didn't want to believe it could be true. I didn't want to think that you were capable of such a heartless act."

He would hate me now. He'd lost a child, a most precious life, and I'd taken the life of another one of his children. All I could do was stand there near him and be condemned. Courage left me.

He held out his arms wide. "You may as well strike me down. You may as well wipe me from your life. You say you did this because of what I needed, but you didn't allow me to be part of the decision. How could you seriously have been doing it for me?" He dropped his arms, helpless before me. What was done was done. "Do you know what I would have done?" He took a step toward me. He was a warrior facing his enemy.

I was three paces away from him. I stood straight and crossed my arms defensively. I felt my chin rise. "Yes, I do."

"You know I would have loved you and the baby, you know I would have done everything in my power to make it work, you know I would have lived my life as well as I could without regret even though we had a child? You know all that?"

"Yes." My response was weak.

"Jesus." He took another step toward me. His finger was jabbing the air. "You killed our child." I took a step back. He took two steps toward me so his finger was practically touching me. "You did this horrible thing. You deliberately chose not to have a life with me."

"I know."

"It could have worked. We would have made it work." His face was distorted with anger but he was softening as the horror of it sunk in. "We would have had the child. It would have been my first child, our first child. Don't you see that when you love someone, you don't do things like that? I thought you loved me."

"I did love you. I loved you more than I loved myself. I loved you so much I only wanted your happiness. But now, all these years later, I can't believe I did that to you either."

He dropped his hand and put both of his hands in his pockets. He looked older. "I thought we had it good."

"You were everything to me. I was ashamed of having allowed it to happen. I didn't want to be an unwed mother."

"You wouldn't have been an unwed mother."

"But you would have had to marry me. You wouldn't have been marrying me because you loved me, you would have married me because you had to. How would we ever have known if we married each other because we wanted to?"

"Oh, Betsy, this is so complicated." He threw up his hands and walked down the street away from me. He was walking fast. I followed him at a distance, uncommitted, not sure what to think or say, and thinking I'd ruined things for us, just when I was loving him again. The hollow ache that comes when you've lost someone came in, and my chest ached. I didn't want to lose him.

We walked like that until we were near the baseball stadium. It was cold, but I wasn't noticing. He was almost a block ahead of me when I shouted, "Tom, wait up."

He stopped. I caught up to him next to one of the lighted columns in the courtyard between the stadium and arena. The anger was gone, but defeat showed in his sloping shoulders. He reached out his hands to me, and I took them. I felt such relief, I started trembling. He pulled me to him and we stood in the cold, feeling the warmth of our bodies through our coats. As if on cue, we both opened our coats and let the other in, my breasts against his chest, my hips against his. He was trembling too. I sensed he was letting it set in. When we had both calmed down, he said, "Let's go back to your place."

He took my hand and we walked the long city blocks back to my apartment. I felt safe and protected by the steady heat from his hand, the way his fingers curled around mine. I felt his strength and steadiness in the way my palm and his palm became united.

The apartment felt warm and inviting. When we got inside, we threw our coats on one of the barstools and our bodies came together like our hands had. We fit. "I don't want to talk about this anymore," he said.

When I started to say something, he put his finger to my lip. "You made a mistake when we were young, but that was a long time ago. It hurts to think about it, not just for me, but for you. It's out in the open, and it's part of who we are, part of our history together, but I want to move past it."

We kissed like we were hungry. Time passed, and all we knew were lips and hands and bodies and the bliss of letting go of everything else in our lives. I allowed elation and delight. I enjoyed the way he felt against me and the smooth power of his back and shoulders that I stroked through his soft sweater. Our embrace said more than words could have said.

When I spoke, I said, "I'm ready. I'm ready to love you."

And he kissed me harder, his hands cupping my buttocks and pulling me to him. He said, "Tell me a story later, okay?"

It had been our game. I promised to tell him a story later. We'd played that game the first time we made love and ever after, and he hadn't forgotten.

I nodded.

He slipped my clothes off before I knew what was happening, and I felt his hands all over me. It was difficult to separate my memories from the present as the way it felt to be loved by Tom came back to me.

I unbuttoned his shirt, luxuriating in the softness of the fabric, and touched his bare chest as I opened the shirt and pulled it from his shoulders. He stood up again, next to me, so I could unbutton his jeans and pull them down to his knees. I had him then, vulnerable, before I claimed him with my arms.

He pulled me up so we could move to the bedroom, walking hand-in-hand towards it, naked, our clothes left in a huddle. He kissed my lips and my neck and drew me down to the bed, laying me down beside him and hugging me close. I snuggled into him, loving the raw closeness, and his lips grazed my ears and my neck, making me squirm. He stopped and we laid quietly together while I touched him. He moved his body so it was full-length on mine, and I wanted him inside me so badly I lifted my hips to try to force him inside. "I want you."

"Not yet."

I had no choice but to follow his lead, trusting in what he knew, a man who knows himself and what he wants, here and throughout his life. When we were both so aroused we were almost delirious, our bodies became one. Despite myself, I moaned and found I couldn't stop because he was so fully within me, all the need I had sated by the way he filled me up, his palms open against mine, strong fingers grasping.

I felt everything I'd lost, all I'd wanted, all I'd looked forward to and not realized, all the disappointments and all the men who I wanted to carry me away and save me but who I wouldn't allow to do that. Here was the one guy who filled my need.

"I love you." The words were whispered in my ear. It was such a mixture of agony and pleasure, this coupling of ours. I waited and let him be there within me and my mind went to white happiness, inconceivable contentment, and I stayed there in my mind, listening to his quiet breathing. I could feel the slow rising of his chest against mine, his heartbeat and mine, together, beating, two as one. I lapsed into the moment, the lingering time together, as he forbid me to move, but to just lie there, my muscles gripping him. We both ached with need.

Then he moved and we built to a crescendo, and he moaned with pleasure, and my hands went to his back and the muscles working there. I whispered I loved him in his ear and felt his response as we climaxed together, knowing in that moment only each other and what we shared.

He pulled up the covers and took me into his arms, my shoulder in his, and we slept the sleep of deep satisfaction, his arm pulling me close to him so I couldn't go anywhere if I tried. Then we turned to spoon close with his arms up under my breasts and our hands together under my chin, and he said, "The story."

I began. "Once there was a man who loved a woman he could not have. He watched her from afar. He trailed her. He wanted to know her in a way he'd never known another woman, so he came to know her walk, the way she tossed her hair, the sway of her hips in her high-heeled boots. He saw her stop to talk to a man on the street dressed in a suit and dark tie, briefcase in his hand, and she laughed, took his hand when they parted, and kept walking to the library. He became incensed that she would talk to another man and respond to him, when she didn't even know he existed. The man followed her small figure through the turnstile at the main library in downtown Cleveland and down the cavernous hall and through the doorway of Literature, where he saw her look up into the stacks on the second floor and make a decision. He loved the curve of her mouth as he stood pretending to look in a display case at books about finding ancestors when he was actually looking sideways over to her as she stood, her head upturned, so he could admire her gorgeous neck and ears jeweled with small pearls. He waited, and then she stealthily walked down the floor looking at the signs showing the letters and choosing an aisle which she turned into. He followed, saw the black heels of her boots as she turned the landing up to the second floor. He didn't know what he'd do when he found her in the racks, but he continued to follow her, trying to quiet his steps on the metal stairs. When he was on the balcony with the first floor dizzyingly below, he saw her a few rows down to the left, and then she went into that aisle. He told himself he'd take it slow and see what happened, and he did. He walked slowly down the aisle until he came to where she'd entered the stacks, and he stopped. She turned with her amazing green eyes, brightened by the cloth of her green blouse, looked confused and momentarily afraid. Then the look flicked away. She smiled in recognition, opened her mouth to say something until he put his finger to her mouth and signaled her to be quiet. He saw her close her mouth and he went to her and wrapped his arms around her and stilled her body and her heart with his body against hers. He had her, there in the stacks with her coat and his to hide the way their bodies joined, the rhythm of their connection, and satisfied, they slumped against each other and she said to him, 'My darling husband, what game were we playing today?'"

Tom chuckled before we fell asleep.

CHAPTER FIFTEEN -- WINDY HILL

I wondered why Tom loved me, what it was I had to offer him. It was a symptom of my inability to love myself that I thought about that question. As the days went by and all was well, I gradually understood that what he'd said was true—he'd always loved me, despite all my foibles and everything we'd gone through. Me as a girl and me as a woman was all the same person to him, and he loved me for all I'd lived and all I was.

I had to look at what I loved about him too. It wasn't quite enough to know that he forgave me and loved me. That wasn't enough of a reason to love him. I loved him for all the same reasons he loved me, for who he was as a boy who carried my books and knew what my favorite flower was, the young man with all the hopes and dreams, the middle-aged guy whose marriage continued while he loved someone other than his wife.

We were reading together again. He came to my place after work, and after making love and eating dinner, we opened up our books, our backs resting on pillows at either end of my couch, our legs entwined. It was like we never stopped being who we were when we were kids, and we relished, delighted, in that shared interest. We read Ursula Hegi's *Stones from the River*, which had been on both our reading lists. We thought the same things, felt the same things, experienced the same things.

On impulse one evening I pulled my *Faerie Mists* out of its drawer and sat it on the table. Tom was at an architectural board meeting, and I was alone. The book was about pursuing lost dreams even if it meant going through unknown territory. I picked it up and started reading, and then I started writing the next chapter, feeling the book within me, moving me to continue, driving me, the words mine but inspired by a power much higher than me. I knew instinctively how the tale needed to be told and what would drive it to the end. The process worked. I connected with the words I wrote, caressing them into sentences and paragraphs. I didn't want the dream to end at two in the morning, yet it was going to be fine because the thread ran through the story line true and taut and would continue to unite the work when I returned to it. I was sure I would complete the book.

The reason I'd stopped working on the book was because of the fairy named Eliza. She didn't interact with the other fairies. The other fairies wanted to kick her out of the kingdom because she wasn't living up to the rules. She wasn't fighting back, she wasn't showing them who she was. She was going to get kicked out if she didn't do something. I tried to get into her head. She became stronger, more sure of who she was, even though the other fairies didn't know it, and by the time the other fairies approached her, she pulled a sword and said she had the right to protect who she was inside and they had no business asking her to live the way they thought she should live. They let her stay, but I showed the reader that Eliza was very much alive and ready to fight for who she was.

I woke at five in the morning and went back to the book. It was flowing remarkably. At eight I called Tom.

"I think you're an inspiration," I said.

"Oh yeah? How's that?" He sounded like he was in the middle of running around to get ready for work.

"I pulled my fairies novel out of a drawer last night and started working on it again. The writing came easily. Then I went to town on it. I didn't want to stop. I've already worked on it for three hours this morning."

"That's great, Betsy. I can't wait to read it." His tone said he meant it.

"I can't wait to finish it. Maybe I should call off work."

"Call off work? That doesn't sound like you."

"What are you trying to say, that I don't have any spontaneity? That I live too much by the book?" My voice raised a tinge.

"No, that's not what I meant. I mean that you don't often go for the gusto and live for yourself. You need to do that. If you're on a roll, go for it. Finish it."

I took what he said at face value then, although my feathers were a bit ruffled. "All right. I will!" I said, and opened up my e-mail and started typing a note to my secretary. "It's happening right now. I'll let Mo know I won't be in."

I finished my novel that day. I'd never experienced the force of having a story tell itself, but that's what happened. The book was going to be published. I knew it.

A new energy was awakened in me. I gave chapters of my current novel to Tom each week, and he read them with amazement. He was still my biggest fan, and hearing his comments made me believe that I'd have other fans, one day. I waited for an acceptance letter from an agent in response to my *Faerie Mists* queries but I had already moved on to another project, a book about my parents based on their letters.

It was Thanksgiving. I was thankful.

Tom walked into the kitchen from outside wiping his hands on his jeans, heavy boots laced loosely. Although it was only thirty degrees outside, his body emanated heat under his flannel shirt. "Whew! That was a lot of work. I have to get used to this country living."

I smiled and walked over where he was sitting on the bench by the door taking off his boots. When my hands stroked his back, I felt the beauty of his muscles, the strength in the width of his back. I loved knowing he was mine to do with as I pleased, in a way. I could touch his back whenever I wanted. I didn't need to ask permission.

When he looked up at me, his face looked as it had when he was twenty-one. He was the same exact guy as he'd been then. I'd been thinking about Tom then and Tom now and Tom, well he was just Tom. I took in my breath to stop the rush of emotion, the realization that I could stop worrying. That life I'd been leading, first with Rick and then on my own, demanding that others perform and demanding affection when I needed it, was behind me. I was moving forward, yet moving backward. Life had become circular with Tom at the center of it. Tom and me. Again, I took in a deep breath. Time froze. I didn't feel the need to explain the look in my eyes or the intakes of breath or the waves of regret and exhilaration drowning me.

He stood up to hold me. The sensation of the years leaving us behind, of being in the now and then, of being just Tom and Betsy came to me again, and my body relaxed into the scariness of tremors and sinking and nerve-tingling skin. I dissolved. My body quivered and he held me closer. Not a word was said as the moment became minutes. I had no sense of time passing. I allowed the ocean to flow over me and take away concern.

When I looked up at his ageless face, his brow was furrowed, and he asked, "Are you all right?"

I nodded. I knew I didn't need to say much because somehow he'd been there in the same shapeless, timeless letting go and letting down experience I had. I caught my breath, and he smiled at me. He knew all this emotion was tied to how I felt about him. It was raging love. It was bigger than me. I couldn't get my arms around it. "I feel like I've been walking in a dark valley looking for my way and now I've emerged into the sunshine and it's too bright to look about much, so I'll take it one step at a time and allow myself warmth in each moment, just the amount I can stand. The sun, it's very bright."

His arms tightened around my waist. I felt he could carry my burdens. No one had ever carried my burdens. I'd been seeking someone to lighten my load, and if I'd only let him help me with that twenty-seven years ago, the nonsense life I'd led would not have happened.

But I couldn't live in "what could have been" in this glorious basking in light I was now savoring. I sighed. When I took in my breath again, it was big. "I'm still having those dreams."

"It will take some time. You never had a chance to process it before and now you're doing what you should have done years ago. You've been living on the surface of life, not expecting much, and not getting much. Now you want more, and more takes some thought."

"Just now the ocean washed over me."

"I hope it took away some of the bad." His voice was soft.

"It did that, but also, I think it took me back, brought us back to where we were. I feel I know you now as I knew you then. I can't pretend I didn't live those years in between; they're part of me. That's why the feeling of coming around to me again is resisted. I can't let go of the 'me' that has been. The person who struggled with love and motherhood and death is still there, but the burden is light."

"It's a pretty sunny place, Life."

I laughed lightly. "Yes, it is."

He pulled me up off the floor into his arms. My legs dangled over the sides of his arms. He looked full into my face and I put my arms around his neck. "Ready to start on a new life?"

I nodded and smiled back at him, then I let my head fall back and started laughing. I laughed so much I lost my breath. We were moving through the kitchen and into the dining room with the table set for twelve, and over the Oriental rugs to the stairs. Tom was laughing too because we both felt silly all of a sudden. He paused at the bottom of the stairs and firmed up his grip. He kissed me through my giggles until I quieted down and gave into the passion of it.

He carried me up the stairs into my room and laid me on the bed.

Slowly, he pulled my long-sleeved T-shirt over my head and traced his mouth down the length of my torso from the hollow between my collarbones to the ridge between my breasts, over my belly button and down to where my skin stopped at the top of my jeans. Then he worked loose the button and zipper and easily pulled off my jeans until I was laying before him in panties and bra.

He stood up to unbutton his shirt and pull the sleeves off his hands. He reached down to pull off his T-shirt and his head emerged rumpled, boyish again above a chest forested with dark hair that wasn't part of his youth. He had a slight roll to his belly, a softness above the muscle that seemed right for his age. I sat up to reach for him and put my head on his belly, my arms around his jean-clad hips. Then I reached down and undid his jeans and they slid from his slim hips down to his knees. I found him ready for me and admired its firmness and resolve.

I couldn't imagine that all this was mine to enjoy. This affectionate and sexy man liked me even though I'd failed him. And then I was caught up in wanting those pants off and in having him next to me so he could touch me and make love to me.

He turned me over as if he owned my body and unclasped my bra, then he pulled my panties off, all the way past my feet. His hands took in the length of my body, from circular rubs of my buttocks to sweeping caresses down my thighs to swirling touching of my feet. Then he moved his hands solidly and steadily up my body again and when he reached the small of my back he whooshed up to my shoulders, kneading them. After his fingers left tingly trails along the soft parts of my back, he worked his fingers up my spine, taking a moment with each vertebra, before he turned me back over.

I was left wanting to touch him. I pushed him down so I could touch the front of his body and trail my fingers through his chest hair. Then I laid on top of him to kiss his lips and feel the full nakedness of him beneath my body. I traced my fingers over his lips and marveled at the fullness of them, the perfect shape that symbolized his classic good looks.

Our lovemaking was infused with goodness. I felt the release from sex and the satisfaction of having been thoroughly savored. Afterwards we slept and when I woke I smelled turkey.

Butterfly kisses on my cheeks and Tom said, "It's eleven."

Our guests would arrive in two hours. I sat up and said, "What a perfect way to start hosting a Thanksgiving dinner."

"I agree with that." He sat up and swung his legs to the floor. "What do I need to do?"

"Make a fire in a little while, chop some vegetables for the salad, make sure the candles are lit, open some wine. I think I have the kitchen figured out."

He was buttoning his shirt when he said, "I like this, Betsy. I like living like we're a couple."

I looked across the bed that separated us, buttoning the top button of my jeans and said, "We are a couple."

He nodded in agreement and blew me a kiss as he headed out the door.

By the time people started to arrive, candlelight flickered on the walls of the house and the pies were proudly displayed on the sidebar in the dining room. Ben arrived first and I appreciated him as a parent. The arrival of his daughter and her family made the house feel full. Cassie was radiant, so radiant I expected her to say she was pregnant even though Beth was only eight months old. I was surprised when I opened the door to my childhood friend Linda, her eyes a bit weathered and her hair streaked with gray, but Linda nonetheless, with Tom's parents. Tom's father's stoop reminded me of our mortality. And then I thought of Mom.

She would have liked the party. There were twelve of us. I had never hosted Thanksgiving in my life, truth be told. When I'd confessed that to Tom the evening before while we were crimping the edges of the pies, Tom's eyes widened. He'd never heard of such a thing, a person who never had people to dinner on Thanksgiving.

I apparently have entertaining in my blood because I managed to engage everyone in conversation as we watched Beth toddle around, holding onto furniture and grasping for things on tables. We had to move some of the candles beyond her reach. I put out crackers and cheese and poured glasses of wine and listened to the steady banter—Linda and Tom reconnecting, Tom's father talking with Ben about town happenings, Mike talking about business with Ben's family. Cassie helped me keep glasses full and finish up the side dishes, and as we stood in the kitchen, I realized she had much more experience with people than I did.

"You know, I haven't done much entertaining."

Cassie looked up from sprinkling dried onions over the green beans. "What do you mean, Mother?" Her voice was tense.

I'd sensed the underlying resentment from the minute she walked in the door. It wafted into the room like a trail of smoke, and I tried to ignore it, but there was no ignoring it. Not now, alone in the kitchen. Perhaps it was time to be done with this, whatever it was. "I mean I rarely have people over to my condo, and when I lived here, it wasn't me who did the entertaining, it was either your grandmother or great-grandmother. And before that, years ago, when I was with your father, I was too busy and unnerved to have anyone over."

"That was because you didn't want to be a mother, so it was overwhelming to you. You had no friends anyway." The last of the sentence was added as an afterthought, for effect. I was reminded of my teenaged daughter flinging insults at me like spears hitting my heart. The first sentence was somewhat true, but I didn't want to admit it, and I hadn't known my daughter knew that about me.

I felt the anger rise, but forced myself to be in control. "Maybe we should look at those things one at a time. Why do you think I didn't want to be a mother?"

She shot me a glance that would kill a firefly, or at least a fly. She was swatting at me. After putting the casserole dish in the oven, she turned to face me. "You let your mother raise me after all those fights you had with Daddy. When you fought, you ignored me. You were so concentrated on each other, I wasn't there. You were unhappy, and this house was our refuge, the place where you couldn't fight, where you had to pay attention to me. When we moved into this house, I felt like you were a boarder, returning after being at your job, not connected with the household."

"I worked hard . . ."

"You didn't have to be at the office so much." Cassie's hands were on her hips, her mouth a scornful accusation. "I could tell you didn't like me much, almost wished you hadn't given birth to me. You ignored me."

"That's not true."

"Isn't it?" Her voice was raised and I looked toward the door. "Grandma got me to my dance lessons and came to my soccer games. If you made it to the recital or a game, we made it a celebration. You were like the father in a divorce having visitation rights a few times a year. When you divorced Daddy, you divorced me!"

My breath caught. The truth was, Cassie was right. I'd allowed life to flitter past me, including my own daughter's childhood. And maybe she reminded me too much of what had gone wrong between her father and me. I'd always been comparing Rick to Tom in those days, missing Tom more than I'd admitted, until this moment. "I tried, Cassie. I read to you."

She softened, hung her head. Then she turned from me to pick up the salad bowl and take it into the dining room. "Maybe you wanted to abort me," she said under her breath as she left.

My breath caught in my throat at what she'd said. Anguish filled my chest as the realization came to me that my daughter didn't think I loved her. She thought I wished she'd never been born.

A few moments later, she flew into the kitchen again and picked up the salad dressing and serving spoons. I stood against the counter with my arms crossed.

"What's that? Armored for combat?"

I was confused.

"Your arms, crossed. Are you waiting for the next blow?"

"I heard what you said." I knew what I said next had to be said well. "I love you. I never regretted having you. I'm proud to be your mother. I'm glad you're in my life." My voice sounded desperate. If my daughter thought her mother didn't want her, if she really believed that, her life had been harder than I had ever imagined.

"It didn't feel like that to me . . . I don't know why I chose today to bring this up. Maybe it's because this house is more mine than yours, and it's yours, and Grandma should have given it to me. You did your best to get out of here, and you took leave of this place twenty years ago. And here you are, hosting a dinner in your house like you deserve to have it."

My anger rose close to eruption. *How could you? I'm your mother, I've taken care of you, and now you hurl this at me?* I opened my mouth, then shut it, took in a deep breath and exhaled. *My daughter wonders why I kept her. She's in pain, has been in pain. And I didn't even know it. Lord, be with me through this.* When I gathered my thoughts, I finally said, "My mother thought I deserved this house and farm. She kept telling me to live my life more fully, to let go of the worry. She knew . . . what you couldn't, can't. She knew . . ." What did she know?

Cassie waited. She stood there with a bemused look on her face, a look that said she knew more than I did about what was going on, and she waited.

"She knew I wasn't normal."

The expression on Cassie's face changed. She was more curious than angry now. Her voice was quiet when she asked, "What do you mean?"

I started crying. The tears came into my eyes and started down my cheeks, and I felt my face crumble. *I wasn't normal.* The admission of something I'd known as true hit me hard. I'd never admitted abnormality before, not even to myself. But that's what I'd been feeling. I searched for the starting point of that change because I was sure I wasn't born that way. "A normal person wouldn't have done what I did, wouldn't have acted like I did," I sobbed. Cassie put her arms around me and after crying a couple of minutes, I forced myself to stop, pulled away, and went into the bathroom.

What a mess, I thought, looking at my tear-stained face in the mirror of the bathroom off the kitchen. I bathed my face with cool water and stood there, looking in the mirror at a woman whose face was different than I remembered, yet it was the same. How infrequently I actually looked at myself. The sagging under my eyes and lines around my lips were a testament to the years gone by. I would have cried again, but my cheekbones were high and my eyes a clear blue, as they'd always been. My hair, long now, waved around my shoulders. The blue of my sweater brightened my eyes. I stayed there long enough to feel that my face was back to normal, but I wasn't sure I'd be able to hide the fact that I'd been crying.

Cassie was mercifully absent from the kitchen when I returned to it. I opened up the upper oven to check on the sweet potatoes and green beans, then opened up the bottom oven. The aroma of turkey was pronounced, the skin browned, and the thermometer popped. I reached for the potholders on the side of the range, and I heard a movement behind me.

"Let me get that for you, Betsy." It was Ben. I turned around and in that split second we looked at each other, I could tell he knew I'd been crying. He stepped in front of me, took the potholders from my limp hands, pulled out the rack, and placed the turkey on top of the stove. "We'll let this sit awhile. Do you need any other help?" He looked around the room and headed to the table where the rolls sat on a baking sheet. Glancing at me, he picked up the baking sheet and put it in the oven, turned the timer to ten minutes, then came over to where I stood and put his arms around my shoulders to give me a hug. "Kids. Even when they're grown up, they can get to you."

I finally looked at him, then tilted into the hug. "And they often know more than we think. I just told Cassie that Mom knew something she didn't, that I'm not normal."

He chortled. "Not normal? What does that mean?"

"That's what my daughter asked. I'm not sure what I mean, but once I wrap my thoughts around it, you'll be the first two to know."

"Don't think too hard on that one. All of us have regrets."

The door opened, and Tom walked in. "Hey, you guys. How's it going in here? Do you need some help?" He could tell something happened, but he was going to get past it for now.

"In about fifteen minutes, I'm going to open that turkey bag and take out the stuffing. You can carve the turkey."

"All right!" He rolled up his sleeves to the elbows. "That's always been my job. If I didn't do it this year, I wouldn't feel normal."

Ben and I looked each other and started laughing.

Tom looked bewildered. "What did I say?"

Ben let his arm fall from my shoulders and said, "I'll be back to help with the turkey." He walked through the swing door and left Tom and me alone.

"Cassie told me I wasn't a good mother, that I wasn't there for her, and that I didn't deserve this house." I hesitated. "She also said that she felt I would have preferred to have gotten rid of her, had an abortion."

"Oh, sweetie," he said, and he came toward me. I stepped back. "Cassie left, then Ben came in and I told him that I'd told her I wasn't normal, and he said I shouldn't think about normalcy too much."

"Oh, so that's why you laughed, because I said something about feeling normal. No, I would think you wouldn't want to think about normal too much." He reached up his hand to stroke back the hair that clung damply to my cheeks. "Why were you crying?"

"You know, I really don't know, exactly. I suppose I'm disappointed in myself. Cassie's right. How do I undo twenty-four years of bad mothering?"

"Betsy," his voice warned.

"No, I mean it, Tom. How do I do that?"

He thought a couple of minutes then said, "Admit it, apologize, then change things. Don't beat yourself up or linger on it or battle it, just deal with it, with Cassie."

Everyone insisted I be the one to say grace. "Thank you, God, for the food before us, for family, for life. Thank you for giving us the opportunity to live fully and the courage to change those things we can and let go of what we can't. We are yours, and in your name we pray, Amen."

We ate our salads with the warm rolls, then the table was filled with a platter and casseroles, which we passed around, refilled, and passed around again. There was laughter as the stories were told and Beth tried different foods and spit them out. Why didn't my granddaughter like stuffing? She couldn't stop eating the cranberry sauce. The pumpkin and pecan pies were appreciated a couple hours later when we ate them haphazardly, some in front of the football games on television.

The usual turkey snoozing took over after dinner and the company left together, as if on cue. The women were good enough to help me clean up the kitchen while the men watched the game. Cassie was solicitous towards me.

It was a joy to wake up in Tom's arms. He'd always been a cuddler in the night. I'd found that most men cuddled until sleep overtook them and they turned on their sides away from me, loneliness afterwards keeping me awake. Tom liked the closeness of a warm body.

I traced the hairs on his chest when he turned over on his back and I laid my head on his shoulder. "Did you sleep that way with Miriam? All wrapped around her?"

"Humph," was his reply. "Hardly. She hated to be touched while she slept. You, on the other hand," he kissed my head, "love to be close and tight and loved all night and day."

I snuggled closer. "What about . . ."

"Do you want to know?"

I sighed. "Not really. I know. She was the love of your life, wasn't she?"

"No. You were. And are."

I let that sink in. I'd known it, but I hadn't believed it. He'd pursued me. "Why?"

His voice held exasperation when he said, "Why do you question it? I wish you wouldn't do that."

"But," I started, tentatively. "I'm not normal."

Another sigh from him. I really needed to leave him alone on this.

I laid back on my pillow. He rose up on his elbow and propped his head on his hand and looked down at me, his turn to trace the skin on my chest. "I enjoy your smile, the way your eyes light up, and your voice when you get excited about something you're passionate about. I love that you read and think about what you read. I like that you're into long walks. I like many of the same things you do. You're a successful writer and editor, and I love the way you use words. Your daughter's a good person."

I sighed. "I need to see the good things."

He watched my face. "Your mother was good at celebrating. And sometimes I see that in you, but other times . . . it's like you forget."

I smiled. "I have my own personal therapist. I like that we get into each other's heads. And do you know I'm always aroused when I'm with you now?"

He laughed and moved his right hand down my body to touch me between my legs. I was wet. "Yes, I feel that."

We made love like honeymooners.

I've always loved the little towns in northeastern Ohio: Hudson, Vermilion, Avon, Olmsted Falls, Peninsula, and . . . Chagrin Falls. We drove to Chagrin Falls to shop for Christmas. The toy store sold wooden blocks and puzzles and collector dolls, and I bought some things for Beth. When I told Tom I still couldn't quite call myself

Grandma or a grandmother in my head, he said grandparenthood isn't the same as it used to be—people in their late forties and fifties just aren't as old as they used to be.

"Remember my mom's mother? I think she visited a lot when we were kids."

"Yes, she was pretty old."

He shook his head. "That's the point. She wasn't. She was only in her early sixties when she died, but when I was a teenager and she was in her fifties, her hair was completely white and she wore house dresses and flat laced-up shoes. She not only dressed old, she acted old, moving slowly and laboriously."

"Yes, I think you're right. My grandmother was very proper, never died her hair, but she didn't wear house dresses, she was too much a lady for that. She seemed older than she was."

"And look at the next generation. Your mother was active until she became sick, and mine still works in the vegetable garden."

We took the packages back to the car, then stopped on the bridge to look over at the falls. It was warm, near 50 degrees. We sat down on a bench, and Tom said, "This reminds me of our first kiss." He leaned over and kissed me lightly, a friendly kiss. "Was it like that?"

"Yes."

We looked into each other's eyes, and he said, "This is the same too," as he took both my hands in his. "Will you go to a movie with me on Saturday night?"

I smiled. "I don't think my mom will let me. I'm not sixteen yet."

"Rules are made to be broken."

"Let's just be who we are, okay? We can talk about the past, but let's let it go."

We squeezed on it.

I called Cassie on Friday night when I knew she'd have time to talk. "I'm sorry I wasn't a good mother."

"Oh, Mom," she began. "That's not really true. I'm sorry I said it."

"No, it's true. I let my mother take care of you."

"You were dealing with Daddy and all that trouble. I remember him coming home drunk. I remember him banging on our door, trying to get you back. I remember how he yelled at you, called you names. I heard you talking to Grandma about his sallies with other women, and I heard you crying. Then, even after the divorce, you got him to AA meetings, went to Al-Anon, tried to help him. He still drinks. He still can't relate to people. He still cares only about himself."

"Yes, but that doesn't excuse me doing what I did."

"Letting me hang out with Grandma was one of the best things you could do for me. We had so much fun. You know."

"I'm glad I spent time with her at the end."

"And you and me, we're doing that more now too. You had a lot on your plate when I was young. I understand. But you know, I'm going to be different with Beth. I'll be at her soccer games and dance recitals."

"I'm glad about that, Cassie."

"I know you have a tendency to be down on yourself. I think you're a good person."

Suddenly I felt as if everyone I knew was trying to build me up. Was I that transparent? I didn't like that weakness in me. Then I said, "Cassie, your Dad and I wanted you. We planned you. When I found out I was pregnant, I was so happy I told everyone right away. I couldn't believe that I was having a baby, that life was in me. I hoped for a happy life with my baby, a happy life for you. I never, ever thought about having an abortion."

"I know. I shouldn't have said that. I'm sorry I did."

"Okay. That really bothered me."

"Sorry, Mom."

When I hung up, Tom came into the bedroom. I was sitting on the bed. "How'd it go?"

"Like you, she doesn't want me to beat myself up over the past. She told me she remembered how her father was, how he came home late, drunk, how he had other women."

"I thought he only had one."

"No, there were several. He always told me it was the last time. When it happened for the fourth time, I'd had it. The night I told him to leave, he called me from a woman's house and a woman was laughing in the background. He told her to be quiet, he was talking with his wife, and she said, drunkenly, 'your wife? What are you calling your wife for, when you're with me?' He was drunk too and he told me to ignore the disturbance in the background. He came home, later, after I'd had the chance to stew over things, and I was so empty from crying and letting go of all my expectations that I'd made up my mind that it was over. I told him I was done. I was so done . . . he started apologizing and I didn't care what he had to say. I was numb."

"For some people, marriage is a noose that doesn't allow them to be themselves."

In the morning, half asleep and before our coffee, I told Tom about taking Rick to AA meetings and going to Al-Anon, working on letting go and how that no longer worked after a while because he wasn't trying. He told me how his children were different from each other, and how Marion cried when they took their daughter to Ohio University and how young and alone she looked as they drove away from her, leaving her in Athens, four hours from home.

I went downstairs to make coffee and when I came back to bed with two steaming mugs of coffee, he was lying full length on the bed, asleep again. He woke when he heard the thump of the coffee cup next to his ear and pulled me back into bed with him, wrapping me in his arms spoon-style, and I basked in his warmth.

"I always wonder how couples are with each other, and whether they fight."

"Me too. The only one I ever fought with was Rick, but those fights were never fair—there was no fighting with him."

"With Miriam, she had to be right, or she walked away."

"Rick has an angry spirit."

We were quiet for a while. I sat up and picked up his coffee and handed it to him. We sat up against the backboard, sheets up under our arms, and sipped at the warm liquid. "I don't think we'll fight," I broke the silence.

"Life's too short."

We did the noon-day milking, checked on the fence, and went to the grocery in town. When we were done and were back in the house in the waning light, I brought the last of Mom's journals into the living room and read out loud: "I'm worried about Betsy. She lives her own life away from us. Family's important, but she doesn't feel that way. Cassie's pregnant and excited, and I'm very happy for her. She's excited about having a baby, and she's ready to be a mother. Betsy and me, we weren't such great mothers."

"My mother told me she's sorry she was a poor mother."

"Interesting. I wonder if women have a greater tendency to take everything too seriously."

"Of course they do. Every woman I've ever known has taken things more seriously than she should have."

I turned on the oven and put leftover turkey and vegetable casserole in to warm up. I made a salad, and we set the table in the dining room. We ate like we were starving, talking non-stop. I cleared the table and brought out the Ben & Jerry's we bought for dessert. Cherry Garcia. It needed no adornment.

"I love this ice cream," he said. "Remember the first time we found it?"

"Yep," I said as I ate another spoonful. "We went to that wedding on Cape Cod."

"My cousin's wedding. We were running here and there, settled in Wellston and we needed a laundry mat. While we were waiting for the clothes to dry, we walked down the strip and there it was, an ice cream store."

"They weren't marketing nationwide yet."

"You picked the best one, and it honors Jerry."

When we were done eating, I picked up the candle and took it with us as we moved into the living room. It felt too formal, but at the farm, there was the kitchen, the dining room, and the living room. "I wonder if I really could live here," I said, slipping onto the upholstered couch. It was a comfortable room, Mom had made sure it was, and wasn't as full of the antiques Grandma preferred, although there were enough of those. I placed the candle on the end table next to me.

Tom sat down close. "Of course you could. This is a good house, a classic farmhouse. You'd have to figure out what to do with all the furniture you have in your place."

I looked over at him with what I hoped was a troubled look. "I don't know if I can give up that condo." But home was a place of family and tree houses and magical ponds and walks along the beach and a downtown where everyone knew me and said hello.

He didn't comment. All of a sudden, his eyes on the piano, he said, "Play for me."

I hadn't played the piano in years. "I can't."

He implored me. "I remember hearing you play at a recital at the church when you were sixteen. Was it Liszt?"

"Maybe. Or Chopin. They're my favorites."

I stood up and walked to the piano. I opened up the bench and pulled out some Chopin I knew. Had known. I hadn't sat down at this piano since I moved to the condo. I opened the book and placed it on the ledge. The bench was heavier than I remembered, but the legs felt fragile as I pulled it straight up and placed it firmly on the floor. I sat down. I played. It flowed like I'd never stopped playing. I felt in touch with the piano and the music.

When I was done, neither of us spoke for a few minutes. I was astonished that I could still play. Finally, Tom said, "The last time I heard that music was when you played it that last Christmas we were together."

"I haven't played it in so long, I didn't think I could."

He came up behind me and put his hands on my shoulders, kneading my muscles. "You should play more often."

"I will if I live here. Pianos aren't easy to move."

"Are you leaning towards that now?"

I turned and looked up at him. "Yes, I think I am."

"I think that would be a good thing for you."

"But I love Cleveland."

My response was so emphatic, he laughed. "I can tell that. You seem to be fully at home on its streets."

"I like the river, but the truth is I feel better when I'm here."

"I noticed that," he said. He drew me up so he could put his arms around my body and his hands on my hips,. I felt the warmth through his flannel shirt and his hardness against the confines of his jeans, and he pulled away to look at my face, his hands in my hair, owning it, splaying it in all directions away from my face. "I like your face."

I liked his intensity, the light blue-gray of his eyes, the smoothness of his skin, the ripples of his muscles. I liked how close we came together, standing there on the wooden floor, the need rising in both of us with immediacy. I wondered at the power of this need, the urgency that consumed us, as he kissed me wetly and fully, our mouths open and wide against each other's, his tongue against mine, taking me as his in a moment. I was lost. I'd been taken over by my love-like of him, my sexuality was aroused, and the real world slipped away as his hands moved from my hair down my shoulders and back to my hips and pressed me closer to him.

    My head fell back as his mouth caressed my neck, and I felt the hardness of his arm muscles as they held me aft. He reached for my right hand with his left and our fingers entwined. We climbed the stairs, our feet stepping side by side. Up in my room, the one that used to be my mother's, he threw the covers from on top the bed to the foot and they rolled off the end in a bunch on the floor, and he sat down and drew me near and carefully pulled my shirt above my head, then worked on the hook of my bra. I felt the warmth and sureness of his fingers against my skin as he unhooked my bra and my breasts were freed and in his face. His breath softly touched my belly. He cupped my breasts with his hands and felt their weight. I was his, lost in him, as he put his lips on my neck, on my breasts. He swirled his tongue around my right nipple. I felt a hunger in my loins, an unbelievable need and I moaned, causing him to look up at my face before he went to the other breast and pulled at the nipple, then bit it carefully, and rolled it with his tongue. My back arched so my breasts were pushed against his face. His lips were on my belly as he pulled my jeans down from my hips and when the jeans were at my knees, I stepped out of them. They fell to the floor with my discarded shirt and bra, and I felt his fingers grip the band of my panties and slide them off smoothly. A purist, no nightgown or lacy bras ever stayed on my body for long when I was with him.

    We were entwined until I woke up in the twilight of the hours between midnight and dawn. A baby was crying but when I tried to find it in my room, under the covers of the bed or behind the half-opened closet door, nothing was there. When I started opening up the drawers in the bathroom, Tom woke up and asked me what I was doing. I woke then, startled, and went back to bed with Tom's help.

    In the morning, I wobbled awake with the gray dawn and unwound from the cocoon of warmth we'd woven around us. The kitchen felt cold, especially the tiled floor. I ground the coffee, started it brewing. The land outside was empty, but when I looked at the red barn, I thought about swinging from the rafters when Tom and I came home from school for Thanksgiving.

    Upstairs with mugs of coffee, I climbed onto the bed and handed a mug to my long lost lover whose face looked happy. I was happy until I remembered the middle of the night, and he did too, looking at my face. "What was that all about?" he asked.

"I don't know."

"I asked you what you were looking for and you said you were looking for the baby."

"I thought I heard a baby crying." It was a half-truth.

"In this house?" He looked concerned.

"I heard it."

"So you thought a stork dropped by in the middle of the night or what?"

"I think I was still half asleep and in my dream, a baby was crying." I said.

"Cassie? Beth?"

I shook my head. "I don't think I knew this baby. It was lost and calling for me to come and help it."

"Our baby."

Christmas always brought memories of decorated department store windows, roasting chestnuts on the fire, and snuggling with Tom. We trimmed a small Christmas tree in my condo after arriving there late on a Friday night. I was on deadline and he was trying to finish filing pleadings before the courts closed for the holidays. I could see the tiredness in the slump of his shoulders and the way he let his briefcase fall to the floor in the hallway. I put my arms around him as he took off his shoes and sensed an everyday tiredness that comes from working hard.

"We work too hard."

He kissed my nose and nodded. "Yes, we do."

I tried to describe the kind of love where there's no distillation of thought before thinking, where the love is so true it's a thing in itself and not to be denied. "If I could give you anything in the world, it would be the gift of waking up and living each day as the best day of your life, a day of warmth and loveliness, and having the same perfect day again and again."

He smiled. "Being a famer is seeming a lot less like a pipe dream."

"And so is the idea of living at Windy Hill," I said as I walked past the bedrooms and dining room towards the open space of the kitchen and living room. I opened up the crock pot and dished stew into stoneware bowls.

"That smells really good," he said, coming up behind me. He sliced French bread on the cutting board. I brought the stew to the table with satisfaction. When I was in my seat, the star-shaped note up against my water glass caught my attention. I read:

If I could give you the world . . . I would find a place where you felt at home and live there with you.

On December 24, I drove out to Windy Hill. My gifts were in the trunk along with nut and poppy seed rolls from the Hungarian bakery and cheeses and cider from Amish country. One of the local radio stations was playing their traditional 24 hours of Christmas music and I listened to "Silent Night" followed by "White Christmas" and then "Jingle Bells," in a medley of memories without rhyme or reason.

The pine scent of the evergreen wreath decorated with bay, holly, and pine cones, greeted me at the back door. When I let myself into the house, cinnamon trembled into my nose. Candles had been placed on the kitchen table and countertop and a bowl of fresh fruit surrounded by pine overwhelmed the dining room table. The oranges were decorated with cylindrical dots of cloves, Cassie's handiwork.

I dragged my suitcase up the stairs, and when I entered the living room, I plugged in the tree. The white lights twinkled and lit up the gold and red glass ornaments and strings of beads. My grandfather's old console radio blinked at me—I tuned in the same radio station I'd listened to in the car, two weeks of Christmas carols.

I unloaded the car and settled down on the chaise to read, but I was thinking about how the last time I was in the house, I'd heard the baby crying.

When I was twenty, in love with Tom the first time, Maria had tried to talk me out of the abortion. I'd had the pregnancy test the week before. We were sitting on a blanket on front campus under the trees, the black squirrels, restless as always, scampered inches from our blanket and up trees, down trees, chased after each other.

I found it hard to put into words. "Maria, I'm pregnant."

She clasped her hands in an excited movement. "Betsy, that's . . ." and stopped when she saw my joyless face. "It's good, isn't it? Tom and you, you're so happy together, so perfect, meant to be. You can still finish school, and so can he."

I shook my head. "I'm not going to be like my mother. I'm not going to have a baby and mess up my life. I'm not going to mess up Tom's life. You should have heard the way he talked when we went to dinner with his boss. They talked about the young women who gave up their babies for adoption like they were ignorant fools."

She rolled her eyes. "Geez, Betsy, you're so weird sometimes. Do you think Tom would think that about you?"

"Yeah, I do. He's become so holier-than-thou lately with working at the law firm, planning to go to law school and become the next Bobby Kennedy or something. He wouldn't say it, no, he'd act like he was happy, but he wouldn't be, not really, and he'd judge me."

"But he's part of this too."

"I know, but . . ."

"But what?"

"Well, what are you going to do?"

"Leave."

She frowned. "Leave?"

"Yep. Tom's going to be a congressman some day and the last thing he needs is people poking around to find out his wife was pregnant when he married."

She sat up straight and looked me in the eye. "You're not even going to discuss this with him? What about the baby, what are you going to do about the baby?"

The word "baby" made me cringe. I had no intention of ever having a baby. I was a student, not a mother. "I'm not going to have it."

Doubt crossed her face, and concern. She was so young. She looked down at her hands and said, "I think that's evil."

"Sometimes we do these evil things, we humans. Look at Eichmann—we do what we have to do. Life happens, and we deal with it the best way we know how."

How crude I'd been, how unfeeling, how determined, how unloving. I opened up the book and took myself to the craggy walks of Britain's shore as Jane Eyre wandered aimlessly, trying to find her soul.

I was arranging cheese and crackers on a plate in the kitchen, when a soft tap tapping on the back door window caused me to jump. He was looking at me hopefully.

I felt ecstatic to be in his arms again. "I'm so happy you're here," I said as I put my arms around his neck. "I feel better now, more myself."

"Because you're home."

"And because I have an idea for the baby's name."

"Our baby?" He looked confused and upset. "I don't think . . ."

I put a finger to his lips. "Hear me out. If we name the baby, make the baby real, think about the baby, sort of relive that time in our lives, we can rewrite history."

He nodded, unsure about my proposal.

"The name is Maddie.'

CHAPTER SIXTEEN – VINEYARDS

Dad came for Christmas. He kept talking about Mom, and I was glad Ben wasn't there to hear it. He remembered the way she wore her hair, the kinds of shoes she wore, the way she tilted her head when she asked a question. I showed him the driftwood sculptures and painting in the sunroom and told him about her art.

It was a warm Christmas. We were able to walk the property without hats, and Dad and Tom helped me bring the cows in when it was already dark outside. As we walked through the orchards, Dad said, "Peaches. You know they're a good indication of whether you can grow grapes, and we're in grape country here on Lake Erie."

"I know," I smiled at him. "What about olive trees?"

"I know no one who grows olive trees in this area." He stopped to inspect the trees, moving his hands over the supple bark. "The trees do well here. Have you thought about growing grapes?"

"Yeah, I have." I looked over at Tom. "We talked about it once when we were picking peaches."

"It's a good thought. You don't have to make wine, but you could sell a lot of grapes in a few years."

"That's what I've been thinking," Tom said.

"But vineyards?" I said. "They're something different entirely. Are you going to work on that project with me?"

"You always seem to need nudging. I'll be there." Tom smiled mischievously.

"It's not like you're pushy. You're just steadily supportive."

My father watched us. "You two, you're good for each other, you know? I can see it. You're friends—that's important."

"Do you want to be just friends?"

Tom tackled me into a hug. "Not JUST friends."

Dad smiled. "If you like each other and love each other, you have something."

At the same time, we said, "We'll see," and laughed as Tom took my hand and we walked back to the house.

One morning while reading the real estate section of the paper at the condo, I saw one of the units in my building was for sale. The asking price was forty thousand dollars above what I'd paid six years ago. My unit was larger, with a better view.

I stood up and walked to the window. The valley was covered in a dusting of snow. Just then, a ship was meandering Collision Bend and the sky was starting to lighten, but the lights of industry still dotted the landscape. The landscape was gritty. The view from the kitchen window at Windy Hill was green and virile. I loved to be part of the city's struggle for renewal, and the river was at the heart of that, but at Windy Hill, crocuses were guaranteed to appear in the next couple of weeks. Their struggle was simpler and richer.

I'd been driving an hour out to the farm every Friday and driving back again every Sunday since November. Nothing changed in the furnishings at the condo or the house, but the house required cleaning time and the farm would devour my time in the spring as the condo was left empty. The African masks and Alaskan totem poles were part of who I was here, and I could see them in the salon at home.

"At home," I said aloud. This was not my home. The farmhouse and acres of farmland at Windy Hill were.

It was time to sell the condo.

I walked a lot at the farm. It was a good thing to walk. It slowed down time. I didn't know how Tom was going to fit into my life but I decided not to think about it. I was just glad he came to visit every other weekend or so. I felt like we were waiting, but I didn't know what we were waiting for. That was all right with me.

In February, the snow was two-feet deep and it was a slippery drive into the city every morning, but I had to do it now that most of my things, including my bed, had been moved from the condo. A young married couple bought it a week after it was put on the market. It surprised me how selling the condo made me feel lighter. It was one less thing to deal with.

I didn't like driving that long highway in and out of Cleveland where semi-trucks shared the road with sports cars. Summer would be better. I'd learned my work at the magazine could be less of a priority but still go well. I encouraged my staff to take on more of my duties, and in letting go of all the many things I had to control, I empowered them to do their best work. And I was out of the office every day by five.

I was driving carefully, aware that a tap on my brakes could cause me to slide into a car in front of me with the anti-lock jaggedly scraping to keep me on a straight path but helpless to stop the forward motion. It was seven a.m. and I was driving west on Route 2. I was looking forward to finishing the February issue that featured included Mayan ruins and Peruvian winery tours. I was going to schedule my trip to Italy with Tom and my Dad, and I would write a feature article on vineyards of Italy for the June issue. I was listening to a National Public Radio program on music in Kenya.

Like an action movie, a semi-truck in front of me skidded sideways, tail jackknifing, time suspended as it continued to roll and then fall on its side, skidding down the highway until it stopped. Cars flew to the side of the highway, into the snowbanks, but six cars, one after another slid right into the mammoth injured vehicle, and I hit my brakes. I had no traction. I steered toward the side of the road and came to a stop in a snow bank as I prayed the drivers behind me would stay clear of me. I wasn't surprised when I felt the impact of a car sideswiping me as it veered to the side of the road as well.

Wreckage was all around me. People were getting out of their cars and running towards those first cars to help survivors. My instinct was to stay in my car but I knew I should help as well. When I tried to open my car door, it wouldn't budge. The passenger side was firmly against the snow bank. Long minutes stretched out as people covered in blood were pulled from the cars. It was ten minutes before the blinking lights of highway patrol cars, ambulances, and fire trucks appeared.

I sat in my seat, helpless and dazed. The scene was horrific. People tried to get into cars that no longer had roofs and a group of firemen flipped one vehicle from its roof to its tires. A rap on the window took me out of my daze. A policeman was shining his flashlight in my face while trying to yank my door open. He opened the back door and asked if I was okay.

"I'm not sure," I said but I was intact, undamaged, protected by the steel shell around me.

"Are you hurt?"

"I don't think so."

"Can you climb into the back seat? I'll get you into a warm car." He held out his hand to help me.

I took it and climbed into the back and let him lead me to his car. People were being moved onto gurneys and wheeled into open ambulances. People were hurt, maybe dying. I felt thankful to be safe and warm. I felt thankful for everything.

The person I chose to call was my father. Somehow, I'd not thought to pull out my cell phone and call anyone until I was in a safe place. He answered the phone on the second ring.

"Dad?"

"Betsy?"

"There's been an accident. On Route 2 near Geneva. A tractor-trailer jackknifed and swerved and landed in the middle of the highway and the cars, they didn't have time to stop. I barely had time to stop."

"Are you okay?"

"Yeah. I feel dazed, but I'm in a police cruiser. It was a shock."

"Do you need a ride?"

"Eventually. I don't know where I'll end up and when. My car's a wreck."

"Let me know when you need a ride. I'll pick you up."

"I will."

As I watched the tow trucks move the cars from the road and saw the line of traffic stretch out forever behind us and the police redirect traffic to the shoulder of the road, one car at a time gingerly continuing its journey toward the city, I had only one thought—*I can't do this any more.*

The snow finally melted in early March after six weeks of feeling like we lived in Alaska. I'd been walking less and reading more. I liked making a pot of tea in the afternoon. I set the kitchen table with dessert plates and cups with saucers, Grandma's good china and silver, when we got together to talk about our trip to Italy. Dad let himself in the back door when I waved, and gave me a quick hug before turning to Tom. They shook hands like old friends, one hand over the others', and gave each other a long look.

"So, you two are going to become farmers?" He asked when we'd settled into our chairs and I was pouring tea.

Tom laughed. "Of sorts. I'll keep practicing law, and Betsy plans to keep writing, and we'll be farmers together."

"I know how to milk the cows," I said as I settled into my chair. "Pedro's showing me how everything works, but he's moving back to California in a few weeks. He and his wife are ready to retire close to family."

"A new way of farming Windy Hill," my father said.

"Not a new way, but my way. And you know what?"

"What?" Father looked over at me, amused.

"You're going to teach me everything there is to know about growing grapes."

It was his turn to laugh. "It's been many years since I planted and grafted and coaxed vines to grow."

"It'll come to you as easily as milking a cow does for me."

"Betsy has a new cow pet," Tom said.

"Cow pet?"

"You know. A cow she talks to."

That time my father roared. "What's her name?"

"Raphaela," I said with satisfaction. I took a sip of the fragrant chamomile.

Raphael, my father, nodded, satisfied. "We'll have to learn as much as we can about grapes when we're in Italy."

Tom and I looked at each other. It was exactly what we'd been hoping for.

I started my memoir with the details of the teacup my mother gave me. I took it from its safe place and put in on the dining room table.

> The teacup is made of white porcelain and painted with tiny brush strokes, shades of pink that come together in the shape of roses. Shades of green and silver make up leaves on vines ringing the cup. The thorns are lovingly stroked but menacing. My mother gave me the teacup when she was dying.
>
> The teacup began its journey in the backpack of a young man in Japan to defend our nation's honor and the freedoms we hold

dear. Later, it traveled on a military ship across the Atlantic, where he gave it to the love of his life, my grandmother, in 1942. She passed it to her daughter, my mother, not knowing that my mother would own it for such a short time. The tale of sin and redemption is a common thread joining us all, like the twining vine linking thorns and roses. We struggle on our life journeys in an unforgiving world. The teacup reminds us we are women of worth and we are well loved.

I took those moments in time from the journals my mother kept and I kept, and wrote our story, entwining my mother's life with my own. I sat in her salon, where I didn't change a thing except to move in the paintings and driftwood from my condo on the River.

Even though it was early May, the daffodils were still blooming around the fence in the back yard. Some white with white centers, some with double petals and all yellow, others white with orange flowers that didn't look very daffodil-like. The more traditional daffodil, all yellow and not double anything, the kind Tom picked for me in high school, the kind he picked for me now, were the ones I liked best. I sat on the steps of the rear stoop and watched the sun fall low on the horizon. Soon, Tom would be home.

Tonight we would begin our own photo album, the first one we would share together, pictures from Thanksgiving and Christmas and the months we'd spent in the farmhouse together, the story of our life together. Telling stories was what we seemed to do best. And we had a lifetime of stories to tell. Some evenings I felt like all we did was talk. Reading books gave us more stories to talk about, and our own stories merged with the stories the writers told, the stories I was putting in my memoir.

I think about how it felt to want to have sex with Jerry, and the pain when he took me against my will. I know being with Jerry changed me forever. That a man could force me to do something and I was so trusting and innocent and didn't know what was happening until later when I knew I'd been used . . . that anyone could use me like that was a wake-up call. People did that, used people and then pretended it didn't happen, not caring how it made the person feel.

How did it make me feel? Like nothing, a person of no worth, a whore, a woman who wears a skimpy dress with high heels and leaves the red light in her window. That's who I became after that rape.

Even though we've named the baby and the secret's out, I have yet to deal with the fact that I was able to go through with it. The situation was bad from the beginning. Everything was bad, and I'd hit rock bottom when I turned my back on Tom, and on God. I hated myself for many years, and sometimes I hate myself now. It's easy to forget about something if one doesn't think about it for over thirty years and I did that until Tom came back into my life.

I didn't know right from wrong. Hadn't I learned that people in the church could be harsh and judgmental? I have a skeptical relationship with the church even today—I don't trust it or the people. It feels like home, because it is, but yet it doesn't. I don't know how that will come off in my book, but that's not the point of the book.

I remember how I hurt Robert and many others. I didn't believe in love, didn't believe they could love me. I thought it weird when I received a call for a second date—it was against my rules. Tom and I were playing against the rules, but I tried not to think too much about it. It seemed like the rules were being broken for a good reason, for our truth.

One section of the fields was cleared for grape vines. We ordered them from Italy. Dad planted the small hard plants and coaxed them to be part of the ground. I tried to imagine the way it would be when the vines are larger and bursting with grapes, but I knew I was better off not trying to see it, just waiting for it to happen.

The sun fell lower. Like blossoms trying to push through the ground, fireflies began to fill the air. It was early for fireflies, late for daffodils. When Tom's car pulled into the gravel drive, I stayed on the step. He came to sit next to me, and we looked out towards the barn and the fence laced with daffodils, the air filled with tiny lights.

How improbable, to have both daffodils and fireflies at the same time. Inspired and happy, I rose from the steps and joined the fireflies in a swirling dance, my long skirt flowing out around me. I laughed when he joined me, doing a dance as ancient as the Celtic runes.

We were living our story.

DAFFODIL DAYS
At Willow Beach

My mother died during daffodil days. It was during daffodil days that I discovered love. Now, a year after Mom died, Windy Hill is my home again. I know the richness of writing down words that are rich and deep. I know the strength of a grape vine and the kind of soil it needs to thrive. I know the honesty of being able to say whatever it is that comes into my head. I know the pleasure of a lover's hands on my skin.

When I walk to ease the anxiety, I find the questions and sometimes discover the answers. Walking is good. The writing's good, the farming's good, the love's good. The fireflies come out at dusk during the summer. Dragonflies flit across the surface of the Magical Pond until the fairies come out at night. The tree house is my favorite place to read. The teacup anchors me to who I am.

My heart is at home where the porch swing waits and the cows need to be brought in from the fields, where I am happy with who I am. Home is where we have begun to grow grapes and it is also within the vineyards of Italy where my father was born. Home is where I can find the goodness that resides within me that is also my connection with God. My heart is full of questions, some of which I can answer.

Last night when Tom and I danced with the fireflies amidst the daffodils, I no longer had a care in the world. We're making a life together, loving each other, and loving all there is to love. Soon, I believe, Tom will live with me at Windy Hill as well. I don't think we'll marry. We seem to have this idea that life is open to possibility and we're going to let things happen as they will. Marriage may close off the pathways to something new that one of us needs.

But when I sold my condo and quit my job, I was not just being open to possibility, I was making some permanent decisions. Anything is possible.

I reach my arms high toward the sun that has now come from behind the clouds and makes a glowing streak of light from the horizon to the shore. I reach for my toes and see the feet that carry me along the sidewalks and fields and take me away from the old me and toward my refinement. As I stand back up, I feel the sun on my face.

The old man continues to doze on the bench. He seems content. Perhaps he's already learned all the lessons life put out there for him to puzzle over. He knows about the ebb and flow of the water, the ebb and flow of life.

The story continues. But first I must make my way back home, to where the daffodils bloom and the fireflies twinkle.

AFTERWARD

I wrote of daffodils and fireflies after reading Virginia Woolf's *Moments of Being* and Alexandra Johnson's *Leaving a Trace*. While reading Linda Olsson's *Astrid & Veronika* I found a kindred connection when I read, "My life's memories take up space with no regard to when they happened, or to their actual time-span. The memories of brief incidents occupy almost all my time, while years of my life have left no trace." This was precisely what Woolf spoke of in her memoirs and why Johnson chose to call her book on memoir writing, *Leaving a Trace*.

With that background, I sat down and wrote *Daffodils and Fireflies*. It wrote itself, in two months' time, and I'm happy to tell it as it wanted to be told. My friend Sheryl said, "Just write the story." So I did. And then I made it better. During the revisions, I was listening to books on tape by Marissa de los Santos and Francine Prose, whose excellent word choices helped me select better words in my own writing; I was reading like a writer, as Prose would say.

And when I thought it was done, I re-wrote it again. Revision is where the real writing takes place. The first draft was merely a telling in which I am the conduit. But since God was in it, it was no mere thing and Anne Lamott says I'm entitled to "shitty first drafts."

The final revisions were made while I was at Mount Benedictine Monastery in Erie, Pennsylvania, while re-reading Sue Monk Kidd's *When the Heart Waits*. I didn't mean for this to be a book about spirituality, but it became more so while reading Kidd and Thomas Merton during my stay at the monastery. I struggled with that because I didn't want it to be spiritual, and definitely not Christian, but I'm the daughter of a Methodist minister through and through, and for me, our lives are always connected with God.

I thank Virginia Woolf, Alexandra Johnson, Linda Olsson, Marissa de los Santos, Francine Prose, Anne Lamott, and Sue Monk Kidd. I've learned so much from all of you, and I have so much more to learn. I thank Skyline Writers and the women at the Willoughby women's writing retreat for reading drafts of my work, for telling me when the characters weren't well drawn or when the words didn't make sense.

But most of all I thank my family for giving me the time to write this book and for understanding that I need to write, even if my words are never published. Having written this book, my words will not die inside me as *The Cleveland Plain Dealer*'s Regina Brett warned could happen if I never set my pen to paper and just wrote.

I've learned to follow my dreams and open up my heart to possibility.

ABOUT THE AUTHOR

Claudia Taller received her Bachelor's Degree in English with a Writing Certificate from Kent State University. While at Kent State, she was the co-editor of the English Department's literary magazine, interned with the Kent State University Press, and worked with then department chair Robert Tener on development of the Writing Certificate Program.

She began her career as a corporate transactional paralegal after college, and spends her days at the office reading and writing. She has written for many legal trade publications as a contributor, columnist, or editor, and has written several hundred travel and lifestyle articles for local Cleveland-area magazines. Her Arcadia book, *Ohio's Life Erie Wineries*, was published in 2011, and her spiritual memoir, *30 Perfect Days, Finding Abundance in Ordinary Life*, was published in 2014.

Her dual careers have led her to speaking engagements and to organizing and presenting at many conferences and workshops. Igniting Possibilities, her workshop business, incorporates Julia Cameron's *Artist's Way* concepts to encourage writers and other creative people to live their dreams. She and husband Paul, who has a doctorate in psychology and makes a living from counseling, live in a Cleveland suburb near Lake Erie. She lived in Conneaut as a young girl, near Vermilion as a teenager, and has worked in downtown Cleveland for thirty years. Claudia and Paul have three well-loved daughters.

Follow Claudia's writing, blogs and other activities at her website:

www.claudiajtaller.com